A Pius Man
A Holy Thriller

DECLAN FINN

A PIUS MAN
By Declan Finn

Published by Silver Empire
https://silverempire.org/

CONTENTS

DEDICATED TO ALL THOSE WHO HAVE BEEN VICTIMS OF THE NEW HOLOCAUST.

FOREWARD

My writing career can be blamed on two people: Joseph Michael Straczynski (JMS) and my father. JMS created a television show called *Babylon 5*. It was essentially a filmed science fiction novel, where the primary author (JMS) was the executive producer. By reading his online posts about writing, learning about construction of story, the elements of character, my interest was piqued. At sixteen I came up with a concept for a novel.

My father encouraged me to write what I had in mind. I designed my own characters, weaving stories out of loose threads of information in Straczynski's universe. After a while, the stories were mostly my own, and it grew into a universe beyond the actual show I based it on. In fifteen months, I had created a science fiction quartet of over 575,000 words that sprawled all over a universe that was mostly of my own design. After that I was hooked on writing. Since then, I wrote multiple novels, some bad, some readable. I'm still working on creating a version of my science fiction series that will not get me sued by Mr. Straczynski. I wrote thrillers, a hostage novel, short stories that were mostly a result of my creative writing professor, James Sheehan.

A Pius Man can be blamed on Professor Ralph McInerny, PhD, of Notre Dame University, and Prof. William Griffin, of St. John's University. McInerny, whose claim to popular fame can be traced back to his Father Dowling mysteries, also wrote a book on Pope Pius XII. I read it, and it spurred me to such anger that when Prof. Griffin wanted a paper, Pius XII was a topic that sprang to mind. May they both rest in peace.

A Pius Man is, in essence, a graduate paper gone completely out of control. It is the result when you cross a student of history, with an interest in Catholic philosophy, and who enjoys your average action film. It was *originally* written in 2004 over a period of only four months.

Some things: I do not speak Russian, and I can barely spell Russian, especially since Russian can be transliterated into English about four different ways. Also, the Sudan referred to in this book is on the Human Rights Commission. This book was written when there *was* an HRC. It's been replaced by a Human Rights *Council*, with a rotational body of nations on it – nothing prevents Sudan being on THIS HRC. And if you tell me it can't happen, you can explain how Sudan got on the Commission for Human Rights in the first place. As the book was originally written in 2004, if there are characters presented as younger than they should be, please roll with it.

A lot of the weapons are gleaned from details I found online. Some of this stuff is vaporware, and sounds nice, but isn't here yet.

ACKNOWLEDGEMENTS

J. Michael Straczynski, for starting me off in this business—sort of. See Foreword.

Ralph McInerny, RIP, for inspiring this book. See Foreword.

To Professors Mauricio Borrero, Joseph Califano, Frank J. Coppa, Robert Forman, Arthur Gianelli, William D. Griffin (RIP), Father Robert Lauder, Alice Ramos and Konrad Tuchscherer of St. John's University, for leading me to most of the factual background of the book.

To my friend Manana, for being a good sport about being portrayed in this book. If the reader believes that the physical descriptions of the character Mani Shushurin is too hyperbolic to be real, I went to college with her.

To Tanja Cilia, Walt Staples (RIP), Ann Lewis, Karina Fabian, and Randy England of the Catholic Writer's Guild, for all the beta reading.

John Santiago, SJU, 2004, hopefully a priest by now—obviously, I made good use of the slides.

I should note that any and all mistakes in combat and moments where "that Bruce Lee stuff won't work" moments are completely my fault...and probably written before I learned a combat system that worked.

To Jason Bieber of the University of Dayton, I would like to thank for his suggestions on the media angle of the Pope and the journalists of the world.

Matt "Funtime" Pryce, James Masciale, for the audio trailers.

Barbara, for the support.

And I'd also like to thank everyone who believed in me, even when I didn't: Allan and Annie Yoskowitz, Colleen Eren, Daniel and Melanie Pietras, Amanda Kennedy.

To Margaret and Gail Konecsni of Just Write! Ink, for editorial services.

To Matt Bowman – he knows why.

To Russell and Morgon Newquist, for dealing with my neuroses during the edits for this rerelease.

Everyone on the Facebook page. We made it.

And to RM Hendershot, author of *Masks*, for everything.

PROLOGUE: A PIUS OBSESSION

David Gerrity had lived with eighty-five years of obsession.

He had been obsessed with learning, which brought him into Harvard; history, which provided him with his Ph.D.; and, later, a wide range of other subjects, disciplining himself to no more than three or four obsessions at a time.

His family was another obsession. When he married, it was to a woman whose interests were as wide-ranging as his, which allowed her to at least partially understand what he was talking about. Between them they raised three daughters and two sons, each of whom was hatched, then matched, then finally dispatched from the home to do likewise.

His third permanent obsession was his religion, primarily in its philosophical aspects. He had even read the twelve shelf-feet of the fifty-volume Thomas Aquinas philosophical opus *Summa Theologica* during one summer break.

His final obsession varied. Unlike many academics who knew one thing and wrote on the same topic over and over, once he had exhausted a subject, it amused him to go back to the student side of the desk. In that fashion, he earned his second and third doctorates in sacred theology and in law. He had made a modest fortune on his four-volume history, *Lies Historians Tell: From Herodotus and Thucydides to Leni Riefenstahl and Michael Moore.* This revision of the revisionists armed a generation of smartass high-schoolers and undergraduates to challenge their professors with all the far-more-interesting facts the teachers left out of the official version. Gerrity was thus superbly equipped by training, talent, time and treasure to pursue his latest obsession.

His latest interest would become his last.

The final obsession explained the pile of books in Gerrity's hotel room in Rome. He bellowed, "God forsaken liar! Suffer eternal freezer burn!" as he hurled yet another volume with the force of a clay pigeon at a skeet shoot. It smacked against a wall, the impact sounding like a gunshot.

In Gerrity's mind, all of these books had been flawed. He had done exhaustive research on the records of the period, so he *knew* the authors had lied. He knew about what happened back then: the backroom deals, the failed assassination attempts, the intrigue, and the incompetent spy games they played, as well as all of the successful ones. Research was made harder because boasting was not in the nature of intelligence. He knew almost a dozen condemnations by heart, as well as how the words were twisted. It had taken 50 years to prove that Alger Hiss was an enemy agent, that the U.S.S.R. was a paper tiger, that Sacco and Vanzetti were guilty... This would be done also.

His new obsession was to correct one simple point of history; to settle the matter once and for all. There were few final victories, but to settle this for one generation would be enough — two generations had been poisoned already.

He rolled out of bed, ignoring his body's screams of protest as his arthritis flared up once more. The eighty-five-year-old had focused his attention on collecting facts; pain could be attended to later, assuming he noticed it.

He grabbed his portable scanner and plugged it into his laptop, wanting to read all he had collected yesterday. When they allowed him into the library, he brought his scanner, as he would not have been allowed to leave with any documents — an official policy he disliked, but one that seemed to follow him everywhere he went. Technically, he wasn't allowed to scan anything either, but he cheated. He had scanned each piece of paper so he could read them later, saving his eyesight and time in the vault. It had been a very well-lit vault, but he didn't like being locked in.

The day before, he had accidentally rammed his head against a top shelf. The shelf came loose and nearly decapitated him. Inside the shelf was a narrow, hollowed-out slit, where he had spotted one more piece of paper. It had been properly preserved, like the other documents, but who put papers inside of a shelf, not on it? Like every other document, he had scanned it, put it back in its proper place, replaced the shelf, and then forgot about it until now.

That image was the last one he had scanned, and the first one he looked at now.

Gerrity's eyes widened and he stood, suddenly knocking the chair backwards. If this were true, he was going to have to change everything - the title of the book, the premise, even his own beliefs.

Damn it, everything's gone to Hell.

Gerrity whirled, headed for the door, intent on demanding to be let back into the vault for the original paper. If this was correct, and if he could find data to support this, he would bring down an entire institution with what he knew. He would grind it under his feet, burn it and scatter the ashes, down to every last member. He would metaphorically kill them all, show them for what they really were. He hadn't exactly intended on doing it when he had arrived, but now, he had no choice.

Gerrity worked the locks and wrenched open the door. Standing on the other side was someone from room service, pushing a full dinner cart.

"Io ho qualcosa!" he shouted. I've got something!

The bellman blinked, and raised the water bottle in his right hand. Gerrity looked down and saw that the mouth of the empty water bottle had been taped to something else. A gun.

Room service fired one bullet into Gerrity's stomach at an upward angle, letting the .22-caliber round ricochet off of the back of his ribcage, into the breastbone, finally lodging in the knotted muscles of his left shoulder. Gerrity staggered back and was shot again, this time under the chin; this bullet did the job, bouncing off of the back of his skull, through the frontal lobe, ricocheted a final time, to finally embed itself in the top of the spinal column. Gerrity landed with a light *thump*.

Clementi dragged the cart into Gerrity's hotel room and closed the door, heading directly for the laptop. His improvised silencer would be good for at least one more shot. He raised his gun to finish the job. He had been instructed not to read anything Gerrity had left behind, only destroy it.

Clementi disobeyed, having caught part of one sentence, and then again, and again… Clementi stopped and stared at the screen. The information in front of him was impossible. Perfectly, absolutely, utterly *impossible*. He could not believe some of the names on that screen. He could not believe the events it described. And he could not make another move without passing the information along.

Clementi whipped out his cell phone and hit redial so he could immediately contact his superior.

"Is it done?"

"Gerrity's dead, but the evidence — you must read it. We can't work for him anymore. Do you know who he is? What he is?"

"Yes, I do," his superior answered.

A moment later, three sticks of dynamite underneath the dining cart exploded. The concussive wave slammed into Clementi like a giant smacking him with sheet metal. It sent the computer across the room, and the assassin out the window, smashing apart all of the glass. The assassin shattered both legs against the frame as he fell to his death on top of a car below.

* * *

Several blocks away, the assassin's superior officer, and his murderer, calmly strode out of the café onto *Via Ottaviano*, tucking his cell phone into an inside pocket. He looked out over the columns of the Vatican. Rome was rather pretty at this time of year.

"Excuse me!"

He turned, and smiled at an approaching mother and infant. "Yes?"

"Father, would you bless my baby?"

* * *

Manana Shushurin was covered with sweat, and half-regretted wearing the T-shirt. The material on this one was definitely too thin. She gently slid the barbell back onto the

5

rack and then swung her long legs over the side. It took three hours to get this much sweat accumulated, and she had barely noticed. She had slept from five p.m.—when everyone had left work — to nine p.m., and had gone down to the gym.

But it was time to go back to work, whether she liked it or not.

After the showers, she slipped into simple gray pants and a white blouse. Then she headed back to her office. She looked around the room. Officially, she lived with her mother. Unofficially, when she wasn't in the field, she was in her office, sleeping no more than she needed to. There were few things in her office that gave a hint that she lived there — her closet, a bookcase, and the DVD/VHS player on her lamp table. All her other clothing and impedimenta were in storage.

Shushurin sighed. *Yes, that should be depressing, shouldn't it?*

She dated, but not often. She had degrees in political science, philosophy and history, but men only noticed her body. She stared down at her well-developed chest, cursing mildly. At least her build was useful when she was sent into the field. It was easier to interrogate a man when he was too busy drooling to use discretion.

She looked down at the paperwork on her desk, and grabbed a chair. She gazed from pile to pile, trying to figure out where to begin.

Working for German foreign intelligence, the *Bundesnachrichtendienst* (BND), had some perks, like the workout room. Her office was tucked in the back end of the building, but was still as crowded as any cubicle. Her job was to sort through intelligence reports for the Israelis. As irony would have it, the BND gave a great deal of information to the Mossad. But some members of her own service thought the creation of Israel had stolen from Ahmed to give to Avram, and hence disliked giving Mossad intel. So, for doing her job to the fullest of her abilities, she was seen as "supporting Israel," and she had been tucked into the back end of nowhere. Fortunately, she was too good to be tied to a desk for any length of time. She could lie, cheat and steal with the best, as evidenced by her generosity every poker night. After she cleaned everyone out, she ended the game by sharing her winnings with the pigeons she called colleagues.

Manana Shushurin flipped a mental coin on what folder to review. Then, she picked up the latest folder out of Rome, and after she scanned the first three lines, her eyes lit up. This was something she needed to pass on immediately.

The phone rang. She answered. The caller told her, "You're going to Italy."

CHAPTER I: A PIUS COP

G iovanni Figlia stood in the lobby of Leonardo da Vinci Fiumicino Airport in a solid black polo shirt and a black suit jacket. The color scheme made him seem shorter than his 5'9" height. His hand ached for his Beretta to reassure himself that he was still armed, but instead he ran his fingers through his thick dark hair.

It must be something about Americans that brings out the Clint Eastwood in people.

He scanned the crowd for his target, comparing each face with the photograph he had memorized down to the dots on the color printout: hazel eyes, brown hair, Germanic cheekbones, not bad-looking. Wilhelmina Goldberg, a former member of the Americans' National Security Agency, with degrees in esoteric languages and mathematics, had transferred into her current profession some time ago, and was supposed to be good at it.

Now all I have to do is hunt her down.

"Looking for me?"

Figlia looked down. Three feet away from him stood a woman just under five feet tall. He recognized her as Goldberg; she wore black jeans and a tight-fitting, long-sleeved turtleneck. Over one shoulder she carried a duffel bag as large as she was. She also dragged a wheeled suitcase as big as Figlia.

"*Io ho pensato che Lei ha…* supposed to be in formal attire," he said in his own combination of Italian and English. He glanced at her. "Not attracting attention."

She replied in crisp, formal Italian. "On the former, you thought wrong. As for the latter…" she looked down at her chest and shot him a look. "If 28B passes for attention-getting in Italy, you people need to open a Playboy, pop a Viagra, and get a life."

Giovanni Figlia stepped to one side. "This way?"

"You lead. I don't want you stepping on my equipment. You want this job done, we'll need this intact."

He led. Goldberg moved forward. "You're Gianni, right?"

"Mi chiamo Figlia, si." I'm Figlia, yes.

"I'm surprised," she told him. "You're the head of this outfit; why would you meet me?"

Figlia shrugged. "Because I like to get out of the office every once in a while. And we'll be working together for a while. We might as well get used to each other, starting now."

"Done. Where's our first stop?"

"The Vatican." Figlia stepped around more passengers just getting in and made his way to the automatic doors. It was still dark outside, despite the fact that it was 6:30 in the morning.

"What are you packing?" she asked.

Figlia blinked. "This is Italy. What do you think?"

Wilhelmina Goldberg rolled her eyes. "Beretta, then." She looked around before answering. "I just got on a plane from Spain with security that's a joke. I'm carrying a Sig and they didn't even *notice*. Forgive me for wondering about Europeans." She pronounced it Euro-*peons*. "We're not exactly in a safe business."

When Giovanni Figlia stopped at a four-door silver Jetta, Goldberg shrugged. "Not a bad little toy. You own it?"

"Depends on my wife." He smiled. "Come on, I'll load the bags."

Goldberg laughed. "No way in hell, buddy. I'll manage. You just start this thing up."

Once she loaded herself into the passenger seat, he sped away.

"You know, I'm halfway surprised that you carry outside of your target area."

Figlia glanced at her briefly. "You expected me to live on a hundred-acre leash? Check my gun at the colonnade?"

"Given your line of work, I'm surprised they allow you to have a gun."

"Don't worry, we're allowed to shoot back. There are some situations where force is required. Mind if I ask you something?"

She shrugged. "Whatever."

"What's your religion?"

"I'm Jewish. Orthodox," she added as an afterthought. "My parents say an Orthodox Jew is a 'real Jew'… you don't want to hear what they have to say about the others." Goldberg shrugged. "So, tell me a little bit about what you do here."

They continued to discuss their mutual professions, the conversation punctuated long enough for her to look out at the city and take an occasional photo with her iPhone. He began to decelerate as he followed the Tiber River and hung a right onto the *Via della Conciliazione*, making a right in front of the colonnade, onto *Via Ottaviano*.

It led right to their target, the Vatican.

At that moment, one of the buildings exploded in a massive fireball, dropping glass, brick and debris down upon their car in a shower of destruction. A moment later, another object smashed into the hood of Figlia's car, smashing the windshield, and denting the hood in front of him.

Giovanni Figlia instinctively swerved away from the explosion, and braked hard. The object on his windshield stayed there.

After a few seconds, Goldberg and Figlia got out of the car and studied the scene, wondering if it was safe to go check the damage. She bounced up on her toes to check what had killed Figlia's car. It was the body of a young-looking, olive-skinned male...without a face.

"Between 25 and 35?" Figlia asked.

"...Sounds like a serial-killer profile," she answered.

Figlia grunted and again wanted to reach for his gun. He glanced at the short, pixie-like woman and muttered, "Damn Americans. Here for fifteen minutes and Dante's Inferno rises to surface level."

The only *carabinieri* in the area ran to the scene, leaving his motorcycle behind. He let out a small string of curses, ran back to his vehicle, and immediately radioed for help.

The police were the first responders, followed immediately by the fire department. The firemen quickly moved to douse the flames with the fire hose. Giovanni Figlia tackled the main man on the hose, grabbing him before he could attach the hose to its water supply.

"What are you doing?" the fireman shouted. He tried to fight back, but Figlia had already locked one arm into place, totally immobilizing him.

"You're going to wash away all evidence of the bomb,"

Figlia growled. "Use a fire extinguisher or buckets."

The other firefighters didn't know what to make of him. He was an utterly unremarkable fellow in basic black. With the addition of a white collar, he could have been wearing a priest's uniform… if the material were better. He wasn't even that big, but held the burliest member of their team immobile with minimal effort.

Figlia shoved the firefighter aside, and reached into his inner jacket pocket before someone shot up. He pulled out a wallet and flashed his identification, as well as his badge. "Commandatore Giovanni Figlia, Vatican's Central Office of Vigilance. That body over there is dead, and not only is my car a secondary crime scene, do you see that line?" He pointed to a white painted line on the cobblestone street. "Sixty years ago, the Nazis put that line down to clearly mark the territory. This side, right now, is Rome." He sidestepped to in front of his car and pointed toward the colonnade of St. Peter's Basilica. "Where I'm standing now is Vatican City."

Wilhelmina Goldberg laughed. "Now you see why American cops call firemen the evidence destruction unit."

The fireman scowled at her. She was short, so she wasn't a member of Figlia's security force. Her dye job was obvious and ugly, so she wasn't working for the Vatican. Her accent sounded more like American actors trying too hard to sound like she was from New York City, and so became a self-parody. "And what are you? His *puttana?*"

She shook her head, unconcerned as she reached into her pocket. "First of all, you're thinking more like a Calabrese." She pulled out a leather wallet of her own and flipped it open. "Second, I'm a consultant: Wilhelmina Goldberg of the United States Secret Service."

Giovanni Figlia looked around frantically, hoping no one

else would try to wash away the evidence. A shiny silver object caught his attention, and he narrowed his eyes, focusing on… the cover for a hotel serving tray?

"And," he continued, "the explosion radius extends into my jurisdiction. I have a body and half a crime scene over here — you only have half a crime scene, I win. I'll head up there myself, if you don't mind… and if you do, too bad. Frankly, if you'd like to do something useful, secure the street!"

Figlia caught a familiar sight at the edge of his peripheral vision. The black cassock of a priest was more than enough to identify him as such from thirty yards away. It looked like the priest gave the crowd more attention than he had given the scene of the crime, which was odd — most of the time, far too many people wanted to look at the destruction. At that distance, the only other detail he could make out was the man's silver hair.

"Padre! Venga, per favore!"

The priest looked up, then left, then right, and finally, he shrugged and stepped forward cautiously, eyeing the building as though he wanted to make sure it wouldn't collapse.

"What's with the priest?" she asked, sotto voce.

"He might be able to provide a barricade between you and the *polizia* when they arrive. Have him standing by ready to give the corpse last rites, while you snap photos of the body. I suspect we won't get another chance for pictures after this."

Goldberg gave him a look as though he had sprouted three heads. "You *want* a murder case?"

He flashed a Casanova grin. "I'm going to check the room. Stay close to the priest."

She raised an eyebrow. Before she could make a scathing remark, Figlia bolted into the damaged hotel and flew up the stairs.

13

* * *

Wilhelmina Goldberg looked over her shoulder at the body-covered car, absentmindedly tapping her iPhone for photos. "And I thought this would be a nice, quiet little trip — some consulting, audit security, but no, I get the one cop on the planet who makes Hoover look mildly sane," she muttered in English.

"Excuse me," came a gentle voice from right next to her, also speaking in English.

She adjusted her line of sight to the priest, only a foot away from her, and tried not to jump. *Do priests in Rome get ninja training?*

The priest was… odd. He had a piercing set of violet eyes. And while his hair was solid silver, there were only a few lines on his face, so he couldn't have been older than forty. If she were sending out an APB or a BOLO for him, she would have actually said he was only about 5'6" – maybe 5'8", she was looking up at him, and his shoulders were slumped.

Goldberg bunched her lips, trying to figure out how to speak to a priest over a corpse. "Uh. Hello …Father… could you wait a moment while I take a few pictures of this poor schlub?"

He nodded. "Of course. Are you a friend of Gianni's?"

She shrugged and turned to the corpse. Goldberg twisted her lip and stepped around the priest to get back into the car. She slid onto the seat and clicked at the corpse through the windshield, getting every possible angle with her phone.

Click. "I'm a consultant."

"From… New York, I presume by the accent." *Click.* There was another flash from the phone flash. "I grew up

14

there… briefly. It's an odd story."

Click. "I don't doubt it." *You've decided to spend the rest of your life without sex, so you must be odd somehow.*

"So what kind of consultant work do you do?"

Click. She checked the quality of the photos, and then slid out of the car. "Security."

I'd ask how you know Figlia, she thought. *But he called you Father without using a name, so I'm guessing he only knows you because of the outfit, and you only know of him because he's papal security.*

* * *

"Ah. Of course," the priest answered.

Commander Figlia wouldn't hire out some lone American gun-toting security hack, he thought. *You're Secret Service, aren't you? Not very talkative, either.*

They turned the body over once she had taken all of the photos she needed.

The priest knew exactly who this man was, and knew him well — his entire life story, in fact. He had been raised as a red-diaper baby in a family loyal to the *brigate rosso*, the Italian Red Army.

He performed the last rites over the body, blessing him as he went on into the next world. *Rest in peace, you schmuck.*

* * *

Giovanni Figlia walked into what was left of the hotel room, and he took it in with a sweep of his eyes. On the floor was another dead man, a hole clearly visible under his chin. This second corpse — Gerrity, according to the hotel people

15

he passed on his way up here — was on its back, hands out like a crucified martyr. Furniture had been scattered across the room, thrown against the wall, much of it shattered.

Figlia rubbed the back of his neck. "*Benone,* a double cross."

One of the hotel staff in the hall raised a brow. "*Scusi, signore? Non capisco.*"

Figlia waved at the room. "The spherical pattern of the bomb suggests a normal explosive, not plastique — plastique tends to be directional. Besides, you can smell the black powder, *si?* Maybe homemade."

He looked into the ceiling, and saw silver forks embedded like shrapnel, surrounded by other pieces of metal. *I wonder if it matches the tray lid that landed outside.* Below the forks were wheels, separated by a flat metal sheet pressed into the carpet.

"Serving cart," Figlia muttered.

"*Che?*" a bellboy asked. What?

He carefully stepped around the body and pointed at the sheet of metal. "The lower level of the serving tray, beneath the forks." His eyes flickered across the room as though they were tracking a soccer ball. "Not to mention the silverware in the walls, the bed, the floor, as well as the plate fragments — either he had a grand celebration with an American fraternity, or they came from a full room-service cart that exploded."

He pointed out the shattered window. "Our *amico* on the street wore a busboy's white coat; assume the cart was his. The cart is in the center of the room; too far inside if he was lugging dirty place settings all over the hallway. He would have stayed outside in the hall and collected them. This person on the floor is dead from the nice neat bullet hole under his chin. Given the position of the cart, it had to have been

16

pulled around this man's body — the poor fool probably opened up for his killer." He made brief eye contact with the men out in the hall. "That killer is, by the way, the one who ruined my car." He waved at Gerrity's corpse. "At least this man's killer. Who killed the busboy is another quandary. He was killed with the explosion from his own cart, so it is either stupidity on the busboy's part, or murder on someone else's."

Figlia walked over to the window, and shouted out, in English, "*Signora* Goldberg, look around for a pistol! I'll check up here!"

He stepped back from the window, looking back as he did so. He opened up his cellular phone and hit autodial. "Veronica, *bella,* could you please bring the team down to the hotel?"

Veronica Fisher smiled; he could hear it in her voice. "Which hotel?"

"Outside the colonnade," Figlia told her. "Follow the smoke; we have a bomb, black powder composition."

"Some priest playing with leftover fireworks?"

"A double homicide."

Fisher paused a moment. "Gianni, isn't the hotel *outside* our jurisdiction?"

"The body isn't. You'll also have to process what's left of our car."

Fisher, who was Figlia's forensics expert as well as his wife, paused a moment. "The bomb destroyed the Jetta?"

"No, the corpse did it." Figlia paused for a moment, wondering if that was a double entendre, as the corpse had done both the first murder and the destruction to the car. *Perhaps in American English.* "I'll have the locals secure the crime scene."

"You sound like the FBI back home."

"Heaven forbid. *A più tardi.* I won't be here when you arrive, I have a guest."

"You picked him up?" Fisher asked.

Figlia furrowed his brow. "Him?"

There was some light laughter. "You weren't sent to pick up Hashim Abasi? Remember, the Egyptian coordinating with you about Josh's visit. What am I, your secretary?"

Figlia felt like the dead man had it easy. "I'll get him as soon as possible."

* * *

The Secret Service agent, Goldberg, leaned against the door of the dead car, glancing at the priest. "When did he start thinking he was a homicide detective?"

The priest said, "You should ask him about it sometime."

Commander Figlia dashed out of the hotel and waved at Goldberg to follow him. She offered the priest her hand. "It's been nice talking with you, Father…?"

"Francis Williams, of the *Compania.*"

"Ah, a Jesuit."

The priest smiled. "Just call me Frank."

CHAPTER II: A PIUS MERCENARY

E ven in Rome, there were not that many people conscious so early in the morning — just people awakened by the explosion, firemen, and a scattering of pedestrians.

One pedestrian was a jogger, moving along the street casually. His gray jogging suit didn't stand out at all, and his build was unremarkable underneath all the cloth. Even his face was covered by the hood. He was short, only 5'6". The only other detail the observant person could pinpoint would be the occasional flash of bright, electric blue eyes.

The jogger slowed as he approached the Vatican, looking over the scene of devastation. He gave a low whistle and pulled back his hood, revealing his pale skin and raven-black hair.

He gave a small, quirky smile. The scene was amusing for multiple reasons, the foremost among them was that a hotel had been wrecked, and he hadn't been responsible for it. For once.

He murmured, in an almost unaccented voice, "Someone had fun."

He scanned the crowd, more interested in the people around the crime scene than destruction itself. It wasn't even all that impressive, as far as destruction went — the only thing really damaged was the hotel room window. And the car.

Well, if you don't count the body. But body bags aren't that expensive in Italy, are they?

One person slipped through the crowd. A figure in black, only a little taller than the jogger himself.

Well, if anyone is going to know what's going on here...

"Ahoy," the jogger hailed, speaking only slightly above conversational volume.

Father Frank Williams heard and looked in his direction, smiling as he headed towards the jogger. "How are you, Sean?"

The jogger named Sean shrugged. "I'm doing well, though I'm wondering why you weren't at our usual meeting. I waited twenty minutes before I started by myself. After a while, I feel ridiculous firing off all of those bullets solo."

Father Frank nodded. "Understandable, considering your profession. What are you calling yourself this week, a prostitute?"

The jogger shook his head. "No, a mercenary. I'm not exactly a big operation like Black Lake, but I count."

The man in black cocked his head. "Black Lake?"

Sean furrowed his brows. "It is Black Lake, isn't it? Blackpool...? Blackthorn...?" he thought a moment, and then his bright eyes lit up and he snapped his fingers. "Blackwater! That's the name. The mercenary company."

The priest shrugged, and blatantly ignored that Blackwater had changed its name years ago. "Sounds better than 'personal demolition unit'."

Sean rolled his eyes, the electric-blue orbs looking like circular lightning. "Again, I'm not *quite* that bad. I've only killed a few… dozen… people? I think? I figure I manage to kill a few more, I win a set of steak knives."

Father Frank was uncertain about whether or not he was joking. "In which case, I will let you get on with your day." He turned away, then paused, and looked back to Sean. "By the way, I should probably mention, I may not be able to train with you for the next few days."

Sean raised a brow. "Really? What's up?"

Father Frank looked back towards the shattered car and the broken person. "Oh, just some business I'll have to attend to, that's all."

Sean nodded. "Okay, then, I'll see you around."

The jogger watched the priest wander off, and then turned back to the devastation. He caught a whiff of something odd, and blinked. He looked up to the ruined window, studying the frame, and the faint, lingering cloud of smoke wafting away from it, like smoke at a fireworks display.

Someone used black powder on this? Wow, talk about bombs on the cheap. What did they do, dissect a box of firecrackers?

Sean shook his head. He was suddenly glad that he had left his bag full of guns at the studio; otherwise, he would probably be in even bigger trouble than usual.

He glanced down at the car, studying at the short woman Father Frank had been talking with. She wasn't too bad-looking, even if she was a few inches short of being a dwarf — and not the kind with a beard and a battle axe. Her eyebrows hair was were a light brown, but her hair was overdone with gold highlights deliberately put in by some hairstylist who may have been holding a grudge.

Then again, what do I know? Sean thought. *I'm from California, a silicon valley that has nothing to do with computer chips.*

21

The short woman walked through the crowd with little difficulty as she followed the taller man in a dark suit. Sean quickly flipped up his hood again, hiding his features.

The last thing he wanted to do was get in the way of the head of Vatican security when he was in a bad mood — and having someone land on one's car was more than sufficient to put anyone in a bad mood.

I wonder if I should make Gianni's life easier, get involved.

Sean considered it, but only briefly. His resume was cluttered with inconvenient events — explosions, assaults, gunfights, and a body count that would have counted as mass murder if they weren't all in self-defense — and offering assistance would pretty much ruin Figlia's day.

After all, it was bad enough that the same person who had slaughtered dozens and had leveled millions of dollars in property damage was also, at that very moment, employed by the Pope.

CHAPTER III: A PIUS VISITOR

Hashim Abasi was tall and powerfully built, his broad shoulders accentuated by the fit of his sandy, tan jacket. At thirty-five, he had enjoyed a moderate professional success — given where he lived and what he did, being alive counted as success. He occasionally wondered how long that success would last since he couldn't leave his job if he tried. Everyone in political circles liked him, mainly because he was one of the few not trying to stab anyone in the back.

He ran a hand over his bald scalp, wondering what had become of his liaison with the chief of Vatican security. He was tempted to slide his reading glasses onto his sharp, angular nose and start flipping through papers on Figlia's desk. Premature presbyopia annoyed him no end: others only needed reading glasses after forty or forty-five. He was just lucky in his ancestors that his good distance vision had saved his life more than once.

Abasi pinched his sinuses, fighting off the coming headache. He crossed his legs, hoping to become even slightly comfortable in the office chair.

If I ran the office, I would have chairs that made people uncomfortable on purpose. But who knows — the head of the papal detail may be a man chosen because of his virtue, and not because of his security qualities.

"Agent Abasi, my apologies, sir, I had a little car accident on the way here," someone said in English as he dashed into the office. Abasi didn't even stand, merely glanced at the head of papal security as he rushed through the door.

Figlia's cheeks were flushed, as if he had run the entire way. Abasi looked over Figlia's suit, and wondered just how much Figlia dressed in basic black because he blended in, and how much it was affected by being on a SWAT team for so long.

"Nothing serious, I hope," Abasi replied in clear, crisp Cambridge English. It was a voice at odds with his body – most people didn't expect a voice that educated to come out of a man with physique like a body builder. Then again, Abasi usually tried to stick to gutter vocabulary when he was on the job, it helped with the image.

Figlia smiled, glad that they had English in common — the wonders of the "new Latin," as the resentful Vaticanos called it. Although that is a good question — were they referring to English as a universal language, or the 2003 Latin dictionary, which had entries for "motorcycle" and "hot dog?"

"I will certainly need a new window," Figlia told him, "but no one was killed... not by my car, anyway."

Abasi nodded solemnly. He cocked his head and furrowed his brows, his dark copper eyes catching the light. "I hope that was not an explosion I heard not long ago."

"It was."

Abasi started, and turned towards the source of the new voice.

Special Agent Wilhelmina Goldberg slid into a chair not far from the corner of Figlia's desk. "Unfortunately," she continued, "the body of his car needs work because it was body-slammed by a corpse."

Abasi looked from one to the other. "Is this a terrorist incident?"

Figlia shrugged. "Unknown. This only just blew up in our faces. My people are looking at it now."

"If I can do anything, do not hesitate to call on me, please." He smiled. "After all, I have plenty of experience with explosives."

Goldberg cocked her head, looking at him sideways. "Excuse me for asking, but why are you concerned? I mean, outside of the Pope's safety during his visit to Egypt, why would you care? Even a lot of *Catholics* I know wouldn't mind if this Pope bought it. He's even more militant than the last two."

Abasi raised a brow. "Indeed? May I ask who you are?"

"Special Agent Goldberg, U.S. Secret Service."

Abasi arched his eyebrows. "Really?" He angled himself towards her. He ran a hand over his bald scalp, and scratched at the back of his neck. "Well, Agent Goldberg, there is something American Catholics don't have to worry about — retribution should the Pope get killed. You may remember the uproar your president caused when he talked of a *crusade* against terrorism?

"For my people, the Crusades are as recent as fifty years ago. Everyone acts as though they've been personally traumatized by them, and that a new crusade could happen again at any moment."

He held up a hand to hold off her protests.

"The idea is absurd, but that's what they believe — if a Muslim should kill Pope Pius XIII', my people believe the West will start their invasion in Morocco and go east." Abasi looked to Figlia, then back to Goldberg. "Now, everyone in

25

this room knows that, if a crusade should start, it will have nothing to do with religion and everything to do with killing religious psychopaths.

His massive shoulders went up and down in a shrug. "In short, I am here because Egypt does not wish to be wiped out in the crossfire between tribes." Abasi shifted again, failing to get comfortable.

Goldberg blinked. "Funny, coming from a government that had a new Nazi party only a few years ago."

Abasi merely smiled. "Regimes change - in the Middle East more often than most. The Muslim Brotherhood alienated many, which is why they're gone now. The current government wants to change our national image. Allowing the Pope to visit is one part of that."

Figlia blinked. "And how do *you* manage?"

Abasi laughed. "Commander Figlia, do you know the key to surviving as a policeman in Egypt? When the Sunnis are in power, all of the criminals are 'shi'a.' When the shi'a are in power, all of the criminals are Sunni. It is all a matter of how you fill out the paperwork." He looked to Goldberg. "And you, Special Agent, what are you doing so far from home? Sightseeing, perhaps?"

She shook her head. "I'm here as a security consultant."

"And they allow this in your country?"

She shrugged. "Yup. Besides, I'm too short to take a bullet for anyone except one of the seven dwarves, so I'm in tactics, strategy, advance work, etc."

"Indeed. So we are all here to keep Kutjok safe."

Goldberg looked from Abasi to Figlia, and blinked. Figlia said, "Abasi means His Holiness. His name before he became Pope was Joshua Kutjok."

Goldberg nodded. "Ah, sorry, it didn't process for a moment. Then again, there's been so much fuss made in the U.S. over 'Pius XIII' ever since he took the name, oy!". She closed her eyes and thought for a moment. "The news coverage, depending on who you believe, the last pope to take the name either *did* nothing about the Holocaust; *said* nothing about the Holocaust; or was actively *responsible* for the Holocaust."

Abasi said, "True. Before then, I did not know that every historian who specialized in Catholic history was a reject from the seminary, an ex-priest who married an ex-nun, or 'Catholics' who, mysteriously, support *none* of the teachings of the Catholic Church."

Wilhelmina Goldberg sighed. "I wonder if CNN could get the same results from a historian who didn't have an axe to grind."

Figlia shrugged, and tried to move away from the third rail of a topic. "As for his birth name, people might not recall where Pius was from if he did not make noises about it every day."

Goldberg nodded. All of the historians were just as enraged that, not only had Joshua Kutjok picked the name Pius, but the Sudanese Archbishop had given two reasons for picking the name: "Like my predecessor, I, too, have a mission to save lives from a mechanism of death, which seeks to 'purify' a country through murder. Like Pope Pius XII, I will put all of my energies toward ending the murder and slavery in Sudan –North and South – as he did to save the Jews of Europe during the dark years of the Nazi infestation. To commemorate this mission, I will start the proceedings to canonize Pope Pius XII."

Like most of his predecessors, Pius XIII was on a mission from God.

"I have to tell you," Goldberg told Figlia, trying to get

27

comfortable in the chair, "I think the only people he hasn't pissed off yet are at Fox News."

At that, even Abasi had to laugh. "This is true. I remember when few people talked about the decades of genocide, over two million murdered before anyone had heard of *Darfur.*"

Goldberg arched a brow. *I don't think I've ever heard of someone say Darfur like he had a personal grudge. Then again, if I saw a genocide go on for decades, but no one paid attention, I guess I'd be pissed too.*

"That's part of the problem," Figlia said, leaning back in his chair. "The bulk of the direct attacks on the Pope are leveled by the Northern Sudanese government, which has labeled the entire Catholic Church as one unnatural entity. As an Archbishop in the Sudan, when it was one country, the Pope's own parishioners dragged him off to Uganda because it was safer. I believe tranquilizers were involved. Heh. He is not one to take anything lying down."

Even Abasi laughed at this. "You are not kidding." He said to Goldberg, "I recall Kutjok's first desire being to canonize 'anti-Semitic' Popes, Pius IX and XI--one had sheltered and supported Jews, and the other had condemned fascists and communists in the same week. It was announced by a new Secretary of State, a Vietnamese priest who spent years jailed by the People's Republic of China... that was well-done." Abasi smiled, obviously appreciative of the political chess in-volved.

Goldberg rolled her eyes. "That's nothing. You should have been in Washington when they talked about making a patron saint of spies out of Dr. Thomas Dooley..."

Abasi gave her a blank look; he had missed that one, apparently.

"He was a full-time doctor and a sometime spy for the

U.S. government in Vietnam," Goldberg answered.

"Ah," Abasi said flatly. "So that would explain why China and North Korea have the uncomfortable idea that Kutjok has them on his short list of things to do."

Goldberg gave a short laugh. "I still like that the press release where they announced that one of the Rothschilds would run the Vatican Bank."

Abasi laughed. "This is true. Though it was still not as brilliantly handled as the elections process."

Goldberg blinked. "What *was* all that about? I'm not entirely certain what went on there. Elected priests? I don't remember the last time a Rabbi took a poll."

Giovanni Figlia frowned. If this was going to be a conversation about politics no matter what he did, he would at least jump in and hope to cut it short. "Catholic critics wanted elected bishops, and the Pope gave them what they wanted. Mostly in countries with a long history of democracy, and on the condition that the elected were ordained priests, and that Rome had final ratification. The candidates had gone on a tour of parishes under the guise of guest speakers. Not even the parishioners had known there was a campaign. Since the critics hadn't gone to church since 1965, they never knew the elections happened until after. The 45% of Catholics who regularly go to church were the ones who voted. By the time the critics had heard of the elections, they were over, leaving them without an argument — there were elections, but they failed to show up, and so failed to get the outcome they wanted." Goldberg stretched her neck to one side. "Anyway, we figure a lot of people want to kill him. So, I'm just here to walk around and point out ways to improve the system already in place. A normal security audit, only more on a theoretical level rather than personally testing the system."

Hashim Abasi cocked his head. "This should be interesting. May I join your audit? If you, Commander Figlia, decide to initiate any of her suggestions, I would already know the details from the same presentation."

Figlia shrugged. "I see no reason not to. Agent Goldberg?"

She shrugged. "I'll ask my boss, but I can't see why not."

Abasi said, "Then you will not get any permission; I would fail a background check, because my English is so good." Abasi's smile broadened into a full grin, as though he was straining not to laugh. "My name, essentially, translates into 'stern crusher of evil.' " He shrugged. "The hopes of a parent. My father sent me abroad in order to learn the language of the enemy, so I could better kill them. While I was abroad, he was killed while tinkering with a mail-order C4 vest. While I have locked away more terrorists than some Mossad officers, I can't imagine passing a background check by any U.S. federal agency."

Goldberg's eyes glittered. "Ah. In that case, we'd better not tell them." She looked to Figlia. "I suppose you can coordinate with Agent Abasi after, or even during, my audit, incorporating my advice as we go… depending, of course, on when or how you want to squeeze it in around your homicide investigation. I mean, you worked so hard to win the case, I'm guessing you want to work it yourself."

Figlia laughed. "I'm certain the autopsy reports will take long enough for me to fit the audit in, between forensics reports."

Abasi's eyes flickered from one to the other. "You fought for the investigation? Why?"

Figlia leaned back in the seat. "I started out in what you may call the… Special Tactics team of the police force. After working abroad, I came back, and took the detective's test, working homicide before coming here. Think of it as a mental game to keep the mind sharp. The Secret Service rotates the members on Presidential duty after a few years, to avoid its becoming routine, yes? This is my version. A little murder to break up the boredom."

Abasi smiled. Figlia was a man whose posture said *cop*.

* * *

Sean, the mercenary, had changed out of his jogging suit only a few minutes after Giovanni Figlia had begun his conversation with Hashim Abasi. Already, he was about to begin the job he was brought here to do.

For several weeks, he had been training men and women into what he saw as a well-equipped fighting force, even if no one else noticed.

He double-checked his box of weapons to make sure that everything was there. It didn't look like much, but he could make an entire army out of what he had there.

He had been doing just that.

He hitched his gear up and started out into the Borgia Gardens. When he had first been assigned that spot, he had found it amusing.

Sean whipped out his tactical baton and opened it with a flick of his wrist.

Now it's time to make the Borgias look like amateurs, he thought with a manic smile on his face as he stepped out to see his trainees; the priests and nuns of the Vatican.

If people thought that the Templars were fun to deal with, he thought, *just wait until the conspiracy theorists get a hold of what I'm doing. They'll go insane.*

* * *

The standard trend for Popes went one of two ways: nobles or peasants. In an age where nobles were disappearing, the noble was usually replaced with the academic. It had worked well in the case of Karol Wojtyla, and Joseph Ratzinger – John Paul II and his successor – who were both academics.

Then there was Joshua Kutjok, the latest Pope. He was both an academic and a peasant. He had been educated by the Church, but had also lived in some of the worst places on the planet earth.

And now he was the most powerful religious leader on the planet. He didn't mind being "the most powerful religious leader on the planet," but he *did* mind being called that to his face. It usually got in the way of getting things done.

Pope Pius XIII was a tall, athletic, dark-skinned man. He was a very solid six feet tall and two hundred and thirty-five pounds, his hair salt-and-pepper gray, his eyes dark brown. He had a shoulder span as wide as the seminary bed he kept in his papal offices. His size made him intimidating, but his build made everyone exceedingly curious about how he moved over marble floors without sound.

That wouldn't have been so crazy-making had anyone had an idea about exactly when he slept: it couldn't have been more than five hours a night. Pius XIII was either awake or at prayer at any time of the day, according to everyone who saw him at such hours, moving soundlessly through the hallways at three in the morning toward his office, or moving down to the office of papal security.

Even though the offices of papal security were in a completely different building, he wanted the *Commandatore* on hand — no one was quite sure if he was just being prudent after the repeated attempts on his predecessor, or if this was a habit carried over from his former diocese. It was rumored back during the last papal conclave that he had once beaten a man who had threatened a parishioner. The rumors were never verified.

A priest walked into *il Papa's* office in a building next to the colonnade. He was a man with short, gray hair, a strong Roman nose, and brown eyes that twinkled with the anarchy so common among the residents of the Mediterranean, descended from the Roman mobs that ran the city into the ground over a thousand years.

The priest said, "We've got a problem, your Holiness."

Pius XIII looked up at him. "Oh?"

"We've got two murders on our hands. Gianni took them from the local cops."

"Why? Don't we keep him busy enough?"

"The body fell on his car."

The Pope nodded. "Most unfortunate. Someone we know?"

"David Gerrity and Giacomo Clementi. Clementi landed on Gianni's."

The Pope's lips twitched with annoyance. "Blast! I had such hopes for both of them. Any word on Figlia's investigation?"

"Not yet, it's only just started. He's busy with the Secret Service and Egyptian police. Thankfully, my best man was at the scene to meet Clementi. Obviously, something happened."

"Obviously," the Pope said, unhappy. He stared hard at the Bishop. "XO, this has happened twice already: I can't let this interfere with what we're doing together, it's too important to me, to our people — I'd say to our survival, but it's too melodramatic. Pius XII *must* be canonized, no matter the cost, *capisce?*"

The other man nodded. "Yes, Your Holiness. I guarantee we will not fail. I'm certain."

"Pacelli thought he could not fail, and look what happened. We can't allow ourselves the luxury of defeat this time. See to it, XO. Remember, any means necessary."

CHAPTER IV: A PIUS MISSION

The summoning had been easy. After all, it was merely, "We lost a target in Rome," on a cell phone. He was then given information about the contact, and his travel information.

Scott "Mossad" Murphy allowed his mind to drift over the information he had been given. According to German Intelligence, a terrorist on the Mossad hit list had been found in Rome with two bullets in him. It looked like a professional killing, and Mossad didn't kill him.

And, since it's Rome, they decided to send in their golden goy, he thought. He looked around the Roman landscape and wondered, *Gee, it's not like a blue-eyed, dark blond Irish Catholic from Boston will stand out in Rome! What have my superiors been smoking?*

Murphy couldn't argue. As a Catholic, he had strong Goyim Brigade contacts in the area, so it sort of made sense. But still, if bullets were already flying, King Saul Boulevard should've known better than to send him.

Now all he needed was to meet his German contact at the alfresco restaurant. Murphy had only been given a contact phrase, and nothing else. At least he would get some fresh air while he waited.

Murphy caught his reflection in the restaurant window. His mix of brown-blond hair had effected profound confusion among his enemies, and the various dyes he employed made him excellent for work around the world. His skin was pale, and his eyes were dark enough blue to be considered a dark brown with improper lighting, which he always managed to find in the West Bank. He wasn't that tall, almost like he had suffered from slight malnutrition in his youth. His build was due to habits formed during his previous existence as an accountant. He was very thin, which his family had always thought to be a genetic aberration, given that both of his parents and all of his five siblings — older and younger — had been tall basketball players.

He sighed. *I'll make do. There's gotta be some tourists somewhere.*

"Is this seat taken, or do you have a wife?" asked a rich, female voice. The voice was young, but over twenty, and had notes out of Barber's *Adagio*.

She also said the magic words. Murphy turned in his seat.

The woman standing next to him was about 5'7", and wore a charcoal-black turtleneck over deep gray slacks — dress so professional she could have been on her way to see the Pope. Her light pink lips were curled into a smile, which made her glittering amber eyes light up. Her eyes were slightly almond-shaped, set above gently sloped, obviously Slavic cheekbones. Her hair was a deep brown laced with flecks of dark gold, and the ringlets stopped about the middle of her well-endowed breasts — full enough to be noticeable, but not intrusive.

Scott Murphy felt his jaw begin to slacken, and automatically regained his composure. "I'm not sure if you want the chair, it looks a little dirty to me," he replied. The chair was as shiny as polished silver.

She smiled, eyes glittering. "I know it does. I'm used to dirty, I come from Germany."

Really? Can't hear the accent. "How is the weather this time of year?"

"It's snowing," she said as she slid into the chair with grace. It was May.

Murphy opened his mouth and moved his lips, but no sound came out. He paused, rubbed his lips as though entering into deep thought, and slid his fingers up his face to rest on his cheek. He mouthed one more time.

She scanned his mouth, reading, "Do you read lips?"

"Yes," she answered.

"Do we need to exchange names?" he mouthed.

"We'll be working together," she replied, mouthing the same way. "So I'd guess so."

He offered his hand. "Scott Murphy."

"Manana Shushurin. Call me Mani." She squeezed his hand lightly. "What have you been told?"

"Someone died, and we're supposed to keep watch on someone... I hope you're not the spy. You're too dazzling. You'll attract attention like you have flares attached to you."

"That's the point. I'm considered the perfect spy."

Scott Murphy blinked. "The perfect spy is a gray colorless little man whom no one would notice if you tripped over him... which is sort of why they call me that around the office."

She beamed. "Exactly. What were your thoughts on first contact?"

"That you're too pretty to be a spy..." He stopped and chuckled. "Point taken."

She nodded. "We were also told you attract no attention; I can be a diversion."

No kidding; you're a weapon of mass distraction. "Can you be inconspicuous for, I don't know, the majority of the mission?"

She took out a cap, one usually seen on muggers in old "Foggy London" movies, and set it so the sweatband stopped just over her eyebrows. No one could see her face unless she was looking right at them.

"Not a bad adjustment," he admitted. *And it would be hard for someone to report what she looked like, even if they stared right at her... and they will be.*

She nodded. "Thank you." She studied him for a moment with those brilliant brown eyes. She looked over his hands, his arms, his face. She took him in, and then took him in again. "May I ask, why did they send *you?* Sorry, but—"

"I don't look Jewish?" he joked. "I'm Irish Catholic."

She cocked her head to one side with curiosity. "And yet you're in Mossad?"

Murphy shook his head. "First of all, we just call it 'the Office.' We never call it... by that name. As for me... Well, you heard about John 'Taliban' Walker Lindh? An American who went to Jihad University in Yemen? Well, I decided that we needed one for our side—" he started talking again, "—and I joined up."

The waiter set down his cappuccino and walked away. Without even looking to see if he was out of earshot — which he was — Murphy continued. "Let's just say," he mouthed, "that I had a good view of the World Trade Center on an unfortunate day."

Shushurin cocked her head, admiring what seemed to be Murphy's own built-in radar.

A pipe appeared in his hand, and he held it up, waiting for her approval. She nodded. He lit up and let the smoke drift up, briefly letting his mind flit back to the morning of September 11, 2001. "Anyway, what about you? Shushurin sounds odd for a German."

"East German," she answered, as though it sufficed for an explanation.

"Ah, Russian father?" He thought a moment, considering the history of the area, and the border shifts over time. "Or is it Polish?"

"It's from Lvov. It used to be part of Poland, then Russia. Do you carry a weapon?"

Murphy shook his head. "I've always been better at just spycraft. I can improvise." He stopped mouthing his words as the waiter drifted closer to them—"I can make use of almost anything they have here for all sorts of"—as the waiter drifted away behind them, he started mouthing as soon as the waiter was out of earshot—"weaponry."

Manana cocked her head. "I have to ask, how did you know he was out of range?"

"It's a gift," he mouthed to her. As he talked, he continued making hand gestures like an Italian Jack Benny, always able to hide his mouth from possible lip readers in the room, but making it seem natural. "As I said, I don't do guns — as soon as you use, you lose. I'm *never* violent." He emphasized that with a sharp cutting gesture. He leaned forward. "So, what's the mission? Who, exactly, has died?"

"Ashid Raqman Yousef."

"I hope he wasn't related to Ramzi Yousef," he joked.

She moved forward, allowing the world to imagine that she was merely about to kiss him across the table. "He was."

Murphy didn't show his visceral, gut-jerking reaction.

This could be bad.

In the early 1990s, Ramzi Yousef had taken the first major swipe at the New York City World Trade Center. Before there had been Osama bin Laden, there was Ramzi Yousef. Even though that bin Laden had already started his career, next to Yousef, bin Laden had looked like a rich playboy who wanted a play at jihad, a mere Gucci terrorist. Yousef had made grand plans for terror across the planet, even making detailed plans for killing Pope John Paul II.

"What was Ashid Yousef doing here? I know his brother wanted to kill the Pope, they found the plans on him when they caught him, but—"

She smiled, almost reading his thoughts, and squeezed his hand to cut him off. "Yousef was doing research. The BND kept an eye on Yousef. He spent weeks going back and forth from his hotel to the Vatican Library. Then he died. Two shots, very professional. One day, Ashid made a phone call to Iran, and woke up dead."

Murphy blinked. "Odd. That sounds more like an Office hit than anything al Qaeda would've done." Murphy continued. "Could friends of his have hired someone to kill him? It's unlikely, but a well-disciplined terrorist takedown of one of their own? They'd sooner steal a page from *The Godfather,* invite him back home, and work him over there. It's either that or it was a CIA hit, but even that makes no sense; the CIA would kidnap him, or follow him around until he led them to someone higher up in the chain of command."

Shushurin nodded, reached out and touched his arm to complete the illusion of intimacy. His eyes brightened in response. "Is there another possibility?"

Murphy took her hand in his. "It was a rush job. It needed to be handled immediately. Which means he was either going to run and talk to someone, or about to compromise an attack."

"Could they have spotted our tail?" she asked.

He squeezed her hand right back, hoping that they would both go unnoticed as they continued with the charade. "This is Rome, not Moscow rules. They don't have counteragents trailing our tails, which means that Yousef would have had to have spotted and reported your people. Unlikely if he was sent here to do research. I mean, if he knew how to empty an assault rifle into the Mall of America, he'd be out in the field, doing it, not locked up in some vault."

"Vault?"

"The Vatican Archives — a large, fully stocked, fully furnished vault. My only question is, what was he doing?"

* * *

Wilhelmina Goldberg blinked at the priests and nuns in the Vatican gardens. The short Secret Service Agent didn't even look away from the bizarre sight in front of her. "Tell me they're not doing what I think they're doing."

Giovanni Figlia grinned broadly, looking like a male Italian fashion model as he kept one hand in his black slacks, and gestured with the other. "Tai chi. His Holiness wanted them to do this, if only to keep in shape. It's only twenty minutes a day, as voluntary as the rest of the hour."

Goldberg raised a brow. "Rest of?"

Figlia nodded. "We've hired someone to train our 'citizens' for self-defense. His Holiness wants to be certain that if someone shoots at him, anyone who feels compelled to attack the shooter could do so safely."

Hashim Abasi frowned in thought at the idea. The Egyptian cop looked at the elderly nuns, the pudgy and middle aged priests, and shook his head. "Surely, you're joking. The odds of such a thing happening—"

"Oh?" Figlia asked. "You mean an apprehension by one of our fine, upstanding nuns?"

Abasi bowed his head. "Of course."

"The first person on John Paul II's would-be assassin was a nun, right before a Swiss Guard. Luckily, the shooter didn't mind being taken without a fight. Should it ever happen again, only with a suicide bomber, the Pope wants our people to have a chance."

Goldberg nodded her obviously dyed blonde head. "Not bad. They're a replacement for CATs – a Counter Assault Team, what we use to support a detail when it comes under fire." She frowned, revealing worry lines all over her mouth, as well as her forehead. "Given the size of Vatican City, there isn't much need for a mobile CAT. Training civilians isn't a bad idea, if your trainer is smart enough to teach them when to approach and when to run."

He nodded. "*Si, Signore* Ryan is very good about that."

Abasi unbuttoned his tan jacket and slipped his hands in the pocket as he watched the Vatican residents continue to go through the motions. The Egyptian counted them and tried to decide how effective they would be. "And where, may I ask, is your trainer from? American Special Forces?"

"No. While *loro sono molto bene*—" Figlia paused, and began again, remembering to stay with English. "These are ordained priests and nuns. We will not have them carry guns. Our objectives needed them to learn how to disarm and disable someone. Special Forces do not have the luxury of taking prisoners. This man teaches mostly Krav Maga, but uses other techniques as well."

Goldberg was intrigued. *Protection that avoids killing?* "Who'd you get?"

Another big grin. "I'll introduce you."

They approached as the final tai chi position was taken. The trainer saw them coming and said *"Tempo finita. Take cinque."*

The trainer took a step off of a box and shrank a foot. While he moved with the lazy grace of an egotistical cat, and beamed with a charming grin, something was... off. He was in his late twenties, but he gave the impression of being younger, just in the way he walked, and how he looked at them with his electric-blue eyes — Goldberg had only seen that color once, in the middle of a particularly bad lightning storm. They stood out even against his pale skin and stark black hair.

"Hey, Johnny, *come stai, mio amico?*" he said grandly.

Figlia tried not to smile. Rusty phrases like that were as far as this man's Italian went, and calling him "Johnny" instead of "Gianni" was typical of how he handled Italian. "I wanted to show you off. Meet Hashim Abasi , Egyptian police, and Villie Goldberg, U.S. Secret Service."

The shorter man nodded and shook hands with each. "Charmed. Sean Ryan, of Sean A.P. Ryan & Associates."

Goldberg cocked her head. "Aren't you a security company? American?"

He nodded with a big grin, the bright eyes nearly glowing. "Yes, ma'am. Have you heard of me?"

She cocked her head and closed one hazel eye, studying him a moment. He was basically neat – professional haircut, clean cut, business casual dress... Her eyes shot open as it occurred to her.

"Oh, crap!" she blurted.

Sean Aloysius Patricus Ryan barked a laugh. "Yup, you've heard of me. Normally, I would say don't believe anything you hear, but one of my employees is ex-Secret Service, so in your case, I would think you can pretty much believe everything." He jerked a thumb over his shoulder at the priests and nuns. "Don't worry, though. I'm just teaching the civvies how to hold their own without killing or being killed. You can have Gianni's boys and girls, I don't deal in such things. Heck, I barely deal in this."

Abasi glanced at him askew, still lost about the conversation. "Odd to hear you say that. If I may ask, what were you before you did... this?"

"Hollywood stuntman." Abasi's deep brown eyes almost popped out of his head. Sean Ryan laughed. "Now you know why they got me — I was trained how to hurt people without *really* hurting them, something the Fathers and Sisters need to learn."

Abasi laughed. "With their bare hands, I suppose?"

Sean paused, turned, and walked back to the box he'd been standing on. He opened it and came back with a small black cylinder in each hand. He flicked both wrists, snapping the cylinders outward — they telescoped into tactical batons. He touched the butt of each baton together and twisted, locking them in place to form a seven-foot staff.

"I figured it would just be easier to teach them previously approved methods. I mean, if a medieval monk could use a staff without being excommunicated, it shouldn't be a problem now."

Goldberg raised her hand. "'Scuse me, isn't this a little much?" She looked at Commander Figlia. "Your Pope seems to take a great interest in security. What is he, paranoid?"

For the first time, Figlia scowled. "Let us take a walk."

They walked for a minute, making certain that they were far enough away from Abasi and Sean to be out of earshot. The head of Vatican security slipped his hands in his pockets, and made certain to keep his movements careful and controlled. "Tell me, Special Agent Goldberg, what do you know about the Sudan? Before the North-South split of 2011."

She shrugged. "Arab Muslims killing or enslaving black Christians."

"*Si.* You know the nearest, strongest, non-Muslim government? Uganda. The strongest religion? Catholicism. *Archbishop* Kutjok was the most hated clergyman in the Sudan. They tried to kill him twice, and that was before he became Pope. He's terrified of a suicide bomber in the middle of Saint Peter's Square killing dozens in an attempted assassination. He wants *me* to make sure that doesn't happen, and *you* to double-check me, and Sean Ryan to make sure that innocent civilians aren't helpless civilians. In the Pope's world, all life is sacred, a gift from God, and *no one* is exempt from that. Trust me, he's less worried about his death than the deaths of those around him. He knows the risk he takes every time he steps outside, and he finds it an acceptable price to pay for doing the work of God. But he doesn't believe it's acceptable that people should die just because they gathered to see him."

* * *

Sean Aloysius Patricus Ryan watched Figlia and Goldberg walking away, and once they stopped, he started reading their lips.

"Hollywood?"

Sean sidestepped to square himself with Abasi, still reading lips around the larger man. "Yes, it was a family business.

45

Now it's security."

Abasi leaned over, blocking Sean's view of the other two — but Sean had already gotten enough details.

"What made you qualified for this sort of work?"

Sean looked at the Egyptian straight on, and quickly analyzed him. Abasi was big and bulky, without moving awkwardly. He certainly lifted, but he would probably take a second or two if Sean needed to drop him. Abasi's tan suit was well tailored, and probably new — which was unsurprising, given the nature of his assignment would include making a good impression to a foreign country. Abasi looked 35, but was probably older, though Sean would have usually laid money on the reverse being true.

Sean gave him a broad grin. "I'm a mick. I beat people up for fun, doncha know?"

Abasi smiled. "I am sure my wife would have liked that." Too bad she's dead, Abasi thought.

Sean chuckled. "I always knew the Irish would marry anybody." He hesitated a moment. "Or is it that anybody will marry the Irish?" He gave a casual shrug. "To tell the truth, I have a few connections here and there that keep me just one step ahead of everybody else. That and a Kevlar suit's all I need."

Abasi looked at the young man, studying his form and how he held himself. He was relaxed, almost languid, but in the way that a panther was lazy. The grace of a well-fed predator. "I somehow doubt it is that simple."

Sean grinned. "Is it ever?"

CHAPTER V: A PIUS DEATH

Maureen McGrail crouched over the dead priest in Dublin. Father Harrington's arms had been spread out at his sides, deliberately posed as though he'd been crucified. The old man had been shot first in both knees, and finally in the heart. On his forehead was a precisely carved swastika. His silver hair was spotted with black, crusted blood, and his pale blue eyes were frozen open, staring at the ceiling.

McGrail sighed into her face mask before rising. She always hated wearing the bright white spacesuits at homicide scenes — meant for the protection of the evidence — but then, except for the occasional public-service murder, she just didn't like homicides. Her green eyes scanned the room, and the luggage on the bed.

"And where were you going, Father?" she asked in a soft brogue. "And why?"

McGrail looked to the police officer in the hallway. For some reason, she could clearly hear him humming, "Come Out Ye Black and Tans." "How old was he?" she asked. "Where was he going?"

Her assistant, Peter Boyle, looked up at her. "Almost ninety. He had booked a plane ticket to Rome to give an affidavit in the canonization thing."

McGrail smiled. "Which one? Is it one of the local boys? One of the Belfast Martyrs?"

"Pius XII, Pope from 1939 to 1958."

McGrail furrowed her milky white brow. As a police officer, McGrail had never needed to know much about history. The most she learned about history she read in what she dubbed "Catholic Paranoid novels." They were stories about the Knights of Malta, Knights Templar, or the Church suppressing the truth about everything that happened before the Enlightenment.

As if the Church were ever that organized.

They were fun reads, but rubbish history.

"What about the Pope?" she asked.

Peter smiled. "You have no idea what I'm talking about, do you?"

She rolled her eyes and patiently shook her head as she walked out of the room. It was true that her fellow citizens might read ten times the per-capita average for Europe. And yes, Dublin might have had one bookstore per block. And she could get a fellow Irishman to argue about anything from microcircuits to "the year of the French." But the average Garda precinct would never have enough people to keep up with omnivorous Irish readers.

Boyle cleared his throat like a professor beginning a lecture. "Pius XII, born Eugenio Pacelli. Died 1958. There are books that blamed him as emissary from the Vatican, as papal Secretary of State, and as Pope, for aiding and assisting Hitler's rise to power. Still another tries to make a case that the Pope did nothing to save Jews in Rome, and the only reason so many survived was due only to the rank-and-file Catholic priests."

McGrail raised an eyebrow at him. "You've specialized in the subject?"

Boyle grinned. "No, but it's amazing what you can fake just by reading the backs of books."

McGrail sighed. "So, our dead man was to testify on the matter? He was summoned?"

"No, volunteered. We talked to the maids about how he's been the last week. Agitated beyond all hell; he was annoying everyone, muttering that 'the truth must come out'."

She grinned. Boyle had a near-perfect memory, so everything he had just said was a near-quote. "He was going to talk about death camps and such?"

"Not quite. You see, Father Harrington was with Father Carroll-Abbing down in Rome when Harrington was still in the seminary."

McGrail cocked her head to one side. "Father Carroll-Abbing?"

He nodded. "Ever read Susan Zuccolti's *Under His Very Windows?*"

"Aren't I happy to let someone else fight out the whole thing and wake me when the last man is standing?" she said with a smile. Boyle tried not to roll his eyes at the way she asked questions for almost every sentence. It was almost a regional dialect – if "Ireland" could be considered a region. It wasn't a particularly urban way of speaking, but she didn't quite sound like she was in county Kerry, as those folks tended to not speak to people, but sing to them, their accents were so lyrical. "She was a Catholic basher, ya?" McGrail asked.

"Not quite. Priests and nuns were the heroes in her book; her main argument was that while the rest of the Roman Catholic Church acted, Pius was asleep at the switch, through either timidity or malice aforethought." He smirked. "Google is your friend, ya?"

McGrail nodded, stepped out in the hall, and then stripped off the hood of the suit, letting her raven black hair fall over her shoulder blades. She breathed in fresh air. "So this Carroll-Abbing is?"

"One of the hero priests — Irish. He died in 2001, in Rome. Father Harrington here — on the floor — was a seminarian in Rome in the forties — in his mid-teens, if my math is right. Who knows, Harrington might have been a footnote."

McGrail sighed. "Well, he is now, isn't he?" She peeled the suit off her body. By the time she was done, she wore only her black suit pants and loose white blouse; throw in the running shoes and she was five-six. "Any sense to this being a neo-Nazi thing?"

He cocked his head.

"Thought not. I was called in because I'm Interpol, and someone wants me to fly to Rome, wasn't I?"

"Father Harrington was killed late yesterday, early today, don'cha know? We left the body *in situ* so you could see everything before it was disturbed. We called Rome. They'd be happy to help with our inquiries. Rome is expecting you soon enough, about six o'clock their time."

"Doesn't that mean I'll—"

"Be leaving almost immediately? Definitely."

McGrail headed for the door. "If you need me, won't I be home, packing?"

McGrail stepped out onto the solid foundation of a Dublin street. She looked out over the early morning emptiness of the sidewalks deeply, enjoying the quiet. All of the doors on the buildings around her — in good old-fashioned tradition — were bright, vivid colors, each different from the other, in an assortment of greens and blues, purples and even the occasional... was that brown?

She looked behind her at the ugliest door on the block, which belonged to the Markist seminary she had just left, a garish color that looked like it wanted to be either brown or black, and only resulted in the color of mud.

"Aren't they all barbarians?" she muttered.

McGrail was about to go about her business when she stopped a moment. She turned and leapt up the seminary stairs, taking them two at a time. "Boyle!"

Peter's head peeked into view over the top of the stairs. "What?"

"Did Father Harrington live here?"

"No, he's diocesan, over in Kerry. He was invited. The Markists were having a symposium on the Pius thing, and this guy was going to give a lecture tomorrow, then be on a plane to Rome not long after."

"Can I go to his place, then? Or will the Captain not allow that?"

Peter Boyle shrugged. "Only if you can be three places at once."

She groaned. "Are the Kerry boys at least searching it?"

He smiled. "Leave it to us to worry about that. I'll let you know when they get around to finishing a report. Okay? Enjoy Italy."

"Maybe." She turned to leave, and then stopped, looking at the Markist brochures for the order and the seminary. She picked one up before heading out the door. The cover read, "Markist Brothers, Founded Berlin, 1958."

The year Pius XII died. Hmm. Anyway, we're off to see the Pontiff, the wonderful Pontiff of Rome...

* * *

Giovanni Figlia took both Hashim Abasi and Wilhelmina Goldberg into the basement of the Office of the Swiss Guard, a building next to the colonnade around St. Peter's Square. The subterranean level looked somewhat new in comparison with the rest of the city, with metal security doors that Goldberg would have sworn she had seen on the vault containing the Crown Jewels of England.

Commander Figlia used a hand print, iris and retinal scan, as well as a nine-digit alphanumeric readout combination panel.

"What is this place?" Goldberg asked. "Where you keep old Nazi war criminals the Church is protecting?"

Figlia cringed, remembering the scolding he had received for joking about something similar once.

The metal vault began to swing open, very slowly. "Here, in fact, is our weapons vault."

The wall of the vault was lined with bullet-resistant glass cases of futuristic weapons, as well as some old-fashioned guns, in addition to the obvious gas canisters, rubber bullets, and beanbags launched from muzzles the size of baseballs. And there were a few normal fragmentation grenades and flash-bangs. The entire weapons collection consisted of chrome and Plexiglas. Figlia stepped inside, and presented it like Tony Stark in the first *Iron Man* film. His black suit and polo shirt meshed so well with the chrome and glass finish, it was almost as though he had dressed to match the décor.

Goldberg gaped and took several steps inside. She tried to see directly into some of the cases, but eventually gave in, and grabbed a step ladder so she could see inside.

Abasi stayed at the door and looked around at the equipment. "I didn't know you could afford weapons like this," he began.

"We can't, really." Figlia stepped into the vault, leaning up against the wall opposite Godlberg. "The older guns, the lethal ones, all... *come se dice?* Ah, yes, they 'fell off the back of a CIA truck' during the 1980s. After the Pope was shot, and because *il Papa* was working with the CIA on the Solidarity crisis in Poland, the head of the CIA then, Bill Casey, delivered these. The latest assault rifles we have are all M16A2s — though I would prefer the M8, or more M4s. The rest are non-lethal weaponry we test for the companies that make them. As a result of testing their product, we are given free samples."

Hashim Abasi laughed. "I almost thought you had paid for all of this yourself, like the Saudis' Wahhabi *mutaw'een* – religious police. The ones that drive American SUVs."

Figlia shook his head. "Our budget is... nonexistent, since we are given this for free, which is odd, because I think we should be the second-biggest market for nonlethal weapons."

Figlia quickly opened a case, picking out a boxy, rectangular weapon that looked like an art-deco version of a Stinger missile launcher. "This is from the Air Force Research Laboratory, a directed energy cannon... a microwave gun. It doesn't burn flesh. It only feels like it, very painful."

Figlia gently placed it on his shoulder to demonstrate how to hold it, then placed it gently back in its case. He removed another weapon, which looked like a glorified water rifle.

"Anti-traction gel gun — anyone who tries to drive or walk on this will not be able to. Nontoxic, biodegradable, and dries up in twelve *ore*... hours, depending on conditions. We've also malodorants, stink bombs so bad they are limited by chemical-weapons treaties... which Vatican City never signed, so it doesn't matter."

Abasi chuckled. "You haven't thought of the U.N.'s ways of doing things, have you?"

Figlia shrugged, putting away the weapon. "They are useful third parties, but in terms of making international law, they think they're God, but without the sense. Some say John Paul II was unable to deal with the West because they gave his homeland to the Soviets. I think this pope cannot tolerate the U.N. because they put Sudan on the Human Rights Commission, which is like putting Hitler in charge of the committee on Zionism." Figlia shook his head. "Anyway, we've also the new soft bullets, as well as the WebShot Kevlar nets from Falls Church. This is the one I'm particularly fond of ..."

He pulled out what looked like a flashlight. "It basically uses ultraviolet laser light to transmit an electric current — a Taser beam that works at a range of two kilometers."

At this point, Goldberg coughed firmly so she could get his attention – and she stayed on the stepladder so she could see eye-to-eye with him. "Excuse me, but before you even tell me what your tactics are, what are you doing with all this weaponry? The range of an MP5 is about the length of Vatican City. Right now, you got more than enough artillery to tangle with a small army. Is the Pope expecting an invasion of the Vatican?"

Figlia's eyes went flat and his voice serious. "No. Why?"

"Where I come from, you need enough firepower to keep the shooter's head down. With the MP5s, you got that. With the M16s, you got that squared. I guess you got sniper rifles too. But you can get the same effect by attaching the beam thingy to a telescopic sight. Hell, it could be made into a medium-sized handgun and you can call it a phaser. What am I missing?"

"Nothing," he said flatly. "We're just cautious."

Goldberg looked at Abasi. "You don't believe him? Do you?"

Abasi held up both hands before him, and took a step back. "It would be rude to say so."

"That's what I thought." To Figlia: "For God's sake, you expect me to believe that a Church as anti-science as *this* one will suddenly turn to devices like this? I mean, come on, you only just cleared Galileo two decades ago, and you threatened to cook *him*."

A soft, polite cough sounded behind them. Goldberg looked over her shoulder, and spotted the priest from the bomb site, evident from the silver hair, young face, and bright violet eyes. "If I may answer," he said in a soft, gentle voice. "There are a few problems with your statements. The Church is not anti-Science For example, Nicholas Orsme penned the concept of impetus and inertia over 300 years before Isaac Newton made it his first law of physics. St. Augustine invented psychology in the confessional 1500 years before Freud was conceived and is so listed in the better history-of-psychiatry texts.

"Galileo formed *his* heliocentric theory using the astronomical devices in his cathedral, and partially plagiarized a theory from Polish Archbishop Kupernick, generally known as Copernicus.. Galileo's theories wouldn't be proven until two hundred years after he died, and he was told to teach his theories as if they were theories, instead of fact. At the time, there was no evidence that it was true, so even by today's standards, Galileo would have been laughed out of the scientific community."

The priest shrugged. "Thus ends the sermon."

Abasi looked down at the priest from his six-foot height.

"You go by Father... doesn't that mean you walk around in a suit and tie?"

Father Frank laughed. "You've been to America! How nice. First, this is as much my uniform as a police officer's; besides, women simply go *crazy* over the collar." He laughed and waved it away. "They used to say back in the seminary that if a broomstick wore a Roman collar, women would chase after it."

Abasi grinned broadly. "You're very odd for an American priest."

"That's because I'm a Roman Catholic American, not an American Catholic."

Abasi laughed. "Thank you. When I went to America last, I visited Georgetown, run by your Jesuits. They had taken down crucifixes because they accepted money from the government. I do not worship Jesus as you do, but even I have more respect than to take down his image for *money*." He said the last with disdain.

Father Frank smiled. "I used to be a Jesuit. I and many Jesuits of the old school have gone over to the Opus Dei... unofficially."

Agent Goldberg looked on curiously. "Funny, you don't seem to be a right-wing fascist."

Abasi and Father Frank glanced at her. Then, suddenly, Goldberg laughed. "That was a joke, fellas." She rolled her eyes. "So, you routinely go around lecturing random VIPs?" she asked Father Frank.

"Not as a rule, no."

"Whew, good to know..." She frowned. "I'm going to

regret this, but what was Galileo jailed for, anyway? Being an arrogant prick?"

Father Frank hesitated. "He had started as being friends with the Pope. Maybe frenemies. That, and malpractice as a science professor. But, he kept all of his church pensions and kept up all his communications with other scientists around Europe. Was it smart to disobey a direct order from the Church, *and* make fun of the Pope during the Protestant Revolutions? No. But, because the Church sentenced him to house arrest for teaching a theory like it was the Truth, it has been labeled as 'anti-progress'; nowadays it's just good science. Some have even charged that *Newton* was prosecuted by the Church — which would have been difficult, as he was Anglican. Contrary to the claims of some best-selling novels, the church has never suppressed a scientist. Although I can think of a few novelists who'd fit the stake better…"

The priest smiled. "The fact is the Church has been a fan of science, especially with the development of the anthropic principle in 1974, which states that, scientifically, the universe seems to be made for mankind. As a cardinal contemporary of Galileo said: 'the Bible tells us how to go to Heaven, not how the heavens go.' The Jesuits even run the Vatican observatory out in the American desert. No other religion has one."

She glanced at Father Frank. "Can we help you, Father?"

"Yes," he said, as soft as ever. "I was sent to assist Commandatore Figlia in showing you around. He knows the technology, but I know the history." He tapped his collar and smiled. "Besides, a collar can open many a door here. You might say I could even get away with murder."

CHAPTER VI: A PIUS SPY

"He was here going through the Vatican Archives," Veronica Fisher said. She looked down at the clipboard, leaning back against the wall of her makeshift lab.

The white spacesuit covered her 5'6" frame as she glanced over the crime-scene report. Her brown hair was up in a hairnet to avoid contamination, and she looked like she just had come out of a bio-hazard area. She was standing next to a freckle-faced man with silver hair who was well past his expiration date, laid out quite neatly on a metal slab next to her.

However, the corpse of Dr. David Gerrity didn't mind all that much.

Figlia raised an eyebrow. "I thought I was supposed to be the cop here."

She smiled. "His entrance slip to the Archives was in his pants pocket. Stomach was empty, so he hadn't eaten any breakfast."

"He couldn't have simply wanted to go out to eat? Maybe even to the hotel lobby?"

She shook her head. "His hotel shows that room service delivered breakfast and dinner to his room every day he stayed there. No lunch. I'm going to take a guess that Mr.

58

Gerrity ate breakfast, spent all day at the archives, and then wandered back to his hotel room."

"How could you tell that?"

Fisher smiled, brown eyes twinkling with mirth. "Because we get a lot of flakes coming through there. Have you ever heard of a serious scholar who wasn't in need of a keeper? I know of a scholar-priest who needed to have a nun assigned to babysit him because he was found passed out in the Library of San Francisco — he fell into the research for two days straight and forgot to eat, sleep, or leave the building. Your man had the alarm on his watch set for five in the evening, probably so he'd know it was time to leave."

Figlia grinned. "Sounds reasonable enough."

Fisher shook her head. "He was a diabetic — the insulin was in the minibar refrigerator — he couldn't afford *not* to eat, and he shouldn't have been playing games with the lack of lunch, either. It looks as though he must have been much heavier at some point — he had stretch marks along the base of his stomach, and I doubt he was pregnant. Between his age and the diabetes, he had a choice between losing the weight or a leg. So he *had* to set the alarm, unless he wanted to die."

Figlia flinched. "So, what was he researching? Was he here on behalf of anybody?"

"He has a faculty ID card for the Universities of Navarre and Notre Dame, Indiana."

Figlia blinked at the corpse once more. "He looks *Irelandese*."

"Irish? With a name like Gerrity, I'd hope so."

"I could understand Notre Dame, they have a heavy Irish population. But Navarre?"

"He had a doctorate in sacred theology and in Thomistic philosophy."

"How do you know?"

She pulled out a slip of paper she had collected from the man's luggage, now neatly encased in an evidence collection bag. "It says so in a letter of introduction. The signature on it is from a professor at Navarre."

Figlia looked at it, then at her. "It looks like someone knew him well; it says he needs a keeper, lest he forget to eat."

She grinned. "Imagine that." She slid it onto the evidence tray.

"So, he was here on behalf of either one or both colleges, doing what?"

"You should have read the rest of the letter." Fisher slid her gloved finger down the front page. "He was here on his own time, for his own research. Come, I'll show you."

In the next room over, there were several books spread out along the tables, each of them being photographed in their current, bomb-blasted state before they were put back together again. What titles he could read depressed him: *The Deputy*, by Rolf Hochhuth; *Hitler's Pope; Papal Sin; Constantine's Sword;* and *Three Popes and the Jews*.

Figlia groaned. "Oh no, don't tell me that I have to deal with the canonization of Pius XII." He slapped his forehead. "The American press already wants to hand Joshua his own head on a stick; this is going to be even worse."

Fisher shrugged. "Sorry about that, but they were at the scene. And you're right. I know some papers will have people swearing up and down that His Holiness put a hit out on Dr. Gerrity here."

Figlia stopped a moment, and suddenly barked out a laugh. "You're kidding, *si*, Ronnie? I'm in charge of Vatican Security; I *stole* this case from the *carabinieri*, and *happened* to be there in time for the body to land on my *car*. Some will say I killed either or both of them."

Fisher laughed. "Well, in that case, Mr. Assassin, you used a very inefficient weapon on Dr. Gerrity - a .22 Beretta with a plastic water bottle for a silencer. We found it at the scene. Granted, the bottle had been crushed in the explosion, but the tape still held it firmly to the gun — our hit man used enough tape to keep an antenna attached to a motor home in the middle of a hurricane."

Figlia thought for a moment. "So Dr. Gerrity was in Italy researching Pope Pius XII; he was executed by our other man, who was killed in the explosion and destroyed my perfectly good ca…"

She nodded. "We're not certain who he is yet, though." She snapped her gloves off. "I'll be able to tell you after we get the prints off the Beretta."

"Why not off one of his fingers?"

Fisher spared him a glance. "No fingers. I'll try running a facial-recognition program on him once I get him cleaned up. Your windshield put up a hell of a fight before it lost to his face. We'll also print out those cell photos you took at the crime scene; maybe his face looked better when it first landed. As it is, any more damage, we'd need to go for facial reconstruction. His was almost shredded, and it's a miracle he looks this good." She undid the hairnet. "So, what happened to your guests?"

"I pushed them off on a priest just long enough to stop by. I didn't want to wind up giving you something only to put it on the back burner."

She gently elbowed him in the ribs. "You could always let me tell you tonight, maybe over dinner, when I have the full report?"

He took her hand, and kissed it. "If only I could. The

problem is I'm working late tonight."

"Ah well. Who's heading the detail today?"

"Minor."

She thought for a moment. "I wish I could tell the Swiss Guards apart — they all have blonde hair and blue eyes, I feel like I'm in a Nazi movie whenever they walk by."

Figlia laughed. "*Tu scherzo, si?* These guys wear costumes out of a comic opera, designed by Michelangelo, and you think of Nazis? Time to take you away from American movies. Anything on the bomb?"

She shook her head. "Run-of-the-mill black powder. It *might* have been a beeper detonator, but I'm not certain. There was a cell phone in the room, so we're not sure what pieces came from what device just yet. I'm not sure I can tell you who called him last — he was on the phone at the time, because a few pieces wound up in his skull, which means he had it at his ear when the bomb went off — there is no last dialed, or caller ID. It's even money this is prepaid."

One of her assistants came over and handed her a sheet of paper. Fisher read it over and said, "Well, we've got a name on your dead man. We got fingerprints off the gun and the serving cart."

* * *

Manana Shushurin and Scott Murphy strolled along the Spanish Steps, using them to travel from *Via Sistina* to *Via del Babuino*. The stairs were solid marble, going from the *Palazzo di Spagna* leading down between a set of elegant homes — the Italian equivalent of a brownstone, but more red than brown — into an oval plaza with a wide fountain in the middle. The steps were bordered by a solid stone wall, waist-high and at least a foot thick on either side. Where the steps met the wall, a thick unbroken line of red roses traveled the entire length.

Murphy was grateful for the tourist attraction; that way, more people would be looking at the scenery instead of his companion. "Has there been anything else in Rome that's odd? Seriously odd?"

Shushurin checked her watch. "There was an explosion at a hotel today, and a murder. From what I heard, the murderer was blown up."

Murphy avoided stopping dead in his tracks only by dint of rigorous training. "*What?* That's stupid — you don't draw attention to a nice quiet elimination like that."

"Unless someone was sending a message." She shrugged, making her shirt tighten across her chest — it briefly attracted the eyes of one man on the steps, who was promptly chastised by his wife; the distinctive slap across his face echoed like the crack of a rifle.

"There was talk of it smelling like a fireworks display in the air," she added, "so I doubt it was an accident."

Murphy arched a brow. "How did you hear about that?"

"It's Italy, people talk… and talk. There was only one cop at the scene, a few pedestrians, and the car."

"Car?"

Manana Shushurin nodded. "The corpse landed on a passing car. I heard it belonged to the head of Vatican security."

Scott Murphy thought for a moment. That was uncannily close to who he and Shushurin were supposed to keep tabs on — Hashim Abasi, an Egyptian police officer who had arrived in Rome to coordinate with the Vatican's Central Office of Vigilance, in order to guarantee a safe papal visit through Egypt.

Given Abasi's terrorist connections and the timing of the visit, the German BND thought it would be a good idea to follow the man. He couldn't find a reason to disagree.

"I guess Vatican security isn't too happy," He concluded. "His name is Giovanni Figlia, isn't it?"

"How did you know?"

"I'm a spy. Figure it out," he lied. He knew exactly who and where Figlia had come from, because his boss kept files on everyone around the world's top leaders, down to the upper echelons of their organizations, and the Catholic Church was no exception; though he had a special "in" with the church that other Israeli government departments only dreamed about.

Shushurin continued anyway. "From what happened, it seemed Figlia took over the investigation, and the Italians let him have it."

He sighed. "They would — the Italians are so non-confrontational that they're only outdone by the French. The Italian military's tanks have one gear forward and three back; French tanks only go in reverse… at least in the jokes in my neighborhood."

"Boston, New York, or Tel Aviv?" she asked.

He gave her a sidelong glance. "How—?"

Shushurin tapped her ear. "You hide the accents well, but you're not really trying."

Murphy smiled. "I'll work at it. Anyway, if Figlia's on the case…" he stopped, and blinked. "Wait a second, why is *he* working it? Did this happen in Vatican City?"

She shook her head, her hair softly moving with it. "In a hotel right outside the Vatican."

He felt the urge to run toward St. Peter's. "That sounds

like a great place for someone to stay if they're working at the Vatican archives, don't you think?"

Shushurin nodded slowly. "Isn't that a little outlandish? Yousef was dealt with cleanly, not with such heavy-handedness."

Sounds like they didn't give her great training at her Charm School; handedness is a word, but who uses it? "How exactly was he done in?"

"On the *Ponte d'Angeli,* shot by a man wearing all black."

Murphy tensed and walked faster, compelled by an odd feeling of dread. His analytic skills were so good that few back at Mossad questioned them, and they questioned everything up, down, and sideways, while hanging upside down and looking in a mirror. The rule was two analysts, three opinions.

"That sounds like a perfect disguise for near the Vatican, don't you think?" he said. "In fact, that's exactly the costume I'd wear."

Murphy stepped onto the *Via del Babuino,* looking for the nearest taxi. Shushurin's long legs kept an easy pace with him all the way. "What is it?" she asked

"We're splitting up," he told her. "I'm going to check out that hotel, see who died. Find Abasi. I'll call your cell when I'm done."

A taxi sped along the *Via del Babuino;* Murphy treated it like any taxi in Boston, and simply stepped in front of it. The taxi stopped an inch away from his knees, and the driver waved at him. Murphy stepped around the car and got in.

"La Basilica di San Pietro. Molto pronto."

He slipped the driver the equivalent of twenty American dollars, which broke any language barrier that might have existed — this passenger wanted speed. Murphy buckled up and held on tight as the driver proceeded to work at breaking the sound barrier.

A man in all black. *I wouldn't be surprised if Yousef's German babysitters had seen a man in actual priestly garb. It would be the perfect disguise: who would notice one more priest? He smiled. I can just see the movie — Vatican hit squads, and they're manned by Jesuits.*

* * *

Father Frank Williams, Jesuit, stood in St. Peter's Square. He was next to the tall obelisk marking the place where St. Peter had been crucified.

Father Frank explained all of this to Abasi and Goldberg in the same gentle voice he might use in talking to parishioners in the confessional — soothing and down-to-Earth.

"If you notice, by standing right where we are, next to the obelisk," he continued, "you can see a nice little optical illusion. If you'll turn your attention to the colonnade, you can see that only one pillar of each row is visible, with the other columns hiding immediately behind. You can actually repeat this on the other side of the obelisk."

Special Agent Goldberg marked the effect, thinking, for some reason, that it would make a great bottleneck. She shook her head. *Wake up, Villie. This is the twenty-first century, not the tenth. Suicide bombers are more likely than an invading army. Bottleneck indeed. You're not even here five hours and already your mind is in the Dark Ages.*

The colonnade was curved in semi-circles enclosing St. Peter's Square. On top of the colonnade, the pillars held up what could only be called a marble roof, or maybe an awning. All of it was solid marble, with the wide pillars made from the stuff of mountains, and God was probably the only one who knew how much it all weighed.

She jotted down one note — *Snipers on the colonnade. Keep the sniper rifles on roof. Add beanbags or rubber bullets if it will keep Pope happy.* Goldberg smiled. *Always keep the big man happy; otherwise nothing gets done.*

While Goldberg pondered the tactical possibilities of the layout, Hashim Abasi merely appreciated the architecture.

Goldberg allowed her hazel eyes to flicker over the square. It was the main entrance to Vatican City, the only gap in the perimeter. "Isn't it a little odd to have walls around the city?"

Father Frank chuckled, pointing at the walls. The sun glinted off of the priest's ring: it was a gold ring with two swords crossing behind a gold crucifix, set on a red background. "The walls, as you can see, are made of solid stone blocks. Those are meant to fend off possible invaders. However, the wall wasn't totally constructed in the 'dark ages,' as some ignorant people like to call them."

She nearly jumped. *What, he reads minds now?* She would have been offended, but he had said "ignorant people" in such a sad way--more disappointed than mocking.

The priest continued. "You'll notice the black, wrought-iron and additional, more modern stonework that adds at least another fifteen feet to the wall's height. This was installed during World War II, meant to keep out the fascists."

Goldberg almost started a discussion on "Hitler's Pope," but she considered it rude to disagree with the priest who had taken the time to show them around.

Father Frank snapped his fingers, and his violet eyes lit up with glee. "I just remembered, in reference to your perimeter security question — during the war, we had a clearly demarked line in front of the colonnade, a narrow white line you can still see. The Nazis had two guards just outside the line to keep troublemakers in, but they weren't all that bright. The wall is ample to keep out most invaders." He looked down to meet her eyes. "However, it's not like we can lock up St. Peter's Square every night."

She smiled. *Perimeter security? How did he know that's why I asked?* The line of patter made her wonder what this priest had been before the seminary. He wasn't born with that collar, was he? He might have been some sort of Vatican history scholar, but that would hardly account for answering security questions before she asked them.

History aside, where the hell does he get off answering the questions I didn't ask?

Father Frank smiled. He read her face like a neon billboard. "As you noticed, the Office of the Swiss Guard is just inside the wall, and immediately next to the colonnade. This, of course, is not a coincidence. As with any protection force, you want your guards at the front door. As it happens, the Pope chose to park his office right across from the Swiss Guards."

Abasi furrowed his brow. "Why is Commandatore Figlia's office in the same structure as the Pope?"

"The Pope takes a hand in almost everything around here, from the Communion wafers to the design of the postage stamps," Father Frank answered, "and Commander Figlia's job is no exception."

Abasi cocked his head. "Most odd. I know many of our Muslim clerics are not entirely otherworldly, especially the religious police, but to be that micromanaging?"

"Entirely too much," Wilhelmina Goldberg concluded for him with a bob of her blonde head.

He nodded. "Just so."

She frowned, then looked at Abasi. "I didn't know 'micro-managing' was a word being taught in ESL courses."

"I read Dilbert comic strips online. Amazing how much it reminds me of my job."

Goldberg laughed. "I hear you."

Abasi nodded solemnly. "Good, I would hate for you to be going deaf. You only just met me."

Special Agent Goldberg was about to correct herself, thinking that he had misunderstood, but she caught his broad grin. *He just made a joke, okay.*

"In answer to your question," Father Frank replied, "from what I know of the life of His Holiness, he believed, as the late John Paul II did, that 'if you don't go to bed tired, you didn't do enough.' As it is, no one is entirely certain that he indeed *does* sleep; he seems to work at an almost obsessive rate; he has personally taken it upon himself to coordinate the devil's advocates for each canonization case, as well as the managing of most of the facilities. There are days in which I believe he may liquidate the Vatican museums."

"Why doesn't he?" Goldberg asked. "I mean, the Church is supposed to be poor, isn't it?"

He grinned broadly. "Ah, you're a fan of St. Dominic, are you?"

"What do you mean?"

"A Pope showed Dominic around the Vatican treasury, and made the mistake of saying 'The descendants of Peter can no longer say "of gold and silver, I have none." ' Dominic replied, 'Neither can they say, "Arise and walk.' " Father Frank smiled.

"In this case, I'm not sure the Italian government, or the people, would allow the treasures to be sold," the silver-haired priest continued. "The Vatican museums bring in plenty of tourist business. Let's not forget we have pilgrims come in weekly, housed by the Italian hotel industry, fed by the Italian food industry. For all of their surface anti-clerical stances, they like us. We're the original Men in Black, if you don't count the Dominicans." He paused, and laughed after a moment's thought. "Maybe that's why we aren't liked by the conspiracy-theory set in the U.S.—they think we're agents of the government. That would be funny."

Father Frank shrugged it off. "In any event, our treasury is less a treasury and more a depository for objects, and many of our 'worldly' treasures are in either our archives or our museums."

"*Scusami, padre,*" a voice cried out from behind the priest. Father Frank turned. Between the columns came Giovanni Figlia, lightly jogging. The former athlete looked worried.

Father Frank smiled, confused. "Tour over already, Commandatore?"

Figlia was four columns away when he was blindsided by a pedestrian stepping out from between a set of columns. Figlia almost ran him over, just catching him as he was about to fall. The collision victim held onto Figlia's wrists as he dropped, and they each managed to keep the other from falling.

The other man breathed heavily, as though having an asthma attack. "*Grazie.*"

"*Prego.*"

He looked back at the ground where he could have fallen, straightened his black beret, and walked on. Giovanni Figlia promptly forgot it and moved on, continuing toward the trio.

"We've got a problem," he told them as he reached into his pocket, where he had tucked the information he received

70

from Ronnie Fisher.

Abasi arched his brows. "And what might that be?"

Figlia frowned as he dug in his pockets. He looked back toward the colonnade, knowing it would be nearly impossible to find the pedestrian amidst the marble towers. "It's about our second victim, the shooter; I guess I dropped the file... Doesn't matter, I can get another."

Father Frank looked up at him. "Is there anything I can help you with?"

"Maybe in a few minutes, Father. If you could meet us in my office in fifteen minutes, there will be something I need to ask you about."

* * *

Sean Ryan stood between two of the columns in the colonnade and watched the trio of Abasi, Figlia and Goldberg depart. His self-defense course for the theologically inclined had finally ended, and he had arrived just in time to see Giovanni Figlia nearly run over what looked like a tourist.

Sean frowned thoughtfully. In his profession as a personal protector for the rich, famous, infamous, et al., he had tendencies which even he was forced to admit bordered on the paranoid. Some people thought he was hyper-aware of everything that went on around him. Instead, he considered himself to be always prepared because he could imagine innocent, everyday events in their darkest interpretation. So, when someone did something as innocuous as collide with a passerby, Sean was prepared for the worst.

But in this case, what possible benefit could there be? His electric-blue eyes locked onto the passerby as the man walked into St. Peter's Basilica. It was just someone in a hurry, that was all. Figlia had not been casually slashed, poisoned, or otherwise molested; there was no bomb in his pocket. All was at peace.

And if something was wrong, Sean had the man's entire features and profile memorized: blond-ish, blue-eyed, anemic.

After a moment, he smiled. "Hello, Father Frank."

The priest glided to a stop just short of Sean's side. "How did you know I was here?"

"I've got better hearing than anyone else I know. I used to hear ultrasonic dog whistles." Sean glanced over his shoulder. "How's your practice coming?"

Father Frank nodded. "Well."

"Still taking prisoners?"

"I have little choice in that regard."

"Pity."

The former stuntman pivoted, directing a sharp roundhouse punch at the priest. Father Frank side-stepped, caught the wrist and pulled Sean forward, off his feet. Sean rolled off his shoulders and back onto his feet with ease.

Sean smiled. "Real pity. You could've worked for me."

* * *

Scott "Mossad" Murphy slipped the beret off his head and ducked into Saint Peter's Basilica, where Manana Shushurin waited. She stood outside the confessional as though someone sat inside it. If anyone pointed out to her otherwise, she could always act like a dumb tourist who didn't see the sign. He smiled. If this were America, being around the confessional would be the best place to keep out of sight, because American Catholics avoided the confessional like it was an anthrax-smallpox hybrid.

Murphy slid into one door of the confessional, and Shushurin sighed softly, just loud enough to be heard in all the background noise of the tourist attraction, and slid into the other side. No one noticed, mainly because half the church was filled with people at prayer, and the rest were treating the place like a tourist trap.

Scott Murphy sat in the wooden box of the confessional. He shoved aside the sliding panel and the metal screen, peering into her dark, glittering eyes.

How does she manage to have her eyes catch the light like that, even when there isn't any? "You're right," he began. "Figlia seems to be the guy to follow rather than Abasi. First, I checked the hotel, I expressed shock and outrage over the double homicide, and then I inquired after the corpse. His name was Gerrity, an American professor of some sort, doing research at — guess where? The Vatican Archives. Since Figlia is heading the investigation, and he was meeting Abasi, I managed to… run into him."

He unfolded the piece of paper he had picked from the pocket of Giovanni Figlia, and quickly scanned it. "This was the shooter. Take a look." He slid the sheet through the panel. "It's the résumé of a Red Brigade terrorist. Granted, he was getting up there, but what the hell, a gunman's a gunman. This man, Clementi, was a nasty bugger, but he's been in retirement since the early nineties. Why he would have taken out Yousef is beyond me; but to have two people, working the same archive at the same time, both drop dead? It's unlikely. But this shouldn't be anywhere near his area of interest. He'd sooner want to take the Pope out than Mr. Yousef. And our boy Clementi isn't a blaster. What do you think he was doing getting himself blown up?"

"Well," Shushurin said carefully, still memorizing the résumé. "It could be he was bad with the explosives he was using, or he was blown up by the people who sent him. The former would just make life too easy on us, so my money is on the latter. I just wish there were more forensic reports."

"It's only been a few hours since this guy died, we'll find something. So, am I crazy, or does this have something to do with our man Yousef?"

She slipped him a small smile that warmed him. "I don't know if you're crazy, but either this has been an amazing coincidence, or something is up. It's also possible that this isn't the same killer both times, but who knows? The important thing is to find out who this... Clementi worked for."

"Which means we'll have to stick close to the Italian, as well as Abasi."

"Not all that hard. We know where his office building is, and he can't leave the city without going through St. Peter's Square."

Murphy nodded. "True, but that still leaves me with that one, annoying question."

* * *

"What the heck is an old leftist gunman doing knocking off some *schlemiel* going through the archives on Pius XII?" Wilhelmina Goldberg asked.

She sat back along the wall of Figlia's office, the Commander behind his desk, with Abasi leaning against the wall across from her, arms crossed over his broad chest.

Giovanni Figlia shook his head. "First of all, Gerrity probably wasn't killed for that. Most of the documents from during the war were released decades ago. I'm not sure Gerrity would have wasted his time, but if he's like some, he would have sifted through everything on the presumption that there was a grand conspiracy going on."

"Or," Hashim Abasi added, "he could just be looking for something that others missed. I used to be in the intelligence section of my police. Trust me, I would rather look at the raw data than what someone just handed to me, even if I *know* the person in question is honest."

Goldberg grumbled. "That still leaves the question — a terrorist who disappears for almost two decades reemerges to kill a history geek? Come on, this is as paranoid as Oliver the Stoned."

Abasi politely coughed. "What makes you so certain that this was the only killing this man — Clementi?—committed as part of his return? Have you checked to see if there have been any similar killings? Was this man, Dr. Gerrity, killed in any specific manner?"

"A shot to the stomach and under the chin," Figlia said, "both with a .22 caliber, both fired at an upward angle. Either or both were meant to be kill shots."

The Egyptian nodded. "Mossad assassination squads appreciate a good Beretta in that same caliber, as do your Mafia, if I recall. Was Clementi an employee of the hotel?"

Figlia shook his head. "I have a few of my men flashing his photo around, but I doubt we'll find anyone who knew him. According to his record, he's been able to do infiltration jobs, and hotel security isn't something to brag about."

Goldberg suddenly had to stifle a yawn. She blinked. "Sorry, I'm still trying to readjust to the post-jet-lag phase. It's about..." she glanced at her watch, "4 a.m. where I'm from."

Figlia smiled. "Understood. How about we try to canvass

the area, see if anyone might know where Clementi is from, or who's seen him, then after three hours, we have... I believe you Americans would call it dinner."

Abasi glanced at the Italian. "We? As in the three of us?"

"*Certo. Quando non?* We can all talk and walk at the same time. We spiral out from the blast site, and if we find nothing, we come back. You can tell me about places His Holiness should not go. I'll tell you why he'll go there anyway, and we can work it out from there."

Abasi held up his hands to stop Figlia from continuing. "It's not that. You're head of Vatican Security. You have men who can do this."

Goldberg nodded. "Yeah, the only higher-ups in Homicide that ever got involved were named Columbo and Kojak."

Figlia grinned. "Where's the fun in that?"

Abasi barked a laugh. "You sound just like my wife."

The commander brightened even more. "Ah? And who might this sensible woman be?"

Abasi's face fell at that. "She was a Catholic charities worker stationed in Cairo."

For a very long moment, the comment that spoke of his wife in the past tense had even managed to make even the talkative Italian hush. Between the "Arab Spring" and the rise of the Muslim Brotherhood in Cairo, both the Secret Service Agent and the man in charge of Vatican security could come up with a whole list of very bad things that could have happened to a Catholic woman in the midst of all that.

Abasi was tempted to tell them what had actually happened, but they wouldn't have wanted to hear that. It would have gotten awkward very quickly.

"Um..." Figlia tried to begin. He paused, and combed

his fingers through his black hair. "Besides, His Holiness is going to lock himself in his office for the rest of today, working on canonizations or canon law, whichever catches his attention today. The rest of the city is still a little traumatized, no Italian Popes for over thirty years, so he makes fewer public appearances than Giovanni Paolo in the hopes they'll get used to him gradually. So my worries are a lot less… at least for now."

"Gianni," a boisterous, heavily accented voice called out, "you're still discounting that the Romans are having problems dealing with black people in Italy, much less one as Pope!"

Goldberg jumped off her chair, and Abasi pushed off the wall, about to defend himself against an attack. In the doorway — the door to which had been closed a moment ago — stood a tall, powerfully built black man dressed in solid white robes and a white skullcap.

He grinned, taking a moment to appreciate the shocked looks on their faces. "I'm only the Pope, no need to stand." He laughed, a sound like the echo of thunder over a flat Nebraska plain. He glanced at both of Figlia's guests. "Neither of you are Catholic, correct?"

Goldberg only looked up at this imposing man and nodded. Abasi managed to do slightly better, but only because he had an inch on the newcomer.

Pope Pius XIII grinned. "Thank the Lord." He offered his hand to Special Agent Goldberg. "That means you won't want to kiss the ring; so many people kiss it, I swear that's how it remains shiny."

She shook his hand, and he replied with a firm grip. "Special Agent Villie Goldberg, Secret Service."

"Pleased to meet you. And please, call me Joshua, or Josh." He waved at Figlia. "It's not like I can get *him* to call me by my first name. He'll use it when referring to me in the third person, but not directly. Neither does anyone else." He shrugged and turned to the Muslim. "And you, sir, are?"

"Hashim Abasi," he took the offered hand.

"From Egypt, yes? It's good to see there are three of you to keep me safe. Having fun?"

"We're working on a homicide right now, Your Holiness," Figlia told him, stepping around his desk.

Pius XIII nodded thoughtfully, clasping his hands behind his back so Figlia couldn't kiss the ring. "I see. Who died?"

Figlia nodded slowly. "One is an American professor, and—"

The Pope's eyes went wide. "Not David Gerrity?"

"Yes, how did you—?"

"I invited him here to do research on the Pacelli canonization! You're going to find the ones behind this?"

Figlia nodded. "Yes, we were about to—"

"Get to it!" the Pope ordered. "Don't let me stand in your way. Let me know when you get back, we'll eat together, the four of us!" With a whirl of his white robes, he was gone, as suddenly and as quietly as he had entered.

After a moment of stunned silence after the papal blitzkrieg, Goldberg cleared her throat and said, "Well, now we can't go wrong, can we?"

They laughed.

CHAPTER VII: A PIUS INTERROGATION

Francis Williams watched the door open as the Pope left. He looked inside the office of Giovanni Figlia to see the three security specialists in place. He took the newcomers in at a glance.

Wilhelmina Goldberg's cheekbones didn't seem all that delicate, but weren't exactly hard, either — they were soft for Germanic features, and fit well on her face. Her nose had an almost imperceptible turn to it — he could see where the bridge of her nose stopped only because the cartilage wasn't parallel, although most people would need a protractor to note the angle. She was well-endowed, at least for her size and build, and her shoulder muscles were definitely well-worked, probably with ten-pound weights.

Abasi was very well-built, especially his muscle mass, and Father Frank concluded he worked out regularly and rigorously. He was well-spoken, and probably had a decent socio-economic background. He spoke English with an English accent, so foreign educated. The tan suit fit him very well, and was probably tailored to his unique dimensions.

Hashim Abasi caught him first and waved him in. "Come in, Father, you are on time."

The priest walked in and smiled shyly around the room. "What can I do to be of service?"

"You know some of church history, *si?*" Figlia asked.

Father Frank thought back to his conversation in the Vatican armory. "You could say that."

Figlia waved him into a chair. "What do you know of Pius XII and World War II?"

"And yes," Goldberg added, "this time, we're asking for a lecture."

Father Frank sat, furrowed his brow and thought a moment. "The Vatican released a whole slew of documents back in the 1970s, after the initial Hitler's Pope accusation came up in the mid-sixties, in a play called *The Deputy.* However, in 1967, Israeli Diplomat Pinchas Lapide said he believed that Pius was instrumental in saving at least 700,000, and probably as many as 860,000 Jews from the Nazis, surpassing those saved by all other rescue attempts combined."

Goldberg blinked. "You're kidding."

Father Frank looked at her with his violet eyes. "No, I'm not. He was even eulogized by Golda Meir and Albert Einstein." He learned back in his chair, recalling what he could. "Born of nobility as Eugenio Pacelli. Nuncio to Germany, later Vatican Secretary of State under Pius XI."

Abasi raised an eyebrow, glancing from one to the other. "Why did he not just say, 'We hate the Nazis?' I know it is not diplomatic, but—"

Figlia shook his head at that one. "Is not Vatican policy — if you condemn Al-Qaeda, they could change the name. If one condemns 'men of violence' in Afghanistan, it is obvious, *si?*"

Father Frank nodded. "Correct. But the policy also maintained *official* Vatican neutrality the year the Nazis took Italy. When Jews were arrested in Rome in October 1943, the Vatican was free to… cause trouble. Adolf Eichmann complained about the Vatican delays because the Nazis only captured a thousand Jews instead of 8,000. Over 477 Jews had been given shelter in the Vatican, and thousands in the Pope's personal residence. Over the years, 2,600 Jews were sent out of harm's way into Spain by Pius XII and a Capuchin monk named Father Marie Benoit, who provided false ID papers. The Vatican gave about four million dollars to the Father Benoit operation.

"The Chief Rabbi of Rome, Israel Zolli, mentioned that Pius XII ordered the convents and monasteries to become refuges. When the Nazis held hundreds of Jews hostage in exchange for gold, the Vatican melted down 100 pounds of gold relics. Rabbi Zolli would later become Catholic, taking the baptismal name Eugenio. Over 150 Catholic institutions sheltered Jews during that time." He stopped.

"Wasn't there a commission to study all of the documents?" Goldberg asked.

Father Frank grimaced. "It was less of a commission and more of a lynch mob. Most of them were asking questions that had been answered years before, and all of them were hacks. They were as insightful as Wikipedia, only with more of their own agenda. Come to think of it, one of them was a major source on the Wiki page – which proves either that the website is garbage, or the historian was. Anything else?"

Figlia shrugged. "Not unless you can imagine a reason that someone could be killed over it?"

Father Frank thought a moment, and lied. "No."

"In that case," Figlia said, standing, *"grazie per il suo tempo,* Father. We need to look into a few things. Canvassing the area, for one."

* * *

Scott Murphy walked out of St. Peter's Basilica, going from one bland, ubiquitous look to another. He had quickly unfolded his light, reversible windbreaker, tucked into the perfect, ever-present piece of tourist garb known as the fanny pack. The windbreaker was a simple black, the best, most nondescript color he could find — it worked well in America, where everyone seemed to wear black, and in Rome, he could easily be mistaken for a priest by the unobservant. He covered his dark blond hair with a dark green baseball cap from Trinity College.

The spy drifted through St. Peter's Square like a lost tourist, staring at the map in front of him, nearly running over a priest, then a nun, and then a police officer; following such "klutziness," he tucked himself away at the start of the colonnade at the entrance to Vatican City, trying not to be run over by pedestrian traffic.

The ruse quickly bore fruit, as Giovanni Figlia walked toward him.

I wonder how long it's going to take him before he realizes something's up, Murphy wondered. *He already knows about the hit man, Clementi, but what happens when he finds out there's something wrong about the murder itself? God forbid the idiot used the same gun twice, or even the same* modus operandi, *but this is an Italian terrorist we're talking about here; they never did anything right.*

He frowned at the map. *Why was I called in* now, *anyway? Because our Gucci terrorist struck again, and then got blown out a window? Before, it looked like someone killed Yousef merely because he's a terrorist. But now, I have to wonder what's the* connection between an old Italian Red Army goon, a dead academic, and a dead terrorist. And what would be the punchline if they all walked into a bar?

Giovanni Figlia walked past the Mossad agent, not even looking his way. He was quickly followed by the Arab and the midget. Murphy made a note to himself to get photos of the woman with Abasi and Figlia and send them back to the Mossad.

Speaking of jokes, what happens when you have an Italian, an Egyptian, and a midget walk into a bar?

Murphy counted to ten, and patiently folded the tourist map, not in any rush. Italian drivers believed that two objects *could* occupy the same space at the same time. Thus, thus the trio he tailed would take their time heading to… where?

To Herr *Yousef. After that, things are going to get* real *interesting, and damned near impossible. Yousef probably had a false ID, which someone will look into and discover he's a terrorist; then my boss is going to get a call, and he'll chat with the Americans. When Mossad and CIA both realize Yousef wasn't killed by either of them, the fecal matter is so going to hit the air impeller.*

Murphy finally stepped out from cover, walking onto *Via Ottaviano*, where the assassin had himself been sanctioned. Even though the body had been moved, and the car towed, someone had left the crime scene tape around one lane of traffic, on the property that was demarcated as Vatican City. However, closing one lane didn't stop any of the Italian drivers, who were all crazy enough to take turns going around the crime scene into oncoming traffic.

The spy smiled. *Someone has a thorough crime scene analyst on the employment register, and I don't think it's the Italians.* The Mossad agent continued to move like a cautious tourist, his thumb still in the map as though he might need to refer to it at any moment — which was possible. He'd been in the city before, but very rarely.

Murphy fought his natural curiosity and stay focused on the trio ahead of him. He wanted to try and put the pieces together, but he didn't even have a general idea. Killing guest researchers of the Archives? That was just too plain strange, even for his overactive imagination. He knew disguises that made his friends at Mossad stand up and take notice, and could spin stories out of whole cloth for anyone — there were days that not even his handlers knew if he told them the truth — but he couldn't put this one together.

Even Mani couldn't guess at why Clementi killed Yousef, but I'm certain that whoever did it, they wouldn't be happy if bin Laden's crew got their hands on them. Sigh... a good question is, was Abasi really sent here to coordinate with the authorities about Yousef? Then he heard about Gerrity, and decided to work with Vatican authorities because of the similarities? Possible, I suppose — and it's time to stop thinking, just keep following.

* * *

Hashim Abasi looked over his shoulder down the street for the third time in five minutes.

"Something wrong?"

He glanced down at Wilhelmina Goldberg. "I'm not sure. I tend to look over my shoulder a lot when I'm home... I'm just having similar feelings right now."

"Why? You think we're being followed?"

"Possibly, but I'm not sure who's doing it."

She nodded, sped up a little bit, and tapped Giovanni Figlia.

Figlia turned. "What?"

"We're going back the other way, and work the other side of the street first. You got a problem with that?" He shrugged. "I care where we start? I care how fast we start. Lead on!"

Goldberg did just that, turning on the ball of her foot, walking back in the direction they had come. A tourist in a black windbreaker almost ran into them — he seemed to be paying more attention to the architecture than the people in front of him. She sidestepped him, and Abasi snapped his fingers in front of the tourist's face before he could run into him.

Scott Murphy leapt at the "sudden sound." His attention seemingly snapped back onto the path ahead and he smiled at Abasi. "Excuse me, sir, but might you know where north is?"

Figlia pointed. "Why?"

"You're sure? Oh darn! Thank you." He reached down and pulled out his map, immediately trying to open it.

Abasi merely stepped around him. Figlia and Goldberg also visibly ignored him. Tourists were mostly annoying — and it was best not to stay around them long lest they start asking more questions.

Scott Murphy kept fumbling with the map for thirty more seconds, waiting for them to get far enough away. He was about to fold the map when he watched them duck into a café, and he suspected it wasn't for a cappuccino. He pursued them patiently.

* * *

Giovanni Figlia flashed the waitress his Vatican identification, which got him instant service. He then flashed the photo of the livelier Giacomo Clementi from his old wanted

85

poster.

The waitress, having heard what he wanted, sighed. *"Non lo consosco. Io ho tavoli—"* I don't know him. I have tables—

"That was the before," Goldberg said in Italian. "Would you like to see the 'after' photo?"

Giovanni Figlia almost rolled his eyes. *The American "bad cop" cliché. God save us.*

However, that didn't surprise him as much as the fact that Goldberg slipped out a photo of Clementi's face after his life, and his body, had hit rock bottom. The waitress dropped her serving tray. Abasi dropped to one knee and grab it in midair.

Goldberg, satisfied her work was done, turned and walked toward an empty table next to the counter.

The waitress, on the other hand, said, "I'll get my boss," and disappeared.

Figlia looked at Abasi and arched his eyebrows. Abasi smiled. "Don't act surprised that it worked; in Cairo, going easy would be to 'accidentally' show them autopsy photos first."

A slender, elderly man walked to the counter. *"Mi chiamo Alfredo Mortati. Che cosa le ha fatto?"* I'm Alfredo Mortati. What did you do to her?

Figlia explained his acquaintance as an American, then flashed the less-gory photo.

"Certo, so lui. Venga ogni Giovedì con una pretta." Sure, I know him. He came every Thursday with a priest.

"What did the priest look like?" Abasi asked in English.

Figlia translated his question, and Mortati's answer. "Three different priests. One was taller, with gray hair, only in a crew cut; obviously Roman, and brown eyes. The other was pale, cheekbones like aircraft carriers, not yet graying, light blue eyes. The last one was short, with silver hair, but he looked young, and… had violet eyes." He shared a glance with Abasi.

* * *

Scott Murphy, five tables away, also made a note of it. *So, what's a Lefty terrorist doing with a Catholic Priest? Or why is a Catholic priest with a Communist terrorist?*

And what if a man in black really did kill Ashid Yousef? Catholic hitmen? Yeah, right.

CHAPTER VIII: THE DAYS OF WINE AND WAFERS

As the three of them wandered back to Saint Peter's Square, Wilhelmina Goldberg looked from Abasi to Figlia as they filled her in on the interrogation. "Violet eyes? Silver Hair? Looks youngish? This sounds a lot like a priest we know, doesn't it?"

Abasi nodded. "It does, a little." He leaned against one of the pillars of the colonnade, folded his massive arms, and settled against the marble.

The Secret Service Agent blanched. "A little? Come on! I'm not even certain how much of Williams' Pius XII history to take seriously anymore. He's been meeting a known terrorist!"

Figlia sighed, and rubbed his temples, a headache forming. "But a priest committing murder? Do you wish to suggest he even dialed in the explosives?"

"Did the priest use a phone while he was in the shop?" she asked.

Figlia answered. "I checked out the restrooms, the phones are on the way, and no one can remember seeing if the priest left the table this morning."

Goldberg blinked. "This morning? I thought you said that the priest met Clementi every Thursday?" She checked the day and date on her watch. "It's only Wednesday."

He coughed politely. "When you reset your watch, did you move it forward or backward to the proper time?"

She thought a moment, said nothing, and reset the watch. "So, Clementi met three priests there. Who was it this morning?"

"The one with violet eyes," Abasi answered.

"We saw Frank outside almost immediately after the bomb went off. How exactly is he *not* someone we'd like to talk to?"

A soft voice said, "Imagine trying to take a rabbi in for questioning in the middle of Brooklyn's Crown Heights, and you'd have the general idea."

Abasi bounded off the pillar and pivoted, muttering one or two curses in Coptic. Goldberg took a step back and put her hand on her gun.

Father Frank Williams smiled at the reaction, amused. He looked to Abasi. "I can only hope I'm not damned yet, sir. But there's always that chance, isn't there?"

"How long have you been standing there?" Goldberg asked. "Better yet, *where*?"

Father Frank jerked his thumb over his should. "On the other side of the pillar."

"Are all of you priests trained to be so freaking quiet? If you are, I'd be happy to have you train the FBI."

He nodded. "If you are all quite finished discussing my whereabouts today, His Holiness would like to have a word with you." Father Frank paused, and a mischievous twinkle appeared in his eye. "As would I. Now, please, come along,

89

he even imported some Italian food just for the guests."

A small smile played across his face, and his eyes shone brightly. Goldberg noted that Father Frank's eyes were right on her. In fact, they were intently focused.

What the? Her eyes narrowed, and a low growl escaped her throat.

Father Frank gave her a broad, sheepish grin, and stepped aside, letting the three of them pass. Goldberg went first. Abasi insisted the priest precede him.

She groaned inwardly. *Well, look at it this way — your rack's good enough to distract a priest; at least this one likes girls.*

Father Frank was content to let her think he had been checking her out. After all, he had already noted exactly where she had holstered her pistol.

* * *

Abasi and Goldberg both had trouble with the image before them — the most powerful religious individual on the planet, the Man in White, was busy assembling a portable dinner table in the middle of his office.

Pope Pius XIII looked at the table, nodded with approval, and before anyone could offer him aid, flipped the table onto its legs. He nodded, slapped the table, and stepped back, running into his desk. With one short push, he slid the desk against the wall.

"Normally," the Pope said, "we have a special dining hall for guests. But I prefer a more informal atmosphere whenever I can. I have scandalized most of the Italians this way – many prefer their Religious nobility to be more... noble. But I'm still training them. Also, in the formal dining room, there are too many ears around," he concluded.

The Jew and the Muslim shared a glance, wondering exactly how strong this man was, and why in Allah's name did they elect a bodybuilding Cardinal to be Pope?

The Pope noted the exchange of looks. "Sorry for showing off, but I have to keep in shape somehow. Using the papal swimming pool isn't enough. Besides, where I come from, you have to be able to protect one's flock."

Goldberg allowed herself a smile. "Is that before or after Idi Amin?"

The Pope laughed. "Oh, you mean Uganda's most famous cannibal? Let's just say that I put him on a diet."

Abasi grinned. "So, Joshua, you were the Scarlet Pimpernel of Amin's table?"

The Pope shrugged. "In my youth. But remember, that was over twenty years ago. I had to wear a Kevlar vest to work in the morning, which never matched my robes."

Goldberg raised a brow. "You mean, you don't wear a bulletproof vest now?"

"Never again!" he insisted. He checked his watch, and then quickly stepped outside.

She looked to Figlia. "He won't wear a vest! This is impossible."

The Italian smiled easily. "You do know they can tailor Kevlar, don't you?"

Goldberg smiled. "White bulletproof vestments? *Nice.*"

Pius stepped back inside, bringing along a tall man with deep brown eyes, short gray hair, and a long, Roman nose. "Hashim Abasi, Wilhelmina Goldberg, I'd like you to meet Xavier O'Brien, second-in-command of the Society of Jesus, the Jesuits."

O'Brien stepped forward. "Pleased to meet you."

Goldberg smiled up at him. *Darn, why can't priests be ugly by canon law? He's even got a nice, strong, manly voice... tell me he's gay, too, just so I don't feel bad. What was it Frank Williams said about priests? If you put a collar on a broomstick, the girls'll chase it?* She shook his hand. "Charmed."

Xavier grinned. "I hope not, then we'd need to burn a witch or two, and the Protestants were so much better at that than we were. Even Inquisitors usually told confessed 'witches' to get lost, get some medication, or simply go away." He shrugged. "O'Brien turned to Abasi. *"Assalamu alaikum."*

Abasi nodded. "You even pronounce it with the correct accent — where did you learn Arabic, Father O'Brien?"

"Detroit. It's not too far from Marquette, where I went to college."

"Ah, so you're a Jesuit."

O'Brien smirked. "I'm trying to change the society from the inside, instead of abandoning the sinking ship."

Abasi chuckled. "To do that, you'd need to be the Black Pope — no offense to Joshua."

The Pope waved it off. "None taken. I know what you meant."

Goldberg raised her hand. "I don't."

"Ah." O'Brien sighed deeply enough to blow out candles. "The Black Pope is the head of the Jesuits... Society of Jesus... and technically answers directly to the Pope — and he's 'black' because that's our societal color."

She nodded. "Ah. You make it sound like you're so high up you can't get out."

O'Brien's eyebrows shot up, and he almost dropped his cigarette. "I'm doomed by my initials... I'm the Executive Officer of the Jesuits — the XO, which is what everyone calls me... But occasionally they make XOB sound like a disparagement."

"Funny, didn't know the Jesuits had military-speak."

The Jesuit laughed. "We were founded by an ex-army officer. He called us 'The Company,' and he didn't mean the CIA; they weren't around in the 1500s."

His Holiness clapped his hands together. "Now, if everyone's acquainted, we need to talk."

Goldberg nodded and tucked a loose strand of hair behind her ear. "For example, like why Frank and XO here have been dining with an old Leftist terrorist."

Abasi laughed aloud. "I believe Special Agent Goldberg has appointed herself the bad cop."

Giovanni Figlia cleared his throat, looking embarrassed at his guest's brusqueness before his boss. "It's an American thing."

The bishop shrugged. "She's right. His Holiness here finally heard the rest of the details about the victims. After that, we knew we had information for you."

"So," Goldberg asked, "why were you folks talking with a terrorist hitman?"

Father Frank Williams stepped from whatever shadow of the room he had disappeared into. Goldberg had hardly noticed he had disappeared until he reemerged. "Because we have a different mission from you. Your job is saving lives; our job is saving souls. If we must talk with and convert an indicted-in-absentia murderer in order to possibly save him from damnation, then that is what we do. We do not arrest people, and I assure you, had any of us known that Clementi was still killing people, we would have called the police. Though, I, for one, would have been tempted to perp-walk him to the cop shop myself."

Goldberg raised an eyebrow. "And why didn't you tell us this sooner, Frank?"

The priest gave her an amused smile. "I could not recognize him after his face had lost the argument with Gianni's windshield," Father Frank lied.

"And don't worry," Xavier O'Brien added, blowing out a ring of cigarette smoke, "it gets worse."

Figlia rubbed his temple before the headache emerged fully. "*Certo.* Of course it would."

The Pope looked at O'Brien and waved him out of the room. The Jesuit looked at him with a raised brow, curious if he meant it. The Pope nodded. O'Brien shrugged, and he waved. "I'm apparently being thrown out. I'll talk with you later, then."

Father Frank watched his nominal boss leave the room, and then continued. "Apparently, there was another murder of someone else we've come across."

"*We* being who?" Wilhelmina asked, disliking the pronoun. *It is starting to sound like an episode of* The X-Files. *Any more conspiracy crap, I'm going to start looking for black helicopters. Come to think of it, we already have a cigarette-smoking man, don't we?*

"We as in the Church," the Pope answered in a deep, resounding voice. "The fact is, we had entertained hopes for the soul of someone else with a less-than-sparkling reputation. In that case as well, the result was not good."

"Who? Jack the Ripper?"

"Ashid Yousef, he's a—"

Hashim Abasi's easygoing, relaxed stance and demeanor disappeared like summer lightning. Before Father Frank had finished the next syllable, Abasi grabbed the Jesuit by his shirtfront and lifted him off the ground.

* * *

"Papal hitmen?" Manana Shushurin asked, slightly amused. "Sounds like a John le Carre novel." She thought a moment. "Actually, it sounds like something his brother might write."

Scott Murphy frowned, running through his memory. "And the brother is?"

"John Cornwell. He wrote *Hitler's Pope,* and a conspiracy theory about the death of John Paul I." She tilted her head back ever so slightly, and let her eyes flicker over the al fresco restaurant. Her eyes never made contact with Scott Murphy, who was on the other side of the fenced-off area.

The two intelligence officers had the choice between eating together in private, to avoid being seen, or continuing surveillance. Murphy had sent a photo of the woman to his boss, and now knew she was Wilhelmina "Villie" Goldberg, of the Secret Service.

"You must have very good intelligence," she had told him.

"That we do."

Right now, as they looked at each other across the open space, both of them had Bluetooth earpieces in their ears, and cell phones strapped to their belts. Scott Murphy had out his map, ran his finger over it, and spoke as if he were actually coordinating with another tourist. Manana simply talked, posing as the stereotypical cellphone user.

"So, tell me about Mr. Yousef," Murphy asked, even as he seemed to take a particular interest in the area around the Coliseum. "What do your people know about him?"

"Not much," Shushurin told him, leaning back in her chair. "I was told he was part of some al Qaeda think tank. Something about honey."

Murphy almost laughed. "Son of a bitch. Al Qaeda once

used honey to smuggle weapons, drugs, and scumbags. Ashid came up with the idea? Oy. Anything else?"

"He also wrote the al Qaeda training manual," she told him. "And that's even more impossible."

He nodded, and spared her a glance. Even from a distance, she looked spectacular. The way her hair looked was breathtaking. *How was it she had lasted as a spy for so long?* He dismissed the thought, and focused on Yousef. "Considering the amount of translation from other military manuals, not to mention cobbling together concepts from different military and intelligence circles, I'd say so. Now here's my problem. If he was one of the great brains, why did he risk coming out of hiding? He's got to be on dozens of watch lists."

"Better question," Shushurin countered. "He walked in through the front door of the Vatican. Why didn't they turn him in? They had to know he was there."

"Murphy's Law of spying – no pun intended: Never attribute to malice what can adequately be explained by stupidity," Murphy said aloud into the Bluetooth as a waiter drifted by. Once the waiter left, he lowered his voice slightly. "You're assuming they knew he was here, had his name on file, that they have facial-recognition software, or… actually, wait, how *would* he get into the archives without backing from another institution? Do you know offhand where was he educated?"

"Oxford or Cambridge, perhaps both, studying geopolitical science."

Murphy grumbled. "He would. The Middle East has ejected so many of their nutcases, half of the terrorists are recruited *after* they leave the region. But still, even if he was *Doctor* Yousef, why risk being out in the open? We've got nothing.

* * *

Sean A.P. Ryan opened the door, and blinked at one of the oddest sights he'd seen for quite some time. A collapsible dining table was on its side, the furniture separating the Pope and his head of security from the other side of the room — where Hashim Abasi held Father Francis Williams up off the floor, the neatly polished shoes dangling a foot above the marble.

Sean smiled gently. "Did I interrupt?"

Goldberg barely spared him a glance, and murmured, "Not at all, come right in."

"Where is he?" Abasi demanded, rattling Father Frank, ignoring everyone in the room. "Where is Ashid Yousef?"

Father Williams gently laid his hand on Abasi's bicep. "Please unhand me."

He closed his eyes and let his usual temperament reassert itself before lowering the priest to the floor, but not yet unhanding him. "My apologies, but I've been hunting these bastards for years, and if you've been harboring him…"

"He came to us a few months ago," the Pope admitted, distracting Abasi from Father Frank. "He wanted to write a paper on why the Catholic Church and Islam should work hand-in-hand for our mutual goals. He wanted it read on Al-Jazeera." The Pope bent down to put the table back in place. "Personally, I was confused, but working with other religions is the only thing everyone believes my predecessors and I do *right*, so what could be the harm?" The Pope straightened the table, then reached for the place settings on the cart next to him. "Maybe he had retired from the field of death. Maybe he had become sane. Perhaps it was a chance

97

to convert him — even if it was only in the sense of bringing him out of the darkness of an Afghan cave."

Before Abasi could follow up, Giovanni Figlia stepped forward and asked, "What parts of the archive did he want to look at, Your Holiness?"

Pius gave a small shrug with his massive shoulders. "He did not mention any specifics to me, though he is required to tell the archivists. They have to give authorization to look at a specific range of documents, and they will bring researchers individual boxes by month, date, and year. You can go to the archives and you can see all that he looked over."

Figlia nodded. "Why are you telling us this, Your Holiness?"

The Secret Service agent glanced at him and smiled. "Thanks for stepping up."

"I have to work here in the morning," he said out of the corner of his mouth.

Father Frank replied for the Pope. "Ashid Yousef, al-Qaeda terrorist, was also murdered."

Abasi finally relaxed and let go of Frank, leaning against the front of a bookcase. "In all likelihood, Mossad decided to end him."

"There is a problem with that theory," Father Frank answered patiently. "Killing upper level terrorists is counterproductive. Better they are interrogated."

Sean Ryan nodded, stepping further into the room. He wasn't quite clear on how anyone had brought the name of a high-level terrorist into the conversation, or how this had all begun, but he picked up where Father Frank left off. "You're usually better off to follow him up the food chain. Get to his boss, or kidnap him, or suck the information out of his head."

Goldberg looked at Sean askance. "And you're a Hollywood bodyguard?"

Sean shrugged. "Any good mercenary must have information to survive. Besides, it's common sense ..." He grinned. "Don't you read spy novels?"

Father Frank gave a small smile. "But he is correct. Why kill the devil you know when you defang him, and get to other devils? Even I cannot believe that Mossad would kill Yousef, unless they had first interrogated him. The romance of killing an entire terrorist group with assassination squads, I believe, went out of favor after Mossad avenged the athletes from the Munich Olympics."

Abasi narrowed his eyes for a moment. "But you're assuming this is like the world of spies instead of terrorists."

Figlia interjected, hoping to cut off this train wreck of a conversation. "Thank you, Your Holiness, for telling us about this. I will definitely follow up."

Pius raised an eyebrow. "Glad to know this might be of some help. And, Mr. Abasi, to answer your question, the chief of Vatican intelligence had a conversation with Director Weaver of the CIA. He, in turn, talked to the Mossad — no one knows anything about Mr. Yousef's untimely demise. In fact, the DCI was quite upset with me, but he goes to my Church, and I doubt he wants me to remind him about reformation, reconciliation, that sort of thing."

The table was just barely long enough for six people, two on either side, and one on either end. Goldberg was small enough to fit Sean Ryan in between herself and Father Frank. The Pope sat on one end, with Father Frank Williams on his left. Abasi was on the Pope's right, and Figlia was to the Egyptian's right.

Once they were settled in, Goldberg leaned forward,

around Sean Ryan, and asked. "So, what exactly is going on in Sudan, Josh? I know it's one of your bigger issues, but I'm not exactly getting all that much in America. In fact, they don't put it on any television stations unless they're running a stupid charity concert."

The Pope leaned back in his chair, and it creaked. "That is because your media dislikes saying anything that might possibly offend someone, or get in the way of their secularism. During the Bosnia crisis of the 1990s, for example—"

Goldberg raised her hand to cut him off. "You could just call it Bosnia."

Father Frank leaned over to her, and Sean Ryan leaned back to let the priest have more room. "Around here, we have an institutional memory that thinks in centuries — we remember that Bosnia was in crisis 500 years ago, when the Turks *first* invaded."

"In any event," the Pope continued, "your media insisted on calling Muslims 'ethnic Albanians,' and Orthodox Christians 'Serbs,' framing it as a racial war instead of an ongoing medieval jihad. The U.S. only acted when it threatened to spill over into other countries.

"In Sudan... since the 1980s, the Arab, Islamic north has killed or enslaved any black African Christians they can get. In 1983, they instituted *sharia* law — theft punished by amputation, armed crimes were capital offenses, and adultery punishable by stoning. What did the great and powerful United Nations do? They put Sudan onto the Human Rights Commission!"

Goldberg saw how the Pope seemed to change color as the intensity of his delivery increased. "I'm sorry to say this, sir — and, sorry, I call *everyone* 'sir'—but even 'white' slavery has been ignored, and they sell sex slaves. What makes *sharia* any different?"

Figlia winced, closing his eyes. He had never, not even once, felt uncomfortable questioning the Pope. He had never been discouraged from being anything less than candid in his conversations, But even he was a *little* less blunt.

The Pope nodded. It was a question so familiar he had an automatic reply. "That is not the only issue. The north has old Soviet bombers, and they targeted *churches* — on Sundays. Some were bombed *every* Sunday. Once, as my plane left, the government bombed the airfield. This was shortly after government troops invaded Khartoum's Anglican cathedral sending in grenades first. Even the Archbishop of Canterbury described their policy as 'torture, rape, destruction of property, slavery and death, and forcible conversion.' It is a case of Christians versus Muslims, but who does the American politician wish to offend? Aid the north and promote genocide, or aid the Christians and risk offending future terrorists?"

Goldberg was about to answer, when Abasi said, "No one can profit. And no one wants to be bothered with a large potential mess over the long run. It's not worth it."

Pius said "Correct. While it is quiet for now, another genocide will probably begin soon. And Sudan is merely one of over a hundred petty little wars on the same continent. I sometimes think I'm the only head of state that cares about people who aren't politically 'mine', whom I can't get anything out of. I've had to yell at, cajole, threaten, plead, beg, borrow and practically steal in order to do what I have. Food drops are hard to arrange, to say nothing of the cost. If the Italian banks ever decided to foreclose on us, we'd be broke."

Special Agent Goldberg couldn't help but laugh. "Why? The Vatican has a deficit?"

Figlia nodded, fielding this one. "In 2007, the Vatican had a deficit of over fifteen million euros. Not to mention one of the recent heads of the Vatican bank embezzling over thirty million dollars into his own private account."

The Pope nodded. "And since taking the position, I have not put us in the black." The Pope smiled, looked at his hands, and laughed. "At least, not in monetary terms."

Sean chuckled. "You can say that again." He glanced at Goldberg. "Let's put it this way; my salary actually comes from one of the local noble families."

Goldberg arched a brow. "You're not doing this for free?"

Sean shook his head. "As much as I would like, I can't afford to — I have a company to run. My own personal share is purely expenses — my money is no good in this city. But I'm the head of an organization that does everything from bodyguard work to kidnap and rescue—"

"So you kidnap *and* recover? A full service, huh?" Goldberg snarked.

"—if I'm not there, my employees suffer," Sean continued, ignoring her. "I'm wanted… dead or alive, by some people." He shrugged. "But the Pope has some good benefactors."

"True," the Pope said with a wistful smile. "It is not enough for my purposes. But still …our Lord said the Earth belongs to the prince of this world, but I am not going to let him have it without a fight. Despite the policy of turning the other cheek, there are lines I will not see crossed. No matter the cost."

* * *

Maureen McGrail's pale green eyes flicked to her watch, hoping that the books she had picked up would at least be useful: she had grabbed several books on Pius XII at random in Keohane's bookstore immediately before she went to the airport. Upon arrival, she discovered that she was in business class — the Vatican had paid for it, which was... odd.

She shook away any suspicions and decided to get back to the case. There was only one real piece of evidence pointing to Father Richard Harrington's killer: the swastika carved into his forehead. Calling card? Motive? Red herring? After all, Harrington's heroics were over sixty years ago.

She smiled at the thought of an eighty-year-old fellow priest doing Harrington in. But aside from that, there weren't many options. Either a neo-Nazi punk had broken into the Markist rectory and killed Father Harrington as revenge for hiding Jews during World War II (ridiculous), or he had been killed by someone who knew him well...

Or someone wanted to prevent him from telling what he had done during the war.

Hmm... the priest who knew too much. All we need now is Alfred Hitchcock, Brian De Palma, and Jerry Bruckheimer to make the movie, and we'll be set. McGrail shook her head. *If Father Harrington was killed over something to do with the Nazis, it might help to know what he did. Now, who was it he worked with back in the forties? A Father Carroll-Abbing, that's right.*

She flipped open *Under His Very Windows*, and went directly for the index. Not long after, she also performed a few computer searches with her laptop. By the end of the flight, she had a small biography of Monsignor John Patrick Carroll-Abbing, founder of the Boys Towns of Italy, the oldest American charity abroad.

Carroll-Abbing... Vatican diplomat... worked World War II in the Vatican... hid Jews and escaped POWs ...set up first-

aid stations between the front lines and Rome, evacuated the sick and wounded, and rescued children and old people from the battle zones.

When she was done, all McGrail could think was, *Okay, great, and Father Harrington was with him all the way. How is that a reason to kill Harrington?*

* * *

Wilhelmina Goldberg looked over the food set down on the table, and was surprised to see that the entire meal was kosher. The lasagna was vegetable, the meatballs were in a separate bowl, and in a country where the most popular fish food consisted of things that slithered or scavenged to survive, almost all of it was edible.

"My compliments to the chef," she muttered. The Secret Service agent leaned back in her chair, angling it to better face the other American. "So, Ryan, what exactly are you doing here with the priests and the nuns?"

Sean Ryan sipped a glass of white wine, gently holding the class. "Aside from self-defense?"

The Pope smiled. "This is why you were invited for lunch, Mr. Ryan. Special Agent Goldberg is here for a security audit, and you are a part of that."

"Yep," Goldberg agreed. "Basically, we're considering using the priests and nuns you train as a roaming assault team. However, if they suck at it, I can't take them into account."

Sean nodded slowly. "Basically, I'm teaching them Krav Maga lite."

Abasi gave a light cough into a cloth napkin. "I did not know you were interested in Israeli martial arts."

Sean smiled. "It's almost standard now for anyone in the

104

business of violence — all the fashionable alphabet-soup agencies use it. It's also nonlethal — for the most part. Mostly what I teach is improvisation and spotting threats, building up speed and reflexes."

Sean looked around the table, trying to spot something useful. He smiled, got up from the chair, and went over to a bookcase. Mounted on the wall were two long rosaries; one of them had beads literally a half an inch around, with more than fifty different beads. He slipped it from the wall, then dangled it in from of him.

"Now, one of these is something you'd see wrapped around the waist of a monk — or a Dominican. This is heavy enough to use as a morningstar. The small beads can be used as a whip or a rake, or even makeshift brass knuckles." He draped it over the back of the chair, then slipped back into his seat. "Basically, something even the little old men can use."

Hashim Abasi chuckled lightly, leaning back in his chair, sipping from his glass of water. "I'm curious. What do your parents think of all this? I have trouble believing that they wanted you to be a mercenary when you grew up."

Sean's smiled dimmed a little. "My mother and grandfather are fine with it. My father? Eh, who cares?" He grabbed his glass again. "You've ever heard of Clarence Ryan?"

Goldberg laughed. "Oh, *him*." She looked at Giovanni Figlia's blank stare. "He's one of these American Leftist nuts who thinks Castros was too moderate. Or every president from Carter to Clinton has been bought and paid for by some corporation or another. Real nutjob. I—" She paused, then looked over at Sean. "You're kidding? You're his *son*?"

"Only biologically," Sean replied, taking a long sip. "I consider my grandfather my dad." He gave a small smile. "Hell, my grandfather sided with his daughter-in-law against his own son. My grandfather taught me terms like duty, honor, and country. Then, he's a World War II vet, he should know. Though he spent much of his time wondering how he had failed to raise Clarence like a human being." He shrugged.

Abasi leaned forward, intrigued. "And what did your grandfather do during the war?"

Sean shrugged. "Killed a few people. Won a few awards. He told some war stories, but not nearly enough to cover his time in the war. So he either did more secret squirrel stuff than I can imagine, or they stuck him on a desk when they found out he was too young to be enlisted."

Pius XIII cocked his head at Sean. "Too young?"

Sean gave the Pope a little smile. "Let's just say that Granddad was eager to join the fight. He was *just* big enough to pass for 18. He grew up in the Midwest, had a rifle since he was seven, and figured that anything after that was just a small upgrade."

The short Secret Service Agent cocked her head at him. "So, homicidal tendencies skip a generation?"

Sean chuckled. "Indeed? Whatever could you mean?"

"I heard stories about you."

Sean laughed. "Oh, they're probably all true."

"Like how you blew up a house because a dozen gunmen came after your client?" Goldberg asked.

"I didn't blow it up," Sean murmured, "I set it on fire."

Figlia laughed. "I prefer the story of how he bombed parts of Harvard to protect a student hunted by terrorists."

He smiled at the pope. "Patently untrue — I only used bullets."

* * *

By the time the Pope had more than bent the ears of his guests about North and South Sudan, and Wilhelmina Goldberg yawned for the third time, Pius said, "Tired?"

"More than a little. I think I set my biological clock the wrong way."

He laughed. "If there's any place to fix that, it's Italy. If the Europeans wonder why America has such a good economy, they should stop sleeping in the middle of work, yes?" He reached over and patted Father Frank on the back. "Frank can take you to your hotel."

Figlia was about to say something when the Pope cut him off. "Go see Ronnie. We can talk later. Yousef and Gerrity aren't going to rise anytime soon, and if they do, then a homicide investigation isn't necessary — the world's about to end."

Figlia smiled slightly at the Pope's odd religious humor. "*Io ho capisco.*"

His Holiness smiled. "Good. You're not doing anything I wouldn't approve of, are you?"

He grinned. "Of course, not Your Holiness. We're married, what do you expect?"

"More children, of course."

* * *

Pope Pius XIII sunk into his desk chair after the three professional security officers departed, led by Father Frank.

Once Auxiliary Bishop Xavier O'Brien came back into the room, the Pope smiled at him. "So, XO," the Pope asked, "do you think they bought it?"

Bishop O'Brien shook his head as he settled into the chair

in front of the Pope's desk. "Not entirely. We're the Catholic Church. Enough people think we're run by pedophiles and misogynists that we're automatically evil, no matter how much proof we can fabricate to the contrary. Heh."

Pius smiled briefly. "I just wish we didn't have to tell them about Yousef."

"They would have found out about him sooner or later," O'Brien told him. "We still would have had to deal with it, only on their terms, not ours. This way, we managed to hand them a reason." XO took a brief drag on his cigarette. "They're in good hands with Frank. He'll take care of them. He's taken care of everything we've given him so far."

CHAPTER IX: A PIUS OPERATIVE

Father Francis Williams led the American and the Egyptian over the gray stone streets of Rome leading out of St. Peter's Square, and was immediately picked up by one of two spies. Scott Murphy was intent on hanging back by at least two blocks. He was relatively certain he knew where they were going, since he had already called into Tel Aviv and had their computer- systems people find out what rooms they were in at the *Emmanus* hotel.

Murphy paused and waited just inside the wall of the Vatican.

This was lucky for him, because Special Agent Goldberg looked over her shoulder, as though she felt she was being watched. However, it was two in the afternoon in Italy. The street behind her was vacant.

Goldberg shook off the feeling. *I've been around Abasi too often today.* She spared the Egyptian a glance, and found him also looking over his shoulder.

Father Frank smiled. "Uncomfortable that I met one of your murder victims?"

Abasi laughed as he turned back to face the priest. "No, I do this all the time. I don't know what Agent Goldberg's excuse is."

"Call me Villie." She looked at Father Frank. "So, what are you going to do now that you've lost your assigned convert?"

The silver-hair priest shrugged. "That was only one day a week; surely you must have guessed I have other duties. Right now, I have tours to give, and people to escort." The priest smiled at both of them a little shyly.

"Sure, you don't think we need protectin', now do ya?" Abasi said in a surprisingly good imitation of an Irish brogue.

Both Frank and Goldberg stopped to look at him. Abasi shrugged. "My wife was Irish."

The Secret Service Agent and the priest exchanged a glance. She said, "Yeah, I know. I would *so* like to hear that story."

Abasi frowned thoughtfully. He debated telling them at least *parts* of the story. After all, who would they tell? The beginning of the tale most people found amusing and entertaining.

"Hey, Father faggot!"

The three travelers forgot the brogue and turned. Ahead of them, on the way to the hotel, were a troop of six young adults with "Occupy" t-shirts and bottles of beer in their hands.

Goldberg rolled her eyes. *Drunk Americans in Rome, Adonai save us. Why couldn't they at least be French?*

"May I help any of you?" Father Frank said.

The teenager in front pointed and said, "Yeah, you can die, you baby rapist."

It was Frank's turn to roll his eyes. The teenagers stopped about five feet away from him. The leader took a step forward, and pulled out a gun from the small of his back. The gun was halfway up when Father Frank stepped forward, grabbed it with his right hand and twisted the gun away. He pistol-whipped the thug across the face, backhanded, and sent him staggering back.

Father Frank tossed the gun to the other hand, ejecting the magazine into his right. He leaned his head slightly back and to one side, saying to Abasi and Goldberg, "Please, the both of you, get back. I would hate to see a stray bullet strike you."

Goldberg frowned, confused. "There's five of them."

"Six," the fallen one muttered as he tried to rise. "And we're going to get you and your friends, you—"

"They are with me," Father Frank said firmly, his voice not rising. "My flock is not to be touched."

There was the flick of a knife blade opening.

Father Frank nodded, and threw the gun magazine like a shuriken, hitting one of them in the temple. In the same motion, Frank dropped to one knee and fired the bullet in the chamber an inch to the right of the leader's skull; he wisely stayed down. The priest grabbed the grip and the slide, and then pulled the two of them apart, throwing each piece as a separate weapon. The disconnected grip hit one in the forehead and the barrel struck another behind the ear as he tried to run.

The remaining two only managed to get one step forward. The first one didn't even see his attacker, until the diminutive Wilhelmina Goldberg punched him directly in the groin. Hashim Abasi lashed out with one, simple, open-palmed right cross, dropping the last attacker to the ground.

Father Frank rose and dusted a little dirt from the knees of his pants. "Well, I am sorry for that. I generally do not have parishioners attacked merely for being around me."

Wilhelmina Goldberg looked down at the one she felled, shrugged, and kicked him where she had first punched him. She looked at Frank. "We're not Catholic."

"You're in my current parish; you're my parishioners."

"Where did you learn to do those combat moves?"

Father Frank smiled. "I wasn't always a priest. Let us get you back to your hotel."

When they were fifteen feet away from the fallen teens, there was another cry.

"I'm not done with you yet!"

The three of them gave a collective sigh and turned. The initial instigator stood, knife in hand. Abasi grabbed the priest's shoulder. "I can do this."

There was a loud snap, and the thug cried out. He fell to the ground, revealing a short, dark-haired Sean Ryan standing behind him. "Father," he said with mock-chastisement in his voice, "what have I told you about leaving people mobile?"

"I'm sorry, Sean," Frank replied. "I'm unused to hurting people anymore. I gave up that profession."

"Pity. You're so good at it." Sean looked over the mess of bodies on the ground. All of them were broken, unconscious, or in pain. One was on his hands and knees, trying to get up, and Sean merely kneed him in the head. "Damnit, now I'm going to have to bring these guys into the police." Sean looked up. "Aren't you glad I wanted to ask you something about your schedule next week? Otherwise, you'd have to wait for the cops yourself."

Scott Murphy, well over a block away, smiled, taking notes in his head.

* * *

Vatican crime-scene analyst Veronica Fisher scanned the analysis reports from the hotel room. It was odd: the killer had first assassinated Gerrity, then moved into the room, and then apparently stopped to make a phone call. Why did Clementi, the assassin, stay in the room? Clementi could have shot the scholar and left, but he deliberately moved inside the room, cart and all, and dialed his cell phone.

Fisher frowned again, flipping back to the explosives report. The lab had estimated the composition of the explosive, and how much force it had generated. She did a few quick calculations based on the landing site of Clementi's body. The force of the blast, the condition of his body, plus his relation to the window indicated that he was standing in front of the desk — more precisely, in front of the foot well in the desk. Which meant he was looking at something on the desk. The laptop?

Fisher frowned and flipped back to the results on the computer. It had been thoroughly smashed, and there was no hope in hell of getting any results back anytime soon. "Damn it!"

"Be careful when you say that around here. Someone may take you up on it."

She looked up into her husband's face, grinning broadly. "When did you get in?"

"I've been here for a while," Figlia answered. "Going over this morning's... what would you call it?"

"A hit?" Fisher tossed the report on the desk and ran her fingers through her light brown hair. "Yeah, well, I'm still trying to figure this out. I think he was looking at something on Gerrity's computer."

Figlia tried not to laugh. "Can I get a hello first?"

She paused for a moment, stood, leaned over her desk — giving him a very nice view — and kissed him on the cheek before sitting down.

He arched his brows. "Only on the cheek?"

"No more than that while in the Vatican, wise guy. I don't care if we're married."

Figlia took a deep breath. There went his siesta plans. This day was only getting longer. He glanced at the report. "He was searching the laptop?"

Fisher shook her head. "He was blown directly out the window, which meant he was standing too far away from the computer at the time to do that, unless he had Inspector Gadget arms. It had to be something on the computer screen at the time. Now, either he called someone else, saw the computer, and died, or he saw the computer, and then made the phone call, and died."

"Which means?"

Fisher smiled. "Which means my forensic electronic boys are going to receive very nice treatment until they put the laptop back together again."

"Have you eaten?"

She nodded. "A little. You?"

He nodded. "Up for a *siesta*?"

"I use the couch in my office… it folds out into a bed."

* * *

Special Agent Wilhelmina Goldberg waved Father Frank inside; she closed the door behind him and said, "Are you in the Vatican SF or something?"

He smiled "You mean, am I a spy? All priests are, to one degree or another. We report what we see, and what we can.

114

Why do you think we're put down in so many conspiracy theories? We're bigger than any Mafia, and in more places than all the intelligence agencies put together." In China, our priests undergo special training before being inserted into the mainland. With His Holiness, you can see the effects of priesthood in Africa — he was once accused of killing a soldier who threatened one of his parishioners."

Goldberg coughed politely as he tried to wander off-topic by being a theological history geek. "Hey, Frank, your little stunt back there didn't exactly scream 'just one of the boys.' And Ryan made it sound like you've done this before."

He gently shook his head. "My apologies, Agent Goldberg, but he merely meant his training — you were shown our clerical hand-to-hand defense system."

She nodded. "I was, but I saw what he was doing, and he was nowhere *near* advanced weapons training and disassembling guns. I'm guessing you picked that up from your time in the Green Berets."

Father Frank cringed. "We're *not* hats."

She grinned. "Why'd you give it up?"

He looked at her intently, with a long, powerful violet gaze. "Because, Agent Goldberg, there are some moments when people ask themselves: who am I? What am I? What am I doing being pinned down in a sand trap?"

"I see that… but they make you give up sex."

Frank blinked and hesitated for a long moment, and Wilhelmina Goldberg thought she had hit on the wrong topic.

Then he laughed, loudly and powerfully. "*Make me?* No. No one's holding a Kalashnikov to my head. Every day of my life for eight years in the seminary, they did two things other than teach me: make sure I wasn't a nutcase-slash- pedophile, and prepare me for a life without sex. Any other stupid questions?" he asked gently, eyes twinkling.

"No." She shrugged. "I'm Jewish, and among us Orthodox, we still believe in 'be fruitful and multiply.' I'm just finding it hard to believe that any man with your background would be put to use as a mere chaplain."

Father Frank let a smile pull at his mouth. "I'll take the compliment and leave it at that." He headed for the door, and stopped a foot away. "Say goodbye to Abasi for me; he's listening at the door. I'm certain you'll both want to compare notes."

With that, he left.

A moment later, Abasi knocked on the door to the adjoining room. Goldberg opened it. She shrugged. "Don't ask me how he knew."

She looked over the laptop, her hazel eyes lit up by the bright blue screen as it quickly switched to a *Lord of the Rings* background.

Over the voice of Orlando Bloom welcoming her back, she said, "In fact, I think he's in Vatican Intelligence, not just on the periphery as he told us. I mean, who do you think escorts foreign nationals around the White House? Secretaries?"

* * *

"Father Frank Williams," Scott Murphy said, "Society of Jesus, Almost definitely in Special Forces, but double check. Obviously this guy is far more than he seems to be."

Murphy paced the carpet of Manana Shushurin's hotel room. He had spent the last half-hour relaying everything he had observed over the course of his journey from St. Peter's Square until the time he arrived at her side, as well as every-

116

thing else he could remember.

Finally, he sat down on the bed behind her. "I would have helped, but I wasn't about to pull a Ludlum—"

Manana raised a hand to stop him. "A what?"

"Robert Ludlum. Wrote *The Bourne Identity*? All of his spies know how to kill people with a penny at fifty yards, that sort of thing?"

She smiled. "Ah yes, I remember reading him when I was a child."

Wow, I feel old. Manana Shushurin looked back to her data phone. On the top of the full-color screen was a laser projector that cast the image of a flat keyboard on the table-top. All she needed to do was tap one of the red "keys" and the corresponding action appeared on the screen.

"Cute toy," he said.

"The keyboard is Sharper Image." She barely glanced at him, but her lips turned up in a smile. She tapped on a few more keys and slid back. "Take a look. See if I've got every-thing."

Murphy leaned over her shoulder. He could get the faint-est wisp of perfume. *Vanilla sugar? Whatever it is, it makes me want to either kiss her neck or get some biscotti. Which is probably an odd sensation to have around her.*

After a moment, he said, "That's all I overheard."

She tapped the ENTER key and leaned back, stretching her arms up and around. Her right hand landed around the back of his neck. She paused, then ruffled his hair.

Murphy chuckled as she mussed his hair. "Sorry, I lin-gered a little too long."

Her hand pulled him forward. She placed a light kiss on his cheek. He gave her a confused little smile, unsure of what to make of it.

Manana patted his other cheek. "You're cute when you apologize… Don't worry about it." She let him go, glided onto her feet and across the room, taking her suitcase out of the closet.

Murphy watched her, and analyzed her movement. He had considered what she said back in Saint Peter's Square about her time behind a desk. Her form was impressive. He had spent enough time around the Kidron killers at the office to recognize someone who was at least on their level. Her movements were fluid, she had at least three knives on her, and she used all of her muscles. She was either a dancer or a killer.

I'm thinking not *a dancer.* Realizing that his eyes had lingered a little too long, he looked away. *Odd. I'm usually not that easily distracted.* "What exactly is the computer doing?"

She threw the case onto her bed, clicking it open. "Hacking through the Special Forces personnel roster at Fort Bragg."

Murphy's jaw dropped. *All this, and she can hack the Pentagon, too.*

Shushurin laughed. "Don't worry, I'm having the computer route its way through most of the planet before it starts working on any American systems."

He glanced at her toy. "How much power does that thing have?"

She dug through her clothes, pulling out a long, lightweight nightgown that reached down to her ankles. "Think in terms of terabytes… Why do you think I plugged it in to the wall socket? It eats batteries like potato chips."

"Ah… How long do you think it'll take?"

"Anywhere from fifteen minutes to half an hour, or more." Shushurin placed the nightgown next to her pillow, then rooted around for something else. "Half the time involved is merely routing."

Murphy, still looking at the computer, smiled. "I really must think about getting tech like this. Heck, I didn't even know the Germans were all that up-to-date."

"They're not, really," she explained. "I sift through a lot of professional-security magazines, and requisition it when I get an assignment."

He nodded, and glanced back to Shushurin. Her hair fell across her face, and he studied it a moment. Her hair was a surprising array of colors: a deep brown with flecks of dark gold, and the ringlets stopped around her collar bone. He frowned in thought. When he looked at her, he was distracted by almost every part of her, and that wasn't something that happened to him a lot.

Or at all, really. I've been alone in this job too darn long. "Looking for something?"

She pulled out a handgun, checked the load, and placed it next to the suitcase. "Found it."

Murphy blanched. "You carry a gun?"

Shushurin clicked it closed and tossed the case back into the closet. "It comes in handy. Why? You have a problem with guns?

"I have a problem with *spies* carrying guns, especially in Europe – let's face it, it's a great way to attract attention we don't need. I'm trying to figure out if I got a fellow spy, or an assassin. Sorry, no offense, but those are two different skill sets. And you're not exactly the sort of subtle and low key that I expect in my fellow spies."

She looked at him. "Are you done yet?"

Murphy nodded.

"Good." She settled on the edge of the bed, facing him, one leg tucked under her. "Do you want to hear my life story?"

He glanced at his watch. "I've got time."

Shushurin's Slavic brown eyes didn't even flicker. She sat back on the edge, crossing both legs in front of her in a lotus position.

Murphy let her take her time, choosing instead to glance at her weapon, a large affair obviously meant to keep someone down when they were shot. In fact, it was Russian… a Stechkin ASP, a Soviet military weapon.

Didn't she say her family was originally from Lvov? Even if her family made it to Germany, what side of Germany? East, perhaps? "Aren't you a little young to be have trained with the *Stasi?* Although, now that I think about it, I know they had Soviet teenage assassins, and one can't be one of them unless one started early."

She gently blinked, once, almost like a woman in a bad romance novel being coy. "The gun gave it away?"

Murphy nodded. "That, and your reluctance to talk. I've dealt with Germans before, and they generally can't shut up."

Shushurin laughed. "It happens."

He shook his head. "Thankfully, I'm less stupid than most."

She punched him lightly in the arm. "Shut up."

"Yes, ma'am, I know when to acknowledge my betters."

She laughed again, smiling just broadly enough to show the whites of her teeth without any gum. "What made you think that being silent meant Russian training?"

"Paranoia — talk to no one, Cold War garbage where no one talked to even their allies. That and the gun; considering my Office, *I'm* supposed to be packing heat."

At that, the BND spy arched a brow. "Heat? You sound like a gangster film."

Murphy reached into his windbreaker, and pulled out a plain meerschaum pipe. He lit the pre-stuffed pipe, angling away so the smoke wouldn't drift into her face. "You tend to drop your articles from time to time — Russian language patterns which I'm surprised you haven't retained more of. However, if you were trained by the Eastern bloc, and spoke Russian..."

She nodded.

He continued. "I can only guess they charm-schooled you into speaking excellent English. If you were trained young, you must have been picked for a reason. Someone wanted you to go into the family business, perhaps. The Soviet Union fell apart when you were... maybe eight? So the indoctrination was nowhere near complete, and you appear to be sane, which is why the BND lets you onto field assignments." He thought it over a bit. "I assume they gave your background a thorough scrubbing."

She almost smirked. "Is this the point where you say that I am German, hence a Nazi?"

Murphy almost laughed. "Nah, if this was a Nazi film, I'd be the one under suspicion — I'm the blond. Let me see, what else? You should be living happily and healthy in Cologne with a husband and two kids."

Manana cocked her head. "What makes you think I'd be married?"

Murphy shrugged. "You have a primarily sedentary job behind an intelligence desk, and, I guess, somewhat stable hours. Germany is a generally sexist little country, and you're ..." He hesitated, looking for a polite way to describe her looks. "Pleasant enough to make a priest reconsider celibacy."

Manana Shushurin arched her brows. "And you consider that a good thing?"

"We're three blocks from the Vatican and I just saw a priest take out four guys with an empty handgun, the thought came naturally …" He frowned, reconsidering. "Should I guess that means you're not married?"

"Who has the time?"

He clamped his teeth over the mouth of the pipe and furrowed his brow for a moment. "I hope you're not one of those entrenched in the job; that would be a waste of material."

Some of the glitter in her eyes went out. "Why? You think I'd make a good wife, locked in a house?"

He shook his head. "You run the danger of becoming a function instead of a person; I can abstract enough great attributes from your actions thus far to determine that you would make a good human being *as well as* an efficient officer."

She watched the hand gently holding the bowl of the pipe. "I don't see a wedding ring on your finger."

Murphy chuckled. "I look like a Palestinian in Israel; as an undercover operative in Palestine, I'm not going to start dating one of the local girls; none of the Israeli women would go near me; and frankly, I'm a goy, so not even the secretary pool would lay a finger on me."

Manana leaned forward and gently touched his arm. "Sorry. That really is a waste of material."

He grinned. "Nice of you to say so. Was it the pipe that convinced you?"

She grinned mischievously, the lights sparkling in her eyes again. "I like the tobacco blend."

He blinked, a little puzzled. "*Okaaaay.* Wow, I'm being complimented by a woman whose initials are a deadly neurological disease."

122

Manana Shushurin didn't blink. "Fine talk from someone whose initials spell out a kinky sex life."

Scott Murphy choked on smoke that went down the wrong way. After he cleared his throat, he said, "Let's just hope they aren't prophetic for either of us."

"You mean you're not into that? Pity." His eyes widened, and she laughed, winking, enjoying his funny faces. "You're so easy."

He cleared his throat. "So, what made you escape that kind of life? Working for the Germans instead of the Russians?"

She smiled. "My mother, actually. She got me away. I spent my time in the better of two failing economies." Her eyes wandered over to the computer. "Odd. It's done."

Murphy followed her gaze, reading off the profile. "Joined the Army at eighteen. Filled out his military service while taking courses to become a physician assistant. Transferred into Special Forces at twenty-two. Trained in emergency trauma for a year in Miami. Cool. He's... thirty-three? How can he be thirty-three?"

Manana's eyes narrowed at the screen. "He served in Europe, the Middle East; service records classified. But he's got a medal... a few of them."

"A classified Special Forces record," Murphy murmured around the pipe. "You don't think he could have been—"

"Part of an assassination unit?" Manana finished. "Green Berets have been authorized for such things. Now he's a priest? That sounds like he's a prime candidate for—"

"Vatican intelligence?" Murphy concluded. "I agree. The question is—"

"Do they have a hit team and call them the Knights Templar, or something like that?"

Shushurin nodded thoughtfully, staring to the left of the computer screen. "It makes sense. Yousef looked like a professional hit."

"So much for this merely *sounding* like a John le Carre novel," Murphy muttered. "Vatican assassins. What next? Assuming Williams is still their tour guide, all we need to do is keep following Figlia, et al. We'll find something."

Shushurin nodded. "If the priest is involved, he'll have to stay close to monitor the investigation. Makes me wonder — what is he doing right now?"

* * *

Father Frank Williams slid the collar off his neck and into his shirt pocket; priests were mandated to wear the white collar at all times, but carrying it constituted wearing it. He slipped off his gold ring, tucking it into a pants pocket. He then slid on a set of black leather gloves, and used a black baseball cap to cover his silver hair, and dark glasses to cover his violet eyes.

Frank looked around. No one was on the street, as expected. He pressed his ear to the window, listening for personnel. He circled around to the front door, pulling on it again to make certain it was locked. He went back to the rear, double-checked his surroundings, and then put on a baseball cap to cover his hair. He pivoted, releasing a vicious spin kick that shattered the security glass and knocked the interior wiring right off the frame.

Father Frank hurled himself through the window and rolled to his feet. He quickly scanned this section of Vatican Infirmarium set aside as a makeshift forensics lab. He spotted what he was looking for immediately — a file had been left on the table, labeled "Gerrity: Preliminary Findings."

The distinctive cocking of a semiautomatic froze him in mid-reach.

"Don't move," Giovanni Figlia told him, framed in the doorway to Veronica Fisher's office.

The Jesuit said nothing, he pivoted, grabbing a beaker as he spun, hurled it at the papal security officer and leapt to one side. He threw himself over the table, rolled to his feet and grabbed the forensics report as the beaker smashed into Figlia's gun, forcing the gun out of his hands and back into the office.

Father Frank swept four probing needles from the table and whirled, throwing all of them in Figlia's direction, but the Italian had already leapt back into the office to grab his gun.

The Jesuit leapt over the table and through the window, and hit the ground in a crouch directly beneath the window frame, hoping Figlia would act as professionally as he would.

Figlia scrambled to his feet and bolted for the window, aiming into the street. He checked to the left and the right of the frame before slowly sliding his head through the window. Father Frank sprang straight up, both fists pounding Figlia under the chin.

Figlia's head snapped back against the window frame so hard, he dropped the Beretta. Father Frank whirled, kicked the gun into the street, and ran off.

CHAPTER X: THE MEN IN BLACK

Cardinal Alphonse Cannella swept out of the building with the air of a man who thought the red of his robes was a princely color, and that he was a prince first in line to ascend to the throne. The Cardinal moved into the streets of Rome, and he looked down on the people on the street as the police carted them away.

Sitting at the curb, Sean A.P. Ryan looked up from his newspaper and glared right at him.

The Cardinal sniffed at him, and then swept along his path.

Sean frowned. Something was rotten in the State of the Vatican, and he wasn't happy about it. The blue eyes followed Cannella, taking in the arrogance that exuded from every motion like a snail's slime trail.

Sean glanced back to the cover article *about* Cannella — or, more specifically, about the Boston diocese the Cardinal ran. *Neo-pagan cult donates to the Boston diocese. Diocese accepts money. Cult then busted on drug-trafficking charges.*

Sean gave a low whistle. *Someone's in trouble. But why would drug smugglers donate anything to the Church?*

He was about to read further when a flash of motion

caught his eye — a priest with silver hair floated across the marble streets with a hardcover novel under his arm. The blue eyes squinted to focus on the small figure.

He kept his eye on Father Frank for only a moment — just long enough to know that the silver-haired priest dropped something like a book into a fountain in St. Peter's Square.

Must be a bad book.

* * *

Scott Murphy glanced over Frank Williams' old personnel file — those parts that weren't classified — and let his mind wander. He'd often been accused of trying to be a mobile analyst unit, and he knew he wasn't, but it helped to come to some conclusions without needing home base.

He gave his partner from the BND a sidelong look, watching her check the adjustments on the television. He very briefly admired her long legs, then turned his attention back to the computer. "I'm guessing you bugged Abasi's room."

"Close enough," Shushurin assured him. "I have my earpiece tuned to *her* room, listening into their conversation; don't worry, it's also connected to digital recorder to make sure we catch everything."

"Anything interesting?"

She pulled herself away from the television, and nodded. "They've figured out that Williams was in Special Forces and is in Vatican intelligence." Shushurin snatched her phone off the nightstand. "I'll hook this up to the TV so we can both see the darned file."

Murphy nodded. "Thankfully, the Secret Service agent is Jewish, and the Office has long reserved the right to call upon the assistance of Jews abroad to aid any of our actions."

Shushurin nodded. "I heard her say something about being Orthodox." She plugged in the last connection to the computer and looked up, tightening the connection.

"But I can't exactly go around introducing myself as Scott 'Mossad' Murphy, I'd like you to aid a foreign government, even if you're already *working* in your own government. Yeah, sure, that'll go over well. If she tells me to stuff it, we're blown; I'll be taken off this case, and worse, maybe even taken off field duty until we can be certain she's not going to report my face to the CIA. If she's Jewish Orthodox, that may not even work — some Orthodox see Israel as anti-theological, more nationalistic than religious. It becomes more of a risk to approach her."

The brunette glanced around the room for the remote control, swept it off the tabletop and sat on the bed. "Why not offer her something in return, then?" she asked.

The television went on, and Father Frank Williams' life history went up on the screen.

"Nice picture," he noted. "What do you suggest?"

Shushurin turned to him. "Offer her resources. It's not like she has access to the CIA at the push of a button."

Murphy's phone beeped with a text message. He looked down at it. It beeped again, and he flipped it open. "Oh dear. This should be fun. My boss finally sent me her full bio — she *is* Orthodox. I guess that's something to come in handy should we get desperate."

Shushurin allowed herself to smile. "Define desperate?"

"When we can't find out everything they know. All we're missing is what the Pope told them over lunch."

"I think we know that already." She tapped the earpiece tuned into Goldberg's room. "They know about Yousef, and apparently the Italian assassin was a target for conversion by the Pope… or so the Pope says."

Murphy sighed. "I'm sure *someone's* suggesting that the Pope was more interested in assigning targets to the assassin. *Oy vey.*" He looked back at the screen. "Anyway, scroll down. He might have been dishonorably discharged."

Shushurin turned back toward the television screen and scrolled down. "Does that help?"

Not being able to see through her head, Murphy frowned a little before scooting up the bed next to Shushurin, side by side as though they were seated next to each other on a bus or train, thighs and arms touching.

"Honorable discharge with no reason attached." Murphy glanced at Shushurin. "Sounds suspicious to me. Wouldn't they have put a reason if it were honorable?"

She smiled. "Do you really think they'd want to put 'he left us for a better offer' on the work form? Especially since he became a priest?"

"Point taken." Murphy frowned, looking off into space, not seeing anything as he pondered the options. They were spies, not detectives, both of them with non-official covers; there was nothing to be done aside from following Abasi and company in the hopes that they would find something. As long as Father Frank remained their guide to the Eternal City, all of them could be kept track of. Once they split up, then it would get tricky. Priority would have to be given to Abasi and the priest …

"Can I help you?" Shushurin asked.

Murphy blinked his way back to reality. "No. Why?"

"You were staring right at me."

He frowned around his pipe and looked off to the side. "Oh, sorry. Just assessing the situation. It's amazing how good James Bond makes us look — walk in, order drinks, kill people; seduce someone over a game of glorified black-jack, slip in witty comments, kill yet more people. I wish my job was that easy. Change the details, and I'm set."

"Why, are you gay?" Manana said with a smirk.

Murphy looked at her sideways. "I don't play cards, and I have no time for seducing women." He glanced around the hotel room, and her equipment. "Although your budget is bigger than mine."

She shrugged. "Yousef made it easy to get the money."

He rolled his eyes. "Ah, the joys of spy work. Although I'm still surprised your guys didn't install a bug in the room large enough to broadcast to a remote, off-site location."

"No time. Besides, we have one better than a laser mic." Shushurin pointed over to the table. "The pen in the stand is the listening device, a directional microphone that can penetrate up to three feet of solid metal, and obviously, the floors aren't separated by solid metal."

Murphy smiled. "Wish my boss would supply me with tech like that. Speaking of which …" Murphy opened his cellular phone and dialed a number.

A moment later, his boss answered. "What?"

"I need to look up something on a priest; you may know him. Francis Williams?"

After a moment of silence, his boss said, "Don't worry about him. He's low priority." *Click.*

Murphy blinked. "That was odd. I almost feel like I got whacked over the head."

* * *

"Nice whack on the head, Johnny," Veronica Fisher said,

examining Giovanni Figlia's head wound.

"It's Gianni if you are going to shorten it," he groaned. "Can you stitch it back together?"

His wife smiled at him. She'd been teasing him like that for years. It never got old. "Of course, I was a pathologist's assistant before I went into criminalistics. Give me a moment. I'll get a suture kit."

Figlia smiled. "Just remember, I'm still alive."

"I'll try to keep that in mind," she called over her shoulder. "You sure you don't want me to take you to the hospital? I checked for concussion, but I'm not an expert on people with a pulse."

"I've taken enough bumps in football and SWAT to know a concussion when I get one."

Fisher opened a medical cabinet.

She grabbed the suture kit, rolling her eyes at the European word for soccer. "Got it," she called. "Tell me, when you were playing soccer, why you didn't kill any of those idiots with the vuvuzelas?"

"They didn't allow guns on the field."

She walked over, irrigated the wound with the spray used to wash down corpses, and readied the needle. Figlia's wife was almost done stitching him up when Father Frank Williams entered the room, noting the stitching equipment. "Oh Lord, what happened?"

Figlia looked up at the short man in black. "I was attacked."

Father Frank saw the stitching needle in Fisher's hand. "Would you like me to look? I was a physician assistant in a former lifetime." He glanced around the room, spotting the needles in the wall. "Did he cut you?"

Figlia was about to shake his head when he remembered

that his wife still had a needle at his scalp. "He missed."

Father Frank slipped the ring off his hand and reached for the penlight near Fisher. "Look straight." He flashed the light in Figlia's eyes. "What did he want?"

"He took a copy of the forensics reports on this morning's event," Fisher answered.

Father Frank nodded, then put the light down, checking the head wound and Fisher's stitches. "You're fine." He straightened. "Do you have a description? I could ask around."

Figlia waved it away. "It wouldn't matter. I couldn't identify him if he were standing two feet in front of me. He wore all black — how many people does that fit?"

Father Frank frowned. "Oh dear. Everyone."

"*Certo.* I am fortunate I avoided serious injury, otherwise there would be blood on the street, and it is hard to get blood out of marble." Figlia sighed. "At least we have a backup on the computers... Is there something I can help you with?"

"This might be a bad time, but there is an Irish detective coming from Dublin. She'll be at the terminal in an hour. She's a member of Interpol looking into the murder of a priest."

Figlia sighed. "Why is she coming *here?*"

"The victim was to arrive here in a week to give a report on Pius XII. He was found with a swastika carved into his forehead."

Figlia closed his eyes even deeper. "Not again. What is this, a tourist convention? Who else is in town? The circus?"

The priest smiled. "You mean the CIA?"

* * *

132

Sean Ryan sat in the police station, pulling out his newspaper again. Who knew that even the police wanted to take a break during *siesta* too? What was this, teatime in London? It was almost as if they expected criminals to be napping between the hours of noon and three in the afternoon.

Then again, there's no one around to rob half the time, he thought wryly. *Except maybe tourists.* He was half-asleep with boredom. Then he opened the newspaper.

There was a brief section on Cardinal Cannella's religious order — the Markist Brothers.

Sean smiled again. His fiancée was a talent representative for various talents — one of which was a young novelist who had a personal grudge against the Markist brothers, due to odd events in high school. As a result, Sean knew more about the order than he liked to admit.

Sean popped open his phone, and dialed. After a moment, a lightly accented voice answered, "Sean?"

"Hey, Inna, how are you?"

"Good ... what is the matter?"

Sean chuckled. "Does something have to be the matter?"

There was laughter several thousand miles away. "What is it, Sean?"

"Your man, the one with the grudge against the Markists? What was his theory on them again?"

Inna sighed. "He will sometimes murmur a belief that the Nazis had created the order before they fell in 1945. But his only evidence there is that it had been founded in Berlin. It became recognized in 1958, the year that Pope Pius XII died and Cardinal Roncalli was made Pope John XXIII."

"That was the Italian peasant built like Santa Claus, right?" Sean asked. "They wanted him to be a 'filler' Pope after Pius's decades-long reign, instead he called Vatican II.

133

Something about it 'opening the windows to let in the fresh air,' et cetera."

Inna chuckled. "You have something against fresh air?"

"Of course not, I'm from Los Angeles. But let's face it, when the train of the church is moving through the toxic gas cloud called the sixties, locking the windows would be better. But the Markists?"

"Well," she said thoughtfully, "in their mission statement, Markists were 'dedicated to education,' and founded several schools in the United States, with others dotting the face of Europe. A few years ago, they became a defunct order in America, after their last stronghold of education had been destroyed."

Sean paused for a moment, restraining the urge to give an alibi. "Didn't one of your authors have something to do with the place being blown up?"

"I do not know," Inna told him. "He has always been vague on the details."

He smiled. "Anyway, what else? They have a Boston Cardinal installed, and everyone thinks Rome was scammed. Maybe his installation was a Markist power play to get them back into the States?"

"That is not something he has discussed with me," Inna answered. "If you want my opinion, it is a good question, but why? Pope Pius XIII has nearly declared the United States missionary country ..."

"Could they want back on the front lines, become a real order?" Sean asked. "As opposed to, you know, an order lite?"

"But why? I could think of better places to work," she told him. "Rome? Paris? The Markists want Boston?"

"Okay," Sean conceded, "different track: this Cardinal guy received donations from a group of Wiccans; why? What could he have gained, aside from the money? Better question: why would *they* have benefited from giving him the money?"

"Oh," Inna answered, "so you have not finished the article. I will wait."

Sean blinked, glanced to the article again, then choked.

"They used coffins to smuggle the drugs into the country, and Markists supplied both the coffins and the funerals. The Cardinal's office refused to comment, citing the Cardinal's recent departure for Rome just hours before warrants were issued. "One step ahead of the cops, huh? Lucky man." He closed the paper, looking around the police station for someone to let him know if he should leave or not.

"I guess it could be worse. I could be from Boston."

* * *

"You're from Boston," Manana Shushurin said, "so you must be Catholic, yes?"

Murphy looked up from the screen of Manana's phone, and discovered her inside his personal space, looking right into his eyes. For some reason, it had only just occurred to him that he was on a bed, sitting next to a beautiful woman, and he hadn't even thought twice about it. He was either very well-trained, very focused, or in desperate need of having his hormone levels checked.

Murphy leaned back against the headboard. "You could say that."

"How did Mossad even let you in?"

He grinned around his pipe. "You're BND liaison to the Office, and you don't know about the Goyim Brigade?"

She tucked both legs under her so she could comfortably face him. "The what?"

135

"The Goyim Brigade. We're a collection of non-Jewish Israeli citizens, many of whom emigrated there after 9-11, like I did. Soon, the Office was so filled with Gentiles. They needed their own little subsection. Thus, the Goyim Brigade. Given the odd variety of us, they needed an intermediary between the head of the Office and the rank-and-file intelligence officers. They picked a Catholic, someone who had a relative in the intelligence business, like Cardinal Dulles of Fordham, the son of the CIA's founder. Now, while it would look odd for a Hasidic Jew to walk into a mosque, or a Muslim to walk into a synagogue, there was one place either one could go without raising eyebrows..."

Shushurin nodded. "A Catholic Church, preferably one that's a tourist trap."

"Bingo. It—"

She suddenly held up a hand. "Abasi's about to move. I can hear him. Let's go."

Murphy slid off the bed, checking his watch. It was a quarter to three.

* * *

At three o'clock, Hashim Abasi and Wilhelmina Goldberg arrived at the section of the Vatican infirmary that had been converted into an interim forensics lab.

Goldberg furrowed her brows as she noted the sharp objects lodged in the office door. She glanced at the damage to Figlia's head. "What happened here?"

"It was not a great miracle," Figlia replied. "Someone stole the report from this morning's crime scene."

Abasi cocked his head. "Why? No one has said that Yousef's report had been stolen from the *carabinieri*. Why

136

steal one and not the other? Either Yousef and Gerrity were killed by two different groups of people, or the thief was independent of them."

Figlia rubbed his temple, feeling a headache on approach. "What do you mean?"

"Yousef was more important than Gerrity, I would think," Abasi said. "With Gerrity, they should know exactly what we have, because everything in the room was left by your corpse — everything except the bomb. If someone used gloves, is there a possibility someone might have left something inside the bomb that's useful?"

Fisher, coming out of her office, shook her head. "Not a chance. Everything was generic, and a hair sample would have been fried. Unless there's something so obscure that we haven't found it yet, I can only tell you what was used to make the bomb, little else."

Figlia blinked. "By the way, Hashim Abasi, Villie Goldberg, this is my wife, Veronica Fisher, originally a crime-scene analyst from America."

Abasi bowed slightly. "Charmed."

Ronnie nodded. "Ditto. Now, if you're right, there are only two real options. They might be interested solely in the computer findings... but if that's the case, why not just destroy the computer? He didn't seem interested in anything other than the report."

Figlia nodded, confirming the statement. "He went right for it."

Abasi frowned thoughtfully. "Then one other possibility is that someone merely wanted to increase his own knowledge, not impede us. Otherwise, if the computer was the only thing that could contain evidence, why not take that?"

Fisher nodded. "Makes sense. Clementi, the gunman, was

probably there to destroy the computer as well as kill Gerrity. He may have been looking at the screen when he was blown up, talking on his cell. If that's so, he was probably killed because he saw the computer. If I set off the bomb, my first priority wouldn't be to find out what we know — it would be to keep us from finding something we haven't already. The computer was in plain sight; why not take it? It was closer to the window than the book… a fact I'll have to discuss with my computer guys."

Abasi and Goldberg shared a glance. "You want to bring it up or should I?"

Figlia looked from one to the other. "I've already got a splitting headache, just tell me."

Goldberg inquired, "First of all, where's Father Frank?"

"He just left."

Abasi slid into a chair opposite Figlia. "We think he's part of Vatican Intelligence."

Fisher put away the suture kit. "What makes you say that?"

Goldberg shrugged. "Well, he managed to take down four guys using the parts of a handgun he field stripped like a pro, after he disarmed the one waving that gun at him."

Figlia raised an eyebrow. "If you're implying he attacked me, why would he steal the book? He could have asked; it's not like we have anything to hide."

Veronica Fisher came back from shelving the suture kit. "Maybe *he* does."

Figlia raised a hand. "He's also—"

"Getting the car."

Abasi and Goldberg turned toward the door. Father Frank stood there, holding a set of car keys in his hand. "*Signor* Figlia is taking out a field expedition to pick up a new arriv-

138

al, taking the train into Rome from the airport. I take it you would wish me not to drive?"

"No," Figlia said. "Ronnie does not want me driving with my head like this. Besides, the three of us are going to do business in the car." He looked at Abasi and Goldberg. "We have to discuss security procedures, and Father Frank can treat it as secret as the confessional."

Father Frank smiled. "I like that. It gives them a way to keep an eye on me." He smiled benignly at both of them. "A few simple moves and you get paranoid; would it help if I said I'm an army chaplain, and my parish keeps me up-to-date on self-defense because they can kill twenty ways with their bare hands? Have you both been reading conspiracy novels?"

Figlia laughed. "I've got to call in another van, otherwise there won't be enough room for... did you get her name?"

Father Frank shook his head. "No. Sorry."

CHAPTER XI: STAIRWAY TO HELL

Sean Aloysius Patricus Ryan coughed slightly, hoping that, somehow, he wouldn't get a cold. While his immune system was damn near impervious, he wasn't superhuman. And spending over two hours in an Italian police station was possibly the most boredom he could stand. Heck, how often could a guy reread the newspaper without dying from weariness?

He turned the corner, still carelessly walking in the middle of the street…

He blinked as a set of black vans came bearing down on him. *I guess siesta is over.*

Sean leapt sideways, onto a parked car, sliding over the roof as the vans screeched to a sudden stop. Sean merely slid off the roof to the ground.

The doors of the van opened, Giovanni Figlia stepping out first. *"Tu pazzo stupido americano! Che pensato? Schmuck!"*

Sean smiled, cocked his head, and said, "Funny, you don't look Jewish."

Wilhelmina Goldberg laughed as she came out of the back. "No fair, I was going to say that!"

Father Frank smiled, leaning out the car window. "While

I do not agree with some of Signore Figlia's language, I must say that the sentiment is shared."

Sean walked around the car. "Sorry about that, I thought it was still *siesta* and everyone was still asleep. You can't imagine what it's like trying to get anything done at a police station between one and three in the afternoon in this town."

"More like this country," Father Frank told him.

Sean nodded. "I'll take your word on it, because I really don't want to test that thesis. Anyway, where're you people headed in such a blasted hurry?" He glanced at the second van with the Swiss Guard driver, wearing all black — he could tell the man was Swiss because he had blond hair, blue eyes, and a neutral look on his face.

Welcome to The Stepford Wives. "And what's with the caravan?"

Figlia counted to ten before he answered. "We are picking someone up, and we need the room."

Sean shrugged. "Okay. Let me know if you need any help." He patted the van's hood as he turned away. "I'll get out of your way. *Ciao.*"

"*Molto grazie.* And unless you know any Irish Interpol officers, I doubt you can help any."

Sean stopped and pivoted, grinning. "I know one or two. I can drive."

Figlia closed his eyes, still shaken by the madman. "Fine."

Father Frank nodded. "I'll get rid of our companion in the other car. You don't need more than two cars, and I'm certain he can be of use elsewhere. I will drive his car... I have nothing else to do."

* * *

As the two black cars pulled away, Scott "Mossad" Murphy stepped back, smiled, grateful he had placed the dual-purpose tracking device and bug on the lead van while it had been stopped. If the short guy with the blue eyes hadn't stopped the car, Murphy didn't know what would have happened.

Thank God for happy accidents. Murphy counted to ten, and then, when a dark blue Jetta pulled up in front of him, he let himself inside.

Manana Shushurin, sitting behind the wheel, reached under her blonde wig to secure the earpiece. "We're wired, and so are they."

Murphy blinked. "I'm sorry, I thought I just heard you say that we're weird."

She grinned broadly. "That, too."

* * *

"So, what's all this about, anyway?" Sean Ryan asked, shooting through the streets of Rome as though the cars weren't actually there, swerving in, through, and around traffic that made the Los Angeles freeways during rush hour look calm.

Giovanni Figlia gave him a dirty look. "I brought two cars so I could talk business, not socialize."

Sean nodded. "Okay." He made another sharp turn through traffic, briefly leaping onto the curb, the sidewalk, around a parked car, and onto the street, all to avoid a triple-parked car. "I feel like I'm back at Cambridge," he muttered. He glanced at Goldberg in the review mirror. "Are Secret Service people as stiff as Johnny boy here?"

"More than you can possibly know."

Giovanni Figlia rolled his eyes.

Sean made another turn that made Figlia grab his seat. Figlia thought a moment. "Is Father Williams still behind us?"

Sean nodded. "He's been on my tail the entire way. That isn't bad for a priest; but then, he'd have had to drive through worse garbage to be in the Army."

Wilhelmina Goldberg leaned forward. "Which one?"

"He told you already — he's an Army chaplain. Why, you think he's something else?"

"Well, with the way he took out those thugs—" she began.

Sean waved it away. "Frank's an Army brat, son of An army brat, with two siblings in the military, and he has military service of his own. And now, his day job is as an army Chaplin. He's surrounded by thousands of guys every day who work well with killing people. Have you all been reading John Cornwell novels lately?"

"Cornwell? Of *Hitler's Pope?*" Wilhelmina arched her brows. "I thought he was a historian."

Sean shook his head. "No, my *girlfriend* is a historian. Cornwell's just a journalist who likes to say Catholics are the center of all that is evil in the world. What do you expect from a British ex-seminarian? *Hitler's Pope* was a hit piece on John Paul II; when JPII died, Cornwell backpedaled on Pius XII because it was safe to go after John Paul. Frankly, most people who claim that Pius XII was an evil genius working with Hitler cite forgeries."

Goldberg sighed. "You're another member of the Pius XII canonization campaign?"

Abasi smiled at her. "At least this one has a pulse."

Sean laughed. "Hell no, I just have a good memory. Also,

143

it's a memorable story when Hitler invites the Pope to Germany, the Pope arms the Swiss Guards with submachine guns, and *then* does the Pope refuse the invite."

Sean made another sharp turn, only this time it was into the train terminal connecting central Rome to the airport. "However, as for Father Frank, I see no reason why he can't be an ordinary priest. I mean, honestly, you think the Vatican actually has an intelligence service with members fully trained in hand-to-hand combat? Granted, they have the hierarchy for it, but having the correct command structure doesn't mean that you have the training. Having a bureaucracy does not bestow all the required discipline. Heck, if you get a few members of Opus Dei drunk, you'll *wish* they were a secret society."

* * *

Maureen McGrail stepped out of the Termini train station, newly arrived from Leonardo Da Vinci airport, carrying a single black bag. Around her long frame she had wrapped a black, lightweight raincoat that made her seem smaller than she was, a style she liked to affect. She had lost count of the times she had walked into the middle of a firefight and survived because no one had even seen her. She ran her long fingers through her rich black hair and wondered exactly how long it would take before her ride would arrive.

Her glittering pale green eyes surveyed curbside. Despite the cars and the train she had just gotten off, the ambiance, even the air smelled old... well, except for the exhaust fumes, but she couldn't completely remove the present.

The sound of squealing tires made her jump as she looked left at the black vans heading almost directly for her. She noted the angle and stepped back. The vans didn't stop, or change direction, until they stopped a yard in front of her, at curbside.

She raised an eyebrow. *If I didn't know better, I'd swear I knew the driver.*

The driver's side door opened. The driver swung himself out of the van, and quickly swept up her bag, then hugged her, lifting her off the ground and swinging her around. She was about to break his neck when he let go and took a step back.

"Superintendent McGrail! It's wonderful to see you again! How have you been?"

McGrail blinked when she saw the electric-blue eyes she should have seen a mile away and through the tinted glass. "Sean Ryan? What the hell are you doing here?"

"Training a few civilians, believe it or not. It's been years. You haven't called, haven't written—"

An official looking sort stepped out of the car and went straight to McGrail. He was taller than Sean – but so was everybody – but about medium height, with a runner's build. He looked local, with a Mediterranean tan, dark hair and eyes. His black suit on his black polo almost made him look like a priest, but the jacket was too nice. He reached forward and offered his hand. "Giovanni Figlia, Vatican Central Office of Vigilance."

She took it. "Superintendent Maureen McGrail, Interpol."

"A pleasure." He jerked his head to Sean. "You know this *scherzo?*"

She beamed. "Aye, I know this joker."

A shorter woman with a terrible blonde dye job slid out of the van. "He called Ryan a joke, not a joker. Hi, Villie

145

Goldberg, Secret Service, and the guy hiding in the van is Hashim Abasi, Egyptian cop."

"I am not hiding," the one called Abasi said, just sticking his head out of the car. He was a bigger, heavier man than the others, packed with muscle weight. "I just don't see a reason to leave the van only to get back in."

Sean Ryan tossed McGrail's bag into the back of the security van, and looked at the toy collection in the trunk. He smiled at all of the electronic stun gadgets and Taser-beam weapons. He spied a nice little stun gun, and thought he'd steal it for the ride back. Sean liked having personal protection, and he had had enough guns jammed into his spine that he waited for the day when someone realized that a handgun was not a contact weapon. He took the Taser before closing the trunk. "I just want to know where everyone sits now."

"And why Superintendent McGrail is here," Figlia said.

"Ah, and can't I explain that one in the van? Shall we?"

* * *

From half a block away, someone wearing a solid black outfit stepped out of the shadows behind a tree. He carried himself well for a man who was only forty, and he slid to one knee, hoping that no one would notice him until it was too late. He leveled his Beretta and aimed at the three cops — Goldberg, McGrail, and Figlia — then fired.

However, all three were professionals. As such, they had all eyed every probable avenue of attack, including the tree he'd been standing behind.

Sean Ryan, who already had a weapon in his hand, was the first to fire, dropping to one knee at the side of the armored van and firing a solid, three-second blast, shocking the man in black in the right forearm, the left bicep and the left shoulder. The beam burned mercilessly, and he fell onto his back. He painfully rolled over, into the cover of the tree, as Figlia and Goldberg opened fire.

The sudden acceleration caught Sean's attention, and he whirled, and nearly opened fire on the car speeding towards them, until he realized that Father Frank was behind the wheel.

And then it was hit with the rocket-propelled grenade.

The impact alone would have been enough to throw the van across the street. But the explosion lifted the driver's side wheels off of the street, and the massive fireball threw the vehicle into a roll, onto the sidewalk, landing on its side.

Sean Ryan whirled around, spying a possible location for the RPG. He fired twice, conserving his battery power. He opened the trunk, threw himself inside, and then crawled over the back seat to get to the front. He started the engine, and prayed the shooters didn't have a second RPG ready and loaded; otherwise, they were screwed. He slammed his door shut, then noted that McGrail, Goldberg and Figlia had already leapt in.

Sean gunned the engine and sped away, riding the sidewalk instead of fighting Rome traffic. The injured gunman who had been shocked had, at that moment, poked his head out to see where the four of them had gone. The bumper of Sean's van caught him squarely in the head. The license plate number embedded in his skull.

"What about Frank?" Goldberg screamed.

Sean, to everyone's surprise, laughed. "Oh, I wouldn't worry about him," "" Sean said calmly "He's harder to kill than he looks. If no one minds, I'm going to take the long way to the Vatican. I don't want to be caught in an ambush by taking an obvious, shorter way there. Any objections?" He paused. "So, Maureen, light of my hour, what brings you to this fair city? Anything to get you shot at?"

McGrail furrowed her brow. "I have a murder victim who was on his way here to give eyewitness testimony on the Pius XII canonization. There been anything like that around here?"

* * *

Manana Shushurin heard the entire fracas over the transmitter planted on the van, and cursed in German, following it up with, "Son of a bitch."

Scott Murphy blinked at the explosion up ahead. "Tell me that wasn't our guys."

"It was, and the RPG hit the van with the priest in it."

"Well, that's stupid," Murphy muttered. "Why bother? Those vans are probably like Sherman tanks."

"To keep Father Frank out of the chase? Give him an excuse not to be involved as they kill the passengers in the other van — the only investigators in the David Gerrity case?"

Murphy shook his head. "Is that supposed to be his alibi, or his luck?"

"Great question," she murmured, eyes locked and focused firmly on the road.

"Where do you think they'll be heading?" Murphy asked.

"I have an idea, and I might be able to intercept them. The driver is Sean Ryan — the man you saw come to Father Williams' aid." Manana made a sharp left. "Your people had me compile a record on him a while ago. He's very colorful."

Murphy gripped his seat tightly. "You mean he's nuts. And you'd know from crazy?"

Shushurin sped up to sixty, gave him a long, drawn-out look and smiled at him. Murphy was certain his heart had stopped, but he wasn't certain whether it was because she was gorgeous or because she wasn't looking at the freaking road. "Where did you learn to drive growing up? Georgia?"

"No, that's Stalin's old place." She looked back to the street. "I learned on the autobahn."

She increased her speed, circling around traffic, weaving through cars and around corners, taking off one car's side mirror.

Murphy white knuckled the chicken grip. He took a deep breath, distracting himself from the terror-inspiring drive, asked, "What the hell is going on around here, blast it?"

"Someone obviously knew where they were going," Shushurin answered. She paused, and listened to the transmitter attached to the car. "They just picked up a woman investigating *another* murder related to Pius XII."

Murphy glanced at her. "Is someone having a bad flashback to the forties? Neo-Nazis on an acid trip?"

Shushurin frowned at a slow pedestrian in front of her and made a slight course correction, shooting around him. "No. This particular victim wasn't in Rome at the time. He ..." she paused and listened to the bug attached to the van, "was a priest found murdered in Dublin, and had a swastika carved into his forehead? Oh, dear... the guys I work for are sensitive about Nazis."

"I can imagine," the Israeli agent said dryly. "So are mine. Listen, are we sure that we don't know is there no way to find out what Yousef was looking at in the Vatican archives? Because if there's one body in Ireland who's connected to Pope Pius XII, how much you want to bet both of our dead researchers here were on the same subject?"

Shushurin nodded, zipping down a side street to circumvent a traffic jam in both road and sidewalk. "Which would make sense. In fact ..." she searched her memory. "When Sean Ryan went on about Pius XII, the Secret Service Agent said 'oh God, another one'."

Murphy furrowed his brow. "They probably meant that Gerrity was working on Pius XII!" He smiled broadly. "We have two dead bodies connected to one pope, and maybe three. All right! We know something of what the hell is going on here!"

Manana Shushurin grinned. "You get so cute when you're excited."

* * *

Sean Ryan laughed as he drove over the sidewalk and around traffic. "If this were a novel, that would mean five bodies are on the deck before page 150—nice going. One dead gunman at the terminal, two dead terrorists, a capped priest, and a dead academic. If I knew that my time here was going to be so much fun, I would have brought the rest of my office with me. We could use them."

Figlia frowned at Sean's enthusiasm, and his driving. "I am sorry you had to enter into the middle of this, Superintendent."

The lady in question waved it away. "Call me Maureen. What's going on, exactly? Your terrorist and this Gerrity fella, what do they have to do with my dead priest?"

"Gerrity was researching the Pius XII archives," Figlia answered, eyeing the road with worry as the ex-stuntman continued driving. "As for the terrorist Yousef, we've not gotten around to the archives yet to see what he was working on.

Thankfully, the archive logs keep track of such things. We can evaluate how important he thought something was by the time he spent reading it."

Sean smiled at them in the rearview mirror, driving with his peripheral vision around a pedestrian, through an intersection, and onto the opposite sidewalk. "However," Sean said, as calmly as though he were cruising slowly through scenic countryside, "you say that Father Frank had constant contact with Clementi, the one who shot both Yousef and Dr. Gerrity?"

Sean jerked the wheel sharply around one pedestrian who wasn't fast enough to jump, then tacked back the other way to avoid a parked car. "If you're right, and Father Frank is Vatican intelligence, then he's been running operations on behalf of the Pope. You think the Pope's in on... whatever this is?"

Figlia was the first to jump in. "First of all, that is an unwarranted assumption. Like blaming the U.S. President for every operative the CIA has in country. We're not even sure—"

Sean sped up *Via Sistina,* slipping between two cars. "Did ya grow up somewhere without speed limits, ya daft bastard?" Maureen McGrail yelled at him.

"Actually, I learned to drive in the FBI's closed defensive-driving course. Mom was so proud." He looked over the turn he wanted, which was a path between two buildings down what was meant to be a walkway. "Hold on."

Sean made a sharp left, a move that almost no one else in the car would have considered. Had they asked Superintendent McGrail, they would have learned that the mind of Sean Ryan was a dark and dangerous place, most likely booby trapped with land mines. She, at least, was not surprised by his crazy scheme. Everyone else didn't have time to process what he was going to do before he did it.

Sean slammed the horn thoroughly, trying to clear the area around the *palazzo* of its civilians. They scattered quickly, used to spending their lives running toward a soccer ball in their youth, or dodging cars in the street since they learned how to walk.

And then, immediately ahead of him, Sean saw his goal — the top landing of the Spanish Steps.

* * *

Murphy tried to ignore Shushurin's speed as she shot up *Via del Babuino*.

"Get ready to take the wheel. We're coming up on *La Piazza di Spagna*."

Shushurin turned the wheel to the right, going swiftly around the fountain, stopping directly in front of one of the two short buildings on either side of the Spanish Steps. The wheels nearly grazed the bottom landing. She opened the door and moved without even putting the car into park. Murphy lunged for the wheel and stomped on the brake.

Shushurin rolled to a crouch behind the car, aiming her weapon at the rooftops, hoping to God that whatever idiots had been shooting before had not been smart enough to make the same mental leap she had. She made her way around the car, to the bottom of the stairs, staying just in the shadow of the building. It was evident that her guess had been correct — she could hear the rumble of the black van starting down the Steps.

Sean Ryan, maniac that he was, had decided to charge down the Spanish Steps without slowing.

Unfortunately, her prayer had been answered.

The answer was no.

Shushurin had worried that someone else could anticipate Sean Ryan; the worry had been valid, only exponentially worse than she imagined. On the roof across from her, she could see four men with assault rifles, and she didn't even want to guess how many were on top of the building she crouched in front of, or even how many had managed to find their way above the *Palazzo* itself.

Manana carefully leveled her Stechkin at the gunman with the best vantage of the van, and fired twice, aiming for center mass. With her first bullet, she hit the man's gun arm, and her second bullet went astray, kicking up stone dust from the building, getting into the eyes of the gunman immediately behind him.

This latter one prematurely let off a stream of bullets that missed the black van, strafing the building opposite them.

On the positive side, the gunfire from both the BND officer and the rooftop shooter had encouraged the tourists to evacuate the steps even faster than the honking of Sean Ryan.

However, the two shooters closest to her turned away from the van, and swung their weapons toward her. She slid back, content to let them both waste their ammunition against the side of the building, grateful that most of the civilians had already run off the steps.

* * *

Sean Ryan looked up at the gunmen on the building to his right, and then spotted shooters on his left...

And then felt the impact of bullets on the back, front, and sides of the car.

153

Wilhelmina Goldberg was already reaching into the back, pulling an MP-5 submachine gun from its compartment, along with two magazines. Hashim Abasi, sitting on the other side of Maureen McGrail, did the same.

Giovanni Figlia lowered his window a crack and opened fire with his handgun. Four more bullets added to the dust cloud obscuring the gunmen's vision, and two more found their way into someone's chest, knocking him out of sight.

The two gunmen who had been firing elsewhere turned their attention back to the van. From the street below, a woman wheeled around the corner of a building and opened fire, causing civilians to simply evacuate the *piazza* altogether. After three bursts, the sound of the strange handgun went from semi to fully automatic.

Sean spotted one of the gunmen on a roof fall down. *I think we have backup from somewhere, and she looks blonde. Or she's a dyed hippie from the Valley. My money's on a wig.*

Sean caught a bit of movement on the roof above the newcomer; a gunman looking straight down, at the bright blond hair of her wig. He leaned forward with his assault rifle, aiming straight down for her perfect blonde head.

Sean was about to honk the horn to try warning the blonde shooter, but at that moment, a new barrage opened up from the street, making the roof in front of him explode.

Across the street, on the opposite end of the *Via del Babuino* was yet another van. Sean could just make it out through the cracks in the bulletproof glass. The van looked like it had been punched in with a giant fist. And, in front of it, a man in black fired an M4 assault rifle.

Father Frank Williams did not look like a happy priest.

He let go with another burst of automatic fire, aiming low, mainly at the wall just below the gunman.

Sean gave a mental shrug. *Well, his vows say nothing about suppressing fire.*

The gunman leapt back, and his rifle swung up.

"Abasi, eleven o'clock high, nail that sucker."

The Egyptian cop opened the window enough to allow the muzzle of his gun to peek out. Since this made aiming difficult, he fired on automatic, using the top of the window as a platform, so he strafed the roof in a line that varied with the bumps for each of the steps.

Sean called back, "Maureen, I saw some gas grenades back there. Send two up front, would you? We can't fire at the guys behind us, so we might as well blind them."

McGrail handed three grenades forward. "Who says we can't shoot them?"

Sean smiled. "Good idea. Everyone, hold on." He made a hard right, and halfway through it, he hit the brakes, letting the back end of the van fishtail, and he put the car into reverse. The armored windshield became covered in a spider web of cracks as it took fire from the rooftop of the palazzo.

As Figlia fired at the rooftop — quickly supported by Father Frank — McGrail pulled the pins on the gas grenades and Ryan opened the sunroof just wide enough for her to slide them through, and quickly closed it again.

The grenades rolled to the front and either side of the car, unleashing large clouds of smoke that made it hard to see a moving target like the van.

However, the defenders inside the van knew exactly where their attackers had been last time they saw them.

Sean felt like he should contribute to the gunfire, but he noted the water fountain in the mirror and swerved to avoid it, barely catching a glimpse of blonde hair as the woman ducked into her Jetta's passenger side door.

Sean wasted no time as he made a ninety-degree turn onto *Via del Babuino*, making a right onto the street and then — in forward gear — making a left onto *Via Della Croce*, speeding away.

* * *

"Who the hell were those guys?" Wilhelmina Goldberg asked, looking back at the Spanish Steps through what was left of the rear windshield.

"Well, darlin'," Sean drawled, "that's the question on everyone's mind right now, followed by how the hell do I get back to the Vatican — that last one is rhetorical, Gianni." He blinked, and thought for a moment he had a ringing in his ear. "Anyone have a cell phone?"

Figlia put away his handgun and answered his cell. "Figlia, *pronto.*"

"It's Father Frank," came the soft voice. "Is everyone all right?"

"We got out. Was that you firing?"

"Yes, conveniently enough," Father Frank answered. "After the RPG hit the van, a few helpful pedestrians flipped me onto the tires. I knew Mr. Ryan well enough to meet you at the steps."

Figlia furrowed his brows. "How?"

"Have you not read his resume?" Father Frank answered. "He does seem to enjoy destroying public places. Also, it was an unconventional route."

"Where are you now?" Figlia asked as Sean made a left onto *Via Mario de'Fiori.*

"*On Via del Babuino*, heading south toward *Condotti.*"

"We're on the way to *Condotti* now. See you shortly." He

closed the phone. "Apparently, Father Frank still knows how to handle a gun. He provided cover fire."

Sean nodded. "I suppose that explains why we got out alive. Had they all been ready and waiting with no distractions, they probably could have leveled us with an RPG." He darted around a slow-moving Vespa. "I just have one question. How'd they know we were going to be there?"

Figlia shrugged. "Maybe the way Father Frank knew. He said he knew you."

Sean frowned thoughtfully. "True... it's a very 'me' thing to do... but who knew I was driving? Six people?"

Everyone hesitated for a moment – that was everyone in the car, Father Frank, and the Swiss Guard they left behind.

"Is the guard we left behind new?" Ryan asked.

"No, he's been here for years. I'd trust him to run an operation in my stead."

Ryan said nothing for a long moment as he sped through the streets of Rome. "Then we have a problem."

* * *

"Damnit," Scott Murphy growled as he finally turned back in the direction of the Vatican. Granted, he thanked God that he had gotten out of there alive, and his partner with him, but getting shot at was usually a sign that he had botched his job.

"By the way, that light says you should stop."

Murphy jerked to a stop. He let himself relax, finally noticing that he shook from adrenaline. "Ah, sorry... haven't been in a firefight for a while. I forgot the aftershocks."

Shushurin watched him shake, and placed her hand over his. "Don't worry, you did fine."

He gripped her hand in a squeeze without thinking. "I know. We probably should leave the car somewhere."

"I'll handle that," she answered. "I'm reasonably certain Father Frank saw me, though."

"Secret Agent Priest?" He let go of her hand. But before he fully let go, he slipped his thumb from under her palm and put it on top of her hand, squeezing it firmly. He put his hand back on the wheel. "You were blonde at the time; I think you're safe." He pressed his head into the headrest. "You were damn good back there."

She grinned. "They love me for my mind, not my scores on the target range."

Murphy chuckled. "Why did anyone allow you to stay behind a desk, aside from the fact that you're too beautiful?"

Shushurin blinked. "You say that like it's a bad thing."

Murphy rolled his eyes. "It's hard to be invisible if everyone on the street is leering."

"Aw," she said in a mock-whine, "but if nobody stared, how would you know that I'm still beautiful?"

Murphy, caught off-guard by the playfulness of the comment, laughed, and kept laughing through the green light, so hard he had to pull off to the side of the road to catch his breath.

Once he quieted down to a breathless chuckle, she said, "Feeling better?"

Murphy glanced her way. "Much. Thanks, I needed that." He smiled, and just looked at her for a moment. He thought for a second, and figured it couldn't hurt. He reached over and around her back, gently taking her by the right shoulder, leaned over, and kissed her on the cheek. "Thank you," he whispered.

"Anytime."

* * *

The silver-haired man in black received a call on his cell phone. He stopped, looked around, then stepped out of the line of traffic.

"What the hell were you doing today, you bastard?" the caller snapped.

He smiled. He was always amused when insiders freaked out. Undercover personnel are just so touchy. "You never respect your superiors, do you?"

"My superior? Hardly. I'm not so damn trigger-happy."

"Speak for yourself. You did a good job on our men."

"At least when I was shooting at you before," the insider growled, "I knew you'd be wearing solid body armor in case I hit your guys. Now why did you pull that crap? You've seen their every move, I made sure of it. Why the hit?"

"It was a likely chance to remove all of the investigators," the man in black said reassuringly. "You're taking far too long. We saw a way of finishing the entire ordeal."

"Hey, I'm lucky I'm not under any *real* suspicion already. Now that might change, considering that they should all be taking a very close look at *everyone* now. We both know that if they look at *me*, they'll find you. Not to mention that I could have been killed."

"But you weren't. And you wouldn't have been in harm's way had you not gotten involved. You were told to stay close to them, but not too close."

"Tough. Next time you guys get involved, I might go for head shots. You know I can, and I would. Stay the hell out of my way, or you'll regret it. You assigned me to this job, and damn it, I'm either going to do it my way, or you're going to

159

get yourself a new agent."

The man in black adjusted his white Roman collar. *Ah, insiders always want complete control, don't they, worried we're going to blow everything. Good thing it's not a valid concern, or else we'd all be screwed.*

CHAPTER XII: A PIOUS GOY

Giovanni Figlia relaxed in his chair, leaning back, letting the adrenaline buzz dull slightly. "Father Williams went to file a report with the *carabinieri*. Given the suspicions of Villie and Abasi, I thought it would be prudent that he leave while we chat with Superintendent McGrail." He glanced around the room at his fellow professionals. "And I refuse to believe him a killer, or that he set us up — Father Williams came to our aid, providing cover fire for us."

Wilhelmina Goldberg nodded. "Conveniently hitting no one, from what I could tell." She shrugged. "As you say, Gianni, I'm paranoid. I came here for a simple security audit and had a body fall on me before I was even in the country an hour."

Sean smiled. "I'd figure guys would've jumped you as soon as you got off the plane."

Figlia looked at his clock with exasperation. "I have had an exceptionally long day, and it's not even close to being over. I must have a long chat with the police about my psychotic American driver riding over a *national treasure*. I am *not* in the mood for any *paranoid* theories that have to do with *Jesuit assassination squads*."

Sean Ryan was about to open his mouth, but paused, blinked, and cocked his head to the side. "Does anyone else hear an elephant stomping down the hall?"

The outer doors to Figlia's office exploded inward as Pope Pius XIII burst into the office. "Gianni! I was just called by the *carabinieri*. What in the Lord's name happened? Is everyone all right?" He looked around the room, noting everyone. "Where's Father Williams? Did he make it?" The Pope's questions continued in rapid-fire speech that was so fast it sounded like a different language... until Sean Ryan realized that he spoke in Latin.

Suddenly, the Pope stopped and turned to acknowledge McGrail, still seated, and still not quite sure of what was going on. "My apologies, miss," he said, in English this time. "I'm Pope Pius XIII. If you're not Catholic, please call me Josh."

She smiled. "I am, Your Holiness."

"In which case, you must be Maureen McGrail, the officer Figlia was sent to pick up. I hope nothing was damaged along the way."

She shook her head. "Aren't we fine, Your Holiness?"

"Good." He was about to say something else when he turned around, noting the short, dark Irishman learning against the wall. The Pope beamed. "Ah, Mr. Ryan, how good to see you again... what are you doing here?"

He shrugged. "Oh, you know me. I hear gunfire, I come running."

The Pope nodded. "I heard that Giovanni was shot at while driving over the Spanish Steps. I had wondered why he would drive over them in the first place. I suppose he was not driving?"

Sean grinned wider. "A good guess, sir. Now, if you

wouldn't mind, Your Holiness, I'd ask that you briefly allow me to walk our guest to her hotel, let her relax, freshen up, that sort of thing. I hear that Giovanni needs to chat with the Rome police department, and I suspect that phone call will go much better if I'm not in the room — especially when they suggest confiscating my passport or booting my ass out of the country."

The Pope's eyes narrowed. "Why? You weren't the one doing the shooting."

Sean smirked ruefully. "Unfortunately, no. However, someone apparently knew I was driving, and they knew me well enough to expect me to do something that stupid. So, tag, my fault."

"I see. And how do you think they knew you would be driving, considering that I do not recall anyone inviting you along?"

Before anyone could hint at a spy planted among their caravan, Maureen McGrail raised a finger. "Because, Your Holiness, doesn't Sean know me? And isn't Sean's presence in Rome openly known?. Couldn't anyone conclude he'd be there to meet me, and then take the wheel once any shooting took place? Or, the shooter they had in position could have spotted him at the terminal." Giovanni Figlia nodded, grateful for the alternate ideas. "The latter was most likely the case, makes things far less complicated." He glanced a little at Wilhelmina Goldberg and Hashim Abasi. "After all, it's not like we had a spy around here, now is it?"

"Indeed," Pius agreed. "My question then becomes, who would know you that well, Mr. Ryan?"

Sean shrugged, pleased to realize that he hadn't had to say a darned thing… he was never a real actor, but he had been known to suck the air out of a room if he were given half a chance. "Anyone who can read a newspaper."

Hashim Abasi leaned back in the couch and crossed his legs, leaning an elbow on the back. "And how did you and Ms. McGrail meet, if I may ask?"

Sean smiled. "There were two bozos who wanted to recruit me into their rather pathetic IRA cell — made up of two members. Maureen here was sent in to arrest them both. Our paths crossed, and she's wanted to stop knowing me ever since."

McGrail nodded. "Isn't that a little true? No offense, Sean, but aren't you a real pain?"

Sean smiled. "That I am. Can I take you to your hotel room?"

"Wouldn't it be nice to have another target if someone else starts shooting at me?"

Sean took her bag and waved her through the door first. "See, Maureen, I keep telling you, you should use handguns a little more. Get used to the bullets."

Sean closed the door behind him.

The Pope stared at the closed door a moment before turning to the other three left in the room and said,

He slid down into the seat McGrail had just evacuated. "Now, Giovanni, what is going on? First, the killings were about the Vatican Archives; perhaps a serial killer watching the vault. Now, someone has murdered an eyewitness coming in to talk about *Pius!*" He emphasized by slamming a huge fist into the chair arm, cracking the wood in the arm. "I want answers, Gianni. I want any theories you have on the matter."

Figlia nodded slowly. "My first thought would be that this is about Pius XII — it's the link between Maureen's dead priest and Gerrity. I would presume it is also the link to Yousef."

Goldberg took a deep breath. "Here's my problem — it's the next century, is all of it really worth killing over now? Who would bother?"

The Pope smiled at her. "Who wouldn't? There are a lot of people who do not like the Catholics, my young friend. If there is absolute proof that Pius XII helped the Nazis, it would do amazing harm to the Church. However, if it is the opposite, then the Church would get to discredit many of its most vocal enemies."

Hashim Abasi shrugged. "Perhaps. If you want to list the suspects merely by your enemies, where do we start? Sudan? The Middle East? I believe the Russians have outlawed the existence of the Catholic Church in Russia, and they would most certainly desire any excuse to keep it that way. Let us not forget that the Chinese lock up Catholics in order to maintain their stranglehold on the people; ideology only has one true adversary—"

"Differing ideologies," the Pope finished. He leaned forward towards Goldberg, explaining gently. "The American Church may be the worst ideologists of all. They push for birth control in every eventuality, whether 'needed' or not, ignoring statistical advantages of natural family planning over condoms and pills; they want abortion to be a sacrament, ignoring many of the side effects. It is harder and harder to keep them from going schismatic."

Giovanni Figlia winced. "I cannot say for certain, but it *may* have gotten worse because of the Pope taking the name of Pius XIII."

The Pope nodded. "But Americans do not say anything, lest they be accused of racism."

Abasi said "And let us not forget that Middle East fanatics

would love to put your head on a stick. One plotted to kill John Paul II." He shrugged. "Of course, let's not discuss what the Mossad would do with any information against Pius XII, shall we?"

Goldberg's eyes widened, and her jaw went slack — unsure whether to laugh or yell. "You're thinking *Mossad?*"

He shrugged again. "I'm from Egypt. Israelis are always the first suspects." He laughed bitterly. "The *second* suspects are my own people."

The Pope sighed deeply. "That is the problem with being a universal organization."

Goldberg smiled. "That you're also a universal hemorrhoid?"

The Pope nodded. "And that is if we are doing nothing but *good.* By the way, Miss Villie, you are a pious Jew?"

Her amused look was replaced with a scowl. "What's that supposed to mean?"

He smiled. "Mossad reserves the right to call upon any Jew on the planet at any time to come to their aid. If there is any Mossad involvement in this…"

"Tag," Figlia added, "you're it, as you Americans say."

The Pope shrugged. "It is just a thought. But, if you wish to get back to a list of people who hate Catholics, start with anyone who ever raised a gun in Northern Ireland. The German government would like nothing better than to shove the entire Holocaust onto our shoulders. The French have made similar noises against us. Then again, they've hated us since, oh, about 1791." Pius merely looked at them casually, leaning back in the chair, which creaked under his weight. "Then there are the others."

Goldberg blinked. "What others?"

Figlia felt his headache returning. "There are some true

Church fanatics out there. *Freaks* would be your word; there are people still in revolt over the Council of Trent. If something really condemned Pius XII, they would want to get their hands on it; and if it cleared him ..."

Wilhelmina Goldberg raised an eyebrow. "You suspect this would clear him because you work here, and he's been the biggest proponent of papal authority in... how long?"

The Pope shook his head. "If Eugenio Pacelli was a monster, it would have been safe to say so after he died. Everyone who damns Pius XII praises his immediate successor, because he started Vatican II. This line of thought ignores that the second most quoted authority in Vatican II is Pius XII.

"If I am wrong, and Pius was a monster, why did all of this not come up when he died? Why did most people get their anti-Pius bias from a play in the 1960s? However, if I'm right, anyone with an opposing opinion would just be ignored, as everyone and everything defending Pius has been. Now, who is organized enough to plan that attack on the Steps? And who wants to keep the Pius secret a secret?"

Goldberg smiled. "Why not you folks? After all, you are a tightly knit organization."

Pope Pius XIII, aka Joshua Kutjok, the leader of a billion Catholics, stared at her for a long moment, a smile on his lips, and then he laughed. "My dear woman, we don't belong to an organized religion, we are Catholics! We have always allowed anyone in, from Oscar Wilde to the American Kennedy family! Yes, we look organized from the outside, but liquor up some of our staff, you'll get a different story altogether."

* * *

Manana leaned her shoulder against one of the columns in St. Peter's Square as both she and Murphy stood outside the papal residence. Her rich brown hair bunched up around her as she settled in. As Shushurin had guessed, Figlia had retreated back to his own office as soon as he returned from the shootout. Murphy had picked the location to keep them as far from the residence as possible while still keeping it within a line of sight.

"Scott 'Mossad' Murphy?"

Murphy leaned back against the opposite column. "When I told my boss I wanted to be the antidote to John 'Taliban' Walker, he said that I would be 'Mossad.' "

"Even though you call it 'The Office?' "

He chuckled. "Scott 'The Office' Murphy doesn't have the same ring to it."

She smiled at him. "And where do you generally operate, because, frankly…?"

Murphy shrugged. "I can blend in well when I want to. Not bad for being an accountant."

Shushurin's almond-shaped eyes widened. "And *you're* in the field?"

"Well, last year I became the accountant for the head-quarters of the American Nazi Party in Chicago."

She laughed in anticipation of what was to come. "You bankrupted them?"

"Nope. I drained enough of their cash to put them on serious life support, but leaving them enough money to survive." He shrugged. "As my boss says, 'There's nothing like a Nazi parade to increase contributions to the Jewish Defense League.' "

Shushurin frowned. "So you're part accountant and part… field agent? I'm trying to figure out how you're qualified for operations."

Murphy smiled gently. "I'd been working forward to this job for a long time. From the moment I saw 9-11 happen. I knew what I wanted to do with my life. Kill terrorists. Sure, I couldn't do anything that athletic, but I could take their money. As Murphy's Law of spying goes, Shakespeare was wrong – you don't shoot all the lawyers, you shoot the accountants, because they're the ones who know where to find the money."

Murphy grinned suddenly. "The Israelis took one look at me and wondered exactly what planet I was from. They decided to give me an assignment I'm sure was meant to send me screaming out of town, assuming I survived. They threw me into a refugee camp."

Shushurin's mouth dropped open. "How'd you walk out?"

He laughed. "With a collection of firing pins for AK-108s and –74s, the names and contacts of several terrorist cells backed by Osama bin Laden and Saddam Hussein, and the detonators on several suicide bomber kits."

She looked at him a moment with a new found respect. "Detonators?"

Big grin. "Mom let me play with her bomb disposal kit while I was growing up. As she watched, of course."

"And the firing pins?"

He shrugged. "I asked."

"And you survived the camp. How?"

He chuckled. "Have you ever walked Cambridge at night?"

"Now that's impressive."

"Until you realize that I cut a wrong wire on one of those detonators, and that I should've been blown up that evening. But, the bomb itself was wired wrong."

"So you spend your time making the world free from terrorists?"

He shook his head. "No, that's how I get paid. I spend my time with books and makeup experiments with CIA DAGGER disguise kits."

She smiled. "I'd think that a man like you would at least hang out in a bar."

"Of course, I was in college once. Unfortunately, bar buddies are not who you can discuss your day job with, and my professional friends… are professional. It's not like there are Office field trips to Syria. I …" He paused. "Is someone coming out of the residence?"

Shushurin looked. "How did you—?"

"Natural born spy. They didn't pick me for my looks." *Or my target practice, either.*

* * *

Sean AP Ryan had Maureen McGrail's bag over his shoulder as he went first through the door of the papal residence, moving between two Swiss Guards with halberds. He looked up at the ten-foot poles topped with an axe, the back end hooked, meant to take cavalrymen off their horses.

Wow, wouldn't it be something to have a fight scene with one of those?

"Doing choreography?"

Sean smiled at McGrail. "Ah, Maureen, you know me so well. How's life been?"

"Hasn't it been grand all of this started? How's Inna?"

He smiled broadly. "We're getting married. I finally said to heck with it and the plans will be finalized as soon as I get back."

"And when will that be?"

Sean shrugged. "Oh, probably in another month, once I finish teaching the locals to kick some ass. I mean, it's not like I'm going to be shot at *every* day this week. I'm not getting paid for it this time."

A corner of McGrail's lip curled. "Isn't it nice to be so mercenary?"

He waved it off. "Nah, it's just the way my luck works — I get paid to be shot at, I *will* be shot at, guaranteed."

"*You!*" a voice boomed.

Sean stopped and glanced to a set of red robes emerging from between the columns; robes which hid a large ugly man with a broken nose, eyes the color of fecal matter, and a haystack of hair much the same color.

Sean smiled. "Can I help you, Cardinal?"

Cardinal Cannella sneered. "Are you the one responsible for the disaster at the Spanish Steps?"

Sean glanced at McGrail. "They know my handiwork."

Cannella stabbed a finger into his chest, and Sean instinctively grabbed the finger and bent it backwards, dropping the Cardinal to his knees. The Swiss Guards dropped their halberds from a standing position to their hands, the hooks poised to yank the bodyguard away from the Cardinal.

Sean stopped, looked at the guards and smiled before he even noticed he had dropped the Cardinal. He smiled sheepishly and let go. "Sorry, but you shouldn't do things like that to a guy like me — I know how to break someone's hand in such a way that it would never set, and I can do that before I even know I did it. So be more careful next time, won't you?"

The Cardinal stood, grasping his hand as if it were already broken. "You thug! I demand the two of you arrest him!" he yelled at the guards. The two blond Swiss took one look at the Cardinal and shrugged before moving back into position.

Sean shook his head. "They don't arrest people, and they're smart enough not to bother — they know me." He grinned at the man, and decided to tweak him. "By the way, are you anyone important?"

"Cardinal Alphonse Cannella! I organize the Vatican Archives! I know the Pope!"

"So do I, what's your point? In fact, I just left him, and he doesn't look too happy, but you're welcome to annoy him at your own peril, and ..." Sean stopped in mid-sentence. "You're the Cardinal from Boston, aren't you? You're one of the freaking Markist brothers!"

Cannella glared. "That's no way to address a prince of the Church!"

Sean cocked his head. "You don't even rate a duchy... unless, of course, you mean you're a prince of the church of darkness, which I can understand. You see, I know someone named Matthew Kovach. Name ring a bell?"

Cannella paled. "You know that, that—"

"Author?" Sean smiled evilly. "Yes, I know him very well," he said, leaning in close. "I know all of the dirty little secrets from your order, and I don't think you want me to discuss them here, do you?"

"I should sue you for defamation of character!"

"You have to have character first."

Cannella glared and stepped around Sean to walk straight into the papal residence. Sean laughed.

"Old friend?" Maureen asked.

Sean smiled. "Nah. It's just that Inna represents an author who's the archenemy of the Markists. Let's get you to the hotel before something else goes wrong."

* * *

Shushurin sighed. "I wonder what all that was about?"

"Who is this Ryan, anyway?" Murphy asked. "You said he was a little nuts?"

Shushurin nodded, then waved her hand to motion him to lower his voice. "He also has good hearing." She looked out to make sure Sean and McGrail had disappeared. "He's a former Hollywood stuntman turned mercenary... same danger, better pay."

"Then what's he doing in Rome?"

"Training the priests to defend themselves."

"Ach," a new voice added in a bad Irish brogue. "Don't forget the brothers and nuns."

Shushurin and Murphy turned to look down the barrel of a Taser beam gun held by a short man with bright blue eyes that held their own demented glow.

"Hi," Sean began, his voice normal. "I guess you two already know me. How about you both introduce yourselves?"

Both Shushurin and Murphy tensed, ready to dodge out of the way, and Sean shook his head. "Look behind you. I'd like to introduce you to Superintendent McGrail of Interpol, and she's more dangerous than I am."

Murphy paused a second and checked his own internal sonar. "Damn." To Shushurin: "I told you you're too distracting; I can generally hear them coming."

She shrugged. "So can I."

Sean cleared his throat. "Excuse me, but you can both beat yourselves up later. Besides, I used to hear dog whistles before one of the pyrotechnic guys overstuffed a charge right next to my ear." He cleared his throat. "Right now, I want to know who the hell both of you are, because I'm getting damned close to marching you up to the Pope and saying, 'Looky here, we wanted people who knew me, and son of a bitch, guess who I found talking about me not a hundred yards from the front door.' Who are you and where are you from?"

Shushurin looked to Murphy. "You want to tell him?"

Murphy looked at her blankly. "You think that either one of us can trust him?"

"He's been entrusted with bigger secrets," she said. "You know that there's an actress related to one of your guys?"

Murphy nodded, slowly, pondering the Hollywood actress related to Mossad officers. Then he blanched, remembering an incident when she had been under fire while attending Harvard. "You mean, *this* is the guy who—"

She nodded. "Yup."

Sean groaned, still holding the beam weapon. "You mean he's Mossad?" Ryan glanced at Murphy again. "You know, that's funny—"

Murphy's eyes flared. "Yes, I *know* I don't look Jewish, damm it."

The stuntman cocked his head. "Touchy… you must be part of the Goyim Brigade."

His eyes widened. "You know about the Goyim Brigade? *She* didn't even know about it until I explained it."

Sean thought a moment. "So what? Mossad certainly doesn't share *everything* with their German colleagues from the *Bundesnachrichtendienst.*" His eyes flickered to the woman.

Shushurin nodded. "Very good."

She studied Sean a moment, and did the math, working the angles on how to best get Murphy out of the way, and remove the threat at the same time. Shooting him wouldn't be optimal, but getting caught wasn't supposed part of her mission profile.

Before she moved, she hesitated a moment, feeling a presence behind her. She looked over her shoulder to confirm that Maureen McGrail was there. "Aren't you going to say anything?"

McGrail smiled slightly. "He's better at sucking the air out of the room. Besides, you try getting him to shut up."

Shushurin almost smiled. "You're not the one he's aiming at."

Sean waved the weapon in an attempt to bring the conversation back to focus. "Hi, cranky guy with gun would like to continue the conversation."

McGrail laughed. "Now Sean, isn't it a rare thing that someone actually notes me?"

Sean paused a moment, and gave her a slight nod. "True. Now that we're done with that, what the hell is going on here?"

"My name's Manana."

"Hi, I'm Scott."

"Can you put the gun down before a tourist walks by and sees you?" Shushurin asked.

Sean lowered the weapon to his thigh. Murphy was in a relatively relaxed pose, comfortable with trying to talk his way out of the situation. Shushurin still looked slightly tense.

She is almost definitely a field officer with a military background. "I'm guessing you both came here because of Ramzi Yousef's brother?"

Murphy nodded. "You could say that. Why, do you know anything?"

Sean arched his brows, amused. "Do I look like a Wiki page? You can get your own damn information, although

I'm sure that you've bugged the hell out of everything and everybody."

McGrail smiled. "Sean, don't you bug the hell out of people, before they even know you?"

"You know what I mean." He looked back to the spies, thinking over the day, using hindsight to fill in the blanks. He glanced and stared hard at Shushurin. "There were gunshots at the Spanish Steps before the rooftops opened up. I caught a bit of blonde hair on a woman — a wig, I presume. You made the shooters prematurely fire. But to do that, you would need to know where we were going… you bugged the car, didn't you?"

Sean smiled at Murphy. "You planted the bug, right? I thought you looked familiar. You were there when they almost ran me over; must have put it on the car while they stopped." He took their silence for agreement. "So, do you two know who the shooters are?"

Shushurin shook her head. "Not a clue. There are too many options so far."

"I'm certain," Sean grumbled. He tucked away his gun. "Well, I'll do you both a favor — I'm not going to do anything to you. I'm going to let you stay on the periphery."

Murphy raised an eyebrow. "I sense a catch."

Sean's eyes narrowed as he smiled broadly. "I think it's a great idea to move everyone indoors. For their own safety, of course. Good luck bugging the Vatican."

"Aye," McGrail added. "Wouldn't you have to do something drastic to get information? Like ask? And isn't information a two way street?"

Shushurin and Murphy exchanged a glance. Murphy would be forced to make contact with Wilhelmina Goldberg. Shushurin and Murphy would be forced to exchange information with her, and thus their information would end up in the hands of Figlia and Abasi as well.

The two spies glared at Sean Ryan, who smiled. "Yes, I am a son of a bitch, but I wouldn't tell my mother that if I were you."

* * *

Giovanni Figlia leaned back in his chair, reaching for the telephone. "As much as this conversation interests me, I need to clear things up with—"

The office door exploded inward, and Cardinal Cannella swept into the room like a Mafia knee-breaker dressed as Santa Claus. "What is this I hear about one of your men shooting up the Spanish Steps?"

Figlia rolled his eyes. *I need to get a new lock for my door.* "Oh, now what?"

Cannella panted from yelling after running inside. "One of your bastards destroyed a national monument."

Figlia slowly leaned back in the chair, his eyes narrowing. "To start with," he said slowly, "the 'bastard' in question was not one of mine. He was brought in by the Pope—"

"I'll bring *that* stupidity up with him later!" the Cardinal barked "Training priests and nuns to kill people, I—"

"Cardinal Cannella, currently of the Vatican Archives," Figlia interrupted, "I hope you remember Joshua Kutjok, *your boss the Pope.*" He nodded behind him, and the Cardinal for the first time acknowledged the large Pontiff's presence.

The Pope rose, glaring at Cannella. "Can *I* help you?"

Abasi looked at Goldberg. "I think it's time for us to leave, don't you?"

"You mean you don't want to stay for the fun?"

177

"I'd rather go through the Vatican Archives' visitor log…"

The Pope almost growled as his large hand clamped down on the cardinal's shoulder. "Hey, Markist, you're looking at me, the Jesuit Pope."

Goldberg's eyebrows rose, wondering if violent tendencies were supposed to be prevalent in any Pope. She glanced to the Egyptian. "You know what, Abasi? I think you're right. Besides, I'd like to get to my own frigging hotel room and—"

"No," Figlia snapped, standing. "You're both staying on the grounds tonight. I don't want either of you getting shot at. In fact, I should have told Ryan and McGrail to do the—"

His desk phone rang, and he answered. "Figlia."

"Johnny boy, it's Ryan," came the voice of the former American stuntman. "I just had a thought, I'm bringing McGrail back to the residence." Figlia smiled. "You read my mind."

"By the way," Sean added, "I wouldn't go home if I were you. You're married to that forensics lady, aren't you?"

Figlia blinked. He hadn't thought of that. "Your point is taken." Figlia bent over to make a note on a memo pad, and when he looked up, he found that all eyes were upon him.

The Pontiff looked at his security chief with raised eyebrows. "Something wrong?"

"Hold on a moment, Sean." Figlia covered the receiver. "Sean wants me to move myself and my family into the Vatican for the evening, at least until we can secure all involved with investigating the …" He glanced at Cardinal Cannella, "… recent incidents."

"Good idea," the Pope replied. "I will have them start making arrangements for you and your children immediately, Gianni, and it shouldn't be too hard to do the same for everyone else, right? I think I can arrange something." With that, he swept out of the office, Cannella following in his wake like a puppy trying to get attention.

Goldberg smiled. "Well, that was interesting."

Abasi nodded. "Most interesting. But what happens if the Cardinal returns?"

Figlia waved it away. "Cannella will probably do as he usually does, and follow the Pope around for hours. Excuse me, Sean," Figlia said into the phone, "I'll get back to you."

The *Commandatore* hung up. "Why does everyone treat my office like a train terminal?" He leaned forward, elbows on his desk, rubbing his temples. At the moment, he wanted nothing more than to get back to his wife and his children, and hide from the number of idiocies he had to tend to. "No offense, Agent Goldberg, but I am quickly starting to have my fill of Americans today."

* * *

The German and Mossad intelligence officers sighed. Scott Murphy slid down the column until his butt hit the stone ground, sitting next to the German spy. "I think I'm going to kill that bastard stuntman."

Shushurin tucked her legs under her and shrugged. "I wouldn't try if I were you. You're not trained for that."

Murphy hmmed. "That is so putting it mildly. When other guys go to the range, I have to pretend to shoot so I don't wind up hitting myself in the foot. How about you? Did the BND teach you how to be Secret Agent girl, kill people fifty ways with a *weinerschnizel?*"

The smile fell from her face. "Not the BND." She leaned her head against the back of the pillar and closed her eyes. "My father was part of the East German *Stasi*, the foreign division. I even think they made a comic book character based on my father. I know I have an older brother named Nikita. He's fifteen years older than I am. I know he was Robert Hansen's last handler."

Murphy blinked, thinking briefly back to the FBI mole for the Russians. "Ah… I guess your father was more Russian than German?"

"That is putting it mildly. He worked *very* closely with the KGB. So closely that I think he *was* KGB. When the wall fell, he had to leave Germany. I can't say that I minded." She paused for a moment.

"They wanted to train me to be one of those teenage spies you read about in novels. Had the Wall not fallen when it did, I would have been fully trained in seduction techniques. As it is, I am *very* good at martial arts."

Murphy nodded. "So that's why the BND sent you here, among other reasons, I'm certain. But why, may I ask, did they hire you considering the family background?"

Shushurin shrugged. "I put myself down as a bastard, fatherless." She smiled. "I think that's the only reason they let me in, I fit in so well with the other bastards… and I graduated college early with minors in political science and philosophy and a major in history… real history, which I never got in the USSR. Then the BND recruited me."

"As an analyst," he prodded. "But you're too good with a gun; lie, cheat, steal, etc."

Her star-lit eyes twinkled. "You should see me on poker night."

Murphy smiled. "I see. Been anywhere interesting?"

"No," she admitted. "I've gone after a few neo-Nazis, some Leftists, occasionally gotten to the UK, and to America, where I can… get information out of anyone on the Senate Intelligence Committee, mostly Democrats from Massachusetts... no offense to Boston."

Murphy grinned around his pipe. "If you're talking about the guy I'm thinking about, then *he* is the offense." He inhaled slightly. "You sound like you have a nice life, and certainly get better missions than I do, except, well, where's the rest of your life? I know that I don't have one."

"Officially, I live with my mother. Unofficially - when not in a foreign country - in my office, on a couch."

"Ugh. That doesn't sound good." Murphy puffed on the pipe. "I guess that explains why you don't have a social life. I at least have the excuse that I look Palestinian in Israel. You don't even have a house to take... someone to."

Shushurin gave a half-frown. "Most men I date want to sleep with me on the first date, and I need to turn them down or break their arms."

Murphy leaned closer to her. "Why? Or should I take a guess?"

She raised a brow. "What do you want to guess?"

"The Soviets were very paranoid. How much of your training has stuck?"

Shushurin gave him a sad smile. "A good deal. I functioned fine before I entered the BND, but once I went in..."

"The old training kicked in."

She nodded. "So no matter how hard I try to break the paranoia, I can't... seem to let myself... get attached to anyone outside the office. Unless I had already met them before BND."

He pursed his lips. "Wow... That's... bordering on the tragic. You're lovely, attractive, and that's just your personality. You're not bad to look at either. While I'm single, there's not much to look at, and I'm only as paranoid as I have to be. You were trained and drilled as a kid in what I'm certain the Soviets did to more children than just you."

Murphy reached a tentative arm around her shoulders and gave her a gentle squeeze. "Well, if nothing else, I'd be happy to ask you out when this is all over."

She smiled. "You're sweet. But why wait?"

Murphy blinked, not really anticipating that response. "We're on a job. And we need to contact Goldberg in a way that looks innocent, and… we're on a job."

She shook her head, an amused smile telling him what she thought of his reaction. "And we have a one-bedroom hotel room all to ourselves. We can at least talk in bed, right?"

He gave her a lopsided smile. "But I'm Catholic; I should probably take the chair."

Shushurin reached over, touching her fingers to the back of his head, making his skin tingle. She then leaned over and gave him a gentle kiss on the cheek. "We'll think of something."

Murphy looked deep into her star-lit eyes, and saw motion reflected there. "Someone's coming."

CHAPTER XIII: CARDINAL SINS

Goldberg was about to say something consoling to Giovanni Figlia — maybe something along the lines of Americans not really being that bad — when Sean Ryan and Maureen McGrail walked into the room.

So much for that idea, she thought. *Maybe it is time to get his mind off of the crap to come.* "So, who was the idiot?"

"Cardinal Cannella," Sean answered, flowing into a chair. "Last year, Boston authorities unmasked a drug-smuggling ring." Sean looked around, spotting a newspaper. He picked it up and thumbed through it. "The news only just printed that the ring had made numerous donations to the Boston Diocese, specifically the Markist Brothers. At the moment, the only real connection is that the drug runners used coffins to smuggle in the drugs. The Markists supplied the coffins and said the funerals. But that doesn't say much. Why bother bribing a Cardinal when you can get the same, probably cheaper, results with a rectory desk clerk? The donations have come out and the indictments just came down, and Cannella ran just ahead of the fallout. He was put in charge of the reconstruction of the Vatican Archives — possibly to give the construction workers someone to feel superior to."

He shrugged at Goldberg. "As for the donations… A payoff? Keeping up a front? Supporting a pedophile-filled 'lavender seminary'?"

Figlia chuckled. "At least you are a Catholic."

Sean laughed. "After a fashion. I'm from L.A. The other choice is pagan or cult-like mega-churches."

Figlia slowly shook his head with a smile. "Funny, I thought that was America."

Hashim Abasi looked at the Vatican security man. "That's supposed to be my line."

Figlia shook his head. "You never heard my boss *really* go after the American Catholic Church. Trust me, you don't want to, you'd be here all day."

Goldberg raised her eyebrows. "What's a lavender seminary?"

Sean groaned. He did not want to explain this. "Places taken over by 'liberal' clergymen, priests who had no intent of following through with their vows of celibacy, and instructed seminarians to cruise gay bars and porn. Plenty of pederasts resided in or controlled them, and that's why most of the pederasts caught lately have been from the 1970s, when most of those priests were at the height of their power, endorsing 'sexual liberation' for 8-year-olds. However, when the Man-Boy Love Association talks about the same thing, the ACLU runs to the rescue."

Hashim Abasi shook his head. "And you wonder why my Muslim brethren call you barbarians." He scoffed.

"I am surprised that no one has considered there may be something more to the 'donations'?"

Figlia thought a moment. "If there were, His Holiness might lay hands on Cannella himself."

Abasi grinned. "Understood."

Wilhelmina Goldberg smiled. "The pope would make a wonderful cop." She rose to her feet and stretched slightly, having been in the chair for far too long. "Now, I'm going to take a look at those blasted archives before I fall asleep."

"Before you do, Villie," Sean pointed out, "you might want to be on the lookout for someone from Mossad."

The Egyptian looked up as though someone had slapped him. "What?"

Sean nodded. "I ran across a Mossad and a BND agent right outside. Since Johnny boy is moving everyone inside, they're going to try tapping you for information, Agent Goldberg. I see no reason not to play nice with them until we can drag them into our little circle. And before you ask, they were looking into Yousef's murder. Now I think they're also on the Pius murders."

Figlia said, "Okay, let's try it this way — since I don't want anyone walking around here alone, take someone with you. I don't care who it is, as long as it isn't me. I've tried to call the damn police several times so far, and every time I do, something happens."

Goldberg nodded. "Okay, I'll head in, take a look at the archive logs to see who looked up what, and split off just long enough to give the Mossad guy some time to make contact." She blinked and turned her hazel eyes to Sean. "It is a guy, right?"

Sean smiled. "The Mossad agent is a guy — blond hair, blue eyes, thin, kinda pale. The BND agent is a taller-than-average brunette who is… way too pretty for undercover work. She's someone out of James Bond central casting. Trust me. You'll know her when you see her."

* * *

Wilhelmina Goldberg paused at the door to the Vatican Archives... the dimly lit room in the practically vacant building. She smiled at Hashim Abasi. "You first?"

He smiled. "If you insist. But I don't have a gun."

Goldberg pulled out her Sig Sauer P229. "You can handle a .357 magnum load?"

Abasi raised his brow. "You fire one of those? The kick is usually enough to knock *me* backwards."

She smiled. "You just need to know how to fire it."

He held out his hand and she handed it over. He slid it into an inner jacket pocket in the hope that he wouldn't need it, and opened the door.

The vault that was the Vatican Archives was locked and secure.

However, the gatekeeper of the archives was dead on the ground, both knees bent the wrong way, and his head at an odd angle.

Abasi had the pistol out immediately, scanning the area. "I hope you know Figlia's number. We're going to need him."

Goldberg grabbed her cell phone, looking behind her to check the hall; she only caught a passing glimpse of a shadow with silver hair, moving fast and away quickly. She blinked and stepped back, into the office, and closed the door behind her, almost running into Abasi.

"I think there's someone out there... he's leaving, but he's out there."

"What did he look like?"

"Father Williams." She dialed Figlia's office. "Gianni thought he was annoyed when people kept walking into his office. Just wait until I tell him this!"

Scott Murphy moved down the marble hall of the Vatican Museum, heading for the vault area that stored the Vatican Archives. He was about to turn the corner into the main hallway when he was pushed aside by a shadow.

Murphy fell expertly and rolled to the side, hoping that if the shadow had a weapon, he would at least be a moving target. He looked up and the shadow was gone.

In his ear, the communication piece registered an "oof!" Murphy tapped his ear. "Mani," he whispered, "you all right?"

"I just got run over by a priest."

Murphy frowned. "Williams?"

"I couldn't tell. Built and moved like him… same hair, too."

Murphy rose and stepped into the hallway, looking at the office door to the Vatican Archives. He saw the door closing, but that was it. "He may have done something to the archives."

"Great, now what?"

* * *

Wilhelmina Goldberg blinked and closed her cell phone. She rubbed her ear. "Ouch. I didn't know that Figlia could get so damn loud."

Abasi pocketed the pistol. "The area's secure… and what did you expect? This has been a bad day. He grabbed a case he probably shouldn't have, and now someone's breached his security twice today — once to steal the murder book and again to kill this poor schlub."

She looked at him. "Schlub?"

He shrugged. "I've visited New York."

Goldberg smiled. "Ireland, New York, Rome, Egypt. You've got to tell me the story of your life one of these days. As for the schlub, I suspect he was killed for the guest logs."

Abasi said, "I'll check, just in case... and yes, I have gloves on me somewhere." He handed her the weapon. "You can stand guard this time."

Abasi moved away. Goldberg glanced at her cell phone in one hand, while holding the gun in the other. After a moment, she simply hit autodial. She let it ring three times until she finally got the classics department at NYU.

"Goldberg."

"Hi, abba," she said. "It's me, *Villie.*"

"You got in Rome okay?" came the voice of her father, laced with just a touch of a New York Jewish accent.

"The arrival was good for about fifteen minutes. You should see it on CNN soon enough. A body got blasted out of a window and fell on a car... mine."

"Oy vey! What in God's name—"

"Well, funny you should say that," she interrupted. "I'm in the Vatican right now. Listen, something's come up, and I need some help."

"Such as?" he prompted.

She took a deep breath, then asked, "Did Grandpa ever tell you about the war?"

After a half-minute of silence: "I thought you'd never ask about that."

"It's really important. I know he left Germany after *Krystalnacht,* and came to Italy; but after that, no one told me. It's come up."

Her father sighed deeply. "He never talked about it. However, there was someone he talked to — an Israeli diplomat who wrote a book about the popes and the Holocaust, Pinchas Lapide. The name of the book is *Three Popes and the Jews*. The thing is, I never kept the book because my father was never in it. Somehow, he got lost in the rest of the *mischegas*."

"Understood. Thanks."

"Not a problem, but I'm glad you called. You should do it more often, maybe even call your mother."

Goldberg smiled. "Whatever you say, Dad. I've got to go, talk to you soon. Love you, bye."

Goldberg hung up. She thought for a moment, trying to remember the nearest library, aside from the Vatican, of course. *Like they'd have a book on Popes written by a Jew.*

She put her cell phone away and slowly opened the door, gun ahead of her. She looked both ways, then stepped out, heading back the way she had come. She stopped, thought about it, and then moved in the opposite direction, heading down the hall, away from the entrance.

Goldberg moved slowly forward. She turned the next corner and found a man dead center of her sights, matching the description Sean Ryan had given her — dark blond, almost brown hair, dark blue eyes, pale skin, vaguely Irish… maybe.

"I was actually looking for you," Scott Murphy said, smiling, ignoring her gun in his face. "Sean Ryan told you about me?"

She nodded. "Good guess."

"Not really, he just struck me as the type. You want to put that away?"

Goldberg smiled. "Not really. Where's your partner?"

"Watching the front door."

Goldberg sidestepped twice, until her back was against the opposite wall, keeping her eyes on him and covering her back.

"You have good timing," she told him. "I need you to help me with something."

Murphy blinked. "Wow, that's fast, I usually have to make the offer first."

Goldberg rolled her eyes and snorted. "Puh-lease. I don't have the time. You going to play?"

He raised a brow and smiled. "I'm guessing you have something in mind?"

She nodded. "Diplomatic papers; notes and papers of your diplomat Pinchas Lapide."

Murphy blinked. "*My* diplomat? You mean Israeli? Okay, where was he stationed?"

Goldberg shook her head. "Can't tell. But your guys should be able to put in a quick search. After that, I can tell you what happened in the Pope's office building."

"Okay. One second." Murphy slowly reached into his pocket and pulled out a cellular phone.

He dialed in a number from memory. "Murphy's Morgue," came a lightly accented female voice.

"Hi," Murphy answered, "I want to order a box. Name: Pinchas Lapide. Epitaph: a very diplomatic person."

Murphy smiled at Goldberg as the hold music of Hava Nagila played in the background.

The Secret Service agent cocked her eyebrows. "You don't even trust your secure lines?"

Murphy just gave her a look, as though over eyeglasses he didn't wear. "I work for Mossad, remember?"

A minute later, the voice came back on the line: "Sorry, that box can't be delivered. It's made of mahogany."

Murphy left on his professional poker face, his eyes still on Goldberg, and he didn't even blink. "And how's that possible?"

"Don't ask me, I just work here."

"Okay, hold on." Murphy took the phone away from his ear, and held his thumb over the microphone. "Is there something in particular you want about him?"

Goldberg's eyebrows arched. "Try the notes for his book *Three Popes and the Jews*."

Murphy nodded and said into the phone, "Can I have some book notes on the subject... you at least know there is a book, right?"

"Yes, sir," the other side answered, rather snippy, "I'm not stupid, but they're the same."

Murphy blinked. "How's that possible? I *know* the book has been published!"

"That's what we allowed to be published," she snarked back at him. "There's always more than is released in the book, you should know that."

Murphy's patience was fraying, and he hoped it didn't show. "Okay, understood. But this is *me*. I can get mahogany." Spy-speak for, *Do you know who I am?*

"Well, this is more like petrified wood than mahogany."

He blinked. "Really? Wow. I'll talk with my guy, see if he can get me some." Translated as, *Do you know who my boss is?*

"Good luck." *IE: fat chance.*

"That bad?"

"Worse." *Ouch. Translation: his boss' boss classified it.*

"Understood. Bye." Murphy hung up, chagrined. "I'm going to have to get back to you on that. Your documents are somewhere between classified and 'we really should burn this.' I need my boss to get them... or maybe even his boss."

"Why? He wrote a book on it."

"Well, some things don't get published. You know the

phrase 'Every spy a prince'?"

He slid his cell phone into his inside pocket. "The version around my Office is 'Every diplomat an officer.' I'll have to send the request up through the chain of command. Now, what about you, what have you found? I know about the Spanish Steps attack and who you were there to pick up. Anything after that?"

Goldberg finally lowered her gun, keeping it out and at her side in case he tried something. "Well, unless you want to talk about a Catholic brotherhood known as the Markists taking money from a drug dealer, no."

Murphy thought a moment. "Does this involve Cardinal Cannella?"

Goldberg stared at him long and hard. "How'd you know?"

"I think I know this story."

* * *

Sean Ryan took a right out the door of the Pope's office building, and interweaved himself through the colonnade. *When you move, they can't get you. Especially if you're covered by marble.*

Sean smiled at the whole ordeal. *Sure, Sean, join the family business in Hollywood, after your father and grandfather. At least grandpa was a real life war hero in a real life war, instead of dad, a Hollywood liberal who regularly made fun of mom's job with the FBI.*

Sean had spent years in and out of production studios, learning the art of the continuity director, the prop man, the arts and crafts designers and forgers, latex and, most of all, stunt work. Like all Hollywood brats, he was raised with a

192

private tutor. His teenage rebellious years had reacted to the artificiality of Hollywood by embracing "really real Catholicism" in a "conservative" Sunday school — conservative in the sense that they knew what the Pope was teaching.

Sean's physical endurance was shaped and molded by the Hollywood stuntmen he so admired. He would copy them, throwing himself into service around the set, and getting up at the crack of dawn to exercise. He wanted to do everything Daddy *appeared* to do in the movies. Sean had known better than to believe the movie magic — he wanted to be like the people who made his father look like an action hero.

Sean's mental endurance also helped, and that endurance had been honed every morning in his youth with a "retired" Jesuit who was a member of the Opus Dei– who had been what the Jesuits used to be — a uniquely situated teaching body that answered directly to the Pope himself. They were intellectual shock troops, able to enter a situation and decode the most complex doctrine into the reality of a simple message, only slightly more complicated than "Little children, love each other."

And he always thought best when his body was in motion. Like the philosopher St. Thomas Aquinas power-walking around his monastery, Sean weaved from one column to another, from one side of the square to another, and back again while he considered Pius XII and the recent murders.

Sean finished walking through the pillars of the colonnade, then practically came to a stop. *Father Williams. What the hell is he carrying now?*

The priest with silver hair had both hands in front of him, carrying five thick books in his arms. There was enough reading there to keep even a speed reader busy for a month.

First dumping a book in the well, and then more of the same?

What the hell is Father Williams' problem with reading?

Then Cardinal Cannella came out of the papal office, at least an hour earlier than expected. Sean smiled. *Oh well. I'm not going to give Frank a problem by letting the Cardinal see me with him.*

Sean stepped behind a column, back against the marble, keeping out of sight. He stepped away once the Cardinal passed him, was about to turn when he heard the sound of flapping pages.

The former stuntman ducked instinctively, letting the first book fly over his head. He whirled around in time to see a whole pile of ten pound books coming straight at him. He dropped to his hands and then bounced back up, feet first into the air, and he connected with… something.

"*Oof.*"

Sean came to his feet, looking constantly to find the attacker. He saw marble columns all around, but little else.

He felt a disturbance of air and threw himself forward, into the column, quickly pushing off of it with his hands, ramming his shoulder into someone. His target spun and leapt forward, over the pile of books scattered on the ground, and rolled easily to his feet. Way too easily.

Sean saw only the man's black outfit and the Roman collar. The bit of light between the columns gleamed off the silver hair.

The next detail that caught his attention was the match held above the priest's head. He flicked the match head and hurled it at the books. The next moment, there was a blinding white-hot flame that sprang up between the two of them.

Magnesium flash powder, son of a bitch!

Sean whirled behind the column, blinded, hoping to buy some time before the priest attacked. He had seen Father

194

Frank Williams in action, and didn't want to be on the receiving end.

I just hope the flash attracted someone. Sean raised his arm and cocked his elbow, ready to strike at the first sign of attack. He thought a moment, and then whirled around and leapt over the already-dying flames — he knew that flash powder went up in, well, a flash — and pounded empty air.

He pivoted, expecting to find the priest on the other side of the column he himself had been hiding behind. Instead, he saw two Swiss Guards coming through the columns, halberds in hand. Both of them were coming for him. *"Halt!"*

One of them thrust with a halberd, and Sean wheeled out of the way, grabbing the halberd and yanking firmly. The Swiss Guard was dragged forward, directly into the back end of Sean's fist, immediately before being assaulted by a right hook.

Sean turned to the other Swiss Guard before the first had even hit the ground, and looked down the barrel of a Beretta. Sean genuflected and thrust with the halberd like a spear, throwing the gun into the air; he followed up by slapping the guard upside the head with the flat of the axe.

"I don't need this!"

Sean looked up at Giovanni Figlia, approaching with gun in hand. He leveled it at Sean, standing at least fifteen feet away, out of range of the pole-arm.

"Thank you for realizing a gun is a long-range weapon," Sean told Figlia. He stood, using the halberd as a staff. "When they wake up, you can ask why the hell they attacked me."

One of the two guards swore at Figlia. Sean looked down and saw the first guy he had decked was struggling to his feet. "Impressive, people usually stay down."

Figlia sighed. "You'd be surprised what they can take."

He turned to the guard and had a quick conversation. When he finished, he turned to Sean. "Apparently, there was a priest on the other side of the column who pointed to you and mouthed that he needed help."

"Can he identify the priest?"

There was another quick exchange of German. Figlia raised an eyebrow. "Silver hair?"

Sean nodded. "I saw that. Eye color?"

The Swiss Guard shrugged.

"It went by too fast," Figlia said. He frowned with thought. "Why did he attack you?"

"I was just hiding from Cardinal Cannella and ..." Sean blinked. "You don't think that was it, do you? In fact, I don't know what else it could have been."

Figlia smiled. "It can join the list of questions to be answered... come on, I think you wanted to tend to Agent McGrail, yes? I managed to get her a room."

* * *

Scott Murphy closed his cell phone and told Wilhelmina Goldberg, "I should be going before your friends show up. I left my boss a voice-mail, and I'll try to contact you once he gets back to me. You have a cell?"

Goldberg nodded, handing over a business card. "Can your partner stay out of sight? I hear she's attractive, which sounds out of character for intelligence hiring practices."

Murphy smiled shyly and looked off to his left, down the hallway, trying to hide his reaction. Goldberg furrowed her brows and cocked her head in an attempt to get a better look at his face.

"That pretty, huh? Amazing. Either that, or you're a bad

spy."

Murphy's face evened out and he looked back at her. "I'm a damned good spy… Officer… I'll see you later." He turned and jogged lightly down the hallway, away from the main path.

At the other end of the hall, Goldberg heard the sound of loud, pounding footsteps as Giovanni Figlia charged toward her. "Now what?"

Goldberg jerked her head to the door. He stepped inside the office and swore. Figlia stopped and closed his eyes.

"You know him?" Hashim Abasi asked, looking over the body.

Figlia nodded. "Dr. Almagia. I mean, son of a bitch! His family has been with the library and archives department since the Second World War!"

Goldberg blinked. She didn't expect a history lesson. "What?"

"His father was Professor Roberto Almagia," he muttered. "Jewish cartographer who lost his job at the University of Rome to anti-Semitic laws in 1940. *Pio Papa* hired him immediately after to work in the Vatican library,

"Pio who?"

"Pope Pius XII," Figlia answered, irritated. "He had Almagia work on a map of the German lands before sending it to the German Foreign Minister. Pius had a talent for annoying people."

Goldberg was developing the headache that Figlia had had for the last day. More history wasn't helping it. "Anyway, I think I saw Father Williams just leaving here with the log books. If you hurry, you can find him."

* * *

Sean Aloysius Patricus Ryan looked around the apartment set up for Maureen McGrail. "Nice digs." He placed her luggage on one of the two beds.

"Shouldn't you be recovering from the attack of the killer priest?" McGrail asked.

He shrugged. "Johnny boy has enough problems right now. Given the way things are going, I think I'd rather be here, out of the line of fire." He smiled. "So, what do you think of the situation?"

McGrail popped open a suitcase. "I came for a homicide, and I have enough dead terrorists, murdered academics, and killer priests — so aren't I just wonderful? It's hard enough just to remember the victims." She bent over to look at her belongings. "Wasn't I asking about Inna before?"

"She's doing well. I miss her like hell, but what can I do? I follow the work."

"Ah? And who's paying for this?"

Sean smiled. "The Pacelli family — an old Italian nobility, apparently. They've certainly kept up over the years. And yes, before you ask, they are related to Pope Pius XII. The family fortune isn't half as big as it used to be, though. Eugenio's cut disappeared into the abyss of time. As for the rest, well, they've still got enough to pay me to teach the little kiddies how to kick some ass."

Sean looked behind him and sat down on a chair. McGrail sat down on the narrow bed. She looked over at the other bed, concluding that must be for Goldberg.

"What else?" she asked.

He shrugged. "Inna's actually coming in a few days to visit a client of hers. If I feel lucky, I'll have the Pope marry us, and tell him to forget my fee."

McGrail's face lit up. "Isn't it about time? You've been together since when?"

"A long time," he smiled.

"What's been happening in Dublin?"

"Damn little. My boss is thinking about putting out a notice on you. I'm thinking he might come up with a new color notice, for spite. He'd like to issue a black notice for your murder, but you're still breathing."

Sean smiled. "Good to know I'm still in form."

McGrail shook her head. "I'm going to omit your presence when I call in."

The bodyguard chuckled. "I seem to have that effect—"

At that moment, the door shattered and two men sprayed the room with automatic fire.

CHAPTER XIV: BANKRUPT

They were both professionals, that much was clear. They had hit the door once with enough force to break the door open, but not enough to have the door hit the adjacent wall and bounce back in their faces. Even more impressive, the breach artist had hit the door with his shoulder in such a way as to wheel into the room immediately — most people had to kick the door so they wouldn't have to break their shoulders, but maneuvers like that took time.

However, at the exact moment the door first vibrated with the impact, Sean Ryan and Maureen McGrail reacted as one, throwing themselves backwards, rolling onto the floor.

Sean had kicked his chair backwards, and tumbled to one knee. He grabbed the back of the chair and hurled it at the breach artist as he came into the room. The object of his attack pivoted his upper body, letting the chair bounce off his shoulder, and twisted back to fire at Sean with his silenced Spectre submachine gun — the Italian version of an Uzi. Sean was already in motion and leapt forward from his kneeling position, throwing himself into the gunman's legs, cutting them out from under him. The gunman twisted as he fell, landing on his shoulder and rolling onto his back, bringing his weapon to bear once more. Sean lunged on top of the gunman, smacking the gun away, and locked his hand around it, keeping it in place.

Sean continued with an uppercut to the man's chin, then an elbow slam into his nose, followed by a hammer blow with the same hand. The assassin stabbed for Sean's ribs with the other hand, a knife flashing. Sean quickly grabbed the other wrist, holding onto it firmly. The two of them stayed locked there as neither one gave ground to the other. Sean arched a brow with interest. He had the ability to bench-press the Pope, so coming up against someone with equal muscle told him more than he wanted to know.

On the other side of the room, as Sean Ryan had hurled the chair at the opening attacker, McGrail had already snapped a leg off the night table and hurled it at the second gunman with the speed and accuracy of a circus knife wielder.

The target didn't even blink. He snapped his wrist with the Spectre and sent the table leg off to the other side of the room. However, McGrail had sent herself after the leg as soon as she threw it, and as the gun came back to focus on her, she was already in the middle of a spin-kick, sending the weapon flying. She followed it with a right roundhouse he ducked under as he sent a jab to her stomach. His blow glanced off an armor of muscle and he threw himself forward, into a roll, and came up with a knife.

McGrail sidestepped, letting him charge past, and then turned to face him. They both paused a split-second to reassess one another. If she hadn't had abs like sheet metal, she would have been dropped to the floor, and still struggling with him, and possibly slashed by now.

The attacker stepped forward, thrusting with the knife. McGrail sidestepped, grabbed the wrist and twisted the knife out of his hand, her knee coming up to meet his stomach. He threw himself backwards, rolling with the way she twisted his wrist. He went down to the floor...

He came up with his recovered Spectre.

* * *

Sean Ryan, still locked in combat, smiled, baring abnormally white teeth right before he bit into the gun hand of his assailant. The gunman didn't cry out or drop the weapon until Sean snapped back, his teeth ripping out a hunk of flesh and muscle. The weapon fell to the ground and his attacker blinked, no longer fighting Sean's grip, but pulling him in for a head butt. Sean, dazed, pushed back with his legs, dragging his attacker up off the floor.

Sean curled both legs between them, rolling onto his back, and kicked forward once the assassin was on top, throwing him across the room.

* * *

McGrail was about to jump aside as a falling object slammed into her sparring partner. Both gunmen fell into the corner of the room. The impact knocked the Spectre out of his hand, and it bounced off the wall. McGrail hooked a foot around the nightstand and kicked it over the gun, putting the tabletop between the weapon and the thugs.

Sean scooped up a fallen submachine gun and spun toward the two who had charged in. They scrambled to their feet, knives at the ready.

Sean lowered the Spectre. "You two are so stupid, you deserve a fair fight." He let the Spectre dangle from his hand,

and suddenly hurled it, smacking a gunman between the eyes, making him slump and slide down the wall. "I lied, but I want at least one of you alive."

The other one merely stared, and McGrail moved toward him. He smiled, and in a flash, he stabbed in an arc, catching his partner in the temple with the knife. Before McGrail could leap forward, he himself bit down on something in his teeth, making him fall to the floor dead.

Sean roared, "Damn!"

McGrail frowned. "And who the hell were they?"

* * *

"I'm not sure," Sean answered, "but they were good, well-trained, and young — couldn't be more than mid-twenties, which means they were trained from a very early age, probably one of the old Soviet Union training programs."

The usual suspects were all in the main office of the Central Office of Vigilance — *Commandatore* Giovanni Figlia's room. Sean and McGrail were both on the couch with Goldberg and Abasi seated in office chairs. Figlia was behind his desk, and the Pope stood right next to him — the Pontiff himself refusing to take any seat, and Xavier O'Brien, like his boss, standing, next to the door.

"Unfortunately," the Commander replied, "that is of no help. The Soviet Union ran terrorist training camps throughout Eastern Europe, and they backed the Red Army Faction, the PLO, the IRA, the PFLP, Carlos the Jackal, the Sandinistas, and Horn of Africa insurgents."

Sean nodded. "So we're talking a long list of a lot of bad people."

Goldberg blinked, looking at Figlia askance. "How do

you know this?"

He gave her a sad smile. "The Red Army here, the *brigate rosso,* planted a car bomb that killed my father, one of the *carabinieri. Io sono un studente bene del'mio avversari.* I am a good student of my enemies."

Sean nodded. "However, *these* guys needed training from the start of their lives, and reinforcement — physical and mental endurance techniques, that sort of thing."

Xavier O'Brien puffed on his cigarette. "Since children learn better than adults, having them trained younger would be sensible, if you were interested in raising murderous fanatics and you were *very* patient to get a return on your investment. So it's not out of the realm of possibility."

Wilhelmina Goldberg said, "You've both been watching too much TV."

McGrail shook her head. "I've worked in martial arts all my life. The bastard I fought was as good as I am — and I'm a black belt with multiple levels in in multiple styles. So he had to have had intense training for years… given his age, I would say it took him his entire life at an accelerated pace."

"Also," Sean added, "the one I dealt with was as strong as I am, and you don't get to be like that unless you've been training since you were… oh, four or six."

Abasi laughed. "Really? And how strong are *you?*"

Sean let his eyelids droop as he gracefully rose from the couch and strode over to the Pope. He smiled, nodded at the Pontiff, slowly reached out with his hands, grabbed the large Sudanese native around the waist in a bear hug, and lifted him off his feet as though he were a ballerina in Swan Lake, holding him in the air with preternatural ease.

Sean slowly lowered the Pope, turned, and moved back to his seat. The pope's face registered shock, Lèse-majesté, and then laughter. "The Pope has many titles, but I had better not hear 'Ryan's barbell' as one of them."

Sean smiled. "Absolutely, sir. We won't call you a dumb-bell either."

McGrail nodded. "And while I can't do that exactly, aren't I just as comparably strong for a woman?"

Sean simply said, "Anyway, I'm starting to get annoyed."

A soft voice inquired, "And who, may I ask, has earned your ire today, Mr. Ryan?"

Sean smiled before looking over to the silver-haired priest, showing no surprise at all. "Someone tried to kill me a little while ago, Father. And you?"

Father Frank closed the door behind him and sat in an office chair. "Something destroyed a stretch of rail — I was trapped on the train for hours. What else has been going on here?"

"Someone killed Dr. Almagia, Frank," O'Brien replied.

"Someone who bears a striking resemblance to you, and who moves like you do, Father," Sean answered. "And attacked me, and burned entry logs for the Vatican Archives."

Father Frank blinked for a moment, tapping his ring on the arm of his chair. "Almagia dead ..." he muttered aloud. He looked puzzled for a moment, as though disoriented.

Father Frank cocked his head, looking at Sean. "Really? Oh, well then. I suppose it's time to substantiate my alibi?" he smiled, amused, pulling a slip of paper from his pocket. "If this man looked so much like me, maybe you should turn on the news and see the train wreck, and then see my ticket stub?" Father Frank looked to the rest of them. "Anything else?"

Goldberg shrugged. "Nothing to burden you with, Father. I'm certain you can take care of yourself." She smirked.

"But I doubt you'd need to — it's not like you're involved or anything."

Father Frank smiled beatifically, ignoring her sarcasm. "I'm a priest; I am always involved in the actions of my fellow men."

"Even if they have automatic weapons?"

"Especially... I'm an Army chaplain after all."

Sean Ryan rolled his eyes at the banter, as well as Goldberg's insinuations. "Back to the issue at hand: does anyone know how Tweedle Dumb and Tweedle Dumber got inside the building?"

Figlia sighed. "They were wearing all black — it's possible my people thought they were priests, and you try pulling over a priest to check his ID in Rome."

The Pope nodded seriously. "That is sound. Even if one asks, 'pardon me, Father?' you are likely to 'get grief' because he's a Monsignor." He smiled at Goldberg. "Priests can be touchy about their rank. You'd be surprised."

"Not really," she said. "I live in D.C., remember?"

Sean looked back at Figlia. "Besides, if any of your Swiss-cheese brigade tried to pull one of these guys over, they would've made him *eat* his halberd — trust me, there's no amount of training that could have prepared your guys for these hitters. You need to lock the place down a little tighter."

"Could we get back to the main topic?" McGrail began. "Who the fock is tryin' to kill us? Sorry, Your Holiness."

Pius XIII grinned. "Don't apologize. All of my curses are *real* curses; yours don't come close."

XO shrugged. "He deals with me all day long. You can imagine the amount of cursing that inspires."

Figlia merely shook his head. "We know they bought their weapons locally, they're well trained, and they're too

206

pale to be local. Aside from that... well, let's say that our forensics folks will have a busy night."

Abasi said, "If I may suggest something?" He looked at Figlia. "Dr. Almagia, you say, has been with the Vatican Library as a family tradition, since the second World War. May I suggest that it is odd that the killers waited so long between killing Ashid Raqman Yousef and trying to burn the Vatican Archive logs he signed? Why not burn them sooner?"

Figlia shrugged and leaned back in his chair. "We didn't know the motive for Yousef. There wasn't a reason to burn the logs until Gerrity was killed, and we knew it had something to do with his research."

Abasi nodded, but raised his hand and ticked off points with his thumb. "But you discovered that *today*. How did *they* know? The attack at the terminal was an attack on all of us — if they were only after Detective McGrail, they could have waited. Someone stole the murder book for Dr. Gerrity's murder, but not Yousef's. Why one and not the other? If the thief is, in fact, not responsible for the killing, then how did the murderers know *Figlia* was involved instead of the local police? It is not as though many people were on-site so early in the morning, were they?"

Goldberg sighed, trying to forget that she'd been up for so long. "Not really. A few cops, the fire department, and ..." Her eyes flicked quickly to Father Frank.

"Or!" Sean Ryan interjected, "they could have merely been hanging around a doughnut shop listening to the cops discussing that sumbitch *Commandatore* who confiscated *their* crime scene." He glanced at his watch. "It's been about ten hours between the initial murder and the attack on the stairs, maybe even more. Any number of things could have happened. Quite frankly, ladies and gents, it's been a long day, and I've been attacked three times, thank you. Giovanni, I'm guessing you have new guest rooms set up for the ladies?"

Figlia nodded. "Down the hall from where you were attacked earlier. Right next to them are you and Hashim. I'll take my office. The luggage from the hotel was brought over an hour ago for the two of you," he added, looking at Abasi and Goldberg.

McGrail took the hint. "Come on, Special Agent Goldberg, I'll show you."

Goldberg nodded, sparing a glance for Father Frank and another for Sean Ryan. Figlia reached for his phone to make the calls he'd been trying to dial for the past few hours. The Pope said his good nights, and Sean followed Father Frank into the hall.

Sean closed Figlia's office door behind him, and walked alongside the priest for only a few steps. He quickly looked up and down the hallway, and was reasonably certain no one was around.

He then grabbed Father Frank by the collar and hurled him with one arm across the hall. The priest quickly bounced back, sliding automatically into a defensive stance. Sean advanced with slow, menacing steps, his body posture going from one martial stance to another as he walked down the hall.

"What the hell is going on here, Father?" Sean growled in a low voice. "Goldberg had you dead to rights, and even *I* suspect you're in this deeper than you let on. You were the handler for Leftist assassin, probably because you could handle him physically. You expect me to believe that you wouldn't have the same job with Yousef? That ties you to two dead terrorists. I saw you dropping a large novel into a fountain — about the size of your average murder book. What do you know that we don't?"

Frank sighed and sagged, relaxing. "Oh, is that all? I can tell you, but only if you keep it a secret, and only if you promise to play along, and trust me."

Sean nodded. "Hit me with your best shot."

* * *

The thick Russian accent grated on Father William's nerves, but he had to stand it. He needed backup, and soon. This was getting out of hand, and nothing worked.

"And vot could you possibly need from me?" his contact purred.

"I'm in the crossfire," Father Frank Williams explained. "I've got the Secret Service *and* Interpol on my back, I'm certain someone from Mossad is creeping around, and I think the Germans are here, too."

The Russian voice laughed. "Wonderful. So you call in the old Cold Warrior against the Germans. This I call irony."

"Trust me," Frank said, "that isn't even the beginning. Besides, you've been in on this for weeks. I'm just calling you in sooner than expected, that's all."

"And who do you want me to kill that you don't want to dirty your cassock with, eh?" his contact asked.

Now the accent was getting on his nerves. "There's been enough of that, and it hasn't worked yet. Listen, just be available. I know you're in walking distance, but I need you here within minutes in case I need you."

"And what type of weaponry do I need?"

Father Frank thought back to Sean Ryan talking about the abilities of the gunmen. "Come as though you're about to go into battle against yourself — they have the same type of training you gave me."

"From birth?"

"From birth," the priest agreed.

* * *

Soviet assassins trained from birth, for God's sake. But after 9/11, even the dumbest reporters agree that a lack of imagination can kill you, Scott Murphy thought as he listened to Wilhelmina Goldberg update him.

Murphy and Shushurin had waited for almost an hour to reunite after the body of Dr. Almagia had been found in the Vatican Archives. Murphy had spent most of that time avoiding the crime scene analysts and trying to get the hell out of there. Shushurin had spent her time observing the security patrols, seeing how they operated and what they removed from the building.

By the time Scott Murphy finally got out of the archives (he was reduced to using two tied ends of a curtain cord from the second-story window that he slid down before the cord snapped like a set of cheap shoelaces), everyone from criminalistics experts to archivists and researchers had left for the night and the entire building had shut down. Once he and Shushurin found an obscure corner of Vatican City to hide in, he dialed Wilhelmina Goldberg for an update on a situation he couldn't really believe.

"How serious is Sean Ryan about this Soviet super-soldier theory of his?"

"As serious as a hull breach on the Mir space station," Goldberg answered. "As if he knew something I didn't. You have any idea what he's talking about?"

"No idea," he lied, looking over at Shushurin. "What's

210

Ryan doing now?" he asked the Secret Service agent.

"Your guess is as good as mine," she told him. "I'll chat with him tomorrow, see what he's doing about the priest. Your turn. What do you know about Father Williams?"

Murphy smiled. He'd expected this, and gave her a full rundown. He laughed to himself, thinking about one of the running gags he and Shushurin joked about. "By the way, my partner and I were thinking, have you seen Father Williams wearing a ring?"

After a brief pause: "Not that I noticed."

"If you do, note it. I'm half expecting a red background with a cross and two swords crossed behind it. Old Catholic joke."

"Whatever." *Click.*

"Touchy, isn't she?" Shushurin noted. "What was that about the ring?"

He smiled. "It's the old symbol of the Knights Templar. If you're going to be in a Vatican hit squad, what else would you be in? Granted, the order died damn near 700 years ago; it lent out money to kings who didn't like paying back loans." He shrugged and put away the phone. "Anyway, with an institution as old as this, why throw anything away, even a name or a symbol?

"Now, what do you think about the program Ryan suggested?" he asked. "You said you had been trained in a program for spies since you were a kid, so you could be a trained assassin when you grew up. Does Ryan's theory sound like what you did?"

Shushurin nodded. "Exactly so." Her eyes narrowed, and she looked off, deep in thought.

He nodded slowly. "You think you know these people?"

Shushurin's eyes focused on him, and she looked like she

was ready to hit him. "What? Just because I'm a German, I must be a Nazi? Or is it because I was given some training when I was a kid?"

He literally took a step back, hands in front of him and spread open in a gesture of submission. "Down, girl. I *meant* how many of them could there have been? A few hundred? We don't know how many are here, and with such a small group, being raised together for years, wouldn't the odds be good that you would know at least *one* of them?"

She leaned against a wall, deflated. She put a hand over her eyes and took a deep breath. "I know. I'm sorry. I just… I've spent *years* worrying about this. Who would know, who might find out, how far it would spread." She lowered her hand, laying it on her opposite shoulder, across her chest. "You must understand, when *Stasi* files were opened, over half of East Germany had been revealed as spying on the other half. Whole *communities* were destroyed overnight. Reminding people of the *Stasi* is like making them recall the Nazis, or the Holocaust, and other things they have all but expunged from their history. Like former drunks, they shun their mistakes with the same enthusiasm with which they had initially accepted them. Maybe more. So, every time you mention it, it feels like an accusation."

Murphy nodded, laying a hand on her shoulder. "I get that." He smiled at her, using his other hand to turn her face towards him. "Don't worry, if I'm ever dumb enough to accuse you of anything, I'll be sure to have you handcuffed first."

She smiled, at least. "I thought you weren't into that sort of thing."

He chuckled, then leaned forward, and lightly kissed her on the cheek. He lingered a moment, then gave her a peck

212

on the lips… and lingered *there* for a few seconds. And a few more seconds. When her hands reached out to him, he blinked and stepped back, his breathing a little faster than before.

Shushurin's hands hovered for a moment, then dropped, and she blushed. They were still in public. Her head was spinning. *Have I been alone that long? Have we both been? We met only ten hours ago.*

Scott took a step back, and blinked, slowly steadying his breath. "I think we should focus on business for the moment," he said, clearing his throat. "I also think making out within sight of St. Peter's is illegal. And if it's not, it should be."

* * *

"Please, pick up the damn phone," Sean Ryan muttered into his cell. He had spent the last half hour getting far enough along the *Via della Conciliazione* to make sure that he wasn't being followed… and that that no one was listening … and that most of all, no one could possibly suspect what he was doing. With all of the bodies dropping lately, he wanted his man to be safe and secure.

Sean glanced at his watch, and figured it was probably still early enough in London for his target to still be awake. During all his years of protecting stars, starlets, and other cult members of the glitterati, he had run into some of the deadliest mercenaries on the planet, but despite all of that, there was still only one person he could really rely on for the facets of intelligence history.

Sean turned sharply, accidentally bouncing off a civilian and onto the ground. He looked up from the concrete and smiled. "Sorry about that, I..." his eyes flicked to the glimmer of moonlight shining off the knife blade, and he promptly rolled into the alley, three seconds ahead of a burst of gunfire.

The mugger caught the burst full in the chest.

Sean pulled out the beam Taser he had taken from Figlia's van. He noted the holes in the mugger's chest, thought a moment, and, crouching, wheeled around the alleyway, briefly firing at a diagonal across the street before wheeling back.

You idiot, they probably had a lookout on the Colonnade and waited for one of us to come out, and you walked right into it.

He glanced at his watch again. *Where the hell are the civilians?*

Oh, wait, what am I thinking? It's Italy. Everyone else is already in the nightclubs and won't leave until three in the morning.

Another burst of fire strafed the ground. Sean smiled. All he had to do was sit there and wait for the cops to come for him. *But why wait? You've got a cell phone.*

He glanced toward the opposite end of the alley. *Wait a second... if there's a shooter up there, why's he still firing? All I have to do is go out the back end of the alley and get away.*

Sean rolled his eyes. *Duh, idiot; there's backup at the other end of the alley. Probably waiting for a few more shots before coming in after me. And therefore? Therefore...*

The automatic fire stopped and a motion from the other end of the alley caught his attention—

It was a hand grenade bouncing down the alley.

* * *

Giovanni Figlia leaned back in his chair. His head was already throbbing, and he wanted to do nothing more than go home, spend some more time with his family, and then sleep. Possibly for the next four days. Maybe by then, everyone would have stopped dying, and all the people with automatic weapons would just go home.

Figlia already had hearing loss in one ear, and he couldn't tell if it was from gunfire or the shouting from several prominent police officials, several of whom he used to report to. And, now that he was head of the security force for the most powerful religious leader in the world, they all didn't seem to think much more of him than when he worked for them.

The bullets were another matter. Figlia had been on the SWAT team for Italy, he had trained with the LAPD SWAT, he had been to a World Cup riot, and he had never seen so much gunplay before in his life. He might have fired more bullets at one engagement that evening than in any real-life exchange of gunfire over the course of his entire life.

And the entire time, Sean Ryan had smiled, enjoying himself throughout the entire exchange. That just pushed Figlia over the edge into a full migraine.

His phone rang once more, and he groaned, picking it up. "Giovanni Figlia. *Pronto.*"

"Hey, Gianni," his wife said. "Look at the bright side. We at least get to spend *some* time together this evening."

He blinked, daring to smile. "How do you mean?"

"There's been *another* attack on a researcher looking through Vatican archives," Fisher answered. "One of my friends in the Rome morgue called me about it, since they heard we were having such an interesting day."

"*Another* dead body?" he groaned.

Figlia frowned. "You don't have to sound so cheerful

about it."

Fisher laughed. "I think you'll enjoy this one."

Fifteen minutes later, Figlia looked around the hotel room. It was nothing fancy, just a king-sized bed, neatly made, a nightstand, a lamp, and a television.

The rest of the room was a wreck. There was one destroyed chair, .22-caliber bullet holes in the walls, the ceiling, and the television. Bullet casings clustered in one portion of the room, and a silencer next to the gun. There was also a clump of hair by the door, and a body on the floor.

The corpse lay in the middle of the room, a bullet neatly lodged in his right eye. In most tactical situations, such a shot was impossible. But then again, the target hadn't moved, just stayed there like an idiot while an armed man pointed a gun at him. He had had all the time in the world to be aimed at, and he died. Simple as that.

The researcher's name was Matthew Kovach. He was a young man neatly dressed in pants and a polo shirt. He had medium-blue eyes with silver wire-frame glasses and was the picture of a stereotypical young academic. The only thing out of place was his blond hair, thoroughly disheveled from the struggle that had ended with a bullet in a man's skull.

Kovach also happened to be a well-published American author, and reviewers compared his *Tales from a Catholic High School* to Jean Shepard meets Jack the Ripper.

The author stayed very still. He didn't move, blink, breathe, and remained as still as, well, a corpse.

However, the dead body and the researcher were two different people.

"This one also looks Russian," Fisher said from the other side of the room, looking at the corpse.

Figlia nodded, looking at the blond man who looked

more Irish than anything else. Not to mention a little too well fed. He could have afforded to lose a few pounds, and the impression he gave made Figlia wondered why he was alive.

He asked Matthew Kovach exactly that. "I'm …" the author began, his eyes going out of focus as he drifted off. They snapped back to Figlia and he smiled. "Sorry, I get fuzzy at times. As I was saying, I'm a little paranoid. Room service came up with an order I didn't place; I sent him away. However, I was told I had a package waiting in the lobby, and when I opened the door, the busboy was still in the hall, but with a silenced automatic." He glanced around the room. "You can ask the detectives who talked to me for the details. But the short version is, my wife teaches self-defense."

Figlia nodded, looking over the room once more. He found it interesting that there were bullets all over one side of the room, but not the other. "You immediately disarmed him?"

"More or less. I didn't want to be ventilated."

Figlia nodded. "Understandable." He stared down at the carpet by the door. It was so scuffed, either an army of cops had moved through, or the young author had some interesting footwork.

The local police authorities were pissed. This was the third body at this hotel today. After all, Rome was a large, sleepy city, very lethargic, and usually didn't mind a murder or two every now and then, but this was ridiculous. Another man shot, more academics involved. Another silenced pistol. Another .22 caliber. Another annoying dead body.

The homicide detective muttered from the hall. "More dead bodies. This *signore* Kovach will be as annoying as the others we have in our freezers."

Figlia looked up at the police. *"E tu pensi che e`...che?"*

The police officer shook his head and told Figlia what he thought this was — a simple attempted robbery.

Figlia wanted to give him a stern dressing-down, but he was simply too tired to fight. Especially after a day this long. He didn't want another long battle. But there was, at least, one thing he could get from this.

"Signore... Figlia, was it?" Matthew Kovach asked from the bed.

He turned and tried for a patient smile. *"Si?"*

"You said you were from the Vatican?" the writer asked.

Figlia nodded. *"Si, signore,* we wanted to make certain that you were all right. We know you are working at the archives, and came as soon as we heard about your assault... Tell me, one last thing, what is your research on?"

"Pope Pius XII," he answered. "I figured he was set up by a lot of people with very ulterior motives. Why do you ask?"

Figlia frowned thoughtfully, and hoped his tired appearance didn't turn it into a grimace. "Just curious."

The author raised a brow. "Right. By the way, you should rest, sir. You look awful."

Figlia laughed. If he had only known the half of it. "I will try."

He sighed. That was the final nail, clinching the motive shut. They had all been right — these weren't attacks on people going to the archives, but on people writing about Pius XII. He would have to make certain there was some kind of protection on the author soon. Preferably without anyone noticing it. "Thank you for your service, *Signor* Kovach."

He put away his pen and paper, and tucked them away in his pocket, when Matthew Kovach said, "Is it just me, or is there a war going on outside?"

Figlia blinked. *Where was Sean?*

CHAPTER XV: BURIED BODIES

Sean sprang out of the alley and threw himself to the side, out of the way of the alley opening and into hiding behind two parked cars. The grenade exploded, contained by the walls of the alley, and shooting the force outward like a cannon, blowing past Sean. He leapt back toward the cover of the alley, preferring that to a car with a full gas tank. He turned the corner and walked into an elbow from another gunman.

Sean tumbled backwards and fired without thinking. The gunman dodged, throwing himself out of the way. Sean tracked him, and aimed for the man's center mass. Instead, it hit the Spectre dead on. The gunman landed on his feet, gasping in pain as he hurled the submachine gun away.

Sean's laugh came out in a sudden bark. "Wow, couldn't do that again if I tried." He pressed the trigger again… and the beam flickered and died.

Sean frowned at the weapon. "Great."

The gunman reached for the small of his back. Sean was already on his feet when the secondary weapon came out. He swung the beam Taser like a stick, swinging his upper body into it. The Taser was built like a heavy-duty fireman's flashlight, so it met the gun arm before the barrel could line up with Sean. The gunman leaned back as the gun went flying, letting Sean's backhanded follow-up go by.

Sean landed on his feet again, cylinder in hand. He lunged forward with a slash across the gunman's path, just missing his jaw. The gunman stepped back to reevaluate his options.

Sean grinned, visibly enjoying himself. His attacker cocked his head, now evaluating Sean — for the former, this was a business, a job, something to be taken professionally, not something to be smiling about.

"None of you guys have a sense of humor," Sean mused.

A burst of automatic fire sounded from down the street, with a returning staccato from the rooftop sniper. The bodyguard's electric-blue eyes glowed. "I also have well-armed friends, who sound like they're already on the way."

The gunman narrowed his eyes, and launched himself sideways, kicking off the alley wall. Sean leapt forward, grabbing the gunman's fallen handgun, rolled flat onto his back and fired straight up into the gunman without stopping, cutting into legs and torso. The gunman twisted in midair with the impacts and slammed against the ground.

Sean immediately rolled to one knee, examining the various wounds. The supine figure blinked a few times, realizing that he was still alive, and violently lurched forward, trying to claw at Sean. Sean twisted, blocking the attack with his left and lashing out with a solid right palm to the face, dropping him back.

Either he's stronger than I thought or... what caliber is this thing? Maybe a .22. Great, these guys think they're the Mafia. They would have done better to drag me down to Sicily and then whack me in broad daylight.

The gunfire on the street stopped. A moment later, there

was motion at the mouth of the alley, and Sean rounded on the new figure, gun raised. Scott Murphy skidded to a stop, hands up. "Wow, down, boy! I'm on your side."

Sean lowered the gun to a rest position. "Sorry, I'm a little jumpy."

Murphy looked around the area, noting the two bodies, and the bullet-strafed street. "I can understand that. What the hell have you been doing now?"

"Very little, for once, but I suspect our new friend can help."

"*Va fungu!*" the gunman growled.

Manana Shushurin ran up next to Murphy, Stechkin at the ready. She also gave the area a once over before relaxing her posture. "Everybody in one piece?"

Sean nodded, then noted her weapon. "You're with the BND and you're using a Russian handgun? Whatever happened to the Glocks of Austria? Even an H&K?"

She shrugged. "Heckler and Koch got taken over by the British, and the Glocks don't have the full automatic setting. Besides, I'd shoot myself before using a Beretta."

He laughed. "Nice to know you've got your tastes down pat. As opposed to these guys trying to use local weapons; I think they're trying to keep an air of being amateurs." He rested both hands on one knee. "Problem is, you do that, you're firing brand-new guns you're not familiar with, which is like the kiss of death in combat and—."

A knife flashed in the hand of the assassin. Before Sean could even roll out of the way, a burst from the Stechkin stopped the knife, and its owner, from going anywhere.

Sean blinked, staring at how close the knife had come to his ribcage. He looked up at Shushurin, her gun still smoking. "Umm, thank you?"

"Don't mention it," Shushurin replied, tucking her weapon away. She looked at Scott. "And you told me I should leave the gun in my suitcase."

"Yeah," Scott muttered. "Well, I think it's time for us to depart before the cops arrive."

Sean nodded, flipping open his cell phone. "Good idea. You people run, I'll do something with this guy. By the way, did you get rid of the sniper?"

Shushurin shook her head. "Doubt it. I may have chased him off, but I'd sooner bet that I only made him duck. You should try moving off the other way, down the alley."

"Gotcha. Did Goldberg update you two on the events of the day?"

Murphy nodded. "Two attacks, no waiting? Yeah. And what about your super soldier theory?"

Sean sighed. "It's *not* a super soldier program. This isn't a comic book. These guys are *not* Captain American, Captain Marvel, or even Captain Crunch." He rose to his feet, brushing off his pants legs. "So, do you two want to come out of the closet yet? Join the party with the rest of the grownups?"

Shushurin shook her head. "Not yet, but thank you. Besides, all of you people are still being shot at, so I do not believe that it is safe to come out of the shadows just yet."

Sean smiled. "Fine. In that case, as long as the shadows aren't hiding something that's hunting you, go with God, but go, okay? None of us want the cops to know about you, and frankly, if you're going to stay in the hole, I want you to be the ace. Vamoose."

Once they vanished, Sean bent over the body once more, gingerly checking for any identification, receipts, clothing tags, and ammunition.

He only found one more grenade.

Why the hell didn't you use this in the first place, friend? Did you think it would have been faster with your gun already drawn?

A grain of gravel fell into the blood in the center of the corpse's chest. Sean smiled.

* * *

Above the alleyway, the sniper who had tried to kill Sean slowly inched his way into position.

Ioseph Andrevich Mikhailov was graying, had been for a very long time. He had neatly combed hair with a part on the side, and swept over the front for a more business-bland look — the type of hair one saw on Washington, D.C. talk shows. His mustache was done in the handlebar style of Stalin, after whom he was named — Ioseph's father *really* knew how to suck up to his boss.

Ioseph came closer into position toward this... *stuntman,* who had already beaten two of his agents today, which was two more than anyone had beaten in years. Ioseph wasn't going to take any further chances. He was just going to kill this bastard. He moved slowly towards the edge, until he could point his rifle straight down.

The stuntman wasn't there.

"You didn't think your guys were the only people who could move fast, now did you?"

Ioseph paused, hesitated, then whirled around, leading with the butt of his rifle. Sean Ryan, only inches behind him, caught the weapon in mid-swing with his right hand. Sean landed a solid left hook, followed through with his elbow, and clamped down on the rifle stock, all in one motion. Sean twisted the rifle from his hands, pulling the gun away from

Ioseph, and simultaneously slapping the rifle barrel across the Russian's face.

Ioseph Mikhailov spun dangerously near the edge. Ioseph could sense it, so he threw himself to the side, away from the edge, as well as out of range of Sean's legs, while whipping out his handgun. Before he could aim clearly, Sean dropped into a roll, drawing the Beretta confiscated from the earlier attacker, and hurled it like a shuriken, knocking away the handgun. Sean popped the magazine out of the assault rifle and fired the bullet in the chamber before dropping it.

By the time both of them were on their feet, Ioseph had drawn his combat knife, and Sean had a collapsed tactical baton in hand. They were fifteen feet away from each other, and evaluated their stances.

And the annoying *stuntman* was still there, and he was still alive. And he was *smirking*. His bright blue eyes twinkled with death. He was shorter than Ioseph, and narrower. How had he not killed him already?

Sean smirked. "You know, with all the twenty-somethings I've beaten today, you're the last thing I expected."

Ioseph smiled. "What makes you think I'm not?"

"The last young guy with silver hair I know is a priest; you're not that young." He looked at Ioseph's hair. "You're also more gray."

"And do you believe everything priests tell you?"

Sean nodded. "Until I get proof to the contrary."

"Pity," the gunman replied with a smile. "You're not going to live that long. Tell me, you had bullets left in that Beretta, why didn't you just shoot me in the back of the head? Or if you knew I was coming, run?"

The stuntman allowed himself a broad grin. "I want you alive, and I'm going to take you, old man."

Sean burst forward in two quick steps and snapped his wrist as though he had a whip, lashing at his adversary. Ioseph lunged forward with his blade. Sean diagonally sidestepped, twisting his upper body out of the way of the knife, using the baton to deflect the path of the strike. He then slashed for Ioseph's temple. The gray-haired Ioseph snapped his head backwards and continued into a backwards tumble. Ioseph rolled skillfully, popping up with the knife still in hand — only to find Sean on top of him again, kicking away the knife before whipping his foot back across his face. Ioseph rolled with the blow and came up again on his feet, ready in a combat stance — grinning

Sean studied his opponent a moment, analyzing him. This man wasn't like the others — they were stiff as a board. This guy enjoyed it. "At least you know how to have fun. The other guys just weren't entertaining enough."

Sean slipped away the baton, reached behind his back with both hands, and smiled evilly. With a quick motion, he hurled the hand grenade he had retrieved from the other assassin. The new assailant saw it, and leapt forward at Sean, trying to get away from the grenade. Sean grabbed him in midair and hurled him to the ground, landing on top of him.

Blows didn't rain on Ioseph's head so much as they came in a monsoon, each hook segued into an elbow, and each elbow segued into a hammer blow, which led into an opening with a hook from the other fist. As the assassin punched back, Sean blocked, drove the fist down, then threw himself forward with a head butt, nailing him between the eyes, and then biting down on his nose. The assassin roared and tossed him aside with a burst of strength. Sean rolled to a crouch, mouth smeared with blood.

Ioseph staggered to his feet, and looked toward the grenade. No explosion. "What was that about?"

"You thought I was going to use a grenade while I was in the same area? What sort of idiot do I look like to you?"

Ioseph narrowed his eyes. He thought of running, but Sean could always come after him, or throw the grenade for real.

Ioseph replied with a wolfish smile, and circled to his left. "You have no idea what you're dealing with, child."

Sean shook his head, circling to match his adversary's range and speed. "No, I think I do, why else would you be in such a hurry? At first, I thought you were just shooting at the first one of us you could get, but why not at least wait to kill the first duo you saw? You've wasted a guy on me before, and then another. Why bother... unless I know something?"

Ioseph laughed. "Maybe."

He reached over and ripped a block from the roof's ledge, hurling it. Sean leaped out of the way with ease, spun, grabbing it in mid-arc, and hurled it like a discus, meeting the next block in midair. Sean hurled himself after, leaping on the assassin's back as he reached for another stone. Sean grabbed the attacker's wrist and twisted his arm behind his back, locking it into place against the spine. Sean pulled him away from the edge and slammed his skull, face first, into the rock. Sean pulled him back, receiving the assassin's elbow in his face, and a second one stabbing into his breastbone, knocking him away. The assassin flipped forward onto his feet before running toward the hand grenade.

Sean leapt after him — but Ioseph grabbed the grenade and drove his shoulder backward in one motion, catching Sean across the face, knocking him out of the air. The assassin spun, driving a roundhouse into Sean's face. When Sean hit the ground, Ioseph quickly put in as many shots as possible, punching downwards. Ioseph pulled the pin out of the grenade, popped the spoon and slipping the grenade itself into Sean's pants before the stuntman could recover. Ioseph grabbed Sean by the neck and belt, and hurled him off the side of the roof.

Ioseph smiled, turned, and ran, leaping from rooftop to rooftop.

Three rooftops away, he heard the explosion, and knew that Sean Aloysius Patricus Ryan, ex-stuntman, bodyguard, and annoyance, was now dead.

Ioseph's laughter floated through the night sky, merging with the sound of the police sirens.

* * *

Giovanni Figlia ran down the street, following the sounds of gunfire and smoke. Trailing behind him was a tactical team of Swiss Guards armed to the teeth with M16A2 assault rifles, MP5 submachine guns, RPGs, microwave cannons and beam-Taser rifles. Wilhelmina Goldberg toted a leftover Uzi, while Maureen McGrail had nothing but her nightshirt and sweatpants on (when queried about a weapon, she answered cryptically, "I am the weapon."). Hashim Abasi carried an M16.

Thankfully, the evening was warm enough to let them all out without needing anything heavier than what they went to sleep in. They had all been armed and ready as soon as Figlia heard that no one knew where Sean Ryan was — Figlia knew one thing about Sean Ryan, and that was if someone went after him, it wouldn't be done quietly (automatic weapons and grenade launchers, at the very least).

Figlia knew he had found the right area when he discov-

228

ered the burning embers of a car in the street. "Here's the place! Guards, spread out and secure the area." He looked at Goldberg, et al. "The rest of you, with me. Superintendent McGrail, you know Ryan, you lead, where is he?"

McGrail smiled. She walked toward the middle of the street and surveyed the area. She scanned the alleyway on the opposite side of the street, and noticed a fragmentation grenade had detonated, and there was only a body and a grouping of shells and bullet holes. She followed the trail of shells with her eyes, to a Spectre, along with .9mm shell casings.

Follow the devastation. There was also another gun involved. Sean's?

She stepped around the burning car into the alley. She spotted shoeprints on the alley walls, and smiled, knowing one of Sean's old tricks. These prints were above a dead body...

McGrail knelt down at the victim's side and noted it closely. It had been shredded by a grenade, as if the explosive were either on top or right next to him when it went off.

She blinked at her conclusion. "Oh, God. I think I found him!"

"Will you people, for God's sake, look up!" someone roared.

McGrail looked up with her pale green eyes to a form dangling from a long rod — each end of the rod seemed attached to either side of the alley, but on closer examination realized it was two of Sean's batons linked together at the base to form a long, seven-foot staff. Each end was jammed into the sides of the alleyway, and Sean was essentially hanging there because of the friction generated by the staff being just a little longer than the alley was wide.

McGrail smiled. "Should we try getting you down?"

Sean sighed loudly enough for her to hear even several

floors down. "Why, do you want to catch me?"

"Can't you just walk down the sides of the alley?" she asked with a smile.

"Get real. At the moment, I'm very lucky I had this on me, assembled, from a demonstration I gave this morning. I had to throw a grenade out of my pocket while falling in mid-air. There's only so much I can do in one take, and unlike the movies, I wasn't going to get a second shot at it."

* * *

"One of them got away, I should add," Sean noted at the end of his briefing out at curbside while the *carabinieri* stood off to the side, taking notes.

These cops, Goldberg noted, were far more respectful than the ones from this morning, and several referred to Figlia by name. *Old cop buddies?*

Sean took a sip of his coffee, blanket wrapped over his shoulders by the firemen who had gotten him down. "Now these guys have been good, but this last guy was better, an older fellow. I wouldn't be surprised if he trained the others. It's also possible he just had more experience."

The *carabinieri* thanked him for his report and moved away, asking him not to leave town. Figlia assured them that Sean wouldn't, and walked off with the cops, deliberately leading them away, shooting Sean a look, as though it were the American's fault that he was being shot at all the time.

Once they were out of earshot, McGrail turned to him. "Could it be our man?" she asked, meaning the last, most-discussed suspect.

"Don't worry, I have an alibi," said a soft voice. Almost everyone jumped except for McGrail and Sean — Sean was too numb to be shocked, and McGrail was always ready for surprises when around the former stuntman.

Frank Williams smiled quickly at the scene. "So, what happened other than that someone made the mistake of attacking Mr. Ryan here?"

"That's about it," Sean lied. "You caught me at the tail end of the story. You want to take a look around, see if I missed anything? I suggest starting with the roof. I slugged it out with a good old boy with a mean right hook, a left hook, and a couple of good jabs."

Father Frank smiled. "Certainly."

The priest vanished as suddenly as he had arrived, just as Figlia walked back. "Did I miss anything?" the Italian asked.

Sean paid Figlia no attention for a moment, listened carefully for Father Frank, and when he was certain Frank had left, Sean turned to the others. In a low, almost threatening voice, he started, "No offense to the good father, or even to any of you, but at the moment, Maureen is the only one I trust here."

Figlia smiled. "You trust no one, do you?"

Sean's bright blue eyes focused on him like a laser. "Not at the moment, no." He looked at each one in turn, making sure that he timed each stare to be exactly the same amount of time. "Either someone's been compromised or someone's a direct turncoat. These guys put a lot of effort into trying to kill me, and I suspect they did it because of my idea of Soviet terrorist training camps. Either I hit the nail on the head with a sledgehammer, or I came close, and they heard about it from *somebody*." He turned to Goldberg. "I'd also leave this conversation out of the next report you file with Mr. Mossad and friend, okay? They both showed up, and his partner killed the poor schmuck in the alley when he pulled a knife on me. Considerate, but also convenient. Yes, she saved my life, but I'm feeling paranoid right now."

Goldberg gave an involuntary smile. "Join the club. I've been paranoid about the priest for a while."

"Why would you be?" McGrail added. "Isn't my victim a priest? Can you see them killing one of their own?"

The Secret Service Agent gave her a half-smile and a glance. "Tell it to the Mafia." Figlia'

Giovanni Figlia smiled. "I am also not, as you would say, their biggest fan. I have a set of choice words I would use on signori Coppola and Scorsese, should I get the chance."

Sean looked at McGrail, and blinked a few times, tuning out the conversation. The Interpol agent raised a brow. "Something?"

He smiled broadly. "You're right! Your victim, the dead priest, what's his name? Harrington?"

Sean hopped up, throwing the blanket off of him. "He's dead!" he exclaimed, excited and energized, from adrenaline if nothing else. "But *why?* He was in Rome during World War II. And he did what!"

"Worked with children," Figlia recounted. "The Boys Town of Italy."

Sean shook his head violently, like a dog thrashing around a bone. "No! You said it yourself, Maureen! The answer's not with him! It's with his boss."

McGrail took a small step backwards, about to drop-kick Sean into next Tuesday if he had finally gone around the bend. Even the others looked at him tentatively, as though he were a bomb approaching zero at an erratic rate of speed. "Father Carroll-Abbing?"

"You've heard about *him!* But you never heard about Harrington! Because Abbing was more important."

232

Figlia was the first to relax, and even chuckled. "Is it just me, or did *Signore* Ryan hit his head harder than I thought?"

Sean growled in frustration. "No, dammit! I ..." Sean cursed under his breath and stood, looked up to the roof and called out "Williams! Father Frank, you up there?"

"No need to shout," the priest softly answered from just inside the building's doorway.

Sean wheeled on him. "Tough. Have you heard about Father Abbing?"

Father Frank raised a brow and quizzically studied him. "Monsignor John Patrick Carroll-Abbing? Of course, he—"

"He wrote a book, didn't he?"

He nodded. "It was—"

"Thanks." Sean looked to the others. "Something I learned from my girlfriend: when you can't trust your secondary source, read *their* sources. If Abbing was in the rescue operations, and he wrote his memoirs, he'd have written about it. I want what he said. Look at the sources, and start breaking it down. I want a list of primary research materials, and I mean as soon as possible. If we're right about involving Pius XII and the Holocaust, we should start there,"

Giovanni Figlia nodded slowly, calmly taking in the erratic thoughts Sean shot off. "Why not flip through everything on the subject? Look at *all* the priests, instead of just the one?"

He nodded. "Good idea. Can you get us into the archives?"

Figlia shrugged. "I am a police officer, not an academic."

Sean wheeled on Father Frank. "You're in with the Pope, right?"

The priest cocked his head. "In what way?"

Sean rolled his eyes. "You're obviously his point man in

certain situations, and that means Special Operations — and don't give me that look, I don't mean intelligence, I mean Special Conversions and Tactics or something like that."

Father Frank chuckled. "I'm sure His Holiness would like the acronym SCAT less than SWAT."

Sean waved it away. "SWAT for you would be more like a Vatican Anti-Vampire Squad. Get us into the Vatican Archives for Pius XII — we're looking at them tomorrow."

"They're not all organized yet, but I'll see what I can do."

Sean's eyes narrowed and he leaned in to the priest. "If Pius wants this thing solved, he'll let us in. Or we'll break in, and don't think I won't."

"You can't even speak Italian."

He grinned. "I'll learn. Get moving. I want to start when daylight comes."

Father Frank shrugged. "If you insist." The man in black faded into the night.

Once Sean was certain the priest disappeared, he whirled on Goldberg. "You never mentioned what Mossad had to say."

Goldberg blinked, then took a step back, gun hand bracing to go for her weapon. He was less erratic than before, but it hadn't helped. "I've been looking into a name, Pinchas Lapide, Israeli diplomat. Lapide apparently has something to do with this, but Israel seems to have locked down his archives, so no one in intelligence knows exactly what's in them, unless they own Mossad. I'm having the goy look check it further. He's already put in an application. However, Lapide's already written a book on the topic."

Sean shook his head. "I'll do that. You speak Italian. I'm guessing you can read it, so you'll be needed in the archives tomorrow, as will most of us. I don't," he lied, "so unless it's

234

not in English, I'll do it. So read through them tomorrow, I'll start on the Lapide book as soon as I find a copy." He was about to move off and stopped. "By the way, Villie, you've got Mossad's number? I want you to ask him something."

* * *

Manana Shushurin leaned up against the side of a building. She glanced up and down the street — what street was it anyway?—and touched her handgun to reassure herself it was there.

"Don't worry, you'll still be able to kill people," he joked. He looked back at her, ignoring his surroundings for once. He lightly touched her arm. "Something wrong? You look tired."

She smiled weakly. "I just feel stupid for killing that gunman. If we took him alive, he would've talked and we could all go home."

He shrugged. "So we're all here a little longer. You're assuming that he didn't have a cyanide cap or something. I mean, those things are common enough in our business, and he didn't even have to bother hiding it in his tooth. He could have swallowed rat poison and we'd not have been able to do too much about it."

She gritted her teeth. "But he *wanted* me to kill him," she argued. "If I didn't get him, he would have killed Ryan, and I probably *still* would have wound up shooting him anyway."

Murphy smiled. "I don't think that Mr. Ryan is too much concerned that you killed the prick. Sean didn't seem all that put out by it, to tell the truth, although I wonder exactly what *would* put him out."

Shushurin pumped her fists at her side, wanting him

to understand. "But damn it, I didn't *have* to. I could have aimed for something else on him."

Murphy looked at her a moment, then laughed. She gave him a glare. "What's so funny?"

He pointed. "You! You save someone's life by taking out a bad guy, so what? We're here a little longer, big deal. You're more concerned by the fact that you put the critter down than by the fact that you saved someone in the process. Lighten up."

She stared a moment, then smiled. He could see the tension seeping from her body. "Did you just call him a critter?"

He nodded. "Cop talk for scumbag. What? My family's crawling with cops. You think I'd speak in Yiddish?"

"You're in Mossad, I'd think so."

"You'd also believe that a dyslexic rabbi would go around saying yo? Oy!"

She grinned, and his heart melted.

Wow, I almost forgot for a moment that she's God-awfully gorgeous, emphasis on the awe. He let his hand drift from her arm up to her cheek. "Hey, you do good work, don't forget that." After a moment, he slid his hand down her cheek, around to the back of her neck, leaned forward and kissed her on the forehead.

Shushurin gave no resistance. When he drew back, he didn't step away, but he reluctantly took his hand off her person, taking the smell of her light, sugary perfume onto his hand.

She stared deeply into his eyes. "Does that mean you want to change your mind about the arrangements for bed?" she asked, laughter in her voice.

"Sure, why not? I managed to keep my chastity at Harvard of all places, and I'm so tired, not even a woman as beautiful as Helen of Troy could get me to do much more than collapse."

Shushurin grinned. "At least I'm not that pretty. I don't even have a face to launch a dozen fishing boats."

"No, you have a face to launch the D-Day invasion. I think they could take Helen's pursuers any day of the week."

His phone rang, and he hesitated. Damn, that was bad timing. He flipped it open. "Murphy here. Agent Goldberg, how nice to hear from you again. What about the Hall of Righteous Gentiles?... Not to my knowledge. They usually plant a tree for each Jew that the gentile in question has saved. Trust me, if Pius XII had a few trees there, I think I would have heard about it. But I'll check it out."

Murphy disconnected, looked up at Shushurin and smiled. "Could we put a pin in this for a moment? I've got to make another call."*

Sean Ryan sat on the steps of Saint Peter's, and waited, his phone next to his ear. Sooner or later, the other end had to pick up.

"Hello?"

Sean's face broke out into a grin. "Hey, grandpa. How are you doing?"

In his home in London, James Ryan laughed. "I'm still alive. You won't get your hands on my millions this week."

Sean chuckled. "I could say the same. Though to be honest, I'm wondering who goes first."

"Hmm. I've seen your clippings. That's a good question." James gave a great belly laugh. "So, what gets you calling at this hour? You usually just send me a letter."

"You know I'm in Rome right now?"

"I figured from the postal stamps. And the turnaround time in mail delivery."

Sean nodded, mostly to himself. "You were in Rome during the war, right?"

James hesitated for a long moment. "I spent a few months. Sure. Why?"

"Anything interesting happen while you were there?" Sean prompted. "Did you meet the Pope, perhaps?"

"I met a few interesting people."

Sean could hear the smile in his grandfather's voice. "Right. Anything interesting happen on your end lately?"

"Oh, two men tried to mug me last week."

Sean's smile dropped. "Were you okay?"

James gave another great laugh. "Of course I was. They didn't expect your Christmas present. Boy, were they surprised."

Sean breathed out a sigh of relief. *The* Christmas present had been a walking stick that had an iron core down the center. "Did they walk away?"

"Nope," James said, matter-of-factly. "The London cops are pissed at me. And they took away your gift."

"Don't worry about it. I'll get you another one. I still know the guy."

"That means I'll be able to see you again sometime soon. Good."

"Soon enough. When I wrap this thing up in Rome, I'm going to come visit. Heck, give me a few days, I'll take a break and come see you forthwith."

"I look forward to it, Sean-boy. And maybe then I'll tell you something about my time in the Eternal City."

* * *

On the other end of the phone, Mikhailov growled. *In-*

siders. "Why the hell did you show up?"

"I've been everywhere else," came the reply. "It would look suspicious if I wasn't there."

"You were at the other attack today."

"Which I *also* didn't ask you to do," the other replied. "I ask again, *are you trying to get me killed?* Or is this the way you pull *all* of your operations — kill first, ask later? Fine, you didn't plan the attack, but you were there, you were *in it.* I *warned* you about Ryan and McGrail, I didn't say *act* on the information. Every time you ignore me and go after someone else, they piece together more and more. They know there's an insider somewhere Goldberg is American Secret Service, McGrail is Interpol, and Sean Ryan is neutral. That doesn't leave very many choices. At the moment, *he's* the one I'm worried about."

"He worried me, too, until I tossed him off the roof with a grenade in his pocket."

There was a pause. "He's still alive."

Ioseph fumed. "*WHAT!* And don't you laugh at me. I can hear you smiling you useless… How is he still alive?"

"He's very resourceful."

"I'll make sure he *dies* next time," he growled.

"You will do no such thing!" his informant told him. "I'm the one on the inside, and you're not going to jeopardize me any further, do you understand? Every time you do something like that, it tightens the noose, and they keep picking up more information about *you.*"

"But he guessed at our program."

"No! He guessed at the nature and training of your men, and you just confirmed his suspicions. Anything else would further exacerbate the situation."

"We can't get a signal from the guys we sent after the old

man in London."

There was a moment of silence. "It looks, then, like Mr. Ryan's resourcefulness is genetic, doesn't it?"

* * *

The Egyptian police officer slid back into bed. There was little Hashim Abasi could do about going immediately to sleep, but he decided to try anyway. His first day was supposed to be simple: look around, observe security, and work out logistics. But no, he had to get involved in some sort of Western conspiracy theory out of one of their Oliver Stone films.

He sighed gently, trying not to let anything perturb him further... especially not his roommate.

Thinking of which... Abasi looked to his left, noting Sean Ryan sitting up in bed, fingers laced together, eyes closed, falling into his own head. Abasi didn't actually think that the odd bodyguard could stop and spend time in thought — he seemed more the type to shoot first, second, and third, only to ask questions later on, if at all, if anyone was still alive.

Abasi smiled. Isn't that what you thought of her at first?

Abasi thought a moment about his wife, and dismissed Sean Ryan as being Irish, like her, only much, much stranger, and more stereotyped. His wife had explained to him about a certain type of Irish Catholic — boisterous, charismatic, with occasional bouts of brooding. Either his wife was correct, or the entire island was nuts, which was not outside the realm of possibility.

But, then again, Abasi did stone her to death in public. There had been no choice. So, there was all kinds of strangeness on this Earth. His associates would almost certainly frown on him for that, just as much as he perceived Sean Ryan as being odd.

Abasi rolled over and smiled as he settled deeper into the bed, thinking of his wife's jet-black hair, brown eyes, and pale skin He tried to forget the rocks he had thrown at her head, preferring to remember her as she'd been before. But that was life.

* * *

Giovanni Figlia slipped into the temporary bedroom for the evening. Veronica Fisher was already waiting. Her brown hair was tied up in a ponytail, and a book lay open in her lap. Her black t-shirt read, in Italian, "Dead men tell no tales — unless you're in forensics."

"The kids have been tucked away?" he asked.

Fisher looked up and smiled. "A while ago. What've you been doing?"

Figlia sat on the edge of the bed. "Talking with the police. Thankfully, I still have friends from the old days; otherwise, we'd still be out there, cleaning up Ryan's mess."

"Hey, you did it, so don't worry."

He smiled. "I wish I could. All of these bullets and bombs just a hundred yards away from the Pope's front door… a good way to lose a pontiff."

She shrugged. "I suppose." She looked around the room. "And he's got a real nice arrangement here… where did he manage to find a king-sized bed as hard as a sheet of wood?"

Figlia chuckled. "Well, it's the smallest he could get without falling off the edge, and he prefers private ascetic arrangements. This is assuming he even uses it, since no one knows exactly when or if he sleeps." He turned to look at her. "So, what do you think about the entire ordeal?"

She shrugged. "You seem to be piling up the bodies lately. The two you sent me earlier today were well-developed, physically fit, and probably able to rip a man's arm off. They look vaguely Slavic, but I'll need a specialist to take a gander at their facial features before I cut them open. We can do DNA, if we have a few days."

Giovanni Figlia nodded slowly. *Russians again. Maybe Ryan was right.*

Giovanni Figlia smiled. "No kidding."

CHAPTER XVI: A PIUS BEGINNING

S cott "Mossad" Murphy awoke, a little confused. Somehow, he had gone to bed with a ravishing brunette.

Then he realized he had gone to bed fully clothed, and it made more sense. He remembered last night only a little after he called in to Tel Aviv. When he asked about the file on Pius XII, he was almost laughed off the phone, but he made the call, as he promised Agent Goldberg. For some reason, he failed to see how any of Goldberg's requests made sense. First an Israeli diplomat, and then a file from the Hall of the Righteous Gentiles; if there was a connection, he wasn't seeing it. Maybe Pius XII was the link between Lapide and Goldberg — Pius seemed to be the primary link to everything.

Next time, Murphy was going to get an explanation from Goldberg. *Or, better yet, I'll simply ask Tel Aviv. After all, if the two are connected, then they'd know.*

He nuzzled deeper into the softness, wrapping his arms around what he thought was the pillow. He paused for a moment, and gave the matter some thought. He was lying on a warm surface, and didn't think that it was his own body heat. He slowly slid one hand up the object, and felt that his "pillow" had ribs. He hesitated a little more, and realized that during the night, his head had settled directly on top of Manana Shushurin's chest.

Oh crap, I am so freaking dead. Let's see if I can disengage before she wakes up.

Murphy was about to move when he felt his hair move slightly, as if someone was gently running the tips of fingers along his scalp, and trying not to let him notice.

She's running her nails through my hair? What do I look like, a puppy?

"Are you awake yet?" she whispered.

Murphy slowly raised his head, keeping his eyes closed. "I think so, though I'm hoping I'm just dreaming; otherwise, I need to offer a few explanations."

"Why?"

"Because I had the sensation of resting on a very soft pillow that's firm under the surface, and I'm hoping very hard that it was a pillow — if not, you could probably just twist my head off and be done with it."

She ruffled his hair. "You're sweet, and dead wrong, by the way. I maneuvered you during the night — if someone burst through the door while we slept, I had my arm wrapped around you, and could merely roll off the bed, taking you with me, grab my gun, and return fire. Why do you think I sat in the bed first, on the side facing the door? Everyone else has been attacked lately, why should we be exempt?"

He pushed himself to his hands, disentangling himself from Shushurin. He allowed himself to look her in the eyes, using his peripheral vision to make certain she was clothed. "Because we're following the investigators, staying far behind the front line of the investigation? No one attacks the researchers."

She cocked her head. "Tell that to the Vatican archivist.

Or David Gerrity, or Yousef."

He paused for a moment. "Point taken. Dr. Almagia was the archivist servicing Gerrity and Yousef; he'd know what they were both looking at. Stealing the archive logs would make no sense without killing him off, too."

She nodded. "But that still doesn't exempt us from attack."

He laughed and rolled onto his backside, sitting up straight, his legs crossed. "Slight problem with your whole theory. I never get attacked. *Never.* Even on the Spanish Steps, I wasn't being shot at, and neither were you until you opened fire. The odds of being attacked are slim. Besides, my Office prides itself on not being caught often." He combed his fingers through his hair. "Although, to tell the truth, I'm a little worried that your guys found out about this before mine did. The Office is usually very good at anticipating problems." He shrugged. "But then, I'm a goy, what would I know?"

Shushurin raised a brow. "They keep you out of the loop?"

Murphy shrugged. "If they did, how would I know? I'm an accountant, not a gunner. I blend in, play with money, incite a riot or two, funnel out information, recruit informants, and disappear." He smiled. "At least you get to shoot people occasionally."

Shushurin chuckled. "Not really. Mostly, I read intelligence reports, and hit the weights or the shooting range. I'm sure you get routine training in at least hand to hand, right? Even target practice?"

"Um... I know how to fire a gun... I can't just, well, hit anything with it. I can run really fast, though."

She smiled gently. "That's all right, I'll protect you."

He laughed. "You mean from the evil super-spooks Ryan was talking about?"

Shushurin frowned slightly. "I've been giving some thought about that. Don't you find it convenient that Sean had that conversation, only to be attacked soon after?"

Murphy nodded. "Hell yes. What do you think it means? That there's an insider?"

She nodded. "Who would you lay money on?"

He thought a moment. "I'd rather not try to guess, but I can exclude a few people — mainly everyone from out of town."

She furrowed her pretty brows. "You mean you want to leave out Abasi? Why?"

He reached to the nightstand and picked up a pipe, already stuffed with tobacco, and bit down, lit up with a match. "My Office is familiar with Abasi's family," he said formally. "While we *never* preclude the possibility of an Egyptian cop as a terrorist, Abasi was raised more by his mother than by his father, and we had... an understanding with her."

Shushurin smiled, slightly surprised. "Okay. And I can see why you'd leave off Ryan, they really do seem to want to kill him. But then, they wanted to kill everyone on the Spanish Steps yesterday."

He nodded. "And we're running out of suspects. Unless there's someone we missed. I'm a good chess player, but damn, this is complicated."

"I think we're covered," Shushurin said with a smile.

Murphy cocked his head and thought a moment, chewing on the pipe stem a little. "Well, I'm not going to question your professional memory."

The BND spy smiled. "Yes, but you've at least experienced my skills firsthand."

"Oh, I'm sure you have more skills than I've seen."

She leaned forward, patting his cheek. Her voice dropped

to a seductive hush as she said, "You have no idea." She then grinned and chuckled. "Come. Let's get ready for the day. I suspect we'll need to find and track Father Williams."

"He's first on my list."

* * *

Hashim Abasi slowly walked into Giovanni Figlia's office, coffee in hand. He was more casual than the day before. His tan suit jacket was thrown over one shoulder, his tie was missing, and his top two shirt buttons were open. His reading glasses stuck out of his shirt pocket, absentmindedly stuffed inside. He chose the couch and laid the jacket on the back before settling in. He nodded at Figlia — already seated at his desk, dressed in a black suit and shirt combination, collar open — and Figlia nodded back before turning to his paperwork.

Maureen McGrail and Wilhelmina Goldberg entered, and Sean Ryan after. The Irish Interpol agent wore her loose white blouse and black suit pants, Goldberg had another black turtle neck and pin-striped pants. Sean wore a dark blue polo shirt and black pants.

The Secret Service agent smiled at Abasi. "You look like an academic."

"Technically, I am. I'm a part of..." he paused to think of the English acronym. "MEMRI."

McGrail sat down in a chair in a corner of the room. "MEMRI? I haven't heard of it."

"The Middle East Media Research Institute," Goldberg answered as she sat next to Abasi. "I didn't know you were a part of the Middle East think tank."

He raised an eyebrow. "Most people do not even know of

it. I am surprised you do."

"It's an Egyptian program. Egypt is next door to Israel."

Abasi smiled. "Most Arabs do not know it — then again, in my part of the world, we do not even have philosophers between 1500 and 1900. There are occasions where my religion has a tendency to put the sources of wisdom as the Koran first, imams second, and reason is somewhere around fourth or fifth on the list."

Sean Ryan leaned against the wall next to McGrail, crossing his arms. Goldberg spared a moment to look over his surprisingly impressive muscles.

Sean smiled at Abasi. "And you turned out sane how?"

He chuckled from somewhere deep in his throat. "When I took courses in England, I realized that, outside of oil, Arab nations have contributed nothing to the world for the last 500 years. We *make* nothing, we *produce* nothing, and unless we modernize and stop fighting the west and each other, we will *be* nothing. Soon, Americans will probably have your precious hydrogen-cars, and that will be the start of the end. Europe would soon follow. And my people will have no choice but to move to Detroit, become a place of outsourcing, or blow themselves up. Once oil fields are outdated, no one will need to put up with terrorist governments anymore. Many of those countries, I fear, will all be bombed out of existence by either the Israelis or the Americans."

"We can hope not," said the soft voice from the doorway, the doors closed behind him.

Goldberg and Abasi nearly jumped, while the others merely turned to look at him.

"Nice to see you, Father," Sean said calmly.

Father Frank Williams smiled gently and stepped further into the room, stopping at the lamp table by Abasi's arm.

"I've told the Pope of your request to see the Pius XII archives. He has no problem. Hopefully, you don't mind having to sort some of the materials."

Goldberg raised a brow. "What's the catch?"

"That *is* the catch." Father Frank allowed himself to grin slightly. "The archives were closed in part because they had not yet been organized. Even though scholars are allowed to examine them, they still have not been totally sorted. So, who wishes to go in?"

Wilhelmina Goldberg and Maureen McGrail looked at each other before they nodded. Abasi said, "I will be happy to."

Sean smiled. "Do you happen to have a book written by Pinchas Lapide floating around? I hear that he was looking into this topic."

Father Frank reached under the table next to him, and pulled out a copy of the book *Three Popes and the Jews*, by Pinchas Lapide. He crossed over and handed it to Sean, who merely smiled. Sean caught a brief glimpse of the priest's ring — gold with a gold cross, two swords crossing behind it, set on a red background.

"Journalist and diplomat Pinchas Lapide," Father Frank recited from the brief biography, "served with the British army in World War Two, and liberated one or two camps in Italy. Later a diplomat for Israel to the Vatican."

Figlia raised a brow. "You broke into my office for your little trick?"

"No. I asked for the keys," Frank replied. "I wanted to recommend it in any case. I had to dig it out of the library."

Figlia sighed. "I'm sorry to say this, but I cannot be bothered *con che* right now." He leaned forward in his chair, pulling himself closer to the desk. "I've an office to run, I'm a day behind, and I've problems from yesterday to fix."

Sean flipped open the table of contents, scanned through them, then said, "Unless you need to throw me out, I'll read here."

Figlia narrowed his eyes at him. "I'd suggest reading outside in the square."

Sean frowned. "Great. I should've told the gunmen last night they just could've nailed me with a sniper rifle this morning. Ah well, what the hell." He raised the book in a salute. "I'll see you all later today. Have fun."

* * *

Sean Ryan settled into St. Peter's Square, making certain to hide himself within the columns, weaving between them as he read. He wanted the fresh air, and would have welcomed being attacked again by these twerps, especially the prick who threw him off the roof. He didn't really mind being shot at – if he did mind, he wouldn't be in this job – but he didn't like to lose.

As he read, his curiosity was peaked, and his brows furrowed deeper. Something had been wrong, and nagging at him, and he couldn't tell what. It had been something about the book, and the attack the evening before. What would the story of the book tell? It was the same story from the archives David Gerrity and Ashid Yousef had both seen--the archives that had almost certainly gotten them killed. But what had it to do with the persons constantly trying to kill Sean and company?

"Mr. Ryan."

Sean jumped, turned and nearly killed him, but Scott Murphy was lucky. Sean relaxed , looking at the Mossad agent with a glare. Murphy was dressed in a light blue corduroy shirt and matching jeans.

"What is it?"

Murphy leaned forward and quietly said, "I wanted to know if you've noticed anything on Father Williams that might mean something more to a Catholic than to a Jew. A symbol for an order, things like that?"

Sean raised an eyebrow. "Well, he is wearing a ring for the Order of the Knights Templar. Then again, I bought one of those from a catalog. Why?"

Murphy raised his eyebrows. "Thanks, happy reading."

Sean stared as the spy darted off. *What the hell was that about?* He shook his head, and was about to bury his head back into the book as a voice interrupted his reading.

"Where have you been?" a voice boomed. Sean looked over at the oncoming mass of swirling red cloak. It was Cardinal Cannella again, this time on a cell phone. The corrupt Boston priest didn't seem to go away. "And what *about* Boston?" the Cardinal continued in the open air, assuming that everyone around him could not understand English. "You promised me it would be settled by now." Cannella paused. "How about the rest of it? How have you been handling the other thing?" Another pause. "I'll get in contact with you later."

Sean only raised a brow, then got back to his reading.

* * *

Giovanni Figlia looked over his desk, glancing at all of the papers and reports that had piled up over the course of yesterday, with more coming in by the hour.

Some days, he thought, *murders might be more interesting to investigate if they weren't so hooked into Vatican politics.*

But then again, how likely was it that I could have co-opted a murder investigation of a man in the Vatican archives? It was practically impossible.

He massaged his throbbing temple. *Bull. Of course, it was possible. Easily believable — the hotel was across the street from the Vatican, where else would an elderly archivist stay in Rome?*

He blinked, thinking about his wife and children being in danger because of this stupid, idiotic case, just because he was bored.

From now on, after this, Lord, the most dangerous thing I will ever do is go to my in-laws, he thought darkly. *Hell, I haven't even seen my kids since the day before yesterday, and we're within a hundred meters of each other.*

He looked at his watch, then to the pile of papers he had dealt with, and then to the slightly lower pile of papers he had yet to get to.

He frowned a moment, thinking it over. *To heck with it. Tthe outbox has more papers than the inbox — victory has happened.*

Time to find Ronnie and the kids.

CHAPTER XVII: A PIUS MAN

S everal hours later, Goldberg sighed over all of the paper-work sprawled over the table. The people who worked at that Vatican archives had come in for only brief periods, almost pained by the way much of the articles were scattered about.

"This is annoying."

McGrail looked up, and blinked firmly to clear her eyes. "How so?"

Goldberg grabbed a piece of paper, checked the date, and said, "December 24, 1939, Pius XII's Christmas address called upon the memory of his predecessor against the Nazis, complaining about human rights violations, and calling for the return of peace — defining peace as, among other things, 'respecting ethnic minorities'."

Goldberg looked down at the papers and grabbed another at random. "May 13th, 1940, after a few thousand priests were massacred in Poland, he laments that he can't say anything, lest the Nazis speed up the process. And this one, from Berlin, September '41, about a Cardinal von Galen pissing off the Germans, and having churches closed and ransacked by *Hitlerjungen* after each sermon. Another letter, ten days later, from Vichy France, warns that Hitler considers Pius XII his 'personal enemy.'"

Goldberg's hazel eyes flitted around the papers about her. "I'm not even sure where to go next."

Abasi smiled, his teeth a bright white against his skin, raising a sheet of paper. "Then allow me. April, 1939, Budapest, the Bishops opposed the first racial laws. In June, the Vatican had a request for three thousand visas, and six days later there was a complaint from Bern, Switzerland about the difficulty of emigration to Latin America." Abasi shifted to another folder. "It makes no sense until you see the note a few days later. The Vatican had approved three thousand Brazilian visas."

Goldberg blinked. "But Latin America?" She thought a moment. "Oh, right, the U.S. closed off Jewish emigration from Europe. Canada wasn't any better."

Abasi nodded. "Oh, and in July, the Pope blessed all 'works of mercy' given to Jewish refugees. There's also a thank-you letter for agents of the Holy See giving help to Jews."

McGrail's eyes were grateful for the rest. She closed them tightly and recalled items from memory. "Aye. There're notes discussing papal aid to prisoners in camps intervention for Croatian Jews, Jewish Slavs, Slovakian Jews , Albanian Jews… the list just doesn't stop. And that's *just* 1939."

Goldberg nodded reluctantly. "Not to mention that half of this paperwork is bureaucratic redundancy."

McGrail smiled, despite her aching eyes. "Och, 'tis better. February, 1944, Rabbi Herzog thanked the Church for help it gave Jews. And in August, for saving the lives of thousands of Roman Jews."

Goldberg cocked her brows. "What? Let me see that one."

She did. "Follow that with a letter from the Vatican demanding that they stop massacring prisoners in Auschwitz," McGrail added, handing that letter over as well. "Dated September 26, and 30, 1944."

Goldberg leaned back in the chair, hands folded together in front of her face like a fist. "I had family in Auschwitz and Krakow, and I've never heard of this. All I hear in the community is 'Pius did nothing,' 'Catholics did nothing, said nothing.' Now there's all of these little official protests with diplomats and governments fighting on a local level — and by the paperwork, with either the blessings or near ordering of the Pope."

McGrail smiled. "Cute trick. I haven't seen a letter like that anywhere."

Goldberg smiled. "I know Italians, and I've dealt with New York politicians. Trust me, these letters are direct orders to meddle in the affairs of Nazis, and drive them nuts — or indirect orders, considering that everything's in bureaucrat-ese. I know it's impossible, but I've never heard of any of this — any. I mean, this can't get worse, can it?"

* * *

Figlia stepped out of his office, assuming that the day couldn't get any worse if he joined his family for siesta, and found them in the Borgia Gardens. Possibly best recognized by most human beings as the place where Michael Corleone confessed his sins in *Godfather III*. He shook his head with a smile. While Figlia had no problem with the idea that anyone could be redeemed, he had problems with the concept that the Mafia were men of class. In some dictionaries, *mafioso* translated as "gaudy dresser."

Figlia's children were playing in the garden, kicking the

soccer ball around, Fisher having already joined them on the grass. He just watched them for a moment, smiling as they played together. His family. He loved them more then he knew how to express. He might have been smarter than the average police officer, especially to have gone so far, but his vocabulary could not contain his passion for his wife and his adoration of his two children.

"Joshua and Raphael are adorable," said a voice to his left and a little behind.

Figlia smiled, catching a whiff of cigar smoke. "Run out of cigarettes, Your eminenzia?"

Xavier O'Brien smiled. "No. I only smoke those indoors. Believe it or not, that's only to hold me over until I get outside. They find it harder to get cigar smoke out of the walls."

He nodded. "I hope no one minds my children being here."

XO laughed. "You must be kidding, *Commandatore*. You may have noticed, most of those who work here, we are old men. Grandfatherly instinct works on the same level as paternal instinct. So far, your children have been babysat by the Cardinals of Chicago, Spain, and Florence. Your kids may well start speaking Latin before we're done."

Figlia chuckled. "They have already picked up street Latin — mostly from priests traveling in from New York."

XO contemplated the scene of family before him, then took a sip of scotch from the glass in his other hand. "Why did you take on this case, Figlia? You didn't have to. And I thought we kept you busy enough around here."

"Oh, you do, do not fret about that. I am just... you know soccer, *si?*"

The Bishop laughed. "I've lived in Rome over a decade, Gianni, I've seen soccer."

"Do you ever watch the players who do not have the ball?"

"Can't say that I have."

"They never stop moving. Even when the ball is at the other end of the court, they continue to move, jogging *pede-a-pede*, foot to foot. They always keep moving. They may slow, but never stop. Even the game is continuous, no breaks, no pauses."

"No mercy on the audience for bathroom breaks," XO continued with a smile. "I know, that's why American sports channels hate it — no chances for commercials."

"That as well." He smiled ruefully. "Even Agent Goldberg's Secret Service only allows their agents to protection duty for ten years. After that, they fret that the job becomes routine. Routine leads to death. In my case... I am more restless, I suppose." He finally turned to the American. "By the way, when exactly did the priesthood require so much paper?"

O'Brien laughed. "Come, Gianni, your family awaits. They wanted to have dinner with you fifteen minutes ago."

* * *

Scott Murphy smiled at the sight of Father Frank walking along the bridge. "He's stopped to talk with someone else."

Shushurin stood at the mouth of the bridge, staying out of sight to avoid attention. "Who?"

Murphy stood at the other side of the bridge, trying to observe. "I can't tell. Williams is blocking his face. For all I know, this guy could be a cardinal."

"Can you hear anything?"

"No, can't even read his lips. I'd get closer, but I doubt it's safe."

Shushurin nodded. Thus far, the priest had been leading them a merry chase all day, leading nowhere in particular. He was the only lead they had, now that the primary investigators were busy in the Vatican archives. So Father Frank became the major focus of the two spies.

"Do you really think that he'd risk having a conversation out in the open with someone who matters?

Murphy sighed. "Probably not, but it's the best we have."

Several hours later, Murphy and Shushurin were on the verge of killing this blasted Jesuit. He had dragged them all over Rome, as though he were trying to lose them, but not coming close to succeeding. He hadn't acknowledged that he had noticed them, which would have been wise after failing to lose them for over three hours. He was either a good yet poorly trained spy, who was just wandering aimlessly, or …

"What if he's been leading us on in order to delay us?" Murphy suggested as he rounded yet another corner, nearing the Emmanus Hotel.

"Well, it won't do any good," Shushurin replied alongside him. "He's heading back to the Vatican. Time to end this."

Murphy smiled. "What did you have in mind?"

She felt for her pistol. "Corner him."

The smiled faded and Murphy stopped dead, touching her arm to stop her. "You mean confrontation? We're spies, not knee-breakers. I know you're with the Germans, but there's got to be a limit."

Shushurin closed her eyes. She liked this less than he did. "He's been leading us in circles all day, and we're wasting time we probably don't have. Sean got attacked after concluding that there was an insider involved in whatever the hell this is. We've ruled out nearly everyone but Williams. Even Goldberg figured out that Father Williams is involved somehow.

If we don't pull him aside for a little chat, who will?"

Scott Murphy said, "All right, all right, when do you intend to jump him?"

She watched him cross the street, advancing towards the colonnade of St. Peter's Square. "As soon as it's convenient."

* * *

Figlia returned from his dinner and *siesta* with his family refreshed and invigorated.

Only to find Sean Ryan already in the office, waiting for him, book in hand. "Hard day of papers?" the American asked with a smirk.

"Who knew that a priesthood like this could generate so much *mishegas?*" Goldberg grumbled as she led the way into the office, McGrail and Abasi behind her.

"Oh, it gets worse," Sean Ryan told them as they walked into Figlia's office.

The Secret Service agent glanced at him and said, "How would you know what we found?"

He smiled. "I've got a few notes from my reading. The Vatican released a whole slew of documents back in the 1970s in relation to World War II, and all the others were deleted because they were redundant. Did you find anything contrary to what I told you earlier? Did Pius XII order a village burned or bless Auschwitz as a service to humanity? Something — anything — to support the Nazis, or did he merely have the priests under his command support, facilitate, and secure the release of Jews during the Second World War?"

Goldberg frowned. "When you're right, you act smug."

Sean laughed. "Oh, Agent Goldberg, I was born that way.

But it gets worse. You see, in 1967, Israeli Diplomat Pinchas Lapide stated that —"

"Pius XII saved about 860,000 Jews in World War II," Goldberg said. "Father Frank told us. And that Einstein and Golda Meir both praised him for it."

Sean nodded and raised the book in his hand to show the title: *Three Popes and the Jews.* "It's all in here." He flipped open the book at random. "Page 168, Pius XII spent his *entire* family inheritance on behalf of the Jews."

Goldberg groaned and sat next to Abasi. "It's been a long day, Ryan, hurry up."

"Fine; from 1933 to 1939, there had been fifty-five Papal protests against Germany, and Secretary of State Pacelli filed each one. The Nazis even tried to talk German Cardinals against voting for Pacelli in the Papal Conclave. When Hitler invaded Poland, the end of the first month saw 214 priests executed, and 1,000 by the end of the year. When Vatican media reported it, the repressions increased so much that Archbishop Sapieha of Krakow asked the Pope to stop talking about it, 'as it only made things worse.' "

Sean nodded. "A month later, Pius XII's first encyclical, *Summi Pontificatus,* called dictatorship 'so abnormal that it is like a tumor,' and condemned everything the Nazis had done. *The New York Times* gave it a three-column, above-the-fold headline, and the French dropped 88,000 copies of it on German troops from the air for propaganda purposes. It was even praised by groups of Rabbis the week it was published, and for weeks after."

At which point even Maureen McGrail raised a brow. "That's all in Lapide?"

Sean chuckled. He lowered the book and showed a piece of paper stuck between the pages. "This is my cheat sheet.

I went through the microfiche and a few other books." He shrugged. "After *Summi Pontificatus,* Catholic persecution skyrocketed. The encyclical itself was banned from Germany – no one was to talk about it, hand it out, and anyone who read it from the pulpit was arrested.'

"In October 1940, Pius told the Bishop of Campagna to aid interned Jews. The Bishop's nephew, the police chief for the city of Fiume, give false papers to Croatian Jews who had made their way to northern Italy, sending them to his uncle's Southern Italian diocese. Pius XII gave their operation ten thousand Italian lire."

Abasi frowned with thought. "And how long did the Fiume operation last?"

"Until the police chief was thrown into a concentration camp, where he stayed until the day he died."

* * *

Shushurin and Murphy followed Father Frank, at long last, to the Vatican. They both smiled their way past the Swiss guards at the front of the Pope's office building, running as though to catch up with the tour group that had just entered.

They managed to catch up to the priest in the papal reception hall — which was designed like most rooms in the Vatican, with floors, walls, and ceiling of solid marble.

Father Frank heard a click, and stopped in the middle of the floor.

"Lieutenant!"

The priest turned to the two intelligence officers, Shushurin already holding a gun on him. "The proper designation," he said softly, "is 'Corpsman'. I'm glad to see you decided to stop playing around and talk with me. What can

I do for you?" His eyes flicked to the gun. "Stechkin? I haven't seen one of those since Iraq. I can't imagine that you're Russian, you're too good. You're not CIA, they would've just called. You're not Mossad, they don't try to use the deadly gorgeous except for a honey trap." His eyes flicked to Scott Murphy. "You're both good enough to be Mossad, but I'm betting you're the man from Israel, and you're from the *Bundesnachrichtendienst*." He waved at the gun. "Would you mind putting that away? You won't need it."

Shushurin shook her head. "We know something of what you can do. I'll feel safer holding on to this."

Father Frank laughed, and with his other hand, he whipped out a long, full rosary, wrapped it around the Stechkin, and yanked it out of Shushurin's hand, sending it to the other side of the room.

The rosary came back as Frank threw it into Shushurin's face. She deflected it as though it was a straight punch, then twisted her upper body around to put power behind a right cross. Father Frank ducked underneath and rolled across the floor, trying to get some space between them.

Shushurin rushed him in the hopes that she could close before he got to his feet. Father Frank was spryer than he looked, and threw an uppercut as he sprung up from the floor. Shushurin deflected it with her left forearm, and countered with a right elbow. The point of the elbow glanced off of his temple, and the blow spun him around, and he used the momentum to turn it onto a left backhand. She swung her left arm down like a pendulum to block it, and reacted with a right cross, smacking him across the face.

Frank Williams dropped one leg into a crouch, and kicked out with the other leg, sweeping Shushurin's legs from under her. She hit the floor and rolled away, making sure he couldn't take advantage of her predicament.

They both came to their feet at the same time, then charged each other once more.

* * *

"By 1941, the Nazis were so fed up with the Church, they suppressed the entire Catholic Press, except for 'strictly theological works.' The German Gestapo was so damned worried about the Pope they bribed officials to read the Pope's mail. Pius even stated, 'We ought to speak words of fire against the atrocities... and the only thing which restrains us, is the knowledge that words would make the fate of those wretches even worse.'"

Goldberg raised her hand to silence him. "Excuse me, but *worse?* After being gassed and cremated, nothing tops it, sorry."

Sean raised an eyebrow. "Two million Jews had been saved in shelters within Europe; you piss off the Germans, maybe they break down that convent door anyway. That's what happened in Holland in 1942 – they protested, and ended with a higher deportation rate than in any country in Western Europe. Upon hearing about Holland, the Pope put away a protest specifically condemning the Nazis, believing that if the Nazis would retaliate against civilians for the protests of bishops, they would retaliate even worse should the Pope speak out.

"Pius also knew that Adolf had a plan to kidnap him."

Goldberg laughed. "What?"

"Operation Pontiff: Hitler's plan to kidnap the Pope and occupy the Vatican. He had to be talked out of it several times by saner colleagues. Pius even signed a letter of resignation in case they wanted to use him as a puppet. He had offers of sanctuary from Ireland and Latin America, but he stayed. Even John Cornwell in *Hitler's Pope*, accused him of 'foolhardy valor' for being involved in a plot to take out Hitler."

* * *

Scott Murphy, confused and uncertain of how to intervene between Shushurin and the priest, looked for an opening Maybe he could get across the room and grab Shushurin's gun? Possible.

The two combatants fired off an attack at the same time — Shushurin kicked for his side, despite her better judgment, and he swung for her stomach, both of them caught nothing but solid muscle.

Father Frank and Shushurin stepped back briefly, and then he unleashed a left uppercut. She swept it to the side with a forearm and fired a left cross. He pushed it aside with a deflecting palm, and clamped down onto her wrist, ready to follow through when she recoiled. She stepped in instead; they grabbed each other by the lapels and by coincidence, they both head butted each other at the same time.

Murphy smiled. This was his moment. With both of them dazed and confused, he'd have a chance to grab the weapon. He was about to go for it when he felt two large hands grab him by the neck and the belt and hurl him against a wall.

Murphy bounced off the wall and fell with a *thud*. He blinked the stars out of his eyes, and looked up to see a large, graying man standing in front of him, totally ignoring his existence.

"And now," he said in a thick Russian accent, "we let your

old mentor handle this, *da*, Frank?"

Murphy blinked harder. Was *this* the man who had attacked Sean Ryan? If so, he had completely discounted Murphy as a factor — did he think he'd been knocked out?

Well, that's an advantage... so what? He's too far out of the way for my pocket knife to slash his tendons, and I can't crawl to him fast enough. Now what?

Step one, get off the floor.

* * *

Goldberg and Abasi almost leapt out of their chairs. *"What!"* they shouted.

Sean sighed. "Pius was involved in several plots against Hitler, one in 1940 when German soldiers tried to assassinate him, and in 1943." Sean chuckled. "You remember that movie with Tom Cruise? The Valkyrie plot? Pius supported that one behind the scenes. In fact, there were five plots against Hitler that we know of, and Pius XII may have been involved with all of them."

"Anyway, there was another problem with protests — they were counterproductive. Condemning Nazi propaganda only encouraged book sales. Reports from the camps said that things got worse every time the Pope spoke out. Even Mussolini said protests from the Church would have no effect on the Nazis 'because they are true pagans.' He should talk, he's Italian. They're almost all pagans." He looked to Figlia. "No offense."

Figlia laughed. "What offense? You should see the Neapolitans."

Goldberg said, "Okay, that's all very nice. But what exactly did he *do?*"

Sean stopped dead. "He ordered priests all over Europe to shelter and hide Jews from the authorities. In 1942, the Nazis believed that 'every Catholic family shelters a Jew.'"

Suddenly, Goldberg put up her hands like a football referee calling a time-out. "Okay, let's stop before we go into a Dan Brown monologue. In short Pacelli – as Pope – emptied his own personal fortune to bankroll rescue attempts, and even used hefty parts of the Vatican funds; he allowed for forged certificates and documents to get Jews out of harm's way all over Europe; he even ran a safe house in Rome itself –"

Abasi raised a finger. "Excuse me, he allowed for safe houses to be made out of Church property in Rome. That does not mean he ran them."

Goldberg arched a brow. "He *owned* Castle Gandalfo, and it could only be opened with his personal approval. That's running a safe house. Is that about the gist of this?"

"Just about."

"So, what the *hell* is going on here and now?"

* * *

Manana Shushurin looked from the Jesuit to the newcomer who identified himself as Father Frank's trainer. The former was on her right, the latter on the left.

She looked back and forth one more time and nodded to herself. "Right."

The graying newcomer attacked with a right hook. She blocked it with her left arm and spun, turning the block into a left across his face. She almost ran into Father William's left jab, but weaved around it, grabbed the left wrist and his belt, and hurled him into his partner using his own momentum.

266

The elder assailant grabbed Father Frank in mid-flight, pirouetted, and hurled him right back at her. She sidestepped the human missile, and Father Frank landed, rolling to his feet without a scratch. The other was about to take a swing at her when—

Scott Murphy leapt on the larger man's back, wrapping the Jesuit's fallen rosary like a garrote around his neck. The larger man stumbled and then threw his upper body forward, trying to throw Murphy off. Murphy let go of the rosary, and changed his hold to wrapping his right arm around the neck and his left arm around the attacker's arm.

The gray-haired man growled and threw his entire body backwards, effectively body-slamming Murphy into the marble floor. Murphy had just barely raised his head in time to avoid having the back of his skull crushed by the impact — a move that saved his head, and allowed him to bite his attacker's ear.

Shushurin turned to the Jesuit at hand, and Father Frank held his ground, not moving forward, and she waited, not eager to start again.

"There was no reason to pull a gun on me, miss," he said so softly she could barely hear him over the sound of Scott's grunting.

"I think there was. We know what you can do, and—"

"I gathered. I noticed you have similar training. I take it you were educated from birth as well?"

* * *

Figlia leaned back in his chair. "So, Father Williams was right. Everything he told us about Pius XII was true."

"Actually," Goldberg said with an almost-pout, "he underestimated it."

McGrail raised a brow, curious about what conversation they were referring to, but moved on to the point. "So Gerrity and Yousef were both killed because they read this?"

Goldberg nodded. "Even I saw the instructions were basically 'save Jews.'"

Figlia smiled. "Well, at least the field of suspects is narrower."

Abasi frowned. "Indeed." He looked to Sean. "The American Catholic Church has disagreed with everything Rome has said for forty years. Americans have disliked everything papist since your Revolution — one British 'intolerable act' against the first colonies was to allow freedom of religion to Roman Catholics in Canada. Even now, your Church has been politically silenced in America, lest they risk their tax-exempt status.

"The supposed inaction of Pius XII has been used to beat upon the dogmas of the Church, using human actions as 'proof' against natural law, an extension of divine law. Pius protested on the grounds of natural law — that we are one, no matter the flesh or the blood, and that blood itself specifically has no meaning. Catholics are against abortion, condoms and birth prevention — *also* using natural law, it is easier to just pretend, ignore, or defame Pius than to attack the principle. Attacking the Pope, disregard the teachings. Say the Church did or said nothing, and thus *they* don't have to defend *their* principles, because there is now no other way — they have already 'discredited' the Church. And that is just America."

Goldberg looked at him sideways. "Where do you come up with this?"

The Egyptian smiled. "As I said, I belong to a think tank,

and religion is important where I come from… and my wife is Catholic."

The Secret Service agent chuckled. "I suppose we should be glad *you* aren't Catholic, or we'd be here longer."

Abasi shook his head. "I *can* continue. The UN recently condemned the Catholic Church for, essentially, being Catholic – specifically, pro-Life. The Chinese have been worried that the Church would destroy them like they believe it destroyed the Soviet Union.. The same holds true for North Korea."

"Why stop there?" asked a new voice.

They turned. At the door to Figlia's office, in all of his bright, white papal vestments, stood the Pope, perfectly still in the doorway. "The Russian Orthodox Church is an arm of the Russian government — has been since the Tsars. Pius XIII looked to Abasi. "As for other suspects, you have every enemy to human rights. And remember, al-Qaeda sent someone to kill my predecessor, John Paul II."

"And that is just, as Americans say, the short list," Figlia added thoughtfully. "The long answer is anyone with a grudge."

McGrail turned her body towards the Pope, and cocked her head. "You've been thinking 'bout this fer a while, haven't ya?"

He smiled. "My darling detective, I'm the Pope." The smile disappeared. "My people are killed in the Sudan, Latin America, China, Libya, Lebanon, in places no one even suspects — Toronto, London, Long Island." His lips tightened, and his fists squeezed so tightly the knuckles threatened to turn white. "I think about this every, blessed, day."

Sean nodded solemnly. "A great tragedy… but do you mean—"

Figlia's phone rang, he answered. After a moment, he dropped the phone. "There's a problem downstairs. Ryan, McGrail, with me."

* * *

The man Scott Murphy wrestled with was tired of this. In a feat of strength Murphy could never have imagined, he pushed to his feet — Murphy still on his back — and dropped forward, this time throwing the Mossad agent across the room. Murphy landed on his back and slid across the floor. He barely even saw the older man as he looked around for something — anything — to use.

And then he found it.

Murphy frantically grabbed the weapon and stood, Shushurin's fallen Stechkin in hand. "Now who the hell are you... two?" He stared at the newcomer, looking at him for the first time. "Captain?"

The gray-haired man nodded, then peered at him for a moment. He cleared his throat In a perfect American accent, he asked, "Mr. Murphy, isn't it?"

The Mossad agent nodded, the gun level on the "Captain's" chest. "I take it the Jebbie is related to you?"

"He's my son." Captain Wayne Williams, U.S. Army Rangers (ret.) smiled. He was about 5'9", with blue-green eyes, and an odd intermingling of silver, iron gray, and fringes of gold in his hair. He had broad shoulders, and at the moment looked like he was about to break Murphy in two.

Shushurin slowly backed away from the priest, moving towards Murphy's side. "You know him?"

Murphy frowned. "We're professionally acquainted."

At that point, Sean Ryan, Giovanni Figlia, Wilhelmina

270

Goldberg and Hashim Abasi all ran into the room in order, weapons drawn, Maureen McGrail behind them.

Sean looked at the Mossad agent, his partner, the priest, then—"Who the hell are you?"

Father Frank looked over his shoulder at Sean. "He's my backup for this mission."

Sean nodded. "Scott, put the gun down."

Murphy glared at him. "Why the hell should I? These people haven't exactly been playing nice."

The Pope walked in behind Abasi. "Murphy, put down that pistol before you shoot yourself."

Sean looked over his shoulder at the Bishop of Rome. "You know him?"

Murphy lowered the gun. "Josh? You have something to do with this?"

Pope Pius XIII nodded. "Father Williams works for me, Mr. Murphy, just like you do." He put his hands behind his back and walked into the middle of the room, speaking to all assembled. "As you all may have guessed by now, Bishop O'Brien is the executive officer of the Vatican intelligence service, a special branch that trains with real intelligence agencies. Officially, I'm in charge of the *de facto* intelligence network, and he is just a bishop." The Pope then smiled. "However, while XO is the current head of intelligence, I used to be involved as well."

Goldberg, who felt like she had been thrust knee-deep into a spy game from hell, lowered her weapon. "And, what, you're in charge of Mossad, too?"

He spared her a glance and shook his head. "Not at all. Before I became Pope, I became the first chief of Mossad's 'Goyim Brigade.' Technically, I Vatican's intelligence network, and aided Brigade. Mossad thought it would be useful to have a Catholic coordinate their many myriad Christians. I was in Rome then, I had international contacts, and they were certain I would not stab them in the back. The position later went to XO." The Pope looked around the room, positioned between the three former combatants and the new arrivals. "And here we are."

Sean cautiously lowered his weapon and added, "I managed to drag *some* of this out of Father Frank earlier, though he told me to keep quiet. Apparently, Ashid Yousef came to make a case that Catholics should unite with al-Qaeda against 'the Jews.' What he saw in the archives changed his mind. He'd probably make announcements on Al-Jazeera, and lead an old-fashioned jihad against the Church."

Abasi craned his neck towards Sean. "Since the Western media pays more attention to Al-Jazeera than the Pope, that broadcast would be spread over the planet, which would have ruffled the feathers of a lot of people. Once he reported what he had found, he had to die."

The Pope nodded, and drifted towards Murphy. "That is what we believe. As for Dr. Gerrity, no one knows why he was killed. We've had other scholars read the archives — they've published again, but not on this subject, not that we've seen. Why Gerrity?"

"For the same reason the hit man who shot him was taken out by the bomb," Goldberg answered. She looked to Figlia. "Something on Gerrity's laptop got both Gerrity and Clementi killed, right? So, anyone who knows about what's in the archive *and* raises a fuss is a dead man. What did Gerrity find?"

Scott Murphy checked his watch. "Nobody knows. Trust me. I've been listening to all of you discuss the damn thing since yesterday. Now, I haven't eaten anything but meal bars since I got up this morning, and Father Williams dragged us kicking and screaming all over Rome. If we're going to continue this, can we at least order food and settle down somewhere?"

The Pope stopped in front of Murphy and put his hand out for the gun. Murphy handed it over and the Pope gave it to Shushurin. "You fill them in on the rest."

"What rest?" Goldberg asked.

Murphy nodded at the Pope as he departed, then looked to the Secret Service Agent. "Obviously, I was sent because of Yousef." He moved toward Shushurin's side. He touched her arm with a questioning look, and she nodded, indicating she was okay. He looked back to Goldberg. "My associates wanted to tail Mr. Abasi, but given his history, I knew it was more likely he'd be here to investigate the incident."

Abasi shrugged. "What do you want me to say? I didn't even hear Yousef was in the city until after I arrived."

Murphy cringed, then snapped his fingers. "Darn."

Goldberg studied the father and the priest. "And he was backing *you* up, Father. You were point man on Giacomo Clementi because he was a not-so-former terrorist, and you could probably break him if he tried something."

Shushurin nodded. "That's what we figured as well." She turned to the priest. "Is that what you earned the medals for?"

The priest's father laughed. "Let me tell you a story."

CHAPTER XVIII: A PIUS VETERAN

After the father of Frank Williams finished explaining a little bit of his son's history, they settled down in Giovanni Figlia's office.

Goldberg frowned at Captain Wayne. "What's with the funny accents?"

Wayne smiled. "I enjoy them."

Frank said, "He merely prefers to talk like Boris Badenov."

Abasi laughed. "Is this what the Vatican call spies now?"

Father Frank locked his violet eyes onto Abasi. "I am *not* a spy," he replied quietly. "My father here, Army Ranger that he is, trained me to go into the family business, and Special Forces took me in. When I joined the Jesuits, Bishop XO noted me and took me into the proactive intelligence unit."

Sean Ryan, propped up against the wall, said with a smile, "Let me guess, the Templars?"

Father Williams nodded, raising the ring on his left hand for the others to see. "Good, you noticed. They used to protect pilgrims to the Holy Land, so they seemed the obvious choice, since we're meant to protect parishioners in *un*holy lands. I'm more of an emergency situations agent."

274

Giovanni Figlia laughed. "Ah, *bene, bene...*" He smiled at Frank for a moment, allowing some pieces to come together. Abasi had mentioned several times that whoever stole the forensics report about the Gerrity crime scene was more likely interested in knowledge — and was most likely a third party who had nothing to do with the killings. "By the way, Father Williams, did you find the evidence book interesting reading?"

Father Frank smiled sheepishly. "Yes, it was. Sorry about hitting you, though. I did not want to blow my cover until it was absolutely necessary. May I ask exactly why you and your colleague came after me?"

Murphy and Shushurin, seated together, exchanged a look. Murphy shrugged, then leaned back in his chair, settling in. "We figured the attack on Ryan was too convenient. He gets attacked after bringing up some sort of Soviet super-soldiers. Then, here *you* are, able to beat the heck out of people, and you're just a priest. All of the information we had on Pius XII says he committed crimes during the Holocaust, and that all those researching him or having firsthand knowledge *about* him have been dying lately. In addition, we ruled out everyone else who knew Ryan's theory — Goldberg is Secret Service, my people knew Abasi, Figlia was being shot at, as was Maureen. The only person who hadn't been targeted was you."

Father Frank Williams shrugged. "Because I am never noticed. They shot at the van I was in, but only because it was another armored van. What about yourselves? Have you been attacked?"

Murphy raised an eyebrow, but it was a reasonable query. XO could vouch for him, but paranoia was a necessary lifestyle choice. He tensed briefly, then leaned back in the chair and laid his arm around Shushurin. "Not unless you count my friend here shooting the attackers on the Spanish Steps, drawing fire from you people."

Frank smiled slightly. "I thought the *bella donna* looked familiar." He saw the way both of them were seated — they had individual chairs, but they had both moved them until they were touching — their easy air around each other, and the way Murphy had his arm around her shoulders. "How long have you two been together?"

"We just met yesterday. Why?"

Goldberg and McGrail smiled, both seeing what the priest had seen, and the Secret Service agent was surprised that he had seen it.

The priest waved it away. "Just asking."

Father Frank nodded thoughtfully. "Speaking of which, I found your fighting style equal to my own, and I've had nearly lifelong training due to my father. Who trained you, miss? If I am correct about your employer, then you are German. I can only assume—"

Captain Wayne cut him off, clamping a hand on his son's shoulder. "Sorry, my son's long-winded. What he means is: did your father work for KGB or *Stasi*, and if he did, did he put you into a spy training program for children?"

Shushurin straightened imperceptibly, and her hand tensed on Murphy's.

Murphy sighed gently. "Sorry, we're not dealing with stupid people."

She leaned back in the chair, attempting to relax. She closed her eyes, trying to figure out exactly how much information she could safely give out. She felt a tender squeeze from Murphy's hand, and she opened her eyes again, meeting Murphy's. He smiled at her, and she returned the look.

Shushurin finally nodded to Wayne. "Yes… but, if you want to go into histories, why not Mr. Abasi's? Murphy says Mossad knows him, but I sort through information to send Israel, and I know that Abasi here personally stoned his wife to death for adultery several years ago, making him, in my opinion, the perfect possible partner for Ashid Yousef."

Wilhelmina Goldberg, sitting right next to Abasi, moved three inches down the couch, and readjusted herself so she could grab her gun easier. Maureen McGrail tensed in her chair. Sean Ryan calmly undid his holster strap. Giovanni Figlia reached into his desk for his gun, and even Father Williams tensed slightly.

Goldberg turned in her chair to face him, and crossed her arms — putting her right hand next to her gun. "Is that true? I thought you married an Irish girl working down in your neck of the woods."

Murphy raised his hand to stall anyone from shooting Abasi. "I can explain. Get your hands off the guns. Mr. Abasi here is an honorary member of the Goyim Brigade."

Goldberg — and the rest of the room — turned. *"What?"* she snapped.

Murphy smiled, then caught Shushurin's look of shock. "We bought that suit for him in Tel Aviv, and he's been on our side since we helped his mother with her husband."

Goldberg blinked, then gave a sharp smile. "I thought he might have made that up."

Murphy shook his head. "Not a chance. His father tossed his baby sister away, literally; we helped his wife tinker with a suicide vest he was to give to Hamas. Abasi met his wife, Maria King, when she started her charity work in Egypt as one of the Irish abroad. She went abroad, in part, to get away from certain Irish factions in Belfast who wanted to kill her.

I forget why, but growing up Catholic in Belfast can get you killed for all sorts of reasons. The Provisional IRA wanted to kill her in Egypt, and they kept getting closer. When she was wounded by the IRA during the 'Arab Spring'" – he rolled his eyes at the term – "Hashim contacted us to help him get her out. We staged a stoning for the benefit of the Provos, and made her disappear."

The room gaped at Murphy, except for Abasi. Goldberg let her hands drop to her sides, her pistol forgotten. Sean even snapped the clasp on his closed on his holster.

Abashi shrugged. "Yes. And after several weeks being taught makeup by Mossad officers, I now have a good Muslim woman… who happens to be the exact size and shape of my last wife, who also works with charity."

Murphy looked to Shushurin. "Sorry, Mani. It wasn't my place to discuss it. My superiors keep things very close to the vest; they generally do not like telling things to the goyim that *work* for them, to heck with the ones that don't."

"I'm always free with the information I've given you," Bishop Xavier O'Brien objected as he walked into the office, a trail of smoke following after him. He pulled out another cigarette. "It's just that we're highly compartmentalized. You *get* information. You're not supposed to need more than you've been given."

Murphy laughed. "You're kidding, right? The only information I was given this time was 'Meet your contact in Rome.' That was *it*. I've gotten more information from this beautiful spy than home base. I ask about Pinchas Lapide, the Yad Vashem files — nothing! Both seem are classified up the wazoo, and for the life of me I can't figure out why. Can you?"

The current head of Vatican Intelligence and official executive officer of the Goyim Brigade shook his head before taking a seat in front of the door. "Once I heard you asked for it, I put in a request to read the file and find out what all the fuss was about. I can't seem to find or get access to it. You'd pretty much need a strike team to get to it, but I wouldn't recommend it unless you had the 82nd Airborne. Even then, I wouldn't want to be you in the following years."

Murphy scoffed. "Yes, my coworkers do have this tendency to kill people who piss them off."

"Excuse me," Goldberg said, slowly drawing out her gun. Her hazel eyes flicked over to Manana Shushurin, and she carefully brushed back a blonde strand of hair. She rested the pistol on her hip, the barrel pointed at Shushurin. "Did anyone not remember what was said about thirty seconds ago? This *shiksa* was *trained by the KGB,* and you *schlemiels* seem unable to hold onto this thought long enough to ask about it? What, you all have ADD?"

Manana Shushurin smiled slyly, ignoring the gun. "I am German, and therefore I am a Nazi?" Her eyes flicked to the top of Goldberg's head. "Funny. You're the one with the blonde hair."

"They're. Just. Highlights," the Secret Service agent ground out from between gritted teeth.

Murphy nodded slowly, and cautiously stood, moving himself between Shushurin and Goldberg. His dark blue eyes seemed black, and his facial muscles were tight with controlled anger — as tight as his voice, "Sure. *Let's* also discuss a few things — like that Mani here saved your asses back at the Steps, even before Father Secret Agent Man showed up." He took a step forward, moving closer to the gun. "*She* came to *my people* about Ashid Yousef's death and the Vatican connection." Another step. "*She* saved Ryan's life during

279

the shootout — she could have capped Sean in the back of the head, or simply let him die."

Murphy closed the distance once more, the gun mere inches from his crotch. "She could have killed me *any* time in the last thirty-six hours, taken out Sean, and most of the people in this room. Hell, exempting the clergy and Captain Williams, she's saved the lives of every *one* of you, *at, least, once.*"

Goldberg looked up at him, her gun not moving. "And she just *happens* to have been trained by the same people who are trying to kill us? That's an accident to you?"

Murphy's eyes narrowed. "These people are world-class killers, almost unequaled. Who *else* are you going to hire to topple an organization two thousand years old, with a billion members?"

Goldberg glared right back at him. "Are you done?"

Murphy nodded, but didn't move.

Xavier O'Brien slid the cigarette over to one side of his mouth and let it practically dangle there. "Now that the melodrama is over, I'll answer Agent Goldberg's initial question. Unlike Scott, I can push for information when needed. Manana is an exceptional agent when she's called for, and she's sent more interesting and valuable information to Israel than practically anyone else in her position. She's not politically popular. There have been no exceedingly large deposits into her bank accounts. She's not rich or anything like what you would expect from a woman on the make. Sorry, but she doesn't win the door prize on the terrorist lottery. Anyway, the Pope wanted me to have food sent up. It's been a long day, and you all still haven't killed each other yet. That's cause for some nice Chianti."

Scott Murphy let out a relaxed breath and moved back

to the chair, next to Shushurin. "While I think of it, maybe we should ask how anyone found out about Sean's theory in time to attack him."

Shushurin nodded as though the entire previous conversation hadn't even happened. "And while *I* think of it, who were you talking with, Father Williams? The one you stopped with today?"

Frank blinked, almost bemused. "Him? No one important. Just a weekly penitent. He prefers a more informal setting than churches. It helps him talk more freely."

Shushurin nodded, thought a moment. "So, that only leaves how they knew about Sean's theory *without* an insider."

Sean shrugged. "I suppose it's possible that they were watching to see who came out that they could pick off. I mean, we've run out of suspects. Can even Mr. Paranoid Mossad Person agree that the Pope isn't a suspect?"

Murphy looked to his boss. "I don't know. Can I?"

Bishop O'Brien nodded. "I think so."

"I am so glad you think I am innocent," came the thick accented voice of Pius XIII. He sidestepped into the doorway, directly behind XO.

Commandatore Figlia sighed. "*Per favore,* Your Holiness, can you stop being so quiet?"

Pius XIII waved it away. "I like hearing what my clergy say about me." He looked around the room and closed the door behind him. He noted Captain Wayne. "Frank's father?"

Wayne smiled. "No, he's the father, I'm just the dad."

"Ah, of course. You also worked with Mr. Mossad?"

Goldberg raised her hand. "Excuse me, but what is this 'Mr. Mossad' business?"

The Pope glanced her way. "That is his name, Scott 'Mossad' Murphy, as opposed to your infamous John 'Taliban' Walker."

Scott Murphy winced. He had kept at least his name safe. Now he'd been outed by the *Pope?*

"Charming," Goldberg murmured.

Sean interjected, "To get back to the topic of a few minutes ago, it looks like everyone is cleared of being a spy ..."

Sean Ryan looked at the agents from the BND, Interpol, Mossad, Vatican Intelligence, the Vatican's Central Office of Vigilance, the Secret Service, the Egyptian police force, and quickly said, "Well, no one's a spy working for the *bad guys,* anyway." He smiled. "Does anyone else feel like we've assembled the *Avengers?*"

Goldberg growled. "But we're no closer to who the enemy is. It's not like they signed their names or left a card. We have an Italian assassin meeting with Father Williams in one week and a different silver-haired priest the next — given that a man with the same hair color attacked Sean—"

"We can assume that they are all the same person," Abasi concluded.

* * *

Ioseph Andrevich Mikhailov loaded his weapon. He checked his watch, then turned to his men.

"Our 'Little Gentleman' will be a little slow this evening, so we can all take off. When I hear back from our insider, I'll notify you of your assignments based on the intel I get. We'll move within the next day or two. They've either come to the wrong conclusion, or they're on to us. It doesn't matter. Either way, it's too late for them to do anything. All that matters is that we do what we came to do.

"We will kill the Pope."

* * *

Sean nodded at Abasi's statement. "That's a good guess." He looked at his watch. "I suppose that it's time we all get the heck out of here. I don't know about the rest of you, but I'm starved."

Goldberg laughed a little, and the others all turned to her. She blinked, then noted the attention. She smirked ruefully. "I was hoping for a slightly more dramatic reveal, but I suppose that now is as good a time as any."

For once, for the first time in what felt like weeks, everyone in the room but Wilhelmina Goldberg looked confused. She gave a pleasant sigh. "Well, this is far more enjoyable than being left in the dust by all of you. I'm not a spy, or a bodyguard, or a tactician. I'm a researcher, a computer geek."

Giovanni Figlia slumped back into his chair, clearing his throat. He had been tired of everyone running roughshod over his office for the past thirty-six hours. "Agent Goldberg, if you do not mind, *per favore,* I do not want you to turn into Signor Ryan on us."

Sean started and blinked, as though being awoken from a deep sleep. "Excuse me?"

Abasi raised his fist to his mouth and cleared his throat, stifling a laugh. "You were a little, um… over dramatic during your presentation of research."

McGrail snickered. "Wasn't it more like melodramatic and over-delivered?"

Goldberg cut in before she was talked to death. "I figured I'd save the best for last. You see, I came across a name in the archives that just smacks of irony — the authorization of funds for a mission led by a James Ryan." Goldberg laughed at it, and even Figlia gave a relaxed grin.

In fact, everyone smiled — except for Sean.

A voice cold enough to frighten the damned souls in the ninth circle of Hell said, "Say that again."

Goldberg stopped laughing and blinked. "There was an authorization note for funds backing a trip for someone named James Ryan."

Sean straightened, and he reached for his cell phone like some would reach for a weapon. He calmly flipped open the cell. He looked to the Pope and O'Brien. "Who hired me?"

The Pope and the head of the Office of Vigilance exchanged a glance. Figlia answered. "The Pacelli family is paying for you—"

"I *know* that," Sean interjected. "I said *who* hired me. Why was I hired?"

Figlia leaned back in his chair. "Again, the Pacellis. You came highly recommended—"

Sean jabbed the cell in his direction like a knife. "*Why* did they want *me?*"

Figlia blinked, mouth open. "You know, I had not thought of that."

The Pope shrugged. "We had assumed that your reputation preceded you."

Sean blinked. "Son of a bitch," he muttered, mostly to himself. "They didn't want me because of my reputation; there are plenty of people on the continent. Why get an American? Because they know my family, they've dealt with us before. The *Pacelli* family knows someone in *my* family."

Wilhelmina Goldberg nodded slowly, thinking that Sean had completely lost his mind — assuming he ever had much of it to start with. "Um, okay, that's good," she said in the voice the Secret Service used when dealing with the deranged. "I'm sure the Pope can call them. Isn't that right, sir?"

"Don't bother," Sean Ryan snapped as he dialed. "I know exactly who it is — there's only one option that makes any sense. That's why they came after me before. These buggers didn't come after me just because I knew something. They came after me because I know someone who does."

Abasi nodded slowly, not certain whether or not Goldberg's assessment was off. "That's good. Who?"

Sean raised his cell phone to his ear. "Villie said it before, James Ryan… my grandfather." Sean waited a few rings. "I was going to call him before I was shot at, since his resume is—"

* * *

The sirens passed by his house, and he sighed, remembering things past.

James Sherman Ryan had hit eighty-five not too long ago, and was fast approaching death, as he liked to put it. The old man was of medium height and build for a younger man, and amazingly strong for one of his age. His face was heavily crinkled with smile lines, and his electric blue eyes twinkled under the airport lights. His hair was solid gray, as if the last of the color hung on for dear life. His limbs were spindly but his torso was thick, bordering on bulky. Most of the muscles weren't as firm as they once were, and he had a noticeable limp from a war wound involving shrapnel.

He had moved to London five years before to try and remember some of the oddness of his youth after the war. The days in the Office of Strategic Services had been fun, and far more dangerous than he had been allowed to tell. There were things he did and people he killed that he still wasn't allowed to reveal, in part because he had performed operations with members of the British SAS, and thus under the British Official Secrets Act, which put him under a vow of silence until the year 2045.

But the British weren't all that bad, certainly not half as bad as the French. He had spent time in Paris after freeing the city. The Parisians had been spitting on him and the other American soldiers. Everyone claimed to be part of the resistance, and many of them really had no problem walking people to the death camps, loading them on trains for somewhere else.

The memories of London were far friendlier, especially since he met his wife there, producing little Clarence Ryan, not to mention finding his movie career after the war. He wasn't all that thrilled that his son had gone into Holly-wierd like he had — by that time, Hollywood had become filled with rejects from the Communist Party, and the Screen Actors Guild had paychecks drawn from Moscow.

But at least here is nice. He reached over to his nightstand, opened the drawer, and pulled out his Colt 1911A .45, his constant companion since the war, cleaned daily, and fired at least once every month.

The gun was still in his hand when the phone rang. "Hello?" he answered.

Half a continent away, Sean turned away from the rest of the room, head bowed as he concentrated on the call. "Hi, Granddad, how're you doing?"

James blinked. "I was about to hit the sack... Sean, right? Not your dad... What's the matter? You said you'd be out of touch for a while."

Sean smiled. "You served in the OSS, right?"

Silence. "I was in the operations division. Why?"

"Were you ever in Italy? I'm in Rome right now, and there's something that involves a man named Lapide, Pius XII and—"

"I'll be on the first plane."

Sean wasn't shocked by the reaction, but just nodded. "Gotcha. Before you hang up! Watch your back, there are people dying over this."

After a moment, James Sherman Ryan laughed. "Sean! Of course they are, you're involved! Anything else?"

"Only if you knew an Israeli diplomat named Lapide."

It was at that point that the door of James' bedroom smashed in. There was death, smoke, and the smell of gun smoke in the air within seconds.

* * *

Sean A.P. Ryan looked at the cell phone in his hands as the line exploded in gunfire. He blinked, caught with the look of a stunned deer. The gunshots were loud enough that he needed to jerk the phone away from his head, and even the others in the office could hear through the receiver.

And then it went dead.

Sean hit redial, ignoring the others, hoping that by ignoring them, he could reach his grandfather by sheer force of will. After the ninth ring, he turned to the others. "Everyone grab a phone. I'll tell you what to dial. Whoever gets through first, wins."

Everyone stared at him a moment, looking as though he had grown six feet and sprouted horns. He narrowed his eyes into slits. "Now, dammit!"

* * *

The phone rang in the London home of James Sherman Ryan, war hero and actor, and there was no answer in the dead silence after the gun battle, such as it was — however, there was no contest between four heavily-armed and well-trained assassins versus one old World War II vet with a handgun. The faint smell of gunshot residue hung in the air, and a body was atop the phone, gun still clasped in its cold dead hand. After a moment, a survivor decided to answer, and picked it up.

"Hello?" he grumbled, disguising his voice.

"Hello, is this James Ryan?"

"Um, yes." He didn't recognize the voice. Was this just a telemarketer with bad timing? "And you are?"

"I'm Superintendent Maureen McGrail, Interpol, aren't I calling on behalf of your grandson? Are you all right?"

"Tell Sean that this old man still knows how to take care of himself."

"Granddad," came Sean's voice, "you okay?"

He blinked for a moment, uncertain of what to do. He cleared this throat, and James Sherman Ryan spoke with his normal voice. "I blew the bastards away — they hit my bedroom, emptied enough bullets to shred my mattress, but I was in the room across the hall, in the guest room I use for storage! I stepped in and fired with my old .45; I think I got three out of four before they even noticed me. Can you imagine? They only sent four, and after I took on an entire squad of Nazi bastards with my Thompson, a box of hand grenades and an anti-tank Piet. Maybe I should've showed them my Congressional Medal of Honor before I blew them all to hell, eh? Ha!"

It was times like this that merely affirmed Sean's belief that a lot of genes skipped a generation between James and himself. "I'm surprised they didn't see it themselves before going after you — they knew me and my patent disrespect for national landmarks. They were waiting for me at one point, like they knew I'd be there."

"Ah well, don't worry about it, I beat those bastards back like disobedient dogs. I'll be down there, don't worry about it. See you soon. Bye." He hung up, looked at the bodies in his bedroom. "Maybe I should call the cops before I go. They're not going to like this, no, not at all. Heck, I think they're still on my case for *the last* time this happened... maybe I should've told Sean about that, too."

* * *

Sean gently lowered the phone, letting out a breath. "Anyway," he said, speaking as though nothing had happened, "I've left out a bit of info. My grandfather served in Rome in World War II as part of the OSS. He's flying in tomorrow, and he can fill us all in from there."

Murphy said, "Great. In that case, we can do some of that thinking later. Maybe all of you can tell me exactly what you know about the Pope — Pius XII, I mean."

Goldberg laughed. "You're going to want a seat."

CHAPTER XIX: A PIUS PLAN

Hours later, Scott Murphy nearly fell into the chair in his hotel room. "Well, it looks like Pius XII is going to be canonized after all."

"Looks that way," Shushurin agreed, taking her shirt off.

Murphy blinked, noted the black bra, and quickly reverted to looking at her eyes only.

She caught his quick, reflexive action, and laughed. "Are you always this cautious?"

"Well," Murphy said. He slid down in the seat. His head came to rest on the back of the chair, looking at the ceiling. He tried to make it look casual, but it was obvious he was uncomfortable. "I'd generally at least appreciate your form, but I try not to do that with women who can shoot me. No offense."

She smiled, grabbed her gun, and put it on the nightstand next to the bed. "None taken. Besides, I get leered at every day, and hell, I can strip naked and not mind — that's the training. Learn to not mind being naked before the enemy, because stripping you naked to shame you is a common interrogation tactic."

Murphy chuckled as he studied a crack in the ceiling.

"Yes, but I should theoretically have more respect for you than an interrogator, right?"

"I'd certainly hope so. But then again, if I found someone who respected me, I wouldn't be single." Shushurin paused for a moment. "All right, but the rest of them are married."

He laughed and finally let himself look at her, keeping his eyes locked above her neck. "Well, I've got some vacation time coming up soon enough, if you want to… what is that phrase? Oh, yes, 'have some coffee sometime.' " He stopped and laughed. "Wow, I can't ever say that with a straight face."

She arched an eyebrow. "And you're a spy?"

"That's what they tell me."

Shushurin lightly laughed. She unhooked the bra and casually slipped on a t-shirt. He jerked himself away from her, fumbled for his pipe next to him.

"You *are* easy, aren't you?" she asked from behind him.

He looked up, sensing it was safe, and then smiled awkwardly. Shushurin was wearing only her black underwear and a t-shirt that said "Shuck me, suck me, eat me raw," and under it said "(New Orleans Oysters)."

He laughed. "Cute shirt."

Shushurin did a mock-sigh. "I'm so glad I'm not trying to seduce you — it would be an act of utter frustration."

He gave a self-depreciating smile. "Probably. Then again, if you did, I'd probably die from either shock or delight."

Shushurin laughed. "You really are a little weird. But you're cute anyway."

"So I've been told by an extremely reliable and attractive source," he looked at his watch, "about thirty hours ago."

She did the math in her head and stretched out on the bed. "Give or take."

He let his eyes wander briefly over her body, part in ap-

291

preciation, partly in analysis, and found she was an enhanced stereotype of every romance novel known to man: long legs, good measurements, flawless face, soft skin, and from what he could tell, a very trim stomach. She didn't have full lips, but they were thick enough to exist without being thin.

In short, she really should have been breaking hearts in high school, not arms. Well, I hope she wasn't doing that literally, though with her training she might have been.

Murphy noted that she had made certain her gun was between her and the door before she lay down — leaving the side of the bed away from the door free for him. *Still trying to protect the poor little spy, are we?*

He gave his next move some thought, figuring he should stay fully dressed, just in case something went bump in the night, so he could easily move while Shushurin bumped right back at them.

Murphy placed his pipe on his nightstand, slipped off his shoes, and slipped onto the covers next to her. He looked at her for a long moment. He could feel her next to him – feel her body heat, smell her delightful perfume, and felt his heartbeat accelerate.

I should have stayed in the chair. This is too close to temptation. "What do you intend to do with me?"

Shushurin turned onto her side, propping her head on one hand. Her smile was amused, and her eyes twinkled. "What do you mean?"

Murphy mirrored her body posture, and leaned in a little, his voice little more than a whisper. "Considering how I woke up, I thought I should ask what would happen tonight."

Her smile grew, and her eyes flared dramatically. "What do you *want* to happen?"

Scott Murphy looked into her eyes, and found that they

had caught the lamps in such a way that her eyes sparkled with a thousand points of light, each one like a tiny star. His heart beat picked up, and he was worried that she would be able to hear it in the silence of the hotel room.

They were too close. He knew that. It was right in the back of his head, alerting him to losing composure – even losing control – during a mission. He was there *for a job,* not to get a date, not to get lucky, to just show up, figure out what was going on, and *leave.* And now, he was too close. He was on a bed that was so broad, if they were at the opposite sides, she couldn't even touch him with her big toe. And now, they were within breathing distance.

Murphy had so many conflicting emotions, he couldn't figure out if he admired her for her mind and skills, or because she was just that breathtakingly beautiful he wanted her body.

After a few breaths, tasting her scent, he realized that he didn't want her body. He wanted *her,* plain and simple.

What did he want to happen? So many things. Not one of them was a good idea.

He cleared his throat. The safe route was evasion. "You seemed a little concerned before when they figured out what you were."

Those points of light dimmed. It seemed that he had successfully killed the moment. Murphy's guts twisted that he had to do that.

Shushurin rolled away from him, onto her back, and she went to look at the ceiling. "Maybe a handful in the upper chain of command of the BND knows about me. Everyone else thinks my last name is fake – that I'm probably a NOC. But *those* people met me for thirty seconds and knew. If I've been that transparent, then—"

Without thinking, Murphy reached out and gently touched her shoulder. He knew instantly that it was a bad move. Her skin was sift and smooth, and warm, and reaching out to her brought him closer, and her breathed deeply.

He swallowed and gave her a little squeeze. "You were outed by the Williams family. They're about six generations of spooks, so they're genetically meant to see everything."

Shushurin laid her hand on his, and slid along his arm, rolling towards him. "You sure?"

He leaned forward and kissed her on the forehead. "Don't worry about it."

Her eyes began to sparkle once more. Murphy leaned in and kissed her on the tip of her nose. He lingered close to her, taking in the feel of her skin, the nearness of her body, and Murphy thought, *Oh Hell, why not?*

Murphy darted forward and kissed her. Her arm wrapped around his waist and drew him into her, pulling him against her. His hand slid down her back, along her shirt, and stopped just at the hem. Murphy's hand bunched into a fist to move the hem up her spine, and his hand slid under her shirt, pressing gently against the small of her back. Shushurin's breath hitched, and her fingers curled, and she racked lightly down his back, sending pleasant sensations shooting all along his nervous system.

Murphy gasped into her mouth, and hugged her closer to him as he rolled his upper body onto hers. He used his other hand to support his weight and not crush her, even though his kiss became more forceful.

Shushurin moaned into the kiss, her hand sliding up to the back of his head, keeping him in the kiss. Her other hand slid under his body, diving into his pants, wrapping around to grab his butt. His hips shot forward, pressing him against

294

her stomach. She gave another, deeper moan of appreciation, and pressed his legs open just enough for her own leg to meet him.

Murphy moved down to her chin, and then kissed along her jaw line. When he got to her ear, he whispered, "We're probably going to want to tone that down in a minute."

Shushurin gasped as he nuzzled her neck, and she pressed her leg gently against him. "Tell that to the rest of your body."

Murphy kissed her neck one more time, causing her to make a cute whimper, and stopped. He sighed, then growled in frustration. He took his hand off her back, placing that on the mattress, and pushed up, pulling back from her. "You're probably going to hate me for this, but not half as much as I'm gonna."

Shushurin's eyes narrowed, and she cocked her head slightly. His hand hadn't wandered anywhere that wouldn't have been covered by a bathing suit. There was only a thin t-shirt between him and her, and he stopped. "You're serious?"

Murphy closed his eyes tightly, and slowly moved his leg off of hers. "Oh, I'm serious about what I would really, *really* like to do with you right now. But we seriously have to stop. You have no idea how much I wish I didn't."

Shushurin's brows furrowed, confused. "Why?"

One corner of his mouth came up in a self-deprecating little half smile. "I'm still Catholic, and we ain't married. And? We've known each other a whole thirty hours."

She gave him a cynical little smile that made parts of him lurch. "That usually doesn't stop most people."

Murphy slowly pulled his hand back, the tips of his fingers grazing along her stomach as he pulled away. "I know. I try not to be like most people. Better control." He chuckled.

"Damn it."

She sighed, and placed her hand on his cheek. She wanted to pull him in and molest him. "I really wish I could rape you right now."

He shook his head. "Sorry, not possible."

Murphy shifted positions so he was merely hugging her, his forehead against hers so he could look deep into her eyes. "You realize that I'm not casually interested in you, right?"

"I know," she said playfully, "you said no one else has been interested."

He chuckled softly. "True, but I've also never been as motivated to try for someone as much as I want... you. I don't want your body..." He blinked, frowned, and bunched up his mouth. "Okay, I do want your body, but mostly because it's attached to the rest of you. I like the way you think. I like that you can keep up with me on a pure spy craft level."

"But we've only known each other thirty hours," Shushurin finished. She sighed, annoyed.

"If you don't mind," he continued, "we should probably stop."

"Then why did you start?"

"Well, I've been with you nonstop for two days, and you were never really down until ..." he looked at his watch, "an hour and a half ago." He smiled goofily. "I like you happy."

Shushurin smiled gently. "Be careful," she said in a teasing tone, "philosophers defined love as wanting someone to be happy and seeing to it."

He leaned up and kissed her lips lightly. "Duly noted," he said in a whisper.

* * *

The next morning, Ioseph Mikhailov looked around at the men gathered. It was a significant portion of his force currently in Rome, but to pull off the actual mission, he didn't need any of them. The problem was, as they say, getting away with it — and that was what they were all there for.

Nikita, still wearing the black priest's outfit that had come in so handy, waited patiently. For some reason, Mikhailov's son had gone unnaturally silver at an early age. Given his son's build, and the way he carried himself — as they all did, like trained killers — he bore a great resemblance to Father Francis Williams. Granted, anyone who looked closely for more than a bare moment would be able to tell instantly who it really was, but Nikita had always been fast.

"Now that we know what they have in mind for this morning," he started, "we'll be moving in early for advance work. We're not going to have any problems this time. If for any reason we get cut off, I want you to all proceed as planned." He looked to his son. "Nikita, I want you to hang back, outside the perimeter, in case something goes wrong. You'll be our path out of there."

* * *

James Sherman Ryan exited the airport, suitcase in hand. He scanned the airport parking lot for a moment before he spotted exactly the people he wanted — he could tell because they had so much armor they had to be friends of his grandson. All of the cars were Fully Armored Vehicles, the kind favored by civilians with a lot of cash and even more enemies.

In this case, this "civilian" was the official leader of about a billion Catholics on the planet (unofficially, the numbers who actually *listened* to the Pope were such that those on the fourth floor of the Vatican didn't want to think about it).

The first FAV stopped directly in front of him and the door swung open.

"Hello," Sean told him, "welcome to Rome."

* * *

Ioseph Andrevich Mikhailov smiled at the kind nun who had offered to be their tour guide through the papal audience hall. She smiled back as she went on in intricate detail about what felt like every square inch of marble.

Of course, no one paid the group any mind. Not really. It was just another group of tourists– just a group of "monks." They were wearing full brown robes and all of them were cowled, because a full robe covered a multitude of guns. The only Swiss Guard they had found so far was walking along with the tour group, more or less sleepily. It was still early, by Rome standards, and the guard was only there to guarantee that the group could be cleared out when the Pope needed the building.

So no one really noticed when the left flank of the monks advanced faster than the main group, cutting off the nun from the sight of the Swiss Guard. A few moments later, the nun turned to yet another piece of artwork, and Ioseph moved. He wrapped his arm around the nun's neck and twisted, sharply, breaking her neck before she had even a moment of terror.

Ioseph let the body hit the floor, then fell to one knee next to her, crying out for the guard to come to their aid. The guard dropped his halberd and ran over, hoping to lend some assistance. He bent over Ioseph, studying the woman over his shoulder, when Ioseph's elbow drove up, straight into the man's solar plexus, doubling him over. He drove his elbow up a second time, into the guard's throat, crushing his windpipe.

Ioseph stood, tossing his hood back. "Everyone, into positions." He pointed at one of his men. "Hide the bodies and get into the guard's uniform. We're going to listen to what they know, and then we're going to end this."

* * *

James Ryan was led into the antechamber of the papal audience hall.

James Ryan glanced at the chairs around the room lined up in circular formation, and matched them to the number of investigators he'd been told about on the way in. He also noted the dozen Swiss Guards, halberds at the ready, and bulges of automatic weaponry under their colorful uniforms.

The elder Ryan smiled. "I've been here before."

"Ah? I hope it doesn't look worse."

James turned to see the large, dark-skinned Pope, who grinned broadly.

James shrugged. "Doesn't look the worse for wear." He reached forward his hand, and the Pope grasped it firmly. "Good grip... I wanted to congratulate you on choosing a fine name. You could not find one better."

Pius XIII gave him a small smile. "And why would you say that?"

James looked to his left, and spotted a lovely, dark woman with almond-shaped, glittering eyes and marvelous skin. He grinned and stepped forward, offering his hand. "This lovely young woman must be the German I was told about. It is a *pleasure* to meet you. If I were forty years younger,

I'd properly show you how much of a pleasure it is, but my knees can't take it, you see."

Shushurin gave a cockeyed smile, and looked to Sean. "Call off the DNA test, he is related to you."

Sean waggled his eyebrows. "This I know."

James looked next to her and cocked his head. Dark blond hair, blue eyes, this was a Mossad agent? "Funny, you—"

"—don't look Jewish," Murphy sighed, "I *know*."

He glanced at the short Wilhelmina Goldberg. "You could, though."

Goldberg rolled her hazel eyes. "Thanks? I think?"

Hashim Abasi offered his hand. "And could I pass for Muslim?"

"So could the Pope, what's your point?" He eyed Abasi's tan suit. "Anyway, I guess that you're Goldberg, you're Abasi, Shushurin and Murphy." He nodded at Giovanni Figlia, all in black. "You're the Italian security, yes? You look like a priest." Figlia arched his brows. "You know a better place to look like one?"

James laughed and nodded. "Point taken." His eyes flicked to Maureen McGrail, wearing a frilly blouse and black slacks. "And you I know from photos Sean's shown me."

McGrail glanced at Sean with her pale green eyes and raised a brow. Sean shrugged. "I'm devious, you know this."

McGrail waved it away. She sat, and looked for the others to do the same, looking for Xavier O'Brien and the Williams family.

James Ryan said, "I see we're missing a few people."

O'Brien walked in a moment later. "Sorry, I'm a little slow. I sent the Williams duo off to fight evil somewhere. I'll take notes."

O'Brien sat on the Pope's right. Next to O'Brien was

Scott Murphy and Manana Shushurin. The German spy was between the Israeli and the Secret Service Agent. The next one over from Goldberg was Hashim Abasi. James Sherman Ryan was next, with his grandson next to him. Sean sat next to McGrail. To her right was Figlia, who wouldn't leave the Pope's side for anything

"You said," Shushurin began, "that Joshua couldn't have picked a better name. Why?"

James smiled at her. "Because I went out to work for him once… Pius XII, I mean."

The Pope nodded. "Explain it to them."

James leaned back in the chair. "You see, in the 1940s, I joined the Army… a little early. I managed to get to Italy through a rather long road — a little recon work, lots of fighting — and by mid-1943, I was in Italy. I crashed my plane, I managed to get out and into the city, and ran right to the Vatican. I did some work with the partisans and the local British SAS. Some of you may have heard of a Msgr. Hugh O'Flaherty. They made O'Flaherty's life into a movie… only it has O'Flaherty take credit for almost everything that happened in Rome."

He chuckled, and continued. "O'Flaherty found me, took me in. In October, '43, after the death trains rolled in and took people away from Rome by force, the Pope…" he drifted off for a moment with a dreamy smile, searching for the right euphemism, "called upon a few of Father O'Flaherty's refugees. There were at least a dozen of us — the healthiest, best trained, the most fluent in German — and he wanted us to do something for him. Pius XII swore all of us to secrecy, no matter what happened, no matter what history said about him, and he had a pretty good idea where everything was going. Unfortunately, at the end of the day, only two of us made it out alive."

Goldberg leaned forward. "What did he ask you to *do?*"

"Establish contact with German generals who wanted to end the war in 1943, and after that, kill as much of the top brass of the SS as possible, and most of all, kill Adolf Hitler."

* * *

Ioseph Mikhailov listened to the entire conversation in an earpiece transmitter. His informant had done quite well, bringing the communication earpiece along.

The insider had been correct; this was the moment of truth. Ioseph had placed his men accordingly, ready to make this moment of truth into a moment of death.

Mikhailov waited, and listened. His men slowly scattered throughout the building of the papal Audience Hall, ready for the kill order. After the debacle at the Spanish Steps, there was really only one last chance to clean up the mess. He would take no more chances. Besides, he and his men were already in the building.

He even had one man who had quietly trailed after the Pope and his entourage, clearing the way of Swiss Guards one by one until he stood outside the main hall, waiting for the moment when he should strike.

Mikhailov knew that risking one of his men wasn't enough to completely crush the opposition, but with his insider already in the room, and the gunman armed with automatic weapons, most of the opposition would be swept away. And shortly thereafter, all of the evidence would vanish along with them.

He raised his MP5 submachine gun, and held back a laugh. He would kill all of them, and the plan could proceed.

* * *

"What?" Wilhelmina Goldberg asked. "Pius wanted to have Hitler killed? Why? He was the Pope."

James Ryan's eyes lit up like a lightning storm. "There is a Catholic concept of tyrannicide – assassinating a leader who, in essence, has it coming. Pacelli was a very well-read man, and he knew natural law. Which is what put Hitler squarely in the column of tyrant who has to go. The Nazis had taken a thousand people from his *city*. True, Pius XII saved nearly all of them, but over a thousand were stolen away, some under his very windows, and he wouldn't have it." His mouth twitched into a near-snarl at the memories of what he had been through. "Houses raided, homes broken into, the screams of the prisoners being taken away, to a final destination.

"By that year, we knew what awaited those being dragged away," he continued. "We knew about the death camps. Everyone had heard about it the year before — the BBC finally broadcast what had been going on. But the Pope had already heard rumors." The veteran's hands balled up into fists. "The bastards took them from his city, despite German promises, despite the money paid out in ransom. It was the last straw.

"Pius had an organization in place — he backed it, financed it and gave it all the weapons of diplomacy at his disposal, from fake passes and passports to clemencies, to smuggling people out of Eastern Europe. It was a simple matter to turn the entire system backwards, and smuggle people *in* to Eastern Europe, and to Germany. To smuggle *us* in."

James Ryan looked to Goldberg, continuing to address her earlier point. "Pius had often stressed that he had commissioned us as a private citizen with a family fortune to finance the mission. He'd often refer to himself in the Royal we. But when he spoke to me and my men about what we were planning, and the assassinations he'd already supported, we never once heard him speak like he was Pope."

He sighed. "But we were found. In fact, we were discovered by one of the men we were trying to kill, one of Himmler's top men. He was technically a second-in-command, but he was in operations, a man named Hans Franke. Only myself and an RAF flyboy named Sinclair made it out. The rest of my men." The glow in James' eye had dimmed. "We were separated, but most were machine-gunned. If not, they wouldn't have made it through interrogation."

Xavier "XO" O'Brien nodded, and asked knowingly, "And why didn't you tell anyone?"

James raised a brow. "Didn't I say that His Holiness asked me not to? He made us swear to never mention the mission, no matter what was said about him or demanded of us. The man had saved my life twice. Once landing in Italy, and then being dragged out of Germany. I couldn't refuse him. I managed to make my way out, with a little assistance, into Spain and into South America, then up into the States, and they sent me back out into the field."

Shushurin nodded slowly, looking from XO to James. "Then why are you telling us now?"

Sean nodded at the reasonable question, and then caught something wrong.

"Simple," James answered. "I've wanted to speak since 1945. Every other academic in the field has earned my wrath time and time again, but I held back." He looked at his grandson and nodded at him. "Now it sounds like my silence will get someone killed. Eugenio, Pius, wouldn't have wanted that. He even said that martyrdom wasn't something you could impose on others. He wouldn't have wanted *my* silence to cost lives."

Sean frowned to himself, trying to be subtle about it as he thought through.

The Pope nodded. "I know. The Church as a whole would have spoken out earlier, but the scandal wouldn't have been acceptable then. Compromising neutrality in a war by *assassinating* the *legal* head of state? No, it wouldn't have looked proper."

Manana Shushurin turned to the Pope. "You knew?"

The Pope shrugged. "We heard stories, but we had no *proof.* Not that anyone had gone looking until Hochhuth's play had come out, and by then there were no written documents for this sort of thing, and in an organization that lives as much on paperwork as the Church, no one would believe we could order a pizza without needing five pounds of paper."

"Sure feels like it some days," Xavier muttered.

"No comments from the Jesuit in the corner," Sean muttered.

Sean thought back of the last few conversations, and the events that led up to this meeting, and tried to figure out if what he saw made any sense. He wasn't sure it did.

James Ryan nodded. "There was no paperwork that I know of, and I'm aware of plenty of paperwork that had been burned. We were summoned, we left, and we memorized very little. Somehow the instructions had been sent on ahead of us. We never needed to carry anything on us that could give us away."

Maureen McGrail smiled. "By any chance would one of the priests you came in contact with be named Father Harrington?"

He cocked his head. "How did you know?"

"Lucky guess," she said. "He was killed last week."

Sean Ryan knew something was wrong, but he couldn't place it. It was almost a beep …

XO sighed. "Harrington was coming to Rome to face down the devil's advocate in the Pius XII canonization, possibly to discuss what you just told us."

Goldberg, who didn't want to believe any of this, leaned back in her chair. "Which means whoever is killing these folks *knows* about the attempted assassination. I'm surprised they haven't tried to kill you yet."

James smiled. "People have tried to kill me twice in the past few weeks, one time just before I got on the plane to come here." He leaned over with a smile and said to Sean, "When you also asked about Pinchas Lapide, I thought you might know everything already."

Murphy furrowed his brow. "Why?"

The old man looked to the man from Mossad, his eyes flickering like electrical bolts. "Because Lapide came to my house once after the war, when he was looking up old veterans, and specifically asked me about the assassination attempt. I told him to never come back, sorry, but I couldn't tell anyone."

Murphy cursed. "*That's* why the file on Lapide's book notes was closed — *he knew about the attempt. Everyone did. Everyone…*" he trailed off a moment. "Everyone in the *Office* knew." He blinked. "But if *we* knew, why the hell didn't anyone say something?"

XO smiled. "Because they were asked by Pope John XXIII to keep silent." He puffed on his cigarette and continued.

Sean knew what it was now, an earpiece! "Figlia," Sean

said, reaching into his pockets. "Could you shut down your local comm systems for a few moments? Maybe five seconds?"

Figlia shrugged. "Sure. Why?"

"Trust me."

Figlia did, and immediately Sean leapt up and screamed, "Turn your earpieces off, everyone!" he shouted in perfect Italian to the Swiss Guards. In his right hand, in his pocket, he pressed the button on a short-range jamming device, making everyone with a working transmission receiver get a sharp piercing noise resembling a tea kettle blasting into the ear.

Manana Shushurin winced in pain, grabbing her head.

The very next thing Sean did was lunge forward and ram his fist into the face of Manana Shushurin with all the grace of a bullet car.

Scott Murphy threw himself on top of Sean, but the stuntman threw him off, and raised a communications earpiece in his hand. "This is what she had in her ear." He looked at Murphy. "Tell me, Mossad, if you're her partner, who's she transmitting to? And who's talking to her?"

* * *

Upstairs, Ioseph felt the blast in his ears, ripping everything apart. His men fell to their knees, and they had to tear out their earpieces. He had turned off his communications network, as Sean had told Figlia to do, but only for the five seconds Sean had asked for.

The bastard mick left on a jamming device! "Everyone!" he snapped to the men nearest him, "attack!"

* * *

The first man who charged into the reception hall had something of a chance. He swept into the room, two pistols already drawn. With arms wide open as he passed the threshold, he casually fired a round into the head of a Swiss Guard on either side of the doorway. His arms closed together, killing another two. Four had been killed with head shots before any had a chance to draw a weapon...

Except for Sean Ryan, who already had a gun in his hand, and fired — one bullet per eye.

The remaining Swiss Guards had all dropped their medieval weapons and drawn their modern ones, running directly for the Pope.

Giovanni Figlia snapped, "Get him out of here!" He drew his beam Taser gun the size of a Maglite. "Redeploy around the room, see if we can't box them in when they try again."

The Swiss Guards, XO and Figlia were halfway towards the back exit when two men appeared in the doorway, firing with Uzis. Three guards were killed before Figlia shot one gunman in the head. The other wheeled around the doorway, biding his time for reinforcements.

Figlia growled, ran at an acute angle toward the door, and then hurled himself sideways like in the soccer days of his youth. And, as in his days on the pitch, he found an opening for his goal in midair, seeing just far enough beyond the doorway to see the killer, and fired as he fell toward the floor. He slid across the marble and rolled to one knee, just in time for another gunman to wheel around to replace his fallen comrade, and fire.

* * *

Wilhelmina Goldberg had her gun out before the fifth Swiss Guard had died, and scanned the room for any other entrances and exits she might have missed. She found Sean on one knee, holding his pistol in classic combat style, using two chairs as a shooting platform.

"Well, Sean," Goldberg said, "you seem to have hit on something. You think you disoriented their attack?"

Sean growled. "Only three down. If I'd planned this, I'd have at least a dozen."

Maureen McGrail was also in motion, heading directly for the side exit the first shooter had entered. She flattened herself against the wall, waiting for someone else to come in.

"Villie," Sean said, "go with Maureen, into the hallway, clear the way, and make sure no one else is coming in. If not, we'll see what else can be done."

Abasi asked, "And myself? What would you have me do?"

Sean handed him the handgun as he pulled out another. "I've got a million of them. Stay here and cover Gianni's flank." He looked to Scott Murphy and frowned.

The Mossad agent had been silent for the last sixty seconds. Even when the bullets started flying, he merely stared at the unconscious Shushurin, his eyes wide and unblinking.

Murphy didn't even have words for what was happening at that precise moment. She was with the other side? That didn't make any sense, did it? She had saved them multiple times — why would she do that if she were the enemy? Granted, he knew how undercover work went — you befriended the enemy, even as you planned to take them out. But to save them all, even though they were going to be slaughtered? He was somewhere between being lost in an enigma like Winchester House, and having all his organs kicked out through his stomach, leaving him hollow inside.

Sean lightly tapped him on the skull with the pistol. "You all right?"

Murphy stopped staring at Shushurin, only to stare blankly at Sean. "I'm... I just... I have no idea what's happening."

Sean frowned. "Look on the bright side, neither do I." He tossed him a gun. "Try not to blow your foot off." He thought a moment, realizing he hadn't brought enough weapons for everyone... for once.

Sean gave another look around the area, sweeping it with his eyes, making certain that the area was secure — Figlia had the gunmen at his end contained — before he turned his attention to his grandfather...

James Ryan was still on the floor, his upper torso covered in blood.

Sean turned to the old man, ignoring the firefight just thirty feet away. He whipped out a handkerchief and pressed down on the wound. "How are you feeling?"

James's eyes flickered, and he looked up at Sean with his blue eyes and smiled. "I got them, Sean." His eyes glowed with mirth. "We got the bastards... before they could get me." His mouth wavered, but the smile remained. "You know now. They'll pay."

Sean smiled. "That you did. We know now, and they're screwed." He combed away a loose strand of hair from his grandfather's forehead. "Don't worry, they missed most of you. You weren't gotten as bad as you gave."

James gave a chuckle that turned into a cough. "Sorry... I took them with me. I missed a straightforward TKO... heh." Blood came out of his mouth, a single drop at the corner of his lip. "I love you, boy..."

At which point a light went out in his eyes, his head rolled to one side, and James Sherman Ryan died.

* * *

Scott Murphy pretty much ignored the scene going on behind him and concentrated on holding the flank along with Hashim Abasi. He looked down at Manana Shushurin briefly, and saw her eyes open, looking right at him. He was about to say something when he saw that look in her eyes — all of the lights in her eyes had gone out. They resembled the eyes of a refugee who had lost everything, especially hope.

Murphy had collected his thoughts just before she gave him a solid uppercut, using that momentum to roll to her feet and run for the platform exit at the front of the room — the one place no one had thought to run to yet.

Murphy picked himself off the floor after a moment and blinked, just in time to see Shushurin hit the exit. For a reason Murphy couldn't imagine, whether it was rage, or concern, or just plain autopilot, he gave chase.

* * *

Sean stared for a moment at his dead grandfather, a man who had meant more to him than his own father. James had taught him honor, morality, patriotism, and everything it took to make a good human being, when his own father was merely a shadow of the man that *his* father had been.

Sean quietly and calmly took his hand away, took James's hands and laid them on his chest. Sean looked up, his eyes alive with malice. Murphy and the traitor were both gone.

"It seems we are alone," Abasi told him.

Sean glared, and even though he did not look, Abasi felt the gaze. "I don't care if he's in on it with her, or she's by herself, we need them both. The first guy came prepared to take on all of us and twelve Swiss Guards. He's got to have enough artillery to hold down the fort." He glanced over his shoulder back at the six remaining guards firing down the back hallway.

Abasi finally spared him a glance, looking directly into Sean's eyes, a sight of rage that made him wish he hadn't looked. "What about you?"

Sean picked up one of the discarded halberds. "I'm good."

He switched the halberd to a two-handed grip, stood, and ran after Scott Murphy and Manana Shushurin. Either she had been involved in killing his grandfather, or they both were.

Either way, someone would pay.

CHAPTER XX: A PIUS ARMY

O utside, the entire Vatican security office went insane in a matter of moments. After Giovanni Figlia shut down the communications net for more than five seconds, everyone not in the papal reception hall charged toward the building. All of them had been dressed as civilians, meaning to blend in with the tourists, all wearing jackets, which meant that they each carried a submachine gun underneath, in addition to those who were already suiting up inside the office of the Swiss Guard in full body armor, picking up assault rifles, beam Taser rifles, net casters, microwave cannons, and enough gas to clear out most of Rome.

However, on top of the reception hall were ten men, all of them very good at what they did, which was kill people. Each of them had an AK-78, a very accurate assault rifle if fired on semiautomatic. This was how the leader of the squad fired it directly into the heart of Jacob Trainor, the first Swiss Guard to fall. He had also been the only guard dressed in formal wear, since he was going to take his wife out to the ballet that evening.

The Swiss Guards all stopped and hesitated, wondering about the position of the sniper. When all ten men atop the roof and two men in the main doorway fired, the guards quickly pulled back to the colonnade, where the bullets bounced off the marble.

They quickly radioed for sniper assistance, and a position was quickly decided on — they would shoot from the office of the Pope.

"We'll be there in five minutes."

"Who has five minutes?"

* * *

The first gunmen Maureen McGrail and Wilhelmina Goldberg came across wheeled around a corner, weapon out, aiming directly at McGrail. McGrail stepped into the weapon, knocking it aside with the palm of her left hand, and sent a deadly shot for his throat with stiff fingers. He tucked his chin, making her fingers hit bone along his jawline, and he hip-checked her into the wall.

His partner, however, was right around the corner and moved a second behind him. The second gunman paused, raised his weapon from McGrail to Goldberg. Goldberg lunged for him. The gunman kicked for her head with enough force to take it off her shoulders. Goldberg dove at the last second, making the kick miss her by a hair, landed on her side and rolled onto her back before he could step on her, then fired three shots up into him. The first shot he felt enter his groin and bounce off his vest into his chest. The next two shots went up his anal sphincter and into his spine.

McGrail absorbed the impact against the wall easily, her shoulders and buttocks taking the brunt of it — it was the same position as though she had been thrown on the floor. She fired a backhanded fist into his nose, breaking it sharp-

314

ly, and jabbed the stiff fingers of her left hand into his dia-phragm. His eyes widened for a moment as he lost all control of his breathing. She reached forward, grabbed his head with both hands, and twisted before he could bring his gun to bear. His neck broke with a resounding crack.

McGrail looked around. *"Villie?"*

Goldberg looked up from the floor. "A little help here?"

McGrail reached down and lifted the second dead gun-man off Goldberg. Goldberg nodded. "Thanks."

"My pleasure."

Wilhelmina Goldberg turned her attention to the man she had just killed and picked the radio transmitter from the dead gunman's belt.

"Now if Sean had turned off his darn jamming device, we could at least send for help."

"Well, it's probably the only reason these people can't be coordinated," McGrail told her. "Can you cut through Sean's jamming?"

Goldberg frowned. "Maybe. I went to the Secret Service from the NSA. If you need a radio put together with spit, bailing wire and a combat knife, you call me. The problem is, anyone we called for help would probably be the bad guys themselves, and I'm reasonably certain we don't want to do that."

McGrail went through her dead gunman and took his primary weapon and his sheathed combat knife. "You want?"

Goldberg shrugged. "Sure." She glanced at her would-be killer once more. "Does your guy have a secondary weapon?"

She nodded. "A Stechkin."

"Just like Manana's."

* * *

Scott Murphy ran after Manana Shushurin through the hallway. He remembered his weapons training well enough that he knew to hold the gun low, and how to chamber the round and turn off the safety, but he wasn't certain he could hit her without coming to a stop and taking the time to aim. Given her speed, he concluded that coming to a stop would mean she'd just keep running and probably get away.

I just have to chase her until she stops and faces me. And do I really want to draw down on a fully-trained, highly intelligent assassin who had arms training from conception?

Murphy turned off his mind, because he knew the answer already. There was only one thing he wanted at the moment: the truth. He had fallen for the woman in more ways than one — her story, her cover, her information, her looks, and the lights in her eyes… that look of joy in her face …

Murphy couldn't decide which would be the hardest to deal with: that he had bought all of it, or what his own personal fallout would be like. Between her personal strengths and occasional vulnerabilities, he had been quite taken by her.

When you have to shoot her, please remember that you're in love with an illusion. Otherwise she will probably gun you down.

Murphy breezed past a Swiss Guard coming out of a perpendicular hallway. Murphy thought of calling to him for aide, but that would mean slowing down.

The one in the Swiss guard outfit took no notice of him as Murphy sped by. He smiled, fully aware that Shushurin could kill Murphy all by herself, and she needed no assistance from him.

The fake guard, whose real name was Sasha Suslov, looked

behind at the real papal guard he had killed, his neck twisted at an odd angle. The nun tour guide lay underneath his body.

The fraudulent guard held up his gun in one hand, his halberd in the other, and waited, making sure no one else would follow.

* * *

Sean A.P. Ryan charged down the hallway, halberd in hands, and felt like he wanted to inflict harm on a great many people.

But one in particular would do.

The traitor.

Sean didn't know how well-trained Scott Murphy would be, but he knew that Shushurin would be able to break him in two over her knee and keep running without breaking stride.

Then there was the difficulty of Murphy's relationship with her. Assuming that he was in fact an innocent Mossad agent — *wow, what an oxymoron* — and was *not* in league with the woman, Sean had seen how they were around each other, and saw Murphy becoming far too familiar with a woman he had only just met.

Then again, I also thought that the affection was probably mutual, even more so this morning. But if he's not in league with her, even if he's as well-trained as I am, any feelings he had for her would slow him down.

Speaking of slowing down...

A Swiss Guard stood in front of him, halberd in one hand, gun in the other.

I wonder what the hell he's doing here?

The Swiss Guard raised his weapon and fired.

*   *   *

The Swiss Guard next to Figlia fired down the hallway, and the head of the office of vigilance stepped back to reload. He glanced back toward the main room. The Pope was pushed against the wall only feet from him, and only Hashim Abasi watched their flank...

And he has automatic weapons at his side... and no one else?

Figlia ran back to the Egyptian police officer. *"Ciao. Come stai?"*

Abasi smiled. *"Cosi-cosi.* I have weapons, but there are no good positions for cover in here."

Figlia nodded. "I've noticed. I'm down to half a dozen men and we're pinned down. Where did everyone go?"

Abasi gestured ahead of him. "Villie and McGrail went to clear the road, and it is possible they may get behind the gunmen at our position, but I doubt it; more likely they will get help from the outside and bring it here."

"But my men should have been here by now, in *forte,* without anyone asking. If Villie and Maureen are to get help, they might be the ones to clear the way for my people."

"Then what do you suggest? Follow them and hope the path is clear?"

Figlia shook his head and pointed to his men exchanging gunfire with the assassins. "That would mean a running battle with these people blocking our way. I feel more secure here. And Ryan?"

"Chased after Shushurin and Mossad through the stage door."

Figlia looked down at the blood-soaked chest of James Sherman Ryan. For some strange reason, he remembered

318

that blood sank into marble and never came out. "Understood. Can I borrow a submachine gun? I'll trade you for a smoke grenade."

"Take three."

Figlia nodded, then slung an MP5 over his shoulders, and grabbed both of the Russian guns, flipping them to automatic fire. *"Grazie."*

"Grenada," Abasi muttered.

That isn't Italian. That isn't even Spanish, for that matter. Oh well. He turned and ran toward his men. The Pope had been held back at first, and now he had relented, hanging back of his own accord. Figlia noted his men were low on ammunition. "Forester, Forsyth, smoke grenades."

"What are you doing, Gianni?" the Pope asked.

"Praying, sir."

"Good man."

Figlia waited for the hallway to fill with smoke. "Anti-traction gel."

Several Swiss Guards drew narrow weapons that looked like a super soaker. They fired at several different angles, covering the floor beyond the doorway, making it almost impossible to stand on. He also made a point of grabbing another of the anti-traction guns.

With the assassins' vision clouded and their footing unstable, Figlia charged. He leapt in under the field of continuing fire, holding both Stechkins at once. He half-rolled, half-slid toward the opposition, until he was almost point-blank with the still-firing attackers.

Figlia held both Stechkins, aiming for muzzle flashes through the smoke, and fired. His first five bullets against their vests drove two of the gunmen from their feet, and the next three caught them in their unprotected neck, and shoulders. He kept firing into the smoke, and there were people shooting back this time.

At which point, the gunman in front of him decided to break off, and he had good reason. With the two point men dead in front of him, there was no one to offer suppression fire, which meant no one could kill Figlia and take up positions before the Swiss Guards arrived.

When the smoke cleared, a third body was dead on the floor, but there were no others.

One of the Swiss Guards poked his head in the entrance to the hall. Heydrich Forester cocked an eyebrow. "Was that all of them?"

Figlia glanced down the hallway, still face down on the ground, the front of his body covered in gel. "No, there was someone else. Stay here, take up positions in case he heads for backup. I need to secure His Holiness."

Figlia rolled, coming off the slick floor, until the ground was stable beneath him, then raced back into the reception area. "Your Holiness, you are all right?

Pius XIII, pressed flat against the wall, out of everyone's way, nodded. "Are they gone?"

"No. Excuse me a moment." Figlia made his way to Abasi and sat down on one of the chairs Sean had set up to serve as a brief cover. "Doing well?"

Abasi almost laughed. "I'm alive and haven't been shot yet. Given the circumstances, that's an achievement."

"Do you think that if I left you here with Joshua, you could cover him until we clear out the building? I'll get you some smoke grenades and flashbangs to hold off attackers."

He nodded. "This I can do."

"Thank you." Figlia turned to the Pope. "I must insist that you stay here with Abasi until the building is secured."

320

Pius nodded.

Figlia smiled. "Thank you." He nodded to Abasi, handing him several smoke grenades and flash bangs.

And then Figlia and his men were off.

* * *

On top of the reception hall, nine men with assault rifles were busy trying to totally eliminate the Swiss and Palatine Guards, and everyone of the Central Office of Vigilance that they had within range. A tenth man calmly took shots at the counter-sniper team setting up in the papal offices.

One floor below, at the rear end of the building, one man opened the wooden window screen outward, and slowly slid himself onto the ledge. He bent his knees sharply, then pushed off, barely reaching the edge of the roof. He grabbed hold of it firmly and pulled himself over. He smiled at the ten men in front of him, firing with discipline; even though they were in single-fire mode, they still sounded like they were blazing away with machineguns.

However, none of them heard him come up, and none of them looked behind at him now.

Captain Wayne pulled out one of Giovanni Figlia's prized nonlethal weapons: a microwave beam gun. After jostling the settings a moment, he pointed the thermal beam at them and hit the button, knowing what to expect.

Essentially, the microwave weapon only inflicts as much damage as a bad sunburn — if used properly — but even then, the sensation was much different. It was more like being set on fire. All of the assassins fell to the roof, screaming in pain, their weapons falling from their hands.

Wayne simply sat back. He was tempted to find out

whether there was any popcorn.

* * *

At the main entrance to the building, the two remaining gunmen doubled their fire, switching to full automatic. The gunmen stepped back calmly to seek cover behind the stone walls of the reception hall, still firing.

The first gunman didn't even see the elbow that struck the back of his right ear. He fell forward, unconscious.

The second gunman turned, finding no one there. He turned to see who had felled his partner, but saw no one.

Above him, next to the ceiling, a priest pressed his limbs to the walls, pushing against them, using friction to hold him up. He held himself there until the gunman stopped to reload, then dropped, falling on top of the gun, feet first, head butting the gunman.

The gunner dropped his weapon and fell, quickly crawling backward to gain space.

"Hello," the priest said quietly. "My name is Father Frank, and you shouldn't have come here."

The gunman kicked into the air and flipped onto his feet, firing a right cross too fast for most human beings to even see. The priest sidestepped and kneed him in the stomach before pounding him with a left pile driver, which spun him around. Frank grabbed him by the collar and belt and slammed him into the wall. The gunman spun out of his grip, and backhanded Frank across the face before going for his knife.

The knife came out, and up, and so did Father Frank's rosary. The loop of beads came up and around the knife blade like a whip. A flick of the wrist sent both the knife and the

322

rosary flying across the hallway. The gunman lunged forward with a sucker punch. The priest slipped the punch, and the fist drove straight into the wall. Frank shouldered him off his feet, and the assassin fell to the floor. This time the gunman rolled to his feet, drawing his Stechkin before standing. Frank kicked out, knocking the gun away, and then drew the foot back, landing the next kick squarely into the man's chest, sending him into the doorway, into a straight line of sight with the outside world.

And into the path of the rifle bullets from the guards.

Father Frank Williams smiled. At least his father was right about there being trouble.

Father Frank headed toward the room where the Pope and the others were to meet, and stopped, turned, and picked up the Stechkin.

Who knew when one would need to blow through annoying locked doors?

* * *

Maureen McGrail and Wilhelmina Goldberg moved through the hallway, Goldberg with the gun ahead of her. The hall came to a blank wall, and a hallway that split off, the crossbar of the T-shaped hall. The two women nodded at each other, and wheeled around the hallway as one, each facing a different direction to clear the hall.

Goldberg barely even had time to acknowledge that she had an attacker before she fired from reflex. The bullet she fired landed squarely in the gun stock of the AK78. The assassin growled and kicked her weapon from her hand before swinging down with his rifle. She leapt forward, past his left side, and landed with a solid thud, her stomach even with his boot. He grabbed his Stechkin sidearm, drew it, and pivoted his upper body to aim. He couldn't miss.

McGrail disarmed his partner in a matter of seconds. She slapped aside the AK78, then pushed the gun into the man's chest. Both hands came down like hooks and spun the weapon from his hands. She chopped into his leg with a low roundhouse kick to the knee.

The gunman twisted, just saving his knee. He stepped back out of reach of kick or punch, drew his sidearm, and aimed.

Wilhelmina Goldberg's assassin had a clear shot, and all the time in the world to take it, in terms of proper assassination technique. Only Goldberg wasn't an assassin, so she didn't play by the same rules, as she had slashed both of his Achilles tendons. He fell flat on his face, and he was about to roll when he felt Goldberg's commandeered commando knife plunge into his kidney. The pain shot through his body like an electric current attached to his genitals, an agony so painful he couldn't even scream.

McGrail sneered at her gunman and hurled the banana clip from the assault rifle like it was a Bowie knife. The point of the top bullet in the clip jabbed him right between the eyes, and the circular spin of the clip caused the bullet point to slash through the skin. Given that head wounds bled profusely, no matter how small the wound, blood flowed directly into his eyes. She threw the rifle into his chest.

The assassin paused for a moment, then staggered back as he saw the barrel of his gun sticking out of his heart. He stared in bewilderment for a moment before he remembered…

He had left a bayonet at the end of his assault rifle.

McGrail rose to her feet and smiled at Goldberg, who was also getting to her feet. "Easy, wasn't it?"

324

The bolts of two assault rifles were drawn back.

Goldberg looked on in disgust. "Guess not."

McGrail's eyes flared to life. *Then I'll die with my nails in their—*

She whirled, and before she could finish the thought, a hand had already gripped the assault rifles from behind and pulled them both up and out of their owner's hands.

Their assailant launched a kick to one side, breaking the knee of the one on his right while his hands shot left to grab a hold of the other's head and slapped it against the wall. Before the assassin fell, a right hand fired a vicious backhand behind the ear of his partner, making the remaining gunman's head ricochet off the marble wall. They both hit the floor at the same time in roughly the same condition — out cold.

McGrail noted her savior and cocked her head at the odd-looking sight before her — Father Frank Williams in full clerical garb.

* * *

Sean dropped under the "guard's" field of fire and thrust the halberd at him like a lance. The sharp tip stuck into the gunman's hand and sent the Stechkin flying. Sean pushed off the floor with the halberd, grabbing it at either end before swinging the axe-head at the fake Swiss Guard. The guard blocked it with his own halberd, and pulled back, trying to hook Sean's axe on his pole Sean jerked the halberd away before that.

Sean launched an overhead blow with the blunt end of the halberd. The guard blocked, and he was also ready for Sean's attempt to swing his halberd's axe into the man's side.

The guard caught the axe edge on the pole itself, which was a bad mistake because all Sean did was pull back, sliding the axe blade down the pole, and thrust forward, jabbing the point for the man's stomach.

The fake guard leapt back and parried. After the parry, he swept his weapon back and thrust at Sean. Sean didn't leap back or try to block it, but instead dropped to his knees, below the halberd's point. He thrust his halberd up to meet his adversary's, using the middle of the pole to intercept it, and then he swung his halberd to hook his adversary's pole. Sean locked the halberd from two different sides — the hooked end of Sean's axe had locked the pole, and Sean used the blunt end to push against his attacker's axe.

Sean sharply twisted his halberd, ripping away his opponent's. The halberd clattered to the floor, and the guard backed up slowly to get out of range. Sean smiled, straightened and tossed the fake guard his own halberd.

"Catch," he told him, as though he were throwing a ball.

The guard caught it on reflex, and Sean dropped into a roll, aiming for the legs out from under the pseudo-guard. The guard jumped up, over Sean...

And Sean stopped his roll and spun, still in a crouch, and jammed an uppercut into the gunman's groin. The killer hovered there a moment before he dropped to one knee, bringing him level for Sean to drive a right hook into him so hard, his head snapped to one side and he passed out.

* * *

The Pope held the smoke grenades as Hashim Abasi and the Swiss Guard who stayed behind held their guns on the doorway, no one saying a word, and no one needing to. They

326

were merely waiting for news, good or bad.

The old saying is that news travels fast.

Bad news just happens to travel faster.

Three gunmen charged into the room. The Pope's bright white garments, and the Swiss Guard's uniform, the brightest objects in the room, distracted the gunmen's attention for a split second – they shot the guard immediately in the head. Abasi fired as the Pope threw his smoke grenade. The grenade hit one of the gunmen in the head, while one felt the full impact of Abasi's automatic burst, dropping dead to the floor.

The third gunman disappeared into the smoke. Abasi paused a moment and emptied his gun into the cloud, sweeping from side to side. After hearing nothing, he shrugged, and charged into the smoke himself, only to literally trip over the gunman he'd been shooting for. The gunman and Abasi regained their feet at the same time, and Abasi slammed himself into the attacker with his shoulder, hitting him so hard that they were both flung outside the room. Abasi backhanded the assailant before violently head butting him. The gunman did the same to him, trying to step back to get a little distance and maneuver properly.

Abasi didn't intend to let him have the chance. If the assessments of the mercenaries' abilities were accurate, he couldn't let this man have a chance to breathe properly, never mind maneuver. Besides, Sean Ryan was a trained stuntman with years of experience and fight training, Maureen McGrail had a black belt, and they had trouble dealing with these men.

Abasi was just a lowly cop with nothing on his side but intelligence.

That would have to do.

* * *

Three additional assassins had charged through the smoke, past the two struggling parties. The Pope stood his ground as the three men charged in with AK-74s, weapons high.

The large Pope smiled at them unpleasantly. "Please, put down your weapons, and surrender."

The one in the middle grinned at him, raised his gun, and fired into the Pope's chest.

* * *

Murphy had apparently chased Shushurin into a dead end, sort of. Basically, Murphy stood at the corner of two hallways, and cut off both of her exit routes, while Shushurin was at the opposite corner of the square. She could come around from either side, but she would have to pass by him either way.

Murphy's pistol was ahead of him, one hand on the pistol grip, the other hand cupping the first. He remembered the basic form from his training, but if it came to real gunplay, he would last about two gunshots. *Probably both to the back of my head.* "Mani," he called down the hallway, "I just want to talk."

"About what?" her voice came from around the corner. The only exit other than going directly past him was to his right. Murphy turned toward it, gun at the ready, steadily making his way down the hall toward her voice.

"I think the truth would be a very good place to start," he called back. He slowly lowered himself to one knee, not to steady his aim, but hoping to make himself a smaller target

"Everything I told you was true," her voice echoed back. It sounded sad and lonely.

Murphy smiled. "I think you might have left out a few things."

There was a moment of silence. Her voice came around the bend in the hallway. She spoke slowly and carefully. "After I joined BND, my father came back. He told me if I didn't help him, he'd make my history public knowledge; what the Soviets trained me for, all of it. I'd be ruined at best, jailed at worst — he even has fake documents about my training and 'proof' of my continued Russian employment."

Murphy winced. He liked her father less and less. He shifted to steady his stance. "What did he want you to do?"

"Give him information, until now," Shushurin answered. "On this mission, he sent me to keep tabs on you. He had me share everything with him — gave me the equipment, the money. The transmitters, bugs, phones, all on a shared frequency so he could listen in."

Murphy nodded to himself. That explained a lot. The gunmen knew to be set up at the Spanish Stepsbecause they were attached to the bug Murphy had placed on the car, the one he got from her. Sean Ryan and McGrail had been attacked shortly after they had caught him and Shushurin. Murphy had heard from Goldberg about Sean's idea of a Soviet training regimen — then Sean was attacked. He had initially thought that the German BND had merely given her a bigger budget than Mossad allowed him... but she had talked about paying for the hotel with money "by other means."

Meaning the bad guys. And that's why she was so down after saving Sean Ryan in the alleyway two nights ago — she had been expected to kill him. One problem. He flipped a mental coin and started working his way down the hall to his right, very, very slowly. "There's a hitch in your story, Manana. The Spanish Steps? You could've plead ignorance and let Ryan drive into the trap. We'd have been too late to do anything. Father Williams was there, but you couldn't have known that. Even if you did, you had no way of knowing he'd draw enough fire to get them out alive. Why did you rush to save them?"

"I didn't want anyone to get hurt, dammit," she objected down the hall. "I could not save Gerrity, but I could stop them from killing anyone else."

Murphy nodded slowly. "And what did you tell your... father?"

Shushurin laughed bitterly. "That I had to keep my cover with you. Thankfully, Father Williams arrived, or it would've been suspicious driving them all off by myself."

"Hmm... and they would've known you weren't playing along with them," Murphy concluded. "Nice version of events. Now what?"

"And now," she replied, her voice filled with sorrow, "you'll *all* have to die. If you don't, I'm dead. So is my mother."

"There's another way," he said, edging closer toward her voice, gun ahead of him. "You could come to work for the Office. We've employed worse. I'll vouch for you. You get immunity, your mother gets protection, and we walk away. If you want, I'll put you up in my place until you get on your feet — you could have my bed, I'll take my couch, and I have a nice bottle of Sabra we can crack open.... Come on, what do you say?" He paused.

The hammer of a gun was cocked not five feet behind him. "I'm sorry. I'm so, so sorry."

* * *

Kevlar does not stop a bullet dead in its tracks. According to the laws of physics that is impossible. The most it can do is diffuse the power of the bullet by spreading it out along the Kevlar armor. The size of an AK-74 bullet, for example, translated into, roughly, a 30 caliber round. However, like any other bullet, it travels at hundreds of meters per second. The power of that is translated to the smallest point of the tip of that bullet.

The very point of Kevlar is to take that power, and spread it from an area 7.62 millimeters around into an area equal to that of the bulletproof vest. Usually, that meant a feeling like being slapped in the chest by a three square foot slab of sheet metal, going at ten miles an hour. The result usually meant broken ribs and a torso the color of a giant bruise. It would suck, but the wearer would live.

However, that was only for a regular bulletproof vest, fit to match the normal human torso.

If the Kevlar vest was over six feet tall, and more than three feet wide, the damage is even more distributed. And when it hits an object weighing over three hundred pounds, much of it solid muscle, the damage is even more limited.

Which is the only reason that Pope Pius XIII, born Joshua Kutjok, was able to simply stand there, looking down at his chest, after having three rifle bullets pumped into his torso. It didn't even knock him down, just made him stagger backwards a little.

The man who shot him, as well as his two companions, had already moved along, leaving him for dead.

When His Holiness realized that he was alive, he turned on his attacker. Both hands grabbed the stock of the barrel as the assassin passed by him, and jerked the assault rifle out of his hands.

The assassin gaped as his AK disappeared from his grasp. He didn't really even notice when the Pope thrust the rifle butt straight into his jaw, the power of the impact crushing the bone, snapping his head around. He was unconscious before he even hit the floor.

The assassin's two companions were caught equally off-guard when the Pope wielded the rifle like a baseball bat. The wooden stock smacked against one man's hip, dislocating it with a crack. The Pope shoved the wounded assassin into the one left standing, and bowled both of them over.

When the other killer, pinned by his fallen comrade, tried to bring his weapon to bear, the Pope put his foot down — right onto the barrel of the gun, pinning it. With one last swing, the Pope used the gun like a golf club, driving it in between the man's legs.

The assassin went cross-eyed, and passed out.

The Pope, panting, looked at the three men and gasped, "And that… is how we do it… in Sudan."

He dropped the gun, and moved to the cloud of smoke, and the noises of Abasi in struggle.

And stopped as the smoke cleared, revealing another gunman, his handgun raised, pointed at the Pope's head.

* * *

The Egyptian police officer struck his opponent with an uppercut, then clamped down with his hand on the gunman's shoulder, continuing to punch him with his left fist. His adversary kneed him in the stomach, and Abasi fought to hold on, biting the bastard's arm, and not letting go. The gunman roared. They landed on the floor, rolling, punching,

332

kicking, all professionalism gone. With one proper punch, Abasi broke one of his attacker's ribs, while the other man went for more damage around the face, usually punches that turned into slaps. Abasi reached up to gouge out the man's eyes, and when the attacker waved the hands away, Abasi changed the direction of his thrust ...

Abasi swept his hands outward, grabbing the gunman's arms and pulling him close, slamming his forehead into the bastard's nose, before literally biting into his throat, pulling with his teeth.

As they continued to struggle, Abasi thought. *Where's the Pope?*

* * *

As the smoke cleared, and Abasi still grappled with his attacker, the gunman the Pope had hit with the smoke grenade was already standing, holding a gun on him.

He smiled, coming closer to the Pope. "Hello, Your Eminence."

Pius XIII cocked his head. "You call a *Cardinal* 'Your Eminence.' I'm *'Your Holiness.'*"

"I hear that you like to shuck the formality of the title," he replied in unaccented English.

"Shuck yourself." The Pope's eyes narrowed. "For you, I will make an exception. What do you want to do now? Kill me?"

He shook his head. "Not yet. Sergei," he gestured to the man who had shot the Pope before, "forgot himself. The point now is to kill the investigators; *they* might be believed. They've heard the truth, and can't be allowed to live. Anyone who lives will come back for you. I'll kill anyone who's left."

A soft, gentle voice said, "I'd like to test that theory."

With an impressive whirl, the gunman wheeled behind the Pope, gun to his head.

Pius XIII cocked an eyebrow as he saw Father Frank Williams, holding a Stechkin.

* * *

"The marble walls around here provide an excellent echo effect," Manana Shushurin told Murphy, her gun at his head.

The Mossad agent let his handgun fall to the ground. "You want me on one knee or two?"

"Either will do," Shushurin answered.

Murphy sank to both knees, hands up, staring straight at the wall. "I used to do this as an altar boy. I think I can manage."

He waited for a count of ten, swiftly going through an Our Father in his head before he asked, "Are you going to shoot me, or just stand there?"

She blinked. "I'm getting to it."

Murphy sighed. "Mani, do me a favor, and kill me now."

She smiled oddly. "You in a hurry?"

"No. But after falling in love with a woman just in time to have her pull a gun on me, I don't want this around the Office." He smiled sadly. "It should have occurred to me that there was more to you being single. While your father had control over you, you couldn't allow anyone in. Generous and understanding of you."

Murphy put one hand on the ground, and slowly turned himself around to face Shushurin. He wound up looking down the barrel of her Stechkin. It looked much larger from this angle — like an artillery piece. "Besides, you have to kill me now. If you're going to do it, I want you to at least have a fighting chance of getting away. If you're not going to do it, then ..."

He let himself relax. The rest of his life was out of his hands. "Make up your mind, Mani. You know better than I do that you need to hurry."

She let out an unsteady breath. The lights in her eyes were dim now. "I know," she said softly, almost weakly. "I just ..." She cleared her throat, and her voice broke as she said, "I don't want to, Scott."

Murphy forced his eyes to lock onto hers. "Fine, Manana, then *don't!* Save yourself and leave, or defect, or... or... darn, I should be able to come up with another option."

"You mean aside from fighting me?"

He snickered. "You're kidding, right?" He looked down at his pale, scrawny form, then looked up at her again. "This is not the body of a Sean Ryan. I'm not a hero, Mani. And besides, even if I could, I wouldn't want to hurt you."

Shushurin smiled at last, and her gun slowly lowered.

Murphy pushed off the ground with enough force to send him within arm's length of her ankles. He grabbed them and pulled sharply, sending her off her feet. He scrambled over her body as the bullet passed through where her head had been moments before.

Murphy glared at Sean Aloysius Patricus Ryan, who held himself in the perfect gunman's stance, the stuntman's eyes alight with rage.

Murphy's eye twitched. "What the *hell* are you doing, Sean?"

Sean Ryan scowled at Murphy. "Saving your life, you fool."

The Mossad spy merely kept up the glare. "I just got her

to *defect*, you *schmuck*."

Sean shifted his aim, and Murphy couldn't tell if it was at him or Shushurin. "And my grandfather just got his chest blown out." He cocked the gun. "You want to talk reason with me now, Mr. Golden Goy? You want to explain why I shouldn't kill you for bringing her and her buddies within *spitting distance* of my grandfather?"

"No," said a voice from behind him. "But I probably should."

Sean grimaced, and didn't even look behind him. "Bishop O'Brien, what the hell are you doing?"

The bishop paused for a moment to light a cigarette. "There were better things I could do than stand around waiting to be shot at. Given your reputation, it was safer following you." He took a drag and let it out slowly. "You generally have a method of clearing dangers away." He let out a puff of smoke. "How are you, Scott?"

Murphy glared around Sean. "Boss, stop acting like an XOB — I mean SOB — and cut out the wiseass routine."

"It's not a routine," Xavier answered. "I'm a Jesuit."

Shushurin pushed her gun away from her so that it slid across the floor. "Scott, get off me."

He looked down at her. "He's going to kill you."

She smiled, her starlit eyes shining once more, and kissed him gently on the lips. "He's going to blow through you to get to me, and that would pretty much miss the point of the last five minutes. So get off before I toss you off."

Murphy complied, sliding off her. She easily flipped to her feet and turned to Sean. "If you want to kill me, please, do it; when my bosses find out about me, I am going to be shot. So go right ahead, save them the trouble."

Sean smiled evilly. "Don't tempt me."

"Why not? You're already tempted, aren't you?"

Bishop O'Brian calmly stepped next to Sean. "Mr. Ryan, I'm certain you're not into 'vengeance is mine, sayeth the Lord,' but—"

Sean spared him a glance. "Retribution is not vengeance. Vengeance is overkill. Retribution is just payment for what one has earned. Re-tribute, re-payment, same Latin roots."

Shushurin was about to interrupt, when she suddenly caught the motion ahead of her, behind O'Brien and Sean Ryan. Her entire universe tunneled down to the hallway directly ahead of her — all three of them.

She saw the gun, the priest, the stuntman, and the motion just beyond. As quickly as possible, with reflexes that some would have thought surpassed the speed of lightning, Manana Shushurin leapt forward. She pushed off of her right foot, twisting and extending her left side forward. Her left hand closed around Sean Ryan's gun and pushed it to her right, moving it off line. Her right hand grabbed the gun as well as she slammed into Sean, toppling him. She straightened both of her arms, pushing the gun straight up. Her finger slid over his in the trigger guard, and she squeezed once, twice, and eventually, six times.

Sixty feet down the hall, a man dressed in a Swiss Guard uniform, holding an MP5 submachine gun, fell to the ground, quite dead.

Sean stared in disbelief at the dead man, half-stunned that the bastard had even managed to wake up after he had put him down not five minutes before.

Bishop O'Brien hadn't moved from his position, and calmly inhaled on his cigarette. "What were you saying, Mr. Ryan?"

* * *

The gunman smiled at Father Frank, still holding onto the Pope. The priest seemed confident about the way he held his weapon, but the Russian mercenary was doubly so about his position. "You can't kill me, priest, we both know that. Your vows forbid it. So just throw away the gun, and we'll call it a day."

The priest smiled serenely, his violet eyes glowing with peace. This was wildly out of place, considering that he held the pistol before him like a professional who had only practiced an hour ago. "I doubt it."

The hostage taker smiled. "Fine, put up the gun or I'll simply kill your boss."

Frank Williams nodded. "I will be happy to do so."

He raised the muzzle of the gun, and fired on full automatic, emptying the entire magazine. The gunman looked up as the sound of shattering crystal filled the room. The giant crystal chandelier above him broke off its chain and came hurtling down directly at him.

The Pope twisted, striking at the hostage taker before leaping aside. The gunman, dazed by the papal punch, barely had time to react before the chandelier crushed him.

The two priests looked at the damage, breathing heavily. After a moment of examination, Father Frank sighed. "I thought he would be able to leap away faster than that."

The Pope rose to his feet, brushing off his robes. "You're forgiven. Say two Hail Marys and call it a day."

He nodded again, about to berate himself again for not taking him alive, and paused. "Do you hear that?"

Pius XIII cocked his head, and heard thumping and growling. "Abasi!"

338

The Pope and Frank ran for the Egyptian policeman, and got there in time to see Abasi holding the gunman high above his head and slamming him into the wall. When the attacker still thrashed about, he hurled him headlong into the opposite wall.

Abasi stared at him for a moment, breathing heavily. When his opponent didn't get up again, Abasi turned to the two priests. He wiped away blood from his forehead, reached to get a handkerchief from his suit jacket pocket, and discovered that it, like half of the jacket, was covered in blood.

"Don't worry, it's not mine," Abasi told them. He straightened, and winced painfully. "But I may be wrong."

The three of them walked — or in Abasi's case, limped — into the center of the main hall.

The first thing the Pope did was move to James Ryan's body and say, *"Ego te absolve in nomine Patris et Filii et Spritus Sancti,"* the words of last rites.

By the time he was done,

Four dozen armed men charged into the hall, guns ahead of them, led by Giovanni Figlia, Wayne Williams, Maureen McGrail, and Wilhelmina Goldberg.

"You're late," the Pope told them. He rose from the floor, then over the rest of the bodies. It was going to take *forever* to perform last rites on all of them.

"Sorry, Your Holiness," Figlia answered with a bow, "we hit traffic."

"You should talk," Sean Ryan answered, walking into the hall with Shushurin in his grasp. Murphy and XO were behind him.

Giovanni Figlia nodded. "She's still alive… so I suppose we *need* to talk."

CHAPTER XXI: AN IMPIOUS PLAN

Sean Ryan nodded at Figlia, his eyes wide and fixed, the fire in them intense enough to blacken his soul — though from what he had seen recently, Figlia wouldn't be surprised if the man's soul had been coated with asbestos.

Sean's usual easy smile had instead fixed into a hard, solid line as he scanned the floor, looking over the dead.

He reached into his pocket and pulled out the signal jammer, turning it off before tossing it to Goldberg. The former NSA agent looked at the device and blinked. "You schmuck. You took this out of my luggage."

Shushurin raised a brow. "You somehow thought he carried that sort of thing on him routinely?"

Goldberg lowered the device and squinted at her. "Shut up, bitch."

Abasi's eyes followed Sean as he moved with purpose to the center of the room, where three of the bodies had been. "Why do *you* have it with you, Agent Goldberg?"

"I'm a techie," she muttered, "I like my toys."

Sean knelt down next to one of the bodies and rummaged through his equipment, then grabbed hold of something and pulled, coming away with a communications unit. He forced a smile and keyed it open. "This is Sean Aloysius Patricus Ryan to all of you Oedipal bastards. The bitch is dead. Repeat, your bitch is dead." He smiled evilly. "You *sukinsyn* had better run. I'm giving you a head start. You just keep missing your target, and your employers won't like that. And Grandpa is mighty pissed with you.

"Yes, you heard correctly: you missed my grandfather altogether. *Oops.* Well, *that* was a waste of time." He sat in a chair by his grandfather's corpse, and took a coming breath. "I nailed your informant runt to the wall, and your crappy assault team with her. So, run, Ivan, before I find you. And I will find you. When I do, I will send you straight to Hell. Every, last, one of you will die screaming. Have a nice day."

Sean took his finger off the button, then tossed the radio to Goldberg. "You're the NSA IT department. They'll have radios, so track them."

Goldberg frowned. "They'll have gone to a secondary frequency."

Sean pointed at Shushurin. "She'll have it. And if they she's dead, they won't change it to a tertiary they didn't tell *her* about."

The Pope nodded. "We'll need the time for Last Rites for everyone. Frank, let's get to work."

* * *

The Pope's office was very crowded after everyone had showered, dressed, and been patched up.

Abasi's skull had been so badly damaged that the stitches in his forehead made him look like Frankenstein's monster. Instead of his suit, he wore jeans and a t-shirt that was too small for his massive frame. Everyone had changed, mostly to get the smell of smoke out of their clothing.

After everyone was seated, Manana Shushurin began. "In the 1920s, the KGB learned that it was easier to penetrate the Russian Orthodox Church than the Roman Catholic. The Russian Orthodox was Caesaro-Papist, and the KGB was Caesar. There were married clergy who could be black-mailed with a honey trap." She smiled wanly at XO. "Trust me when I say that the KGB files on the Russian Orthodox Church will never see the light of day. They would show just how many of them were KGB agents.

"But Rome was harder. The agents sent to seminary didn't survive... the rules, the screening, the celibacy, all did them in."

XO nodded. "The Nazis tried the same thing, and had much the same problem."

Shushurin nodded. "But, they had a solution: a little blackmail, the support and promotion of drunks, cowards and weaklings; the occasional subversion of those already or-dained. The Soviets' biggest friend was a neck-and-neck race between John XXIII and a priest who called himself Xavier Rynne. *That* Pope was easy to manipulate. He gave away his chance to condemn Communism so two Russian Orthodox representatives could be present at Vatican II — and they were both Soviet spies! So *he* had no condemnation of the Soviets, despite that they had already murdered more of their own people than the Nazis had.

"The KGB helped popularize phrases that meant *noth-ing* except what they wanted them to mean. John XXIII's *aggiorniomento* — to open the windows of the church, to update it — what could be more *up-to-date,* more *modern,* than communism? Many useful idiots, like Rynne, portrayed the Vatican II politics between evil, conservative curia and good, sainted laity.

"The Soviets even *sponsored* Rolf Hochhuth's play, *The Deputy,* slandering Pius XII, and he *almost* got away with his second play blaming Winston Churchill for World War II."

She shrugged. "But, the spin on Pius *wonderful,* because everything he says that was *not* anti-Nazi could be read that he was not sufficiently pro-Communist — which was tantamount to *being* fascist. Religion is either on the side of Communism, or the enemy.

"Once that happens, you get pseudo-intellectuals at their weakest. If you get rid of religion, if there is nothing worth fighting for except yourself... then duty, honor, country mean duty to your own concern, honored by an op-ed page in the *New York Times,* and what country? You're now an intellectual! An internationalist! All head, no heart, and only the groin for company."

Goldberg glared at Shushurin, tightening her fingers on the arm of the chair, as though she were trying to keep every motion under tight control. "Is there a point?"

Shushurin nodded. "Ever notice how most of Pius' critics are ex-Seminarians, ex-Priests, or the most *un*religious Jews imaginable? Who, for high 'moral' reasons, of course, are in favor of birth control, abortion, and female priests? They are *very* useful idiots. In the late 1970s, the mission was to separate the American Church from Rome, and in the meantime, let them screw their little hearts out in the name of 'conscience' and 'freedom,' and encourage them to tell stories to make them feel better about it. And while the KGB is no more, a weaker Rome can't make headway into Africa like a good Russian Orthodox missionary can – and Africa has a lot of interesting natural resources Russia could use."

Shushurin smiled. "The nice thing about the slanderers

of Pius is that they treat the testimony of all the Jews supporting Pius like *dreck,* and Jihadists enjoy that. So to kill the person, the legacy of the Pope, these slanders actually have to be more anti-Semitic than Pius himself."

Abasi nodded. "It was of great amusement to my grandfather; our people took in the Nazis that never made it to South America."

Goldberg groaned in annoyance and frustration. "All right, you've given us why. Give us what — as in what's going on?"

Shushurin looked directly at Pope Pius XIII. "You, Joshua, have a few enemies."

The Pope smiled. "I've noticed. It's a gift."

"The Chinese, the North Koreans, North Sudan, all of them want you dead. You've put them on your human-rights hit list, and they, in turn, put you on their literal hit list."

Figlia nodded, following the train of thought slightly faster — mostly because he was more familiar with the Pope's enemies than anyone else. "And they would have less of a terrorist network, and more like terrorist networking."

Shushurin nodded. "They… we… members of the youthful Soviet agent program, had been tapped by certain elements who wanted you dead. These mercenaries would, in turn, call upon all of their resources."

Abasi leaned forward. "What resources?"

"Are any of you familiar with the KGB chief, Andropov, and his plans for the church?"

Giovanni Figlia blinked, before the Pope or even O'Brien could open their mouths. "I read about this years ago. He had penned a plan to disrupt the church at every level possible." He looked to Pius XIII. "I know about it because he wrote about it some years before Ali Agca shot your predecessor."

Shushurin nodded. "You're very good. But not all the details of this were put to pen — no one wants an assassination order on paper. Pope John Paul II was supposed to be killed, and replaced by someone more reasonable."

"He survived the USSR by 15 years," the Pope said, thinking it over.

Figlia nodded thoughtfully. "And the children in the Soviet training program? What happened to them?"

Shushurin smiled, like a teacher who saw that her student's mind at work. "You tell me."

"They became mercenaries," Figlia murmured. "Just like everyone else in the Soviet forces. If these plans were in place, the mercenaries — your people — could continue Andropov's plan. It would have to be rewritten, but it could be done."

She nodded. "If you had money, which required *clients.* There were enough funds to put it in action. Under this *new* plan, they've been trying to increase the drumbeats of 'priests are pedophiles,' and 'Pius was a Nazi,' and every other slander they could find as a buildup to a strike."

The Pope frowned. "I had believed that this was just about countering any research about Pacelli from the archives."

"No," Shushurin told him. "Though that's why your Dr. Gerrity was killed; he was interested in the truth. Yousef was also killed for the truth; he came to Rome believing the papacy hated Jews as much as he did. He was wrong, and was killed when he wanted to declare a jihad on Rome. In fact, that's why Giacomo Clementi — the Red Brigade assassin — was called in on the pretense of fighting the revolution, and was to assassinate anyone who discovered the truth of Pius XII."

Shushurin looked to Giovanni Figlia. "That included Dr. Gerrity."

She glanced to Maureen McGrail. "And Father Harrington of County Kerry, your victim."

She looked down. "And James Sherman Ryan."

Shushurin took a deep breath and continued. "The rest of the plan was simple. Once it was 'proven' the papacy was with the Nazis, or once they removed all evidence to the contrary, the next step was to crash a plane into the papal offices during a speech." She looked at the Pope. "Once St. Peter's Square was blocked by a plane filled with burning jet fuel, the Pope killed in the crash, the gunmen ... my fellow students… would invade and ransack the city — rob the vaults, museums. And you would have been replaced with someone more… reasonable."

The Pope's face went darker. "Such as?"

She shrugged. "I'm not sure who."

Sean Ryan growled. Everyone's attention turned to the bodyguard. "I am. Cardinal Cannella. Remember the news article about strange 'donations' made to Cannella? It was a war chest, something to support his bid for election."

Goldberg let out an aggravated sigh. "We should have seen it." She glanced to the Egyptian. "Hashim, remember when we made the arrangements to move everyone into the Vatican? Cannella was there for that."

Abasi nodded. "And we had mentioned going to see the archive logs."

Father Frank shook his head. "The entire College of Cardinals, and the bishops would have to be killed for Cannella to be made Pope. No one wants Cannella to wear his *red* hat. But Pope? No."

Sean Ryan frowned and furrowed his brow, his electric blue eyes staring into the walls so hard, Murphy expected a hole. "How would it work? What could they…" He winced.

"They would use another plane! When they kill the Pope in the first plane crash, they'd use another to crash it into the papal conclave! And narrow the field as much as possible"

The Pope nodded slowly. "How would we prove this?" he asked.

"It's simple," Maureen McGrail answered, a clue coming to her mind from back in Ireland. "The Markists were founded the year that Pius XII died? Given their overall conduct, Pius XII didn't allow them to come into existence as a society — and I'll bet neither did John XXIII."

Sean and McGrail looked at each other. "The Soviets forged the paperwork!" they chorused.

He whirled on Shushurin. "You left something out. I heard something about your father being involved in all this?"

She bowed her head. "My father trained us, and now leads my fellow alumni of the school as mercenaries. He told me he was going to say I was still on the Russian payroll, and he had documents 'proving' it. The German government would've arrest me, and probably my mother as well"

Wilhelmina Goldberg eagerly leaned forward. "What does your father look like?"

Sean Ryan stood, unfolding a sheet of paper from his inside jacket pocket. "I'm ahead of you. I took a crack at making a computer composite while we all collected ourselves."

"In short," Abasi said, "while I was being patched together again."

Sean shrugged. "Whatever you say, scarecrow." He handed Shushurin the paper. "This is the one that threw me off the roof. This him?"

She took a quick look, then nodded.

He nodded. "Thought so. But this isn't the guy who

burned the archive log books. He was slighter built, with silver hair — more like Father Frank."

Shushurin sighed. "That would be my brother, Nikita, an assassin like our father, like our grandfather, and like I was supposed to be. He assassinated Ashid Yousef."

Scott Murphy, who had been sitting next to her the entire time, said, "One question: how would this plan have worked? The plane hits the Pope, chaos ensues, theft ensues. Then what?"

Hashim Abasi laughed, and then grabbed his head. "Ouch... I know exactly what they would do. Think of it as RICO — with the Americans, they take everything used in the commission of a crime, and the profits: if you can 'prove' that the Vatican issued orders to support the Nazis, or gave no resistance to them, and throw in something else..."

"They could ransack Rome and say it's ending a criminal empire," Captain Wayne Williams concluded. "Sudan could even say that they endorsed it legally — they are, after all, on the Human Rights Committee at the U.N."

Father Frank nodded. "But do you know how out-of-hand this could get? Invoking RICO with such a claim... If others were dumb enough to pick up on the idea, governments could start *legally* raiding every church around the world."

Shushurin nodded. "Exactly. That's the idea. They aren't stupid — they want the Church *dead,* and they're hoping that everyone else goes along with it."

Goldberg blinked. "Even *I* know you can't kill an organization like yours"—she glanced at the Pope—"by taking out the buildings; it's like a Washington hierarchy... as much as we don't like to admit it, you could take out the government from the entire Congress on up without the country slowing down, because the permanent bureaucracy is in charge."

The Pope nodded. "In the case of the Church, we could merely move the location and start again. One could destroy Vatican City, and the remaining Archbishops would merely move to elect the next Pope, who could select the curia. Given that most of the planet's cardinals have been selected by either JPII, Benedict XVI, or myself..."

Father Frank smiled. "The next batch of Vatican employees could look something akin to a right-wing extremist group... In comparison to us, anyway."

Goldberg laughed unexpectedly. "I just thought of something. Aside from the countries where they're already trying to take out the Church, what world powers would even let them get away with this?"

Amusement twinkled in the Pope's dark eyes. "Look to your own country a moment, Ms. Goldberg. Did not a President say there was no freedom of religion, just a 'freedom to worship'? Whatever that means. Why do you think statists have always hated God? If God exists, the state doesn't have absolute power – there is always a higher power. With *this* plan, those countries that don't crush the Church for money will do it for power. Imagine, no Council of Bishops to come out with inconvenient statistics about cohabitation and doomed marriages, or that abortion causes post-traumatic stress.

He shrugged. "Money and power. It's the same story since Abraham — unless the state controls the religion, the state doesn't want the religion. Be it the pharaoh of Exodus, or the wars of Josephus, the message to those who worship Yahweh is simple: you are not of us, you are made too free by your own religion; come to us, where you can be 'liberated,' indulge yourself, and be slaves to your own hungers and to the state."

Goldberg nodded. "Okay, point taken. My people have lived with that since, well, forever — every Jewish feast is 'they tried to kill us, they didn't succeed, let's eat.'"

"Exactly," the Pope concurred. "It does not stop. Ever. This is… is…"

Father Frank sang, "Still the same old story, a fight for love of money, a case of do or fry—"

The Pope gave him a sidelong look. "Thank you, Frank."

"The fundamental things go die, as the *Times* rolls by…" Captain Wayne Williams continued.

Scott Murphy looked from one Williams to the other, then took out his pipe. "Whole damn family is cracked," he murmured.

Shushurin looked at Goldberg. "This is a multilevel campaign. Attack the Vatican, discredit them historically, steal it blind, and if there is anything left when they're done, it will be securely in their pocket with a Pope Cannella."

Goldberg lightly thumped her head against the wall behind her. "We three listened to Frank talk about Pius XII, and it was all true. I hate being stupid about this. *Dammit,* I feel like Dorothy at the end of that bloody movie."

At which point, the Pope laughed. "Agent Goldberg, in three days, you have become a believer in a historical fact that goes against what you *knew* was true? How many *know* the truth and reject it? In your faith and mine, we know those who were raised to believe in the Truth that is God, but would rather cling to *anything* else, desperate to avoid what they know to be true. They prefer their envy, their lust, their greed, and their cycles of revenge. It happens. If we were perfect, there would be no covenant, no cross."

"It doesn't stop me from feeling stupid about it," she

complained with a rueful smile.

Scott Murphy, this time, raised a finger to get attention. He paused, lit his pipe, and once he got a good head of smoke going, said, "One question."

Shushurin arched a brow, turning to face him. "Yes?"

"Your father created an army of comic book villains, *and* a Bond-like plan to destroy the Church." He leaned back and readjusted the pipe. "Who the hell *is* this guy?"

"Ioseph Mikhailov, but that is not important," she told him. Manana Shushurin looked to the others in the room. "It is, however, important who his father is. My parental grandfather was named Hans, Wilhelm, Franke."

Sean blinked. "Excuse me, you must be confused. My grandfather just told us that Hans Franke was Nazi in *World War II*."

Shushurin nodded. "Yes. After the war, Soviets believed that 'reforming Nazis' meant replacing the swastika with a red arm band. Franke would become Mikhailov. His son would be named Ioseph, to suck up to Stalin. My father used 'shushurin' as a professional cover."

Pius XIII sat back and frowned thoughtfully, balancing the enormity of the situation. Harrington, James Ryan, Yousef, Clementi, a dozen Swiss Guards, all murdered. And for what? Because people from his past had decided to come after him? Because some tyrants were terrified that he might shake up their cozy cocoons?

So many have been murdered just to keep me silent... After a long moment, he looked to the others. "In my life, I have helped liberate meals from Idi Amin. As a bishop, I had broken an AK-47 over the head of a soldier who threatened my parishioners. Now *these men* come into my city, attack my guests, make attempts on my life, and murder friends of the

Church." His voice deepened in pitch and rose in volume. "I — won't — *have it. Find* these men, with the police or without them. Take them into custody, and *throw* them into jail! If they resist, act as you see fit." The Pope looked from one person to the other. "In short, ladies and gentlemen, *get them.* I leave the how to you."

On the floor, Goldberg's laptop — in the voice of Viggo Mortenson — announced that her program was complete.

Goldberg frowned thoughtfully, then looked down at the screen. "Well, it seems they took your advice, Sean, they're all on the way out of town. Unless, of course, someone can tell me that this *isn't* Leonardo da Vinci Airport that all the little red dots are converging on."

Figlia was already on his feet and taking extra clips of ammunition from his drawer with one hand, and his other hand dialing his phone, barking out orders in rapid-fire Italian.

"What was that?" Abasi asked. "It went too fast."

"Gianni's calling the vans and troops," Sean translated.

Figlia slammed the phone down and checked the chamber on his pistol. "I see that your Italian pronunciation has improved since we met… or should I say, since you ordered my Swiss Guards in perfect Italian this morning?"

Sean smiled. "I like to hold some cards back, just in case. I'm not as dumb as I look."

"Do we have time to coordinate with the locals?" McGrail asked.

Figlia shook his head. "No. Perhaps the head of airport security. I worked with him in the *carabiniere*." Figlia looked around the room, and settled on the stocky American, Father Frank's father. "Captain?"

Captain Wayne Williams snapped to. "Yes?"

"You're the only one Mikhailov has not seen yet. We need

352

you."

353

CHAPTER XXII: FINAL DESTINATION

Ioseph Andrevich Mikhailov grumbled as he walked through lines at the airport. He didn't mind, actually, but it would have looked odd if he were the only person who was happy about the situation. The old mercenary wasn't even concerned about airport security — he had dealt with it countless times before.

While Ioseph did want to personally attend to some of the various and sundry people who had botched his plans in Rome, that wasn't his major concern right now. The primary goal was unchanged, even if some details had to be improved. The original plan had come crashing down like a helicopter without a rotor...

But, upon reflection, Ioseph Mikhailov wondered if that hadn't been a good thing.

He wanted to destroy the Church, and that required public apathy, if not support. If the Vatican could defend itself, stop a conspiracy by highly-trained, well-funded assassins, then who would think anything about any further attacks? Like the Israelis after the first major wars, people would automatically assume that the Vatican could hold its own. That would be useful.

"Scusemi, signore," said one of the transit security agents.

Ioseph blinked, making it look like he was a tourist who had been baffled by the sudden attention. The security guard was built a little like Ioseph, with blue-green eyes, and oddly graying hair, an intermingling of silver, iron gray, and fringes of gold.

"Excuse me?" he said in a voice lightly tinged with a British accent, to match his forged British passport.

"Sir," the guard said in a thick accent, "please come with me. How do you say... you have won the lottery?"

Ioseph rolled his eyes. It was almost as though these people could sense his profession. Out of the last ten plane rides he'd been on, no matter what alias he used, he was always pulled out at random.

In this case, it didn't even seem to matter that he was dressed in an immaculate black suit, made of silk and cashmere, and a simple black tie. If he looked any more professional, his teeth would hurt.

Ioseph sighed. "Of course, my good man."

Ioseph followed the guard without comment or complaint to a little side room. The guard opened the door for him, then let him go in first. The room was dark, except for a single lamp, which illuminated a chair and a table.

The guard's radio burst out a bit of static, and said, *"Scusemi, ma... io...* I must take."

He closed the door, locking Ioseph in. He had been in this situation more than a few times over the years. It was tiresome, but he could live with it.

"Hello, Ioseph," came a voice from the darkness.

Ioseph started, peering into the darkness of the room. "Who's there?"

A shape moved. A hand reached out of the darkness, and

a little sticker was placed on the table that read: "Hello, my name's Sean Ryan."

The shape spoke again. "Don't even try to leave. We have a microwave cannon that will cook you halfway to hell the moment you break open the door, so any further move you make will only end badly for you."

Ioseph leaned back in his chair, smiling broadly. He folded his hands in front of him on the table, and said, "Oh? And who do you think I am?"

"I think you're a butcher who's killed more than his fair share of people in the last few days." The shape shifted position, moving to the other corner. A glint of reflected light caught the man's eyes, and they briefly flashed a bright blue. "After all, what kind of sloppy, second-rate killer would leave so many people on the ground, missing his mark time after time?" He scoffed. "I mean, let's start with Gerrity. I don't know why you had your guy kill him, but come on; the man was a diabetic who played Russian roulette — if you'll pardon the pun — with his blood sugar. Your hitman posed as room service — you couldn't have seen to it that he wound up with the sweetened tea at dinner? Shipped up some sugared cannoli, saying they were sugar-free? He could have gone into shock and been dead soon enough." The shadow smiled, his bright teeth practically glowing. "Or should I just blame it on the hired help, and Clementi's stupidity?"

Ioseph found himself smiling. "I suppose you could... if I had any idea what you were talking about."

A chuckle from the dark. "Of course, I forgot, this is Europe, not America, they don't have Guantanamo Bay or the Patriot Act. You forgot, however, that this is the home of the mafia, of *vendetta,* of *some* people who take their religion very seriously. Just enough people, I think."

356

Ioseph waved it away. "How could you even be certain that I am who you think I am?"

Another voice, from a darkened corner of the room, where he had seen nothing and no person, came a simple two words. "Hello, father."

Ioseph froze, his eyes peering into the darkness where he thought his daughter was, and blinked. He knew of Sean Ryan's temper, and found it hard to believe that she had lived so long.

Sean Ryan laughed without mirth. "I can only assume she takes after her mother."

Ioseph said calmly, "So, if that was a lie, is your grandfather dead?"

"Does it matter?" Shushurin said slowly and patiently. "We have you."

Sean leaned forward, letting his eyes catch the light. "Now, I have one question — how did your father ever live long enough to spawn you? Especially after the Pope sent a hit team?"

Ioseph growled, and nearly leapt for him. The bear of a man looked like a grizzly about to eat his handler. "Good living."

Shushurin laughed musically. "More likely lying through his teeth — the Nazi hierarchy had more infighting than academia."

Sean nodded. "Lying works. After all, all of the ones sent after Hitler and company had been killed, except for the ones who got away. So, like other Nazis who lived until the fall of Berlin, Hans Franke — your grandfather, Shushurin — was brought into the Soviet Union." Sean looked to the Russian. "What happened, did Hans hold a grudge?"

Ioseph's eyes narrowed. "To say," Ioseph Mikhailov said,

his control remarkable, considering his impulse to kill, "that I have a grudge is to put it in the most placid language conceivable."

"And yet," Shushurin said, her fluid form coming into the light, "you decided to wait until you had people who would pay you to take your revenge." She pulled out a seat and took it, her eyes glittering bright with anger. "Convenient."

"Indeed," Sean Ryan agreed, straightening. "Now, I know some of the details. There was an elegant plan to bring down the Church through slander and internal corruption, all very complicated. Much of that slander centered on Pius XII. The plan was kept alive even after the U.S.S.R. fell, and you kept the embers glowing while you looked for backers. You found them, eventually, but by then, Pius XIII, our man Joshua Kutjok, had opened the archives. You became cautious, trailed people who might find an inconvenient truth.

"And one day, Ashid Raqman Yousef, officer for al-Qaeda, appeared, wanting to unite radical Islam and Catholicism by citing Pius XII's *support* for the Holocaust. You bugged him, tracked him, and when Yousef figured that Pius XII was really on the side of the Jews, and must be publicly 'disgraced' on Al-Jazeera, you had him killed."

Ioseph Mikhailov nodded slowly. "If so, why didn't I simply report him? Israelis or the CIA? Others could kill him." He grinned.

Sean shrugged. "You had no idea how fast anyone would move on the intel. And you couldn't waste time. Intelligence agencies can be so slow at times, checking and rechecking facts. Bureaucracies can be such a hassle when someone has to die.

"Your next problem: you heard about this upstart in Rome — a man named *Ryan*.

"*Uh oh,* could he have *any* relation to the Ryan from sixty years before? Nah, can't be... oh crud, he *is.* Now, that would *really* cause problems, wouldn't it? Even better, reports from Ireland told of a Father Harrington going to Rome to testify on Pius XII..."

Manana Shushurin finished the line of thought. "Well, that last part wasn't a problem, was it? He had stopped off at a Markist Brother house, and was easily executed."

Mikhailov finally blinked. The Markists had been compromised? Manana had never been told.

She chuckled darkly, enjoying dismantling his life. "Yes, father dearest, as Sean has said... you're screwed."

"Yup," Sean agreed. "The Markists will be gone within the year — or as fast as Rome can move. Now, after having Dr. Gerrity — a revered historian and an honest man — whacked by your pet killer, Clementi, you do Clementi as well. He must have seen something Gerrity had, like the name of your grandfather."

"Hans Franke," Shushurin said. "A name you've used quite a bit, lately, as your alias."

Sean nodded, and grinned. "Then — oh crap — you have cops crawling all over your plot: Mossad would certainly hear about Yousef, a private mercenary is on the scene already, you hear that an Egyptian cop and the Secret Service are coming to town, what to do? Answer: play your trump card. Manana. If Mossad's coming, bring them in with someone you control — or kind of control."

Ioseph Mikhailov ground his teeth, ready to kill the bitch. He looked at his daughter, who seemed almost as angry as he did. "Oh? And what did she tell you?"

"That you blackmailed me," she answered, her voice calm, betrayed by the murder in her soul. "Threaten to have me declared a traitor by my government. Threaten to kill my mother, my friends, and anyone I was ever close to since you left my life." Her eyes narrowed as she leaned forward. "I'm done with you."

Ioseph cocked his head. "And all that is because of your little spy? My, my, and what do you think you're going to do with me?"

"Scott and I," Shushurin continued, "are taking you to Israel with us. They're allowing *me* to interrogate you."

Ioseph's mouth tightened and he looked to Sean. "You think you are better than me?"

Sean shrugged. "Unlike your men, I'm creative. They're well trained, but lack imagination. You're good, and at the top of the Soviet food chain, you were allowed to show initiative. But, right now, it's just you, Mani, me, and the closed door. We let most of your other members escape. They can't carry on your work, now can they, Ioseph? You're not that trusting."

Ioseph Mikhailov smiled tightly. "Maybe so, Mr. Ryan, but I will win, in the end." He grinned. "You see, my men are still here." He leaned back in his chair. "You didn't, by any chance, take the liberty of jamming our radios, this time, did you, Ryan?" He casually — albeit slowly — slipped two fingers into his front pocket and drew out a cell phone. "Oh, look here, I have five bars."

A moment later, shots rang from outside, and Ioseph was up at the moment of the first shot. He pushed off his feet and sprang back against the door, putting his shoulder into it. The deadbolt broke open easily, and Ioseph was about to be home free.

That's when he slipped on the anti-traction gel, spread liberally over the floor outside the interrogation room. He slid on his belly, right past the shot-up broken microwave weapon set up in front of the door. He leapt off the pool of vile liquid, slamming to a stop at the metal detectors, right at a guard's feet.

Ioseph grabbed the guard's ankles, bringing him down to the ground. An elbow to the throat crushed the man's windpipe as he scrambled over him, taking his sidearm.

Bullets flew as the other guard — Captain Wayne Williams — returned fire, trying to shoot around the stampeding crowd.

Ioseph nodded thoughtfully as the chaos unfolded. Fleeing civilians ran past the metal detectors, right between the Russian and Sean Ryan — and running on top of the ocean of anti-traction gel, creating a wall of bodies between him and the door he had just fled.

Ioseph had to laugh at the scene. Pure anarchy, and he would *still* get away.

He scrambled over the guard's chest, wiping his feet off on the clean shirt, and ran in the direction of the other civilians — away from the gunfire, the front door, and Sean Ryan.

A guard stepped in Ioseph's path, and the mercenary smacked the gun out of the way, and shot the muzzle of his pistol into the guard's throat, making him gag. With a twist from his left hand, Mikhailov availed himself of the man's other pistol.

"Mikhailov!"

Ioseph turned at the roar. Sean Ryan was already stepping on the fallen civilians, creating a bridge over the anti-traction gel. His gun was raised, and already firing.

The first bullet caught Mikhailov in the right side, then two bullets in the left, both of them heart shots. *I am grateful*

I wear body armor.

When the next bullet clipped his ear, he ducked and ran faster. *I have made better moves.*

* * *

"Mani," Sean said, making his way over the civilians, "take the front. Your father is *mine!*"

Shushurin grimaced, but complied, running to the front of the airport as Sean dove into the swarming mass of civilians crowding the terminal. She had out her own gun — given to her over the griping of Wilhelmina Goldberg — and nodded to Captain Wayne Williams as she passed him. He grimaced, torn between the gunfire out front and the leader getting away. He growled at himself and turned to the front, following the spy.

Outside, the airport was a hurricane of bullets. Five pedestrians were down, and the shooters Sean had brought along were already pinned down in front of cars parked near the entrance ramp. Maureen McGrail and Abasi were already hunkered down behind the back of the black Vatican security van, and Father Frank was behind the front hood.

Shushurin and Wayne hurled themselves behind the truck as the next hailstorm of lead burst out. "This looks positively pleasant," she murmured.

"I don't know, it looks like fun."

McGrail looked at him. "Are you sure you're not related to Sean?"

Shushurin smiled. "You'd think that, wouldn't ..." her reply drifted off as she noted the blood running down one side of McGrail's face. "What happened?"

"A bit of gravel, that's all. One of the bullets didn't like

362

me much."

"Do we have any advantages?"

"I have a sparkling personality, not sure about the rest of you," Wayne replied. He slid down, looking underneath the car, and fired three rounds, catching one of the shooters in the leg. The man went down to one knee, then flattened himself, aiming back at the American with a rifle. Wayne rolled out of the way, back behind the wheel well. "And an armored car."

"Figlia is up on the roof providing cover fire," Hashim Abasi added, firing several rounds around his end of the van.

"This is a Vatican security car, yes?" Shushurin asked. "Back at the Spanish Steps, you had all sorts of things. Can we use any of them?"

McGrail and Abasi shared a glance, and smiled.

* * *

The civilians swarmed the airport, running in terror of Ioseph's weapons. People ran every which way, as long as it wasn't into Ioseph's path. He would have laughed if he had the time, or breath, to spare.

He rounded the corner, into a whole new situation — the crowd had fled from him, yes, but they had given advance warning to other people in the airport.

Ioseph cursed — this problem came from the Israeli airline terminal: two El Al air marshals had apparently been awaiting their next flight.

And like all Israeli air marshals, they had Uzi submachine guns.

"Everyone down!" they shouted.

Ioseph dropped to the ground in a roll, firing as he went.

363

He expended all the bullets in his pistols, winging and wounding six different bystanders, but precisely hitting the mark more than enough to drop both the marshals. He spun, watching Sean Ryan come around the corner, and hurled both guns at him like throwing stars. The former stuntman dodged them ably, but it slowed him down for a split second — more than enough time for Mikhailov to sweep up the two fallen Uzis. As the Russian whirled around, Sean leapt back the way he had come, behind the corner.

Mikhailov fired once, a simple burst, just to increase the panic, but then kept running — otherwise he would be completely exposed in the middle of the hall, relying solely on the varying paths of civilians to act as human shields.

* * *

Sean Ryan waited a breath, and then the communications earpiece sounded. "He's gone," Wilhelmina Goldberg told him from the security control center, watching Mikhailov run through the airport via the cameras.

"The bastard's trying to go for another way out," Murphy added, also from the control center.

"You mean they have a back door to an airport?" Sean muttered, getting back to his feet, charging out into the corridor. "Do I have support?"

"Figlia is on the roof," Goldberg told him, "but that's about it. Remember how you wanted him boxed in? Well, his little friends stomped all over that plan. At the moment, everyone's out front keeping the assassins contained."

"Great," Sean murmured as he ran past the two fallen Israelis. "If Gianni has a shot, tell him to take it. If Mikhailov doesn't leave here in cuffs, he doesn't leave alive. Mani, I changed my mind. I'll need help."

Manana Shushurin's voice came on a moment later. "I'm on my way."

Sean was about to run into a horde of civilians running for their lives, then tacked to the right. He took two steps, sideways, up the wall, looking like something out of a Fred Astaire dance routine. The route took up both around and above the crowd.

Once he landed, he jogged a few more feet, then stopped at an intersection of halls, wondering which way Ioseph had gone.

A scream came from his right, and he took off after it. He leapt over two sprawled bodies, well-built bruisers who were obviously interfering in the matter, their temples almost cracked open.

Sean didn't need to see where Ioseph went; a bright red sign told him where to go — the jetway to an airplane. He growled and charged at the door, running through it, running right into Ioseph as he charged out as well.

Sean's gun and one of the Uzis went flying, and Sean's hands went directly to the Uzi still in the Russian's right hand, twisting the barrel to keep it pointed away.

Ioseph eyes shone with triumph as he drove his fist into Sean's kidney. Then again, and a third time, until Sean diverted his right elbow, driving it into the assassin's temple. With one hand clamped on Ioseph's gun hand, and the other on the barrel, Sean jerked it over and above his head, then around and down — keeping himself off-line of the barrel and rotating the Russian's hand clockwise, forcing him to turn around with his arm straight behind him. Sean twisted the Uzi out of his hand just as the mercenary mule-kicked him in the gut.

Sean fell to the floor of the ramp, still clutching the Uzi — upside-down, and every finger at least an inch away from the trigger. Before he could correct his hold, Ioseph pivoted into a leap, curling his left arm around the Uzi, and driving down with his right, the blade of his hand aiming for Sean's throat in a stab.

In a move he knew would hurt, Sean closed his eyes and tucked his chin, causing the stiff fingers to jab against his jaw. At the moment of impact, Sean rolled to his right, taking Ioseph with him, trapping the Uzi under the weight of the Russian's own body. Before the killer could head-butt him, Sean snapped forward — literally snapping with his teeth, driving deep into the flesh of the Russian's right hand, then yanking back hard, spitting Ioseph's own blood right back in his face.

Ioseph growled and rolled away from Sean, the left arm still trapping the Uzi beneath it. The two came to their feet at the same time, and Ioseph didn't even try to grab the submachine gun properly — he deliberately dropped it as he wiped the blood from his eyes.

Sean hurriedly stepped toward him, his right foot forward, almost walking into Ioseph next right jab.

Sean quickly stepped forward on his left foot, turning his upper body with the motion, and grabbing the attacking wrist with his right hand. His right leg whipped around and behind Mikhailov's right knee, bringing him down to the other. Then, with a practiced move, Sean pivoted, his front to the assassin's back, and brought back the arm in a hammer lock, pressing the fist against Ioseph's own spine. With a push of his knee, Sean brought Ioseph to the ground, arm hammer locked behind his back, knee ground into the small of his spine.

366

Sean's other arm wrapped around his neck. "Game over, sucker."

Ioseph slowly drew his knee up under him, fighting Sean's weight. "You forget something, Ryan," he said through clenched teeth, his Russian accent reasserting itself. "Kevlar..." he grunted, as he pushed up off the ground with his free hand, "is... good ...padding," he said in a puff as he brought his left foot up underneath him, pushing from the floor to his feet — Sean Ryan dangling from his back.

With a roar, Ioseph charged down the ramp. And it suddenly occurred to Sean that Ioseph had run into him while running away from the ramp exit. Now he knew why.

The ramp didn't have a plane waiting at the gate.

The Russian assassin charged the ramp's opening, running for thin air.

Sean pulled back, trying for a blood choke, but Ioseph had tucked his chin, fighting the grip, and there wasn't any time for it to effectively knock him out.

The real problem happened when the assassin grabbed on to Sean's arm when he tried to let go — and then leapt into mid-air, twisting, so Sean Ryan's broken and shattered body would break his fall.

* * *

Abasi and Captain Wayne kept firing from the van, changing their positions each time, providing cover fire for McGrail and Father Frank as they crawled into the security car.

The first thing the two did was bring out a box of smoke grenades, which the three shooters immediately grabbed and lobbed over the car.

The next items however, were three large microwave beam weapons.

"Villie," Abasi said into his own radio, "tell Figlia to lay down heavy fire."

"Gotcha," she replied from the control room.

The noise from the roof intensified as Giovanni Figlia switched from a rifle to a light machinegun, liberally spraying rounds all over the concrete island in the middle of the road.

McGrail leapt out of the car, turning on one microwave beam weapon to full power, holding it up like an RPG launcher. The energy pulse hit the assassins like a flamethrower. They pulled back behind the concrete columns, safe from the assault

Father Frank rounded the van on the other side, wielding the same weapon, closing the area to which the assassins could be exposed. They both set down the weapons on the roofs of two cars, placed forty feet apart. The gunmen were all huddled behind the pillars, protected by the concrete.

"Like dog with bus," Captain Wayne said, slipping back into a heavy Russian accent, "we caught them, but what do we do with them?"

* * *

Wilhelmina Goldberg swore in Yiddish, and a smattering of Hebrew, and some Aramaic for fun — because the ancients *really* knew how to swear — and watched as all hell broke out over the entire airport.

At one end, she had a small contingent of the army of darkness at the front door, spraying automatic fire as though an armistice had been declared for five minutes from now; at the back, she watched as Sean Ryan had the stuffing beaten out of him by the evil little schmuck causing all these problems.

Well, at least the front door had been relatively covered — Hashim Abasi had managed to get to one of Figlia's Vatican trucks and get a third microwave emitter. Unfortunately, the bastards in question had managed to find enough cover to keep themselves protected. They were isolated, but still causing havoc.

She turned back to another camera, watching Manana Shushurin running across the airport like a sprinter seeing that she may be second to the finish line. In fact, Goldberg had to switch to another camera every few seconds, because she ran out of frame just that fast.

Three security guards tried to stop Shushurin, arms out like a football line, then found themselves bowled over as she dove and rolled, cutting their legs out from under them, and was up and running before they even hit the ground.

Watching the woman run was almost hypnotic, and she looked pretty cute, too. She hated her just a little bit more for that.

The Secret Service agent went back to Sean Ryan, watching him as he was clutched to Ioseph Mikhailov's back while the Russian ran off into space, twisting so that Sean was beneath him as they went down.

Goldberg blinked. Then she remembered that the average height of a plane like a 747 was six stories off the ground.

* * *

Sean floated in the air for a moment, feeling weightless and almost numb as he went down. It was actually rather surreal. Coming from a man who had once been trapped in a burning orc suit, that was saying something.

Then he hit bottom. The impact happened with a crunch of hard objects shattering into thousands of splinters.

He lay there for a moment, with a brief instant of pain, looking straight up, his entire field of vision a wall of solid white. *Well, it only hurt a bit... I guess I'm dead then.*

Sean blinked... then he noticed he had blinked. He tried moving, and discovered that he hurt, badly, but aside from some aches, he was still functional.

There was some grunting from his left, and he saw Ioseph disappearing over the side. *The side?* he thought. *Of what?*

Sean groaned as he tried to rise to his feet, and realized that someone had parked a luggage truck underneath the exit ramp. Not to mention that he had landed on luggage. "Oh, hell, that *hurt.*"

Instead of rising to his feet, he decided that crawling would be preferred. He could at least pull himself along without hurting... too much.

As he made his way over the edge, he figured that Ioseph had planned this. The Russian could have easily jumped onto the parked luggage truck. However, that wouldn't have slowed Sean — jumping onto a padded surface from heights was what he had trained for as a stuntman — but driving Sean into it, and landing of top of him, was something else.

And Sean saw it had worked as Ioseph ran across the airfield, already obviously ahead of him. Sean stopped at the edge of the luggage container as Ioseph ran off into the distance, then groaned. "Aw, frig." He reached for his earpiece. "He's out in the open... could somebody shoot this son of a bitch? I really don't want to run after him right now."

He was answered with a gunshot, not from Ioseph, but

from the roof. The shot whistled past Ioseph's ear as he made a turn, Giovanni Figlia doing his best to pin him down.

* * *

"I didn't know you could shoot a sniper rifle," Wilhelmina Goldberg told Giovanni Figlia via his earpiece.

"Of course I can," Figlia said from the roof of the airport, readjusting his aim. "I'm former SWAT, we at least have to know how to fire it."

"What about your beam Tasers?" she asked. "Nonlethal force and all of that."

"For him, I am making an exception."

"Works for me."

The crosshairs followed Ioseph's back. He knew the man had body armor, but that was the best shot he had. Going for a headshot was always troublesome, even with a normal person who was stationary. A slight move of the head the moment you pulled the trigger could mess up everything. But shooting for something the size of a large hardcover novel while in motion, from over a hundred yards and increasing, was just begging to have a sniper's bullet miss the mark.

* * *

Ioseph continued to dodge and weave, certain that any sniper would go for his torso only, and that was covered with Kevlar. Unless they had armor piercing bullets — which he doubted — he was safe.

He ran for the nearest building, which looked like a small hangar for a private plane. Even if there wasn't a plane in there, it didn't matter — he would be sheltered from the sniper's bullets.

Even better, he thought, *I can lie in wait for Ryan, and when he finally catches up, I'll kill him, and then make it out of here without anyone following behind me.*

* * *

McGrail, Abasi, and the two Williams men all but sagged by the van, grateful that the problems of psychotic gunmen were over with.

And then the first explosion went off.

A car, about sixty feet away, exploded, and another, smaller explosion happened a few feet closer than that.

The four of them literally hit the ground as the shrapnel flew.

"What the fock was that?" McGrail asked.

Wayne winced as he saw the metal pineapple fall, a little closer this time. "Grenades."

"Damn it! They're throwing them around the columns?"

Wayne nodded. "They're avoiding the beams, but their accuracy is shitty."

Another one went off, this time from the other end. "I think they'll be making up for it soon," McGrail muttered.

"We need another beam," Abasi stated, eyeing the third, unused weapon. "One at right angles with them." His mouth hardened into a firm line, and then he nodded to himself, coming to a decision.

He slapped his hands on the concrete and pushed himself to his feet, grabbing the third microwave weapon before he pushed himself into a run.

Abasi charged around the two currently set up beam weapons, staying out of their field of fire.

But not out of the assassins' field of fire.

Abasi knew that he would be exposed the moment he stuck his head out from behind the van, since he was running at an angle to the killers he was after — and running directly into their line of fire.

The smoke grenades from the van came quickly, almost furiously as the Egyptian cop dashed toward his goal. The priest, the Irish cop, and the army man each threw smoke bombs, hoping to conceal Abasi's moves before any of the gunmen caught on to his audacious idea.

It worked well enough that he was three-quarters of the way to his target when he was shot through the smokescreen.

* * *

Giovanni Figlia took several more shots at Mikhailov, and none of them stopped the man, though they did seem to slow him down. "He has gone into the hanger… it is marked N28."

The sound of Sean Ryan's groans echoed in Figlia's head as Sean asked, "How far out is Manana?"

"A few more minutes, now that you're outside," Goldberg said. "She doesn't want to take the same way you did."

"Works for me," came the reply.

Figlia swung his scope back to Sean a moment. The American actually looked tired. He didn't even leap gracefully out of the container… he practically fell out, not quite landing on his feet. "*Come stai,* Ryan?"

Sean panted, and tried to smile. "It's just been a busy morning." He leaned against a crate and looked out, over the airfield, watching Mikhailov's retreat path along the crates, planes and cargo. "I just feel rather stretched right now, and… I …" Sean paused, his eyes locked on a truck in the distance. "Gianni boy, how good are you with that rifle?"

"Average, why?"

"I have… an idea." He panted. "Goldberg, did you see Mikhailov leave the airfield?"

"No, but I guess he could have gotten past my cameras, if he wanted."

"I don't think that's his plan," Sean continued. "I'm close enough to be the only threat." He straightened up and walked toward his objective, his normally graceful stride stiff and robotic. "After knocking me off, he would be covered from Gianni, and Mani would get here too late to continue the pursuit. No, he's in there, and he's not leaving."

"What makes you so sure?"

Sean walked up to the door of the truck he had spotted, and opened the door. "Because it's what I would do."

Figlia blinked at Sean, looking again through his scope to see what the American was doing now. "Sean," he began, "what are you doing with that fuel truck?"

* * *

The first bullet took Abasi in the leg, turning his run into a lopsided, fast limp. The Quasimodo-like walk explained why the next bullet entered his shoulder, instead of his right ear — which was the intended target. A third round scraped along his upper back like a line of fire, shattering his right scapula into several pieces.

It was the fourth bullet that felled him, raking his right side, shattering two ribs, and puncturing a lung.

As he fell onto his undamaged left side, Abasi cleared the smoke screen, landing on the concrete to the immediate right of the assassins who had been shooting at him.

The nearest gunman drew down on Abasi and paused, smiling. He chuckled, and shook his head, carefully taking aim with his assault rifle. His finger wrapped around the trigger—

And his entire world exploded into realms of pain he had never imagined.

Abasi smiled as the microwave emitter worked. He grinned broadly before he slumped over on the sidewalk, his still form draped over the high-tech weapon he had risked so much to turn on.

"Abasi is down! So are the bad guys!" Goldberg screamed. "Move in and get them." She tapped another button. "This is Secret Service Agent Goldberg, we need medical attention now!"

* * *

Ioseph Andrevich Mikhailov breathed a sigh of relief. He had already found and disabled the power for the hangar, and had decided on which exit to take on his way out — thankfully, there was a back door.

So he waited, in the dark, near the back; waited for the insufferable stuntman to show himself. He even knew how he would do it — there was a particularly sharp pole lying around that looked like someone had dropped a heavy piece of machinery on it, breaking it. As soon as Sean Ryan came in he would be shish kabob.

Which is why it was a surprise when all hell broke loose.

* * *

Sean Aloysius Patricus Ryan started the truck's engine, shifting it to first gear and, soon after, switching to high. His finger hovered over the fuel release button, and he waited a beat before saying, "Releasing... now!"

Jet fuel spilled from the hose at the back of the truck, flowing all along the tarmac. Figlia noted the spill, and spent his time from then on spotting where in the spill he could shoot. He already had a fresh clip in the automatic sniper rifle after driving Ioseph into the hangar. All he needed was for Sean to give the word, and then empty all the bullets into the target.

Sean looked at the door of the hangar, and all he could imagine was his grandfather's face at the moment of death. While he had been somewhat peaceful when he died, the image made Sean's foot become heavier on the pedal. The bastard responsible was in that hangar, and he was waiting for Sean.

"You want me, you little prick," Sean murmured, "you're going to get me... and this truck, right down your throat."

The truck's engine protested at the speed Sean pushed it, but he was oblivious to the roar of the engine, the smell of the gasoline, or the planes that passed near him. He thought of the number of people endangered, the lives destroyed, all so this petty little Russian could act out a petty little vendetta.

Sean had had enough.

He pushed the speedometer to the limit, and stared at the walls, watching as he closed. Thirty yards... twenty... ten...

"Figlia, now!" he yelled.

* * *

The former *carabiniere* fired at the line of jet fuel that had spilled out along the ground. The bullet struck, and sparked, igniting the jet fuel.

With terrifying speed, the fire raced towards the truck, the hanger, and Sean Ryan.

* * *

The truck hit the hangar door at full speed, and Sean jerked the wheel sharply, making tires squeal to the point where three of the eight tires exploded, and the fuel tank nearly rolled over. Instead, the truck jackknifed, and the trailer broke off, the whiplash effect throwing it across the hanger like a grenade. Sean leapt out of the cab, breaking out into a run.

A makeshift spear flew by his head as he ran past the line of jet fuel. He would have laughed, if he wasn't so tired.

A sharp pain in his leg brought him low. He fell to his hands, wondering what had happened. He looked back and found a knife sticking out of his thigh.

Sean noted the hilt and realized that it was made of ceramic, nothing metal ...the sort of thing you could use to get past the airport screeners.

Ioseph came out of nowhere, stomping on his back. "Leave me to die, would you?" he asked. "Think you can kill me, little man?"

The Russian dealt him a swift kick to the stomach, doubling him over. "I do not think you are about to have a good day," he added.

Sean coughed, in pain, his eyes locked on the swiftly advancing line of fire coming straight for him, a fuse attached to a very large bomb.

Sean rolled onto his stomach, his knees tucked up against his chest, then pushed off on his good leg.

Ioseph looked at the advancing flame, then at the fleeing, wounded man at his feet. He calculated he had enough time for one more shot.

The Russian laughed aloud and leapt for Sean, ready to pound on him one last time.

Sean flipped over, coming up with Ioseph's own knife, driving it into the Russian's stomach as he landed.

Ioseph gasped as he looked down, blinking at the point of impact. He gaped in wonder.

Sean grabbed Ioseph's face with the other hand, making him look him in the eyes. "Tell your father that James Ryan kicked his ass. Again."

Ioseph Mikhailov was a blur, knocked off of Sean by a swift kick to the ribs by Manana Shushurin. Ioseph rolled across the hangar as Shushurin bent down and lifted Sean off the hangar floor with one hand.

"What took you?" Sean gasped as Shushurin raced for the exit, literally lifting him off his feet. His feet dragged for five seconds before he had the presence of mind to add to her motion with a limping rhythm from his own wounded leg.

"*My* ramp had a plane parked there," she told him, looking at the advancing line of fire. The flames licked and lapped at the air, the intense heat warping the air around it.

"You're no fun," he murmured.

Shushurin burst out into the sunlight and pivoted, taking Sean with her, and made a break for the left wall of the hangar, made of solid concrete.

The jet fuel burned so hot and so furiously that Shushurin was halfway towards her goal, and she could feel it as it crossed behind her.

With a final burst of speed, she came within two yards of the hangar wall, and threw Sean behind it, leaping after him a moment later.

And then, with a sound almost loud enough to break the human eardrum, the hangar exploded, ripping apart the inside, and turning the main hangar door into a massive source of burning-hot shrapnel that ripped into the surrounding area like a shotgun. Protective tarps for the next twenty yards caught fire just from the heat, and the tarmac on the ground liquefied. Sand that had been poured to cover up a small oil slick turned to glass as the fire raged over it. The vibrations traveled so far, they set off every car alarm in the parking lot. The smoke cloud could be seen all the way to the Vatican.

* * *

Scott Murphy, who stood directly behind Wilhelmina Goldberg, looked at the monitors and said, "Where's Manana?"

Goldberg frowned, looking at the screens. "I can't see through the smoke, and I think that thing took out every camera in the surrounding area, or at least the ones that could give us a good angle." She tapped into the communications network. "Sean, Manana, you want to tell us you're still alive?"

She paused, waiting a second before she did it against, repeating her message. "Hello, anyone?"

Murphy's hand gripped her shoulder intensely, so hard it hurt. Who knew the little goy could be that strong? "Hands off, loverboy. We felt that thing from here, they may have just lost their earpieces."

"If you believe that, you're dumber than I look," Murphy

answered.

Goldberg pried his hand off her, then tried something else. "Giovanni, can you see anything from your position?"

"No," the Commander said, "and right now, I don't think anything other than the fire department will be able to get near them, if they're still alive."

"Bull," Murphy said, already walking out of the room. "Tell Figlia that I'm going out there, he should try not to shoot me."

"Yeah, yeah, sure."

Figlia's voice came back to her. "How is the situation out front?"

Goldberg hmmed and flipped the main view back to the front of the airport. Apparently, guys with heavy body armor and assault rifles had shown up on the other side of the Russian mercenaries, and they had their own means of neutralizing a situation. She couldn't tell if they were local cops, or more of the Vatican shock troops, but either way, it looked settled.

"That's apparently old news. Some friends of yours have apparently shown up."

"Bene."

* * *

Scott Murphy was not the first to arrive at the scene of the explosion, but he was the first person crazy enough to approach the building through the smoke. He did his best to come at the destroyed hangar from the side, avoiding the bulk of the smoke.

Five minutes of exposure turned his shirt black, and he used a heavy cloth handkerchief over his mouth to breathe...

And then he remembered that most people who died in fires died from smoke inhalation.

Murphy ran faster.

However, he almost ran into the wall. The only thing that saved him was that the wall itself had provided a windbreak, and the smoke was blown around the shadow of the concrete wall.

And there, in the same shadow, were Manana Shushurin and Sean Ryan.

Murphy ran over, already pulling pieces of cloth off his own shirt to make smoke masks for them. He slid to Shushurin's side, reaching for her throat.

A hand grabbed him fiercely, then pulled on him.

A moment later, Murphy realized he was being hugged.

"Good to see you," Shushurin said groggily. "Did we get him?"

Murphy almost laughed. "By now, I think you even got the roaches."

Shushurin squinted, looking at Murphy. "I can't hear you. My ears are ringing. Say that again?"

* * *

Sean sat in the ambulance, his wounded leg dangling off the edge. Had Mikhailov gotten him an inch lower, he would have had a knife coming out of his kneecap. Aside from the muscle stab in the thigh, and some smoke inhalation, he was miraculously going to be fine. He was going to be taken to the hospital anyway. McGrail sat across from him in the ambulance, smiling, a bit of blood at her temple.

"What happened to you?" Sean asked.

She shrugged. "Oh, I'm fine. A bullet caused some concrete chips to fly into my skull, but that's about it. I think there's still a piece in there. Better than Abasi."

Blink. "What do you mean? I didn't see him anywhere."

"He was shot. Maybe six times, they thought."

Three blinks. "He going to live?"

McGrail nodded. "They think so. The only vital organ they hit was a lung, but he'll need months of physical therapy. He saved our butts back there."

"Great. Just great," he sighed. He leaned back, closing his eyes slightly. "I'll need to call Inna, tell her I'm all right. Lord knows that *this* is going to be hard to keep quiet."

The ambulance door opened, and Figlia smiled at the two of them. "I am glad to see that the both of you are doing well." He looked over at Sean. "You look like hell, however."

Sean shrugged. "I get that a lot."

"Is there any place you have gone where you have *not* blown something up?"

"I'll have to get back to you on that."

"Was it necessary to drop the building on him?"

"I couldn't drive a stake through his heart."

Figlia shook his head. "I will see you both later. And thank you both."

Sean stirred. "It's not over, Gianni. We still need the guys who hired them."

Figlia nodded. "Governments hired them, and governments will take action. Italy will be filing an appeal with the United Nations, and they're essentially going to take on all of the governments involved."

"Even if they don't do anything about it," came another voice as the other door opened. Scott Murphy stood there, wearing what was left of his shirt, face so black he looked like a coal miner. "I gave Israel the sketches of Manana's brother — the Father Frank clone." Murphy smiled evilly. "I'm sure my people can call in a few favors and break a few legs." He looked at his watch. "I suspect we'll soon be hearing the screams of someone having his gonads connected to a car battery. And I suspect Cardinal Cannella will find himself transferred into Darfur."

McGrail said, "Och, and won't loose ends will be clipped soon enough? Haven't I talked with me boss at Interpol? Don't we have enough notices on these bozos that if the Mossad doesn't get them, we will?"

Figlia nodded. "Given what I know of the Mossad, I suspect all those that Manana can describe for us will be begging Interpol to arrest them before Mossad gets to them."

Sean nodded slowly. "I wouldn't worry in any case. Without Mikhailov, the plan doesn't work." He chuckled. "Besides, if we have any leftover history we need to take care of, my fiancée is bringing in a professional historian to look over what we have."

Figlia closed the door, patting on it twice, firmly, to let the drivers know that it was time to leave. It pulled away, leaving Murphy and Figlia walking to the other ambulance.

"How is Manana?" Figlia asked.

"She's good. She's even better than Sean, but is going to be taken to the hospital anyway."

Figlia nodded, picking up his duffel bag with his rifle, handing it off to one of his men without looking at him. "And what about her end?"

Murphy smiled. "I've already put in a word with my people to allow Mani immunity in Israel. Despite her being blackmailed, we worked pretty well together. She even managed to put together a lot of the case with details she learned the moment I did. She'll be okay… we'll be okay."

Murphy gazed off at the ambulance with Shushurin, and Figlia patting him on the back. "*Buona fortuna,* then. I will see you later."

"*Ciao,* Commander." Murphy turned, and walked towards the ambulance.

"So, that was fun," Wilhelmina Goldberg said behind him. He turned. "So, when will we be continuing the audit?"

Figlia stared at her a moment. "Tomorrow, please."

"Certainly..." Wilhelmina Goldberg shrugged. "*Arrivederci, e grazie per tutto i pesci.*"

Figlia blinked. "Goodbye, and thank you for all the fish?"

The Secret Service agent just rolled her eyes and moved on.

Commander Giovanni Figlia, of the Pope's papal protective service, stood in the middle of the airport, where he had been fifty-four hours earlier, and smiled.

And he walked towards his car. His next stop was home, and his family.

EPILOGUE

Pope Pius XIII sat down at his desk, reading over the report. It was a compilation of mostly Sean Ryan and Maureen McGrail's statements to the police after all hell had broken loose at the airport.

"Good God." He looked up at Father Frank. "And Abasi survived all of that?"

Father Frank nodded. "He's still in surgery having the fragments pulled out of him, but they avoided anything vital."

The Pope arched a brow. "A lung is not vital?"

"Not when he has two of them, Your Holiness."

The Pope sighed, leaning back in his chair, fingers pressed into his temples. "I cannot say I am enthused with that view."

"Perhaps not, Your Holiness," Father Frank said softly. "But you lived in a war zone, you should be familiar with how this works. He has all of his limbs, will have full use of them, and he has his life."

"I know. I never accepted it, though." With a sigh that turned into a groan, the Pope closed the folder with the report. He looked over at the priest's hands, noting the flecks of black on them. "You told me once how you were trained as a physician assistant, and a corpsman in the military."

Francis nodded. "Yes, Your Holiness?"

"That would include gunshot wounds, would it not?" He paused, but not long enough for Father Frank to answer. "How soon were you there to help Abasi?"

"As soon as he turned on the beam, Your Holiness."

"Indeed… you need to wash your hands more thoroughly."

Father Frank frowned and looked down at his hands, with the blackened crusts of blood under his nails. "Oh."

"What about the others at the airport?"

"There were plenty of people wounded," Father Frank said, "but no one was actually killed. Mikhailov crushed the windpipe of a guard, but another doctor on the scene performed a tracheotomy. Two more guards had been shot, more than enough times to kill them, but they were wearing armor to counter most of the impacts."

"How is that possible? So many bullets, and only one person died? Mikhailov himself?"

"Ironically, not even by bullet." Father Frank smiled.

The Pope's eyes widened and his mouth hung open slightly. "Should we be discussing a miracle?"

"Perhaps. But keep in mind, firing rounds on full automatic creates great inaccuracies during firefights. One American shootout in Los Angeles, in two gunmen with fully automatic weapons had a forty-eight-minute firefight with the police. Thousands of rounds were fired, but only the robbers themselves were killed." He shrugged. "It happens. Thank God."

The Pope nodded slowly. He gingerly rose from the chair, careful of the massive bruising on his chest from the bullets that morning. He looked out his window, over the square.

"This has cost everyone a great deal, Francis. Greater than I could have imagined. It should not have happened."

Father Frank looked up at him and said, "We did not start this battle, Your Holiness. We were fighting with words. They shot first. We fought in defense of the truth... if Satan is the Prince of Lies, then, logically, we should be fighting for the truth. We could allow the popular lie to win... but we haven't yet considered it."

He shook his head sadly, and the humor faded. "Where is Figlia?"

"With his family, Your Holiness. He wanted to spend the rest of the day with them. Mr. Minor is in charge of your detail for today."

The pope smiled, which almost looked like a pained wince. "As though I will be leaving this office today. I will be having meetings on this morning alone from now until next week. How are the other arrangements going?"

Now it was Father Frank's turn to smile. "To start with, Cardinal Cannella has been restricted to quarters until further notice."

The Pope laughed, a loud, booming sound, like rolling thunder. "God in Heaven, XO must have enjoyed that."

The smaller priest nodded. "You could say that, Your Holiness. He had my father throw the Cardinal in and lock the room."

"And lose the key, one presumes?"

"Something like that. I believe XO mentioned mourning the fact that we do not have any good dungeons to throw people in."

Pius nodded. "For the Cardinal, even I would consider an exception. But I am certain we have some reasonably uncomfortable places to put him." He paused, then looked at

387

the other priest intently. "How certain are we that Mikhailov is dead?"

"Did you ever see *The Wizard of Oz*, Your Holiness?"

"I have heard some things about it, yes."

"Sean Ryan did everything but conjure up a tornado and drop the hangar on him," Father Williams told him. "It is a reasonable assumption to conclude that he is deceased. Even if they find parts of his body after the explosion, the parts themselves will be small enough to put into Tupperware. Sandwich-sized Tupperware."

"But we still have other members of his organization alive and not captured, correct?" the Pope asked.

Father Williams nodded. "True. But from what Manana tells us, Ioseph Mikhailov was the moving factor behind the operation. Revenge and some profit were his motives. The others were interested in naught but money."

"Possible. In any event, I think we can keep Cardinal Cannella under arrest until the plot is brought up at the United Nations. The Italian government is quite put out about it, thus far."

"With the countries involved behind this, or with Sean Ryan?"

The Pope gave a small cough. "According to the reports they received, everyone responsible for the destruction at the airport has been arrested."

Father Frank raised a brow. "Indeed?"

"Of course. After all, if the assassins had not been there and resisted arrest, then none of the damage would have occurred, and therefore, they are responsible for it."

"Of course, Your Holiness… you do realize that this is the reason that 'Jesuitical' is sometimes regarded as having a negative connotation?"

388

"Why, Father Williams, I am a Jesuit, after all."

"So Sean Ryan will not be deported."

"No. He will stay to finish training our priests. He thinks it'll take another few weeks." Pope Pius XIII smiled. "They should be interesting."

"Indeed. They certainly will not be dull."

AUTHORS NOTES

Some of you may be wondering how much of this novel is true and how much is false. Unlike some books, I'm not going to say "everything with politics, the Roman Catholic Church, and Russia is true, except for the obvious," and leave it there. That's just an invitation for everything to go sideways.

Many of the footnotes and texts quoted from in this book are found in the novel. Pinchas Lapide is a real author, and his book and his resume is painted in this book as accurately as I can manage. Concerning the references on Pius XII, it depends on which side of the fence you prefer. If you are interested in the case for Pius, you can also consult the works of Ronald Rychlak, Sister Margherita Marchione, Rabbi David Dalin, Robert Graham, Pierre Blet, Ralph McInerny, and Martin Gilbert. Most recently, there is Mark Riebling's *Church of Spies,* where we discover that Pope Pius XII, in real life, put a hit out on Hitler more than twice. It's been suggested that there have been five assassination attempts on Adolf that were all backed by Pope Pius XII. Yes, really. Eugenio Pacelli always stressed that he backed the assassination attempts as a private citizen, *not* under the auspices of the Papal Office, trying to distinguish between his actions as Pacelli as opposed to his actions as Pope Pius XII. To my knowledge, Pius XII never directly commissioned an assassination attempt, as I have presented with James Ryan. That part is completely fictional — as far as I know.

The best modern work in this area may be Rychlak, if you're seeking a general, overall look at the topic, though Riebling has made the Pope's personal war into a great, readable work. For personal testimony, and reasons why Pius should be included at Yad Vashem, read Lapide. The cause for sainthood is well looked at by Marchione. Alan Bullock's Hitler: A Study in Tyranny had nothing to do with the Pope — but you can find footnotes on plots to kill Adolf Hitler, where the Pope was an intermediary.

The Vatican spy hunter, Robert A. Graham, SJ, had an amusing look at Nazi espionage against the Vatican during World War II titled Nothing Sacred — however, it is only amusing if one has a dark sense of humor. He had an entire chapter dedicated to Nazis attempting to infiltrate the Church, only to flunk out in the seminary. Also, the additional security precautions on behalf of the Vatican are mapped out there as well.

The "anti-Pius" side could be summed up by Susan Zuccolti, John Cornwell, Rolf Hochhuth, Michael Phayer, James Carroll, and Gary Wills. I have noted only a few of the factual errors I have found inherent in each of these works spread throughout the novel. As George Orwell showed in 1984, the easiest way to rewrite history is to ignore the inconvenient parts, shoving them down the memory hole. Personal motivations attributed to the authors in this book are the opinions of the characters — who, it should be noted, all have heavy doses of paranoia as part of their jobs. If you take offense, well, Sean Ryan offends a lot of people, not just you.

The history here is completely true, with the exception of Pope Pius XII personally sending assassins after Hitler and his upper echelon. Most of the arguments that have been presented in real life, for and against Pius XII, have been inserted into the book. The author of *Hitler's Pope,* for example, really did backpedal about Pius, turning his attention towards Pope John Paul II not long after the Pope died in 2005. At least one source used false documents by a convicted forger, and yet other researchers have used real sources, leaving out data that exonerates Pius XII — some have argued deliberately.

The discussion of the Soviets' policy toward religion in general and the Catholic Church in particular is well documented. Rolf Hochhuth's play, *The Deputy,* which first accused Pius XII of supporting the Nazis, really was supported by the USSR. *Try The Sword and the Shield* by Vasili Mitrokhin and Christopher Andrews for the history between Rome and Moscow. Andropov's plan to separate the Church of Rome from the American Catholic Church is real — the details, obviously, are made up. The list of terrorist groups whom the Soviets had supported is real, and is longer than is portrayed in the novel. Additional material can be taken from the works of Robert A. Graham, SJ. The Mikhailov family is, to my knowledge, a complete fabrication, though the history around them isn't.

The idea of raising children to be assassins is not a new concept. Military training of children goes back as far as ancient Sparta, and continues today. On another note, there are children with black belts in various martial arts.

Much of the situation in the Sudan is historically true; obviously, Joshua Cardinal Kutjok was not there. Any Lexis-Nexis search on the war in Sudan can footnote what has been mentioned.

The Goyim Brigade, anything on a "new" Knights Templar, or Vatican Intelligence, is completely a product of my deluded imagination. I hope. Any and all similarities between the characters in the book and real people are completely miraculous. If any of them are real, I would like to meet none of them in a dark alley anytime soon. They're probably hired as Vatican Ninjas.

Everything political, and referred to in past tense, is true — about the Soviet Union, the United Nations and their resolution against Israel, legal action against the Church in the United States, etc. The analysis of those facts is purely that of my characters, who are, again, paranoid by profession.

The technologies of the nonlethal weapons in this book are real, and not science fiction. See the Time Magazine article from July 21, 2002, "Beyond the Rubber Bullet." How much of it is actually manufactured in reality is anyone's guess — preferably, someone who can guess better than I do.

Dear reader,

Thank you for taking the time to read my story. I hope you loved it! Reviews like yours are the lifeblood of independent authors. Please take a moment to stop by Amazon.com and leave an honest review of this story. Even something as simple as, "I really loved it - 5 stars!" is a huge help. Even if you completely hated the story, please let us know!

Declan Finn

ABOUT THE AUTHOR

Declan Finn lives in a part of New York City unreachable by bus or subway. Who's Who has no record of him, his family, or his education. He has been trained in hand to hand combat and weapons at the most elite schools in Long Island, and figured out nine ways to kill with a pen when he was only fifteen. He escaped a free man from Fordham University's PhD program, and has been on the run ever since. There was a brief incident where he was branded a terrorist, but only a court order can unseal those records, and really, why would you want to know?

He can be contacted at DeclanFinnInc@aol.com

Follow him on Facebook and Twitter @APiusManNovel

Read his personal blog: declanfinn.com

Listen to his podcast, The Catholic Geek, on Blog Talk Radio, Sunday evenings at 7:00 pm EST

MORE FROM DECLAN FINN

LOVE AT FIRST BITE

Honor at Stake
Demons are Forever
Live and Let Bite
Good to the last Drop

THE PIUS TRILOGY

A Pius Man
A Pius Legacy
A Pius Stand
Pius Tales
Pius History

THE CONVENTION KILLINGS

It Was Only On Stun
Set To Kill

URBAN FANTASY FROM SILVER EMPIRE

LOVE AT FIRST BITE

BY DECLAN FINN

Honor At Stake
Demons Are Forever
Live and Let Bite
Good to the Last Drop

THE PRODIGAL SON
BY RUSSELL NEWQUIST

War Demons
Spirit Cooking (forthcoming)

PAXTON LOCKE
BY DANIEL HUMPHREYS

Fade
Night's Black Agents
Come, Seeling Night (forthcoming)

CPSIA information can be obtained
at www.ICGtesting.com
Printed in the USA
LVHW090002120520
655396LV00003B/1063